D1521082

Or So It Seemed

by Moira Leigh MacLeod
author of The Bread Maker

◆ FriesenPress

Suite 300 - 990 Fort St
Victoria, BC, V8V 3K2
Canada

www.friesenpress.com

ISBN
978-1-5255-1734-1 (Hardcover)
978-1-5255-1735-8 (Paperback)
978-1-5255-1736-5 (eBook)

1. Fiction, Literary

Distributed to the trade by The Ingram Book Company

Saturday May 25, 1946

CHAPTER I

The loud rap startled Mabel. She pulled her hands from the soapy water, quickly dried them, and looked out the screen door.

"Myrtle!" Mabel said, pushing the door open for her to step inside. "Come in."

Myrtle handed her an envelope. "Can't. I picked up yer mail for ya."

"Thank you. Are you sure you can't stay for a cup of tea?"

"Gotta get on with my rounds," Myrtle said, pointing to her wagon. "Ya haven't seen Lucky have ya?"

"No. But I'll keep an eye open," Mabel said. Except for Lucky, with his clumpy fur, bobtail and half-eaten ear, Mabel couldn't tell one of Myrtle's cats from the other.

Myrtle pulled her knit hat down over her forehead. "That's all I can ask. Hopin he didn't get into another scuffle with a pit rat. He's ugly enough," she said, turning and heading down the steps.

"Are all your preserves spoken for?" Mabel asked.

"Got extra dills."

"I'll take two." Mabel went to the cupboard, took out her money can, and met Myrtle on the back step.

Myrtle held out the mason jars. "That'll be forty cents apiece."

Mabel gave her a dollar. As always, Myrtle kept the change. "Good luck," Mabel hollered after her, as her neighbour picked up the handle of her wagon and towed her colourful array of beets, mustard pickles, jams, and jellies noisily around the side of the house and down the driveway.

Mabel returned to the kitchen, pushed the curtain of the pantry aside, and placed her dills next to an assortment of Myrtle's other untouched preserves. "Well, JC, looks like it's time to do another dump," she said, recalling the day Myrtle had dropped by looking for her empty jars. Mabel had to come up with a fast lie. She had told Myrtle that she needed to clean them first and that she and the baby were just on their way out. As soon as Myrtle was out of sight, Mabel dumped Myrtle's sweet and sour creations into the trash, soaked the sticky jars, and headed off with JC for an unexpected walk to the dam, making sure Myrtle saw them leave the house. "Can't let that happen again," Mabel said, as JC shovelled a mushy cracker, along with half his fist, into his mouth.

Mabel finished the dishes and thought of her strange neighbour. In the two years since she had moved next door, Myrtle had never once stepped inside despite being asked on numerous occasions. She'd come as far as the front yard or back step, but that was it. And neither she nor Stanley ever stepped foot in hers. They'd never been asked. Probably not a bad thing, Mabel thought. Unlike Myrtle, Mabel wasn't particularly fond of cats. She thought of Lucky and his dozen or more furry companions happily feasting on field mice one minute, then sniffing and lapping at the sweet jams cooling on Myrtle's counter the next. And who knew what the house looked like inside. No matter what the weather, or time of day, Myrtle's doors were never open, and her drapes were always closed. As far as Mabel knew, no one ever entered Myrtle's small bungalow or saw her in anything other than her blue dungarees, plaid shirt, black rubber boots, and the grey toque she always wore pulled down over her ears. Mabel knew Myrtle struggled to make ends meet, but that wool cap in this heat. *Strange. Strange. Strange,* she thought.

Mabel poured herself a cup of tea, sat at the table, and opened the envelope.

Dear Mabel,

I hope this letter finds you well. I was so sorry to hear about Muriel's illness. I've been praying for her and thinking of Ted. He barely got to put his feet up after retiring from the police force and then this happens. I wonder if they will sell the farm and move back to town. And, of course, I continue to pray for Luke. He's such a nice young man and so smart. He's experienced more tragedy in his short time on earth than most people do over a life time, losing his parents, then Margaret and James, and then the war. But then again, so have you. Hopefully he will look to you and your amazing strength and overcome his melancholy. Please give him and his brothers my best. John sent Victoria a sweet letter saying he liked school and that Mark had a girlfriend named Alice. Would that be Alice from the bakery?

A lot has happened since I last wrote. We moved into a larger flat in Wandsworth in Southwest London. It's more expensive than I had hoped but the proceeds from the sale of the Bistro help offset the monthly burden. It's also within walking distance of Michael's office and Victoria's school. Both are adjusting nicely, although Victoria claims her new classmates sometimes make fun of her accent. She's also enjoying getting to know her cousins who have taken her under their wings. It's hard to imagine they're twins. Their personalities are so different. Louise is very quiet and Lorraine very outgoing, if not a little mischievous. As for me, I'm starting to find my way around. When you see the destruction from the bombings, it's hard to believe we were on the winning side of the war. Many parts of the city are still in ruins and thousands remain homeless or in shelters filled to capacity. The area around St. Paul's Cathedral was devastated and yet the church itself escaped largely unscathed. I can't help but think it was the result of God's providence. I imagine it will take years for the city to rebuild. With Michael at work and Victoria in school, I've kept myself busy volunteering with the Red Cross. It's often heart wrenching work, but also very gratifying. I've also met new friends who have gone out of their way to make me feel welcome. They even invited me to join their monthly Whist night, saying they would teach me, but I'll defer for now not having much of a mind for cards.

I will say goodbye for now as I am volunteering this morning and want to post this long overdue letter today. It's hard to believe it's been almost a year since we moved. My how time flies. I miss our view and the smell of ocean and, of course, all of you so much. I imagine JC is growing like a weed and saying a few words by now. Please give him a hug for me. I would love to have a recent photograph. And please pass on our best to Stanley. I was delighted to hear he is expanding the business and that the bakery continues to do well despite the depressed conditions that continue to weigh down the town. Will call before too long. Love you and miss you dearly.

"Aunt" Amour.

PS. Don't forget the liners sail in both directions and that we would love to have you visit.

Mabel folded the letter, walked over to JC, and gave him a hug. "Amour said she misses you. I know I sure miss *her*," Mabel said, thinking back to the night James and Margaret had come to the shack to tell them Johnnie was adopted and that Amour wasn't his sister or her aunt. "So many secrets and so many surprises," she said, lifting the wooden tray off JC's highchair and placing it on the floor. She picked his freshly polished shoes up off the newspaper, pulled their tongues back, and gently urged them over his chubby feet. She tapped their undersides at the heels, laced them up, and pinched them at the toes. "You're going to have clodhoppers like your father by the time you're twelve," she said, undoing the straps holding him in his chair and setting him down. He charged forward, pushing the squeaky screen door ajar. It sprang back and banged shut. "Hold your horses young man. We need our hats." She plopped an oversized straw hat on her own head, then tied JC's navy blue, brimmed bonnet under his chin. She walked to the counter and picked up a box, resting it against her hip. She then grasped JC's tiny hand, elbowed the door open, and led him out. "Look at this glorious day," she said, squinting against the brilliant sun and the sparkling blue ocean that melted into the horizon. "Let's get planting," she said, holding his arm high in the air as he awkwardly took one step at a time. When he reached the ground, he took off. Mabel ran to catch up. "Look!" she said, reaching into the box and handing him a small, plastic shovel.

They sat across from one another, a narrow swath of freshly-tilled earth, rich with manure and the promise of a small, but gratifying crop of potatoes, onions, and beets, separating them. JC stuck his shovel into the soft, rich-smelling soil and flung it into the air. Mabel ducked as it rained down on her. "You're as much a gardener as your daddy," she laughed.

Myrtle Munroe made her way through town. She was approaching Commercial Street Bridge when she spotted the *little darlins* on the corner of Water Street. She bent over her preserves, smiled, and continued on, awaiting the familiar refrain.

Myrtle needed a girdle
But she bought a brassiere
Now her chest is flat as a pancake
And her tits …stick out her rear

The boys all laughed. The laughing petered out when they saw that Myrtle was smiling. Myrtle never smiled. "Crazy old woman," Kenny Ludlow called out. Myrtle reached into her pocket and dropped a dozen or more nickels at her feet. The boys rushed forward, pushing each other out of the way as they scrambled in the dirt for the shiny coins that offered the promise of a few pieces of penny candy or a couple of smokes. The scrambling stopped as they felt the remains of Myrtle's still warm, puce-coloured beet juice drip over their heads and roll down their necks. They became quiet and sat back, each taking in the ghoulish, red-streaked faces of their companions; each frantically licking their hands and roughly rubbing them against their permanently stained clothes.

"It's witch piss and it won't come off," Myrtle said, laughing. The younger ones started to cry.

"Will so," Kenny said with a hint of uncertainty.

"Fraid not," Myrtle said, shaking her head and wagging her finger in his face. "Not only that, but bad things are gonna start happenin to ya. You wait. Your peckers are gonna shrivel up and fall off."

Harley Woodward leaned back, pulled on his waistband, and peeked down his shorts.

"Oh, it won't happen overnight. But, mark my words, it'll happen. Maybe in a month. Maybe two or three. It may even take up to a year. And here's the thing. If any of you little brats tell a single soul I doused you in my powerful witch piss, your dicks will drop off." She snapped her fingers. "Just like that! So ya better keep yer friggin mouths shut."

Myrtle picked up her nickels, put them back in her pocket, and walked away; satisfied the little bastards would be so worried about their privates, they wouldn't be tormenting her again anytime soon.

Mabel held up the eyed-remains of a withered potato. "In a few months this will be your supper. Po…ta…to," she said, plunging it into the warm soil. She held up another, urging JC to say the word. "Po..ta..to," she repeated. She then pointed beyond the high, dry grass and partially-constructed fence at the edge of the cliff. "Okay then? Can you say water? Wat…ter." A gust of wind came up. She quickly reached up to hold her hat from blowing off.

"Wa…da," James said.

"Very good," Mabel said, beaming. She reached down, grabbed a fistful of soil, and rubbed it between her fingers. "Now, say dirt. Dirt."

"Baw…ren," he said.

"Nooo. Not barn," she said, laughing. "Dirt. Dir…it."

"Baw…ren."

Mabel grinned. "I see Daddy's been teaching you too." She, once again, reached up to hold her hat in place, turning her head to the side to protect her eyes from the dusty wind.

"Baw…ren," JC said again.

"Yes, barn," Mabel said, turning and pointing over her shoulder. "Jesus!" She jumped to her feet, roughly scooped James up under the arms, and ran to the front step. She plopped him down harder than she intended. "Stay here! Don't move!" she screamed, running toward the black smoke. She entered the barn. The horses started to rear and wildly scratch at their stalls. She picked up a shovel and ran to the back, frantically whacking at the flames fuelled by the wind and dry grass that were licking the inside of the grey, wooden structure. Mabel threw the shovel down and shooed the agitated horses out. She was heading back to JC when she saw Gussie and his nephew running through the field.

"Wife rang the fire department," Gussie panted. Sweat poured down his face as he picked up Mabel's discarded shovel and began frantically beating at the swirling flames.

"Grab the horses," she hollered to his nephew.

She ran to the house, tore up the steps, and looked up and down the veranda. "James," she called out. "JC! Where are you, honey?" She jumped to the ground and peeked through the lattice. "JC? Are you in there? Are you playing with mummy? Where are you?" She bounded back up the steps and threw the screen door open. "JC!" She looked around the kitchen, tore back the curtain to the pantry, looked under the sink, and then ran into the living room. "JC, honey! Mommy's not mad at you," she said, looking behind and under the furniture. "I didn't mean to holler. Where are you? Please! Come out!" She could hear the clanging bell of the approaching pumper as she charged upstairs and looked under every bed, and in every nook and cranny. "JC! JC!"

He's in the field. "Please God be in the field," she said, running downstairs. She lost her footing halfway down, sliding on her backside to the landing. "Dear Jesus in heaven, let him be safe," she cried as she ran through the tall grass that grew along the forty foot cliff that held the now angry, black ocean at bay. She looked down at the wild surf crashing against the cliff face, then ran along the bank to the steep narrow path leading to the shore. She slid to the bottom, got down on all fours and scrambled over a pile of slippery rocks to get a clearer view of the coastline. She looked up and down. There was nothing; nothing but angry black swells exploding against a jagged wall of shale. "JC," she cried, "Are you down here?" She could barely see. She wiped her face clear of the salty spray and clawed her way back up the embankment. She stood, looked back at the ocean, then slumped to the ground, sobbing.

⊏◻▷

Stanley rounded the bend and looked up at the bluff. He could see more than a dozen people in the field and wondered what they could be doing. Curiosity grew to worry as he made his way closer and saw that they were holding hands and kicking the high grass as they walked forward. He sped up, his truck churning up a long wake of brown dust in its path. He shut the engine off, opened the door, and stepped out. He looked at the blackened clumps of burnt grass to his left. He then turned to his right and saw Mabel running toward him. He held on to the open door of his truck, frozen by fear.

Mabel's face was red, her eyes were puffy, and she clutching something in her hand. She stopped and fell to her knees.

Stanley could feel his heart pound. He ran to her. "What is it?" he asked. He squatted beside her, rubbing her back. "Mabel? What's wrong?"

"It's…it's JC. We can't find him," she sobbed. She held up his blue bonnet. "Myrtle found it in the field…near…near the cliff. Um…um afraid he…he—" she cried, bringing it to her face.

Stanley felt like he couldn't breathe. He pulled her into his chest. "He's hiding that's all," he said, praying he was right. "He loves to play hide n' seek."

"No!" Mabel shouted. "I looked everywhere!"

Stanley jumped to his feet. "I bet he's under the veranda, or crawled into his toy box."

Mabel shook her head.

"How long?" Stanley asked.

Mabel put her hands over her face.

"How long?" he repeated, this time with more urgency.

"I don't know," she cried. "Hours!"

He ran his hand through his hair. "Maybe he ran down the driveway."

"No," Mabel said, shaking her head. "Everybody's been scouring the area. They've been going door to door. We can't find him!" she shrieked.

Stanley tore into the house. Mabel could hear him call for his son, and the doors bang shut. "JC! Daddy's home! JC! Come give Daddy his hug!"

Mabel was sitting with her knees bent up to her chest and her hands over her ears, rocking back and forth. Mary Catherine tentatively approached her. She gently touched her friend's shoulder. "Mabel, why don't we go inside? Your face and arms are burnt. You should have something cold to drink."

Mabel got to her feet and glared at her friend. "I don't need a Goddamn drink! I need my boy!" she hissed and headed to the house. She walked down the narrow hallway and into the kitchen, still clutching JC's bonnet and staring through the screen door. Stanley was on his knees at the end of the bluff, weeping uncontrollably. Captain Dunphy rounded the corner of the house, slowly approached her husband, and squatted next to him; idly plucking the tall grass. Mabel couldn't hear their conversation. She didn't need to. She knew he wasn't bringing good news, but rather comfort. The two sat near the edge of the bank for a half hour or more before Dunphy finally got to his feet and slowly walked out of sight. Stanley stayed where he was, looking out over the horizon.

Mary Catherine whispered into the phone. "No, not yet. You stay with the kids. Yes, he's here now. I don't know. Maybe an hour ago. No, not good. Not now, Sam. It's not...," Mary Catherine cupped her hand around the receiver and spoke even more quietly, "it's not a good time. Did you reach Dr. Cohen yet? Oh, when will he be back? No, I'll be fine. I know. Yes, I'll tell them. And Sam, give the kids a kiss for me." She slowly put the receiver back on its cradle, tiptoed into the kitchen, poured a glass of water and placed it on the table in front of Mabel. She then walked over to the white, grey-speckled, Formica countertop and cut several uneven slices of crusty white bread. She was struggling to see through her bleary eyes as she went through the motions of preparing mustard and bologna sandwiches she knew would go uneaten. She brought her hand up under her wet eyes and runny nose, rubbing it along the front of her mauve, cotton top. She looked down at the dark, wet streak left behind, then at her friend sitting quietly with her eyes fixed on her husband. Tears were streaming down Mabel's face. Stanley was pulling apart the fence, board by board, and hurling them into the ocean below.

"Mabel, do you have a number where I can reach Amour?" Mary Catherine asked as she put the sandwiches on the table next to Mabel's untouched water.

"No! You're not calling her!"

"But, she'd want to —"

"No," Mabel said more firmly.

"Mabel, please try and eat something."

"I'm not hungry," she said, shoving the plate aside.

"At least drink your water. I'm sorry, I don't know what to say or do. I want to help."

"Go home and hug your kids," Mabel said. She loved her friend dearly, but not now, not at this moment. She needed to be alone with her anguish and her husband. No one could say or do anything to help them get through this day, or any day that would follow. No one but themselves.

Mary Catherine bent down and kissed the top of Mabel's head. "I love you, Mabel," she said. She turned and walked out the front door, sobbing.

Stanley watched the Annabelle Lee and Sarah Elizabeth bob close to shore. He knew they weren't there to haul in their traps. He also knew in his heart they would never find his boy's small body. It was lost to the Atlantic and to God. It was getting dark when he got to his feet and entered the kitchen carrying JC's small, red shovel. He put it on the counter next to his bonnet. Mabel was slouched over the table with her head resting on her folded arms. Stanley sat down heavily across from her.

"How did he get out?" The question was blunt and the intent clear.

Mabel slowly lifted her head and looked at him. "It all happened so fast. We were in the garden. Then I saw the fire," Mabel said. She put her head back down, grabbing fistfuls of hair and roughly pulling at the roots. Stanley watched her do it over and over again. "It's my fault. I should have put him inside," Mabel said.

Stanley didn't protest. "Where are the horses?" he finally asked.

Mabel looked up. "Gussie's nephew took them to Donkin. He'll bring them back in a day or two."

"It's not the horses I want back," Stanley said.

Mabel started to sob again. She knew that, like her, he was dying inside. She also knew that while he spoke softly there was a harshness to his words. She didn't blame him. If she had only taken those few extra steps and brought James inside they'd be both be sitting next to their son enjoying their evening supper and counting their blessings. Mabel reached across the table. "Your hands are bleeding."

Stanley quickly pulled them away. "So is my heart." He pushed his chair back and walked to the sink. "How long was he left alone?" he asked with his back to her.

"Maybe a minute. Maybe two. It wasn't long."

"It was long enough," Stanley said. He turned and stormed out of the kitchen and through the front door. Mabel heard him slam the truck door, rev the engine, and tear down the driveway. I lost my son and my husband today, she thought. She stood up, walked to the squeaky screen door, and pushed it open. She looked at the brilliant red sun hanging over the horizon and the shimmer it cast on the now calm, black waters below. It had always been a moment that brought her great peace. But not on this night. She stepped out, letting the door bang behind her. She then slowly walked down the steps, past the garden, and through the high grass leading to the cliff.

Over and over again, the image played out in her mind. JC running happily through the swaying, flaxen grass toward the ocean and toppling over the edge. His small body bouncing off the jagged rocks below and being carried off by the unforgiving swells that crested and crashed against the cliff, spewing their anger high into the air. She sobbed and swayed, then grew quiet. She raised her head to the heavens and blessed herself. "Mommy's coming," she murmured.

⊏⟨⎯⟩⊐

Sam was waiting at the door when Mary Catherine arrived home. He hugged her and led her in. Irwin was sitting on the couch. Mary Catherine walked up to her son and brought him into her chest. She wiped her eyes. "Did you colour that?" she asked, trying to smile.

"Yes," he said, showing her his bright red pony with a green mane. Mary Catherine examined the scribbled image. "It's beautiful. Can I have it?"

"I made it for you. Papa said it would make you feel better."

Mary Catherine pulled Sam aside as Irwin started on another page of his colouring book. "Does he know?"

"He knows you're sad. I thought we should tell him together."

Mary Catherine nodded. "Where's Ruth and the baby?"

"Fast asleep in our bed. No doubt done in by the heat. There's some cod cakes warming in the oven."

"I'm just going to check on the girls," she said. "I'll be down shortly."

Two hours later Sam and Irwin walked upstairs hand in hand. Mary Catherine was curled up next to Ruth and Liddy with her arm protectively wrapped around them. Sam gently lifted his wife's arm away, tucked the girls into their own beds, and walked Irwin to his room. He then returned to his bedroom, turned off the light, stripped down to his underwear, and crawled in next to his wife. Mary Catherine stirred. "Sorry," Sam said.

Mary Catherine reached for his arm and placed it over her belly. "I don't know what to do," she said.

"I know. I can't even imagine. I cancelled my appointments for tomorrow. I'll look after the kids."

"I love you," Mary Catherine whispered, choking back tears.

"Mabel! Please! Don't!"

She turned slowly toward the familiar voice.

Luke was standing behind her, wringing his cap in his hands.

"Another spectacular day proclaiming the greatness of God," she said, laughing at her words. She wiped her hand under her nose.

"He works in mysterious ways," Luke said softly.

"He sure does," Mabel said, turning her back to him, looking up, and shaking her head.

"Mabel. I think he sent me here tonight. I wasn't going to come. Everybody told me to leave you and Stanley alone for the night. But here I am."

"Your timing couldn't be worse."

"Or better," he said. "How about stepping back a bit."

Mabel hesitated, then turned and walked toward him. Luke didn't move. She stood next to him and tried to smile. He wrapped his arm around her shoulder and guided her back to the house.

They sat across from one another in the dimly-lit kitchen, both content to sit in silence. Luke finally walked to the counter, filled the kettle, and put it on the stove. "Would you have done it? I mean, if I didn't show up," he asked nervously.

"Yes," Mabel said firmly.

"But, *you won't now?*"

"Not tonight."

"Mabel, I know how you're feeling."

"You have no idea how I'm feeling!" she snapped. She immediately regretted her sharp tone, remembering the day she heard Stanley say Luke's father *fell* off the same cliff.

Luke put his head down. "I'm sorry. I just want you to know that in time, you'll start to feel less …less pain. When my da died. Then James —"

Mabel cut him off. "It's my fault he's gone."

"It was a terrible accident. You can't blame yourself."

"I can and *I do*," Mabel said. "And so does Stanley."

"I'm sure he doesn't," Luke said, returning to his chair.

"Oh, but he does. That's why he's not here."

"I'm sure he'll be home in an hour or two. He just needs time to—"

"Luke, I don't think he'll ever forgive me. I doubt he'll ever come back."

"Mabel, he loves you. He'll be back before you know it. He's just trying to come to terms with the shock of it all. Grief makes people react in different ways. Believe me, I know. Give him some time. He'll come home and life, as hard as it is, will go on."

It was a familiar phrase Mabel had heard before. She thought of her mother saying the very same thing after Mabel's baby brother died.

The kettle rattled on the stove, vented its hot vapors, and let out a shrill whistle. Luke stood, but Mabel motioned for him to sit back down. She walked to the stove and removed the kettle. The whistling stopped. She lifted the lid off the brown canister adorned with a bright sunflower, retrieved two gauze bags, and dropped them into the dull, tin pot sitting on the counter. She felt a wave of guilt at the thought of doing something so routine, so ordinary as making tea and momentarily thought of pouring the scalding water over herself. She started to shiver.

Luke took the kettle from her and led her back to her chair. He reached in his pocket and placed a tiny blue pill on the table. "Take it with your tea," he said.

"No."

"Please? It'll help you sleep."

"Then I'll have a hundred more," she said.

"One is all you get. Go on, take it," Luke urged.

Mabel's shivering intensified and her teeth started to chatter. She felt as if she were back in the coal shed about to die, regretting she wasn't.

Luke ran to the living room and grabbed a sweater off the back of a chair. He wrapped it around her shoulders. "No doubt shock, a mild case of sunstroke, or both," he said. It was Stanley's threadbare grey cardigan. A handmade treasure from his long-since deceased aunt. He wore it every night, no matter how warm it was. Mabel inhaled the lingering scent of MacDonald's tobacco and thought of him sitting in his favourite chair reading *The Story about Ping*, with JC nestled in the crook of his arm. Mabel snorted. Wet snot dripped down her upper lip. She wiped it away and put her head down on the table, sobbing and shivering. Luke walked behind her and began rubbing her back.

She pulled away. "Please! I want you to go home."

"Not until you take the pill."

Mabel picked it up off the table, took a drink of her tea, and threw her head back. "Done. Now go!"

"Let's get you to bed first," he said, helping her to her feet.

Mabel paused at the bottom of the stairs. "I don't think I can go up there."

"Would you rather sleep on the couch?" Luke asked.

"No."

Mabel held on to the banister and slowly took one step after the next. When they reached the top, she stopped outside JC's room. She walked in and picked up the quilt hanging over the foot of his crib. She unfolded it and held it up. A colourful bear holding a lone daisy; a christening gift from Sam and Mary Catherine. Luke went to take it from her. Mabel quickly pulled her hands back. "Noooo!" she screamed. She was dizzy and nauseous, and stumbled backwards. Luke reached for her arm and, with all his energy, pulled her screaming from her son's room into her own. She was clutching JC's quilt and crying more softly when he put her on the bed, removed her shoes, and put a blanket over her. This was the room she shared with her husband, he thought. Tonight she would share it with him. He pulled an armchair close to the bed, stretched his good leg over an orange ottoman, bent down, and lifted his damaged leg up beside it. He watched her breathing fall into a deep, steady rhythm, satisfied the pill helped momentarily conquer her torment. Where are you Stanley, he thought. "You should be here for your wife and your son," he whispered.

It was dark and Stanley was driving too fast along the winding, dirt road more accustomed to slow moving horses hauling hay. The truck fishtailed. He slammed on the breaks. His blue Ford pickup came to a stop and sat sideways in the narrow road, blocking the path of any oncoming traffic. He put his head on the steering wheel and closed his eyes. He finally backed up, pulled to the side, and walked to the cargo bed. He reached for his tool box and removed the top tray. He felt for his quart of rum, unscrewed the top, and chugged a generous amount. He then slid to the ground, drank more, and cried more.

It was almost midnight when he reached his destination, pushed the door open door, and stumbled to the couch. He sat in the dark thinking back to his conversation with Dunphy. *"It was probably just someone taking a shortcut to the shore and they threw away a lit butt, or the heat of the sun against a broken bottle. Let's let Skinny and the boys take a look. It couldn't have been Dan McInnes. He hasn't been back since he got out of Dorchester. He's somewhere along the Great Lakes."*

Stanley took another swig. "Bullshit! Two barns. Two fires. I know McInnes was behind it. Vengeful bastard put someone up to it. No doubt that greasy little prick, Billy Guthro," he slurred. He drained the remains of his ninety-proof Navy Rum. "I'm gonna fuckin kill ya! D'ya hear me! I'm gonna fuckin kill you, you fucking bastard!" he shouted, as the empty bottle sailed across the black room, shattering against the unlit fireplace.

Sunday, May 26

CHAPTER 2

The sky was a somber, morning grey when Stanley woke. He turned on his side and emptied his stomach onto the floor. He then laid back down as snippets of his dream faded in and out. *Mabel was holding JC's hand. They were watching him throw shovels of wet mud over his charred ponies. The ocean quickly rose up over the bank and washed them away. He was swimming toward them. Mabel's grey, bloated face and wide, red-rimmed eyes were haunting against the clear blue water as she tried to grab hold of JC's out-stretched arms. He frantically swam toward them, but couldn't find them. They disappeared into the deep.*

Stanley sat up, walked to the kitchen sink, and cranked the long arm of the pump. He heard the rumble, cupped his hands, and gathered up the cold water gushing forth. He splashed it on his face and around the back of his stiff neck. He picked up a dishrag, roughly wiped his face, and looked out the window at the water beyond, wondering if this would be the start of every morning to come. How could she have been so careless, so stupid, he thought. He straightened up and slammed his fist on the counter. He never dreamt he would be waking up and mourning his son. He never imagined that he would feel such heartbreak, such anger toward his wife. He threw the dishrag on the floor, kicked a chair over and started to sob. Things will never be the same, he thought.

⊏▭▭⊐

Luke heard the front door open. He eased himself off the chair. His neck, back, and bad leg ached. He looked at Mabel who seemed dead to the world, quietly left the room, and softly closed the door behind him. He could hear someone rummaging around the kitchen as he descended the stairs. He walked in expecting to find Stanley. Mary Catherine had her head in the Frigidaire.

"Hello," he said.

Mary Catherine closed the door. "Luke? What are you doing here?"

"I came last night. I thought I should stay."

"How are they doing?"

"Mabel's sleeping. I have no idea about Stanley. He's not here."

Mary Catherine looked past Luke toward the front door. "He's not here?"

"No. He left before I arrived and never came home."

"You mean Mabel was home alone?" Mary Catherine said, looking at the floor and feeling a wave of guilt for leaving when she did.

Luke decided not to tell Mary Catherine about finding Mabel at the edge of the cliff. "I arrived shortly after eight."

"Thank God!"

"Mabel doesn't think he's coming back."

"Stanley? Of course he will! Why wouldn't he?"

"She said he blames her for what happened."

"That's ridiculous! Mabel's not to blame. It was a tragic accident."

"I know, but Mabel agrees with him. She was pretty hard on herself last night."

Mary Catherine walked toward the phone in the hallway. "I'll call Sam. You two go to Mira and bring him home. I'm sure he's at the MacPhees taking his anger out on the walls." Luke gave her a look to suggest otherwise. "What? You don't think he's there?"

"I know he's not," Luke said.

"How?"

Luke looked down the hall and whispered. "I was there yesterday, after Sam called and told me what happened. Nobody's stepped foot on that property in years."

"But Stanley's been fixing the place up. He's been going there for weeks…months. That's why he's been working weekends and late into the night. I heard him tell Mabel he'd finish it up by the end of June."

Luke pursed his lips and shook his head. "He wasn't there yesterday and I know he's not there now. The place is all boarded up. I couldn't even drive down the lane. It's all grown over."

"You must have gone to the wrong spot."

"He's not there," Luke repeated.

"For Christ sakes, Luke! Just go and check!" Mary Catherine said, immediately regretting her impatient tone.

"I know the place. It's the lane to the right of The Stitch'n Post. I even talked to Joe. He told me the MacPhees are trying to sell it. Old man MacPhee offered it to him for a song, but Jacquie put her foot down. Said she wouldn't buy it for love nor money."

Mary Catherine stared at Luke unsure of what to say, wondering why Stanley would lie to Mabel and everyone else about his whereabouts. "Then he's probably at Murphy's Inn."

They both looked up when Mabel appeared in the hallway, still clutching JC's quilt.

Mary Catherine walked up to her and wrapped her arms around her. "Did you get some sleep?" she asked, worried Mabel might have overheard her conversation with Luke.

"Yes," Mabel said and looked at Luke. "I thought you were going home?"

"I got tired, so made myself comfortable."

Mary Catherine opened the Frigidaire, took the ice tray out, pulled the handle back, and dumped the frozen cubes onto a tea towel. She held the icy cloth to Mabel's swollen eyes.

Mabel took it from her and put it back on the counter. She sat down, still feeling faint and nauseous. "I think I'm going to throw up."

Mary Catherine grabbed a bucket from under the sink and placed it at her feet. "Tea always settles my upset," she said, rushing to fill the kettle. "Sam's father gave me some fresh eggs. Do you think you can eat?" she asked Mabel.

"No."

"I can," Luke answered, thinking he didn't have much of an appetite either, but Mabel might eat once it was prepared.

They heard a rap. "Hello. May I come in?"

They all turned at once and looked through to the front door. It was Father Gregory, the much younger priest who took over St. Anthony's Parish after the much loved Father Vokey ironically dropped dead on the altar during a Mass of the Resurrection. Before he arrived in town, it was widely rumoured that Father Gregory, with his more modern ways, would cause a backlash and the congregation would move en masse to St. Agnes'. But the opposite happened. Numbers swelled as young women, desperate spinsters, widows, and even a handful of curious men caught a glimpse of the handsome, young man in his white collar and black vestments. Folks from all the local parishes quickly began to flock to St. Anthony's for Sunday Mass, morning worship, and daily confession in hopes they could convince Father Gregory he was more a man of the world, than a man of God. Saint Anthony's once small, harmonious choir grew to a large, discordant ensemble, and the once short list of volunteers signing up to help with the annual church picnic, to polish the altar's brass rails, or to wash and press the corporals, now stretched beyond manageable levels, forcing Father Gregory to repeatedly invoke God's help in keeping peace among his enthusiastic congregants.

Mabel looked at Mary Catherine. "I'm not ready to see him."

"I'll talk to him," Mary Catherine offered, greeting him at the door. "Father," she said, pushing the screen door open and extending her hand. "I'm Mabel's friend, Mary Catherine. Mary Catherine Friedman. I was Catholic, but I'm Jewish now. Not that I minded being Catholic. I married a Jew so I had to convert. Not that I mind being a Jew either," she said, thinking she shared too much information, too quickly.

He took her hand in his and smiled. "We all pray to the same God. I just came from Mass and heard the news. How is Mabel?"

"Heartbroken. She's not sure she's ready to see you," she whispered.

"And her husband?"

"He's not here, Father."

"I won't stay long. Maybe just a quick prayer," he said, smiling and walking past her and into the kitchen.

Mabel watched him approach. She didn't see the black, wavy hair, perfectly aligned white teeth, or the chiseled jaw everyone else did. She was focused on the starched white collar digging into his throat and irritating his neck.

"Hello, Mabel," he said in a soothing, priestly voice reserved for moments of bereavement. "I won't stay long. I know you're hurting deeply. Perhaps even questioning God's will. I thought that if we —"

"If we what, Father? That if we prayed all will be good. The agony I feel will just magically disappear. That I'll get on with my day…my life…like I suffered some minor inconvenience?"

"I'm sorry. I didn't mean to suggest…just that at a time of great sorrow, faith in the Lord and prayer can bring comfort. It can be a powerful —"

"To hell with that!" Mabel said in a tone that surprised even her.

Father Gregory looked at Mary Catherine and then at Luke, standing with his head bowed; not as if in prayer, but as if he wished he were anywhere else.

Father Gregory turned and smiled at Mabel. "I understand… perhaps my visit has been…precipitous. If you should change your mind and wish to pray, or just talk, please let me know. I'll see myself out." He nodded to Mary Catherine and headed down the hallway, followed by Luke. Mabel could see them talking on the front step. Father Gregory patted Luke's shoulder, bounded down the steps, and jumped into his shiny black Buick.

Mary Catherine was cracking eggs over the hot skillet when Luke returned. "You two should go about your business. I'm going back to bed," Mabel said and walked down the hall.

"But you need to eat," Mary Catherine called after her. She listened for Mabel's footsteps on the floorboards overhead and dabbed at her eyes. "Luke, go find Stanley and bring him home."

Luke put his cup down, hugged her, and limped out without another word, or breakfast.

Mary Catherine was clearing the dishes. She jumped when the phone rang. It was Alice. She was crying so hard Mary Catherine could barely make her out. Little wonder, Mary Catherine thought. She was like a big sister to JC. When she wasn't baking beside Mabel, she was reading to him, taking him for a walk, or settling him in for his afternoon nap in Luke's upstairs apartment. Ted Collins, who had retired from the police force to a farm in Iona, was the next to call. Then her father in-law, Sam Friedman Sr. When the phone wasn't ringing there was someone at the door dropping off food; so much of it that there was no room left in the Frigidaire, and the kitchen table and counter were piled with enough pies, muffins, tea biscuits, molasses cookies, and oat cakes it could easily sustain the customers at Cameron's Bakery for a week. Mary Catherine wanted to take the phone off the hook, but was worried she'd miss a call from Stanley. She finally decided enough was enough and lifted the receiver from its cradle. She looked at it wishing she could reach Amour, knowing that she was going to be furious with her for not immediately letting her know what happened. She hesitated, then placed the receiver under a pillow to mute the irritating beeping.

Mary Catherine crept upstairs and put her ear to Mabel's door. "Dear Jesus, let her sleep. Mother of Mary, bring her strength," she whispered, looking upward and making the sign of the cross; the childhood rituals of her Catholic upbringing momentarily overshadowing those of her adopted faith. She quietly made her way back downstairs, opened the front door, and sat on the front porch to ward off the next person who would unwittingly disturb Mabel's sleep.

She had no idea Mabel had been awake for hours, wishing Stanley had never found her in the coal shed. Wishing she would have frozen to death right there and then, sparing him and everyone else a ton of grief. Mabel thought about all they had come through together. The trial, the rape, Margaret's and then James' death. The heartache was supposed to be behind them. They had the baby. They were happy. They weren't supposed to be waking up to more misery and apart from one another. *How could I have been so stupid? How could a merciful God be so cruel?* She picked up her pillow and put it over her face. "I trusted You! I believed in You! Why! Why!" she cried.

⊏▭⊐

Stanley pulled into Wilson's Auto and asked to use the phone. The operator patched him through to the fire station.

"Skinny here," Edgar Buchanan said in his always loud, cheerful tone.

"It's Stanley."

Skinny wiped his forehead with his hankie, softened his voice, and offered his condolences.

"Just called to see what you might know about the fire?"

"Me and the boys are on our way to your place now. Should be there in ten."

"I'm not home," Stanley said curtly.

"Will ya be home later this morning?" Skinny asked. "With this heat n' all, I booked the afternoon off. Heading to the *Gut* for a dip. But Eddie One-Eye will be here. He can fill ya in."

"Actually, I'm in Mira now. Can you meet me at Burkes?"

"Yeah. Probably take an hour or so for us to take a look at yer barn and another hour for me to get there. Say around eleven?" Skinny said.

Stanley drove to Burkes and sat on a stool looking out the dusty window, smoking his pipe, and sipping his tea. He closed his eyes, picturing Mabel laughing as she danced around the living room with JC in her arms. Two days later she was sprawled out over the kitchen table, pulling her hair out, and crying over their dead son. He knew she would never deliberately put JC in harm's way, but yet he couldn't help but be furious with her. JC would still be here if it weren't for her. They both knew he was never to be left outside alone.

He tilted his head back as tears pooled in his eyes, seeping out the corners and down the side of his face. His waitress appeared, offering to top up his tea. He quickly wiped his face, forced a smile, and held out his cup. He was relieved when Skinny finally pulled up in his red half-ton and squeezed his 360 pound, five-foot, eight-inch frame out of the cab. He was wearing his department-issued black jacket, adorned with brass buttons and bursting at the seams. He hugged Stanley. The stench of BO, along with the leftover eggs languishing on the greasy grill made Stanley want to gag.

"Thanks for coming."

"Ain't no trouble. Here to help in any way I can," he said, placing his hand on Stanley's shoulder.

"What can you tell me?"

Skinny turned sideways, urging his bulk onto the stool next to Stanley. He undid his buttons, exposing a pale blue shirt saturated with sweat from the collar down; an affliction not confined to the humid temperatures of the unusually warm spring. "Boys all agree it's suspicious. We figure it started in the barn. In the far left corner. A coupla boards are scorched on the inside, but not on the outside. Wind was gusting from the east and yer barn ain't what ya'd call airtight. Flame blew along the inside wall and outward. The wind took it from there. No sign of any accelerant but, then again, there was plenty of straw round to feed the flame."

Stanley's jaw started to flex.

"Fred stopped by when we were there. He said you just need to replace a couple of the rear posts and some of the cladding. Said he and Dirty Willie could have it done in a day."

Stanley nodded, thinking he had better call Fred and sort out the week's work. "So, you're sure it was arson?"

"Always room for doubt. But how else do ya explain the scorch patterns?" Skinny wiped his forehead with his yellowed hankie. "It ain't Billy Guthro if that's what ya think. He's been laid up at St. Joseph's. Apparently his da put a pretty good poundin on him. Bashed his head in with a baseball bat."

Stanley turned to face him. "Obviously not hard enough."

"So who d'ya think done it?" Skinny asked.

Stanley knew to keep his suspicions to himself. "Don't know. But I'm gonna find out and then I'm gonna kill him," he said, bringing his cup to his mouth.

Skinny wasn't sure what to say. He sat awkwardly before asking about Mabel. Stanley kept his eyes forward and sipped his tea. Skinny laid his hand on Stanley's back, squeezed out from behind his stool, and waddled back to his truck. Stanley nodded to him as he pulled away, put his cup down, and asked the waitress for the nearest place to pick up some rum.

Monday, May 27

CHAPTER 3

Tommy Simms squatted beside the brook, trying to catch skaters darting in and out of the mounds of crisp grass at the edge of the water. Twelve year-old Kenny Ludlow, ring leader of the Number Eleven Blackheads, came down the hill. "We're headin to town. Ya comin?"

Tommy looked up at St. Anthony's. "I dunno. Da said if he caught me hookin off again, he'd yank me outa school and put me in the pit."

"Don't be such a girl," Kenny said, holding up a couple of smokes.

"But we just had Mr. Spencer for English. Don't ya think he'll notice when we don't show up for math?"

"We'll tell him we got the trots."

"All six of us?" Tommy said.

"Suit yerself. But I'm not wastin a day like this. C'mon guys," Kenny said.

Tommy watched his buddies walk along the brook, jump across on the flat rocks, and scamper up the steep hill.

"Wait up," Tommy hollered, running to catch up. They crossed the trestle and headed down the high-brushed path.

"Where we goin?" Harley Woodward asked.

"Town," said Kenny.

"But won't we get caught?"

Kenny stopped to think and have a smoke. That's when he spotted them. He turned to his fellow truants, put his finger to his lips, and whispered for them to crouch down.

"What are they doin?" Harley asked, looking down at the grassy clearing.

"Screwin," Kenny said. He lit his smoke, took a couple of drags and passed it to Tommy. Tommy took a drag and passed it to Harley. Harley took a drag and began to choke.

The couple below looked up and scrambled to their feet.

"Holy fuck, Tommy! That's your da!" Kenny laughed.

Tommy stared down at the young barefoot woman chasing after his father with her blouse covering her head. "Yeah, but that ain't ma," he whispered.

Kenny gave him a playful push. "Well, think of it this way, if we get caught hookin off you ain't goin to no friggin pit."

Except for a suddenly quiet Tommy, the boys joked and laughed as they made their way to the ravine. They climbed the hill to the park and stopped at the *Chimney* for another smoke.

Kenny sat on the grass next to his best friend. "Hell, Tommy. Ya got him by the balls!" he said, leaning back on his elbows. "I almost wish it were my da."

"Yeah, but what about my ma?" Tommy asked, tearing up.

Kenny jumped to his feet. "What she don't know won't hurt her." Kenny put his hand out. Tommy grabbed it and got to his feet. They were walking down the Catherine Street extension from the park when Walter Boone a former school trustee came out on his front step. "Shouldn't you boys be in school," he yelled.

"Mr. Spencer got sick. They let us out early," Kenny said. They all turned when they heard the rattling of the jars.

Myrtle was walking toward them hauling her wagon. "Bullshit!" she said. "They're truants."

"I'm calling the school," Walter said, disappearing inside.

Myrtle walked between the boys and stopped next to Kenny. "How's my witch piss working?"

"It ain't. Ain't nothin wrong with my privates."

Myrtle smiled. "Oh, but there will be. See, Kenny, one of these nights yer gonna be all comfy in yer bed. And ya get that urge. And ya start pulling on it. It feels sooo good. Then ya start to get all hot and sweaty, and ya pull faster and faster. Next thing ya know, it just pops right off and yer holdin it in front of ya. Just you wait. Only a matter of time before you wake up dickless."

Kenny laughed. "Yer full of crap."

"Think so, *Kenny*?" She nodded to Walter Boone who reappeared on his front step.

"Walter?" she said. "Tell em yer nickname."

"Wally One-Nut."

Harley pulled on Kenny's sleeve. "*It's true*! That's what my Uncle Emerson calls him."

"Well it ain't because of no friggin witch piss!" Kenny shouted.

"I'm afraid so," Walter Boone said. "Myrtle caught me playing hooky. Just glad she let me off easy. Oh, and I checked with the school. Mr. Spencer seems to have had a miraculous recovery. You fellas are in one pile of shit."

"C'mon," Kenny said. The others ran to catch up with him.

Tommy looked at Kenny. "Hey, Kenny? Do ya think Myrtle will give me some of her witch piss? I could put it in Da's tea."

Sam dropped Irwin off at school and the girls off at his sister's, then drove across town to check on Mabel and Mary Catherine.

When he entered the kitchen, his wife was carving a ham and crying. "How's Mabel?" he asked, giving her a hug.

"She won't come downstairs and doesn't want anything to eat or drink. She's been asking about Stanley."

"I'd like to see her."

"Okay. But if she's asleep, leave her be."

Sam tried to collect his thoughts as he made his way upstairs. He paused outside her bedroom door. He tapped lightly. No answer. He quietly opened it. She wasn't there. He made his way down to the spare room. Again, no answer and no Mabel. He looked at JC's closed door. He stood outside and tilted his head back, trying to contain his emotions. He tapped again. And again, no answer and no Mabel.

"Mary Catherine!"

She jumped, immediately annoyed at him for hollering. "Keep your voice down!" she said in a loud whisper. Sam was slouched over the banister.

"What is it?" Mary Catherine asked.

"She's not here."

"Of course she is! Be quiet!" she said, mounting the stairs and opening one door after the other. "Where did she go? Oh my God, Sam!"

"Maybe she went looking for Stanley," he said, trying to reassure her.

"Sam, she's distraught!" She ran to the front step and looked left and right across the field for any sign of her friend.

Sam walked out the back door, through the tall grass to the edge of the cliff, and looked down.

Stanley drove back to Wilson's and pulled into the pumps. A skinny kid, stinking of gasoline ran out in his grease-stained, navy coveralls.

"Fill it up and check the oil. And how about checking out the rear tire on the driver's side. I think I might have a loose lug nut." The kid nodded. "I'm going to get out of the heat," Stanley said.

He entered the dingy, oil-scented office, picked up the phone, and watched the kid unscrew the oil cap, insert the dipstick, and wipe it along his pant leg. Stanley dialled the operator and waited for the connection to be completed. "Hello. Is this Gladys Ferguson? Dan McInnes' aunt? Yes, I met Dan in Dorchester. I might have a job for him. Any idea where I can find him? Ontario? Do you have a phone number or an address? Oh, Leo…," he looked down at the receipt pad. "Leo Wilson. Then, do you know the company he works for? No, that's fine. And that's the last place you know where he stayed? Yes, I know. They go where the work is. No. No need to tell him I called. Sounds like he's got a better job than I could offer." He hung up just as Gladys Ferguson was asking him his name a second time.

The kid came through the door. "Can't find nothin wrong with yer back tire and the oil's good. So it's four-fifty for the gas." Stanley handed him a ten. The kid went out back to get his change. Stanley was driving away when he looked in his rear-view mirror. The kid was running out of the garage, hollering for him to stop, and waving his change in the air.

Two hours later Stanley put his bags on the counter. He hadn't eaten in almost twenty four hours, but didn't think he could. He removed his quart of rum, unscrewed the cap, took a long swig, then another, and another after that. He plopped down on the couch, put his head back, closed his eyes, and considered his next steps. He'd track McInnes down and kill him, turn himself in, and go to jail for the rest of his life. It would be hell for sure, but then he was already there. He felt woozy. The booze on an empty stomach, he thought. He reached in one of the bags, took out the eggs and milk, and put them on the counter. He then reached into a second bag and removed his store bought bread. He thought of Mabel's reaction after having tasted it for the first time. She had spit it out, examining the mush in her hand. *"They call this bread,"* she had said. *"Ya might as well chew on a wet box."* He had to promise her he'd never bring it home again. He felt himself well up. "Christ, Mabel. How could you have been so fucking stupid?" he whispered.

Sam convinced Mary Catherine there was no need to call the police; not yet at any rate. The two jumped in their car, scouring the neighbourhood for any sign of Mabel. Sam was squeezing his wife's hand. "She's fine. Don't worry, we'll find her. She's not going to do anything stupid."

Mary Catherine turned sharply to face him. "You didn't seem so sure when you were peering down over the cliff," she barked. She softened her voice. "I'm sorry. It's just that I'm scared for her. You should have heard how she spoke to Father Gregory. She's not thinking straight."

"How could she?" Sam said.

Mary Catherine turned her head to the side, looked out the window, and brushed her hand over her wet cheeks. "I wish I knew what to do. How to help?"

"Look, she probably just needs some time alone. Let's try the footbridge," Sam said.

Mabel wasn't there. She was at the cemetery. She laid her hand on James' grave. *It's been a while since I visited. Forgive me. I miss you both so much. You always watched out for me. If you can hear me now, I need you to watch over my son. You and Margaret are responsible for anything good that's come of my life. If it weren't for you, I would never have met Stanley or have been blessed with JC. We named him after you, hoping he would have your gentle ways and generous nature. Please, if you hear me, take JC and hold him to you. Ask him to forgive me and to help daddy through his pain. Tell him I love and miss him more than I fear my soul can bear, but that I will carry him in my heart and thoughts until the day we are reunited. Even as I pray, I'm no longer sure there is anyone to hear. Like you, I have come to a place where I am questioning my faith. But if there is a God, and he believes me worthy of his love and forgiveness, I hope he will show mercy upon my weary soul. I hope he will assure me my son is safe and happy with you and Margaret, and with Ma, Percy and my baby brother.*

Mabel blessed herself and turned to Margaret's grave. *It'll be nine years in a couple of weeks since you've passed. Like you, I'm holding on for dear life and trying to get through every mother's worst nightmare. I feel like I'm condemned to hell on earth. I don't know what God thinks we did to deserve such cruelty? Margaret, my baby's gone. Like yours, he never got the chance to learn to skate, kiss a girl, fall in love, or work with his father."* Mabel wiped her hand under her eyes and nose. "*Anyway, you'll be happy to know I'm still reading up a storm. I read The Little Prince by some French author whose name I can't remember. It was good. Very sad. But then again, no sadder than life. I think you would have liked it. I hope you know how much you and James meant to me and how much I miss you. I think of you every day. I hope to someday find your strength.* She blessed herself a second time. "I'll come back again soon and bring daisies," she whispered. She stood, took a few steps and knelt at the foot of the third grave. A lamb was etched into the grey, speckled stone above his name and the dates denoting his brief stay on earth. James F. Cameron, June, 15, 1925 - May, 12 1926. Cherished son of James and Margaret Cameron. Mabel began to sob. *Hail Mary full of grace, the Lord is with thee...*

Mabel put her hands out, pushed herself up, and walked along the well-travelled path separating the dead according to their faith. Catholic on one side, Protestant on the other. A beautiful Black woman was placing daisies on a grave. Mabel stopped. "They're my favourite flower."

The Black woman smiled. "They were also my son's favourite. He was just twenty-two. Killed in the war."

"I'm very sorry," Mabel said, reminding herself that she wasn't alone in her sorrow. She thought of her mother and of Margaret, and of all of the other heart-stricken mothers who had lost their sons to war or the mines, and wondered how they could forgive an indiscriminate God who could steal away the young and leave the old to suffer.

The Black woman pointed to where Mabel had been kneeling. "Your parents?"

Mabel smiled. "Yes. Yes, in a way they were," she said. She walked away recalling how nervous she had been the day she went to Cameron's store with the hope of getting a job baking bread. She had instantly fallen in love with James' warm eyes and gentle manner. She began to laugh and shake her head, thinking it took a lot longer for her and Margaret to warm up to one another. "It was my fault not yours, Margaret. I'm sorry I misjudged you. You were a wonderful woman and dear friend," she whispered and headed for the brook.

A half hour later, Mabel was sitting on a bench overlooking the hollow and watching a group of kids play pick-up baseball; their jackets and sweaters spread out over the ground for makeshift bases. She closed her eyes and raised her face to the warm sun, picturing JC at their age. *He was slim and tall, with dark hair and a strong chin like his father. He had a natural easy swing.*

The cracking of the bat connecting with the ball generated a spontaneous chorus of cheers. Mabel bent forward and looked down into the expansive pit below. The batter was rounding second and heading for home. He didn't make it. His foot got caught up in the third base sweater. He stumbled forward, hit the ground, and was tagged out. His teammates ran laughing toward him, helping him to his feet. Everyone began gathering up their gear and brushing the dust off their dirty clothes. That was that. The game was over. "Just like my life," Mabel whispered, as she watched them cross the footbridge; the same footbridge where she would often come to pray and where she and Stanley were married.

Mabel kept her eyes on the boys as they climbed the steep incline to Commercial Street and disappeared out of sight. She hoped their mothers would greet them with a smile and a hug, and not scold or punish them for coming home caked in dirt. She heard a rumble, looked up at the clear blue sky, and thought about her visit to the graveyard and her shattered faith. She then closed her eyes and thought about her last moments with her son. *JC running off the step to the garden. JC sitting across from her,   trying to scoop up the soil with his little, plastic shovel. JC charging through the tall grass and tumbling off the cliff.* There was another, louder rumble. Mabel turned sideways and looked over her shoulder. It wasn't, as she had thought, the DOSCO train with its load of coal. A thick, black cloud hung low and rolled closer, quickly overshadowing what remained of a sunlit patch of shimmering grass. Mabel closed her eyes and lifted her head to the heavens. The weather, she thought, mirrored her life. Bright and sunny one moment, dark and stormy the next. She didn't move. She wept, as the thunder roared, the lightening sliced through the angry sky, and the rain came pouring down.

Mary Catherine was frantic. She was pacing back and forth waiting for Sam to finish up on the phone. He finally put the receiver down.

"So what did he say?" Mary Catherine asked.

"He said they'd keep an eye out for her."

"That's it? They'll keep an eye out for her!"

"Honey, what more can they do? The police have no more clue as to where she is than we do."

"I'm so scared. Out in this weather and God knows when she ate last."

Sam hugged her. "I'm sure she's fine."

"You should go home and give your sister a break," Mary Catherine said.

"Sonya and the kids are fine. I spoke to her earlier. She said she'd stay the night. And I'm not going anywhere," he said, urging her down the hall and into the kitchen.

Alice was making ham sandwiches. Luke and Ten-After-Six were sitting at the kitchen table drinking tea. They heard the front door open. They all rushed into the hallway. It was Dr. Cohen.

"Any sign of her?" he asked.

Sam shook his head.

Dr. Cohen removed his trench coat, shook the water off, and draped it over the banister post. He laid his hat on top and looked at Mary Catherine. "I'm sure she's fine."

Mabel rounded Sterling Road and saw the lights on the bluff and three or more cars parked out front. She stopped, uncertain whether to continue. She wanted to be alone. Her legs, weak from the lack of food and three mile walk back from the brook, convinced her she had no other choice but to continue. She made her way up the long driveway, slick from the inch-deep muck. As she suspected, there was no blue pick-up.

"Mabel!" Mary Catherine screamed when she came through the door. She rushed past everyone and wrapped her arms around her, pushing Mabel's wet, stringy hair back off her forehead. "Thank God! Look at you! You're soaked to the bone. I was so worried. Where were you?"

"The brook."

"But we went there looking for you?" she said, looking toward Sam. Sam grabbed a blanket off the sofa, wrapped it around her, and ushered her into the living room. "I was on the high side watching some kids play baseball. I lost track of the time," she lied.

Mary Catherine bent down, slipped off Mabel's muddy shoes, and passed them to Luke.

"Any word from Stanley?" Mabel asked.

Sam shook his head. "Not yet. I'm sure he'll be home soon."

Alice tried to collect herself. She finally walked out from the kitchen and put a cup of tea on the end table next to Mabel. Her lips were quivering. Mabel stood, dropped the blanket to the floor, and hugged her. Alice started sobbing. Mabel stepped back, smiled, and kissed her forehead. Everyone teared up, including Dr. Cohen.

He cleared his throat. "How are you feeling, Mabel?"

"My body's fine. My soul is torn to shreds."

"And when did you eat last?"

"It would have been the same time JC had his last meal." Mabel watched everyone exchange awkward glances. "I'm sorry," she said. "I don't mean to make you feel worse than you already do. And I'm sorry for causing you to worry. I just needed time to be alone. I still do."

"First, you need to have a warm bath, get into some dry clothes, and have something to eat," Mary Catherine said.

Mabel knew it was the quickest way to get everyone to leave. She nodded and headed upstairs. She stopped at JC's room, kissed her hand, rested it on his door, and walked down the hall to her room.

Mary Catherine urged everyone else to leave. She'd see that Mabel was fed and that she'd get her rest. Dr. Cohen reached in his coat pocket and handed her a vial of tiny blue pills. "Try and get her to take one of these. It'll help her sleep." He bent into her and whispered in her ear. "But don't leave the bottle with her. You keep hold of it. I'll call tomorrow to see how she's doing."

Tuesday, May 28

CHAPTER 4

Stanley's eyes fluttered open. He wasn't sure what he was looking at. He put his hand out and touched the leg of the kitchen table. Christ, he thought, I'm on the floor. He pushed himself up onto his elbow, rolled over onto his back, and kicked his bent legs out; sending his empty rum bottle noisily spinning across the floor. He stared at the ceiling and tried to remember his night. He finally struggled to his feet. A stabbing pain shot across his forehead. He closed his eyes and flopped down on the kitchen chair, resting his head on his outstretched arms. "Goddamn you. How could you!" he whispered. He started to cry. He lifted his head back up, wiped his wet face with his hands, and looked around. "Jesus Christ!" The newly plastered walls were riddled with huge gaping holes, and one end of the heavy, wooden mantel was sitting on top of a pile of broken beach stones and crumbled mortar. Stanley slammed his fist down, pushed his chair back, and walked to the sink. He splashed some cold water on his face, and looked down at the maul hammer on the counter. He picked it up. "Fuck!" he screamed, sending it across the room. The one end of the mantel still precariously clinging to the punctured wall came crashing down. Dust from the dry mortar rose up, then slowly drifted back, leaving a feathery, grey coating over the polished stone.

Mary Catherine had another restless night on the couch. It wasn't her only option, a spare room offered more comfortable sleeping arrangements, but she didn't want to take the chance Mabel would come downstairs and sit alone in the dark or, once again, leave the house. She looked at the clock. It was almost seven-thirty. She threw her blanket off and went upstairs to check on her friend. She quietly opened the door, then pulled it closed. Mabel was out like a light. She tiptoed back downstairs, put the kettle on the stove, and looked out over the bluff. The waters were calm. She could see fishing boats in the distance. "Dear God," she whispered. "What if it was my child?" She ran back to the stove as the kettle started to rattle and quickly took it off the heat. Hopefully that little blue pill will help Mabel sleep another few hours. She reached in her pocket, took out the small vial, and read the label. *Luminal.* She was glad Mabel took it without a fuss. She returned it to her pocket, sipped her tea, and watched the gulls circle over the shore. She jumped when she heard the light rap and the front door open. It was Sam.

"You're here early?"

"I miss you. So do the kids," he said, giving her a hug.

"I know. I'm sorry."

He put her overnight bag on the floor. "I brought you some fresh clothes." Mary Catherine peeked inside. "Hun, isn't there someone who could give you a break? Maybe Alice?" Sam asked.

"Alice? Alice is a mess herself. Sam, I'm her best friend. I have to stay… at least until we find Stanley."

"Any improvement?" he asked.

"Not really. Barely eats. Keeps asking about Stanley. I'm worried. Only time she came downstairs was to speak with Captain Dunphy."

"I assume he told her it was arson?"

"Yes. Sam, she asked if anyone checked out the MacPhees. I told her he wasn't there. I didn't dare mention anything about the place falling into the ground."

"Good," Sam said. "She doesn't need to deal with that on top of everything else."

"Dunphy said McInnes is somewhere in Ontario and Billy Guthro's in the hospital. I just don't understand. This is the second time someone set fire to Stanley's barn. I mean, who would want to hurt them that way?" Mary Catherine asked.

"I have no idea. But whoever it is, they'll be facing some pretty serious charges." He looked at his watch. "Look, I gotta go. I have to be at the courthouse by eight."

"How are the kids doing?"

"Good. Irwin and Ruth are on their way to school and Sonya's taking Liddy to her place for the day."

"Sam, where the hell is Stanley?"

"I have no clue."

"I don't understand. Why would he tell everyone he was renovating the MacPhees when he's not? Why would he lie about something like that? And where has he been every night and practically every weekend for the past two months?"

Sam shrugged.

"They need each other right now. I know he's hurting too. But I'm so damn mad at him right now, I could strangle him," Mary Catherine said, making a choking gesture with her hands.

Sam kissed his wife on the cheek. "Everybody deals with grief differently. He'll be home soon."

"He damn well better," she said. "Sure you can't stay for a bit? At least a cup of tea?"

"No. I need to make up for lost time. I'll come by after work." Sam squeezed her hand. "You look like you could use some rest yourself."

Mary Catherine nodded, walked him to the door, and watched him drive off.

Mabel heard the car door close and opened her eyes. She pinched her eyes shut, knowing that the stark reality of day would be no less daunting than the painful quiet of night. She looked at the clock. It was almost eight. Enough is enough, she thought. Her bed brought her no relief. Nothing could. But her heartache was becoming an unwelcome intrusion on everyone else. It wasn't fair to Mary Catherine, Sam, Alice, or Luke. She needed to allow them to get on with their lives. She needed to bake.

She got up, walked to the dresser, and pulled on a drawer. It opened part way. She pulled harder. It didn't budge. She opened the bottom drawer to investigate why it was sticking. Margaret's Bible was caught up under the wooden slats. She removed it, sat back on the bed, and ran her hand over it; thinking of how Margaret loved to read her favourite passages to Luke and his brothers. A thin red ribbon marked a page. She opened it. *"For this child I prayed, and the Lord has granted me my petition that I made to him. Therefore I have lent him to the Lord. As long as he lives, he is lent to the Lord. And he worshipped the Lord there."* Mabel slammed it shut and threw it on the floor.

Mary Catherine heard the thump and then the water running through the pipes. *Thank God she's up and taking a bath.* She placed a dozen strips of thick bacon in the frying pan and put the kettle on. A half hour later, there was still no sign of her friend. She walked upstairs and knocked on the bathroom door.

"Yes?"

"You okay, Mabel?"

Mabel was running the washcloth over the back of her neck, trying to recall the foggy remnants of her dream. "I'm fine."

"I have some bacon and eggs ready," Mary Catherine said.

"I'll be down shortly."

Mabel returned to her room, put on fresh clothes, and sat on the edge of the bed combing her wet hair. She closed her eyes and thought of happier times. *Dr. Cohen placing JC in her arms. Stanley crying when he saw his son for the first time. JC squealing when they shook his toy bunny Boots into his belly. She and Stanley putting him in his crib, then creeping downstairs, and snuggling on pillows in front of the fire.* She opened her eyes and looked at Margaret's Bible on the floor. She stood up, stepped over it, and walked out.

Mary Catherine put Mabel's breakfast in front of her. "Sleep okay?"

Mabel nodded. "That little blue pill everybody's been passing around no doubt helped. Crazy dreams though. One minute I'm seeing JC as a grown man. Then I realize it's not an older JC, but James. He's giving a small boy a piggyback. All of a sudden he rears up and the child starts floating up in the air. He hangs there for a while, then starts hurtling to the ground. That's when I woke up." Mabel picked up her fork, pierced the top off her egg, and watched the yellow yolk ooze over her plate. "Do you really believe there's a God?" she asked.

Mary Catherine was taken aback. "I think so," she said, pouring Mabel's tea. "Honestly, I'm not really sure."

Mabel smiled. "You know, James...Mr. Cameron asked me the same thing the night before he died?"

"And what did you say?"

"I told him I had no doubt."

"But you do now?"

"Yes. Imagine, I told him both Ma and Margaret never lost their faith because they knew their children were safe in the arms of the Lord." Mary Catherine leaned against the counter and waited for Mabel to go on. "So easy for me then. But now," she said, dipping her toast into the yolk and taking a bite, "it's *my son* who's gone." She dropped her toast on the plate.

Mary Catherine took the chair beside her and reached for her hand. "Mabel, Margaret and James both found happiness despite all they went through. You can too. It will take time, but you're strong and —"

Mabel jumped to her feet. "I'm going to the bakery."

"But you haven't eaten your breakfast?"

"I'm not hungry."

"But how are you going to get there?"

"I'll walk."

Tommy Simms sailed down the dirt path and bounced over the rocks in the dry stream.

"Holy shit, Tommy! Where'd ya get the wheels?" Kenny asked.

Tommy applied the handbrake and rang the bell. "Da. Early present for gradin."

"My ass," Kenny laughed, running his hand over the fender and wishing he could be so lucky. "He bought it for ya so ya'll keep yer mouth shut."

It wasn't long before the Number Eleven Blackheads and half the school were gathered around admiring Tommy's shiny new bicycle.

"Here, let me have a spin," Kenny said, grabbing the handlebars and nudging Tommy out of the way.

"Careful," Tommy hollered.

Kenny jumped on, pumped his way up the steep hill, and turned to face the gathering below. He stood up and pushed down, speeding down the hill with Tommy and the boys in his sights. As he got closer he started moving the handlebars from left to right, like he was losing control. Tommy was screaming for him to stop as everyone began to scatter. Kenny stopped in the nick of time.

"Get off!" Tommy cried.

"Jesus! I was only kiddin. Here, sook," Kenny said, roughly thrusting Tommy's bike at him.

Mr. Spencer entered the classroom and singled out his truants. "Hope you guys enjoyed your afternoon off, because they'll be no recess for you for the rest of the week. Here, take these notes home and have your parents sign them." He dropped one on Kenny's desk. "And if I find out it was forged, you'll automatically be held back a year. So don't do anything stupid."

The recess bell rang and Mr. Spencer's truants watched their classmates run to the door. "Kenny! Tommy! Take the erasers out and give them a good clapping. Then come straight back," Mr. Spencer ordered.

Kenny and Tommy gathered up the erasers and headed outside. Tommy checked on his bike. Kenny pulled out a smoke.

"What are ya doin, Kenny? Ya get caught smokin and you'll get expelled."

"Then I won't get caught. C'mon," he said, pulling on Tommy's sleeve.

Kenny squatted between the cars in the school lot with Tommy crouched down behind him. He pulled on the door handle. Kenny turned and gave Tommy the thumbs up. "Stay low," Kenny whispered as he and Tommy slid into the back of Mr. Spencer's Pontiac. "What's under the blanket?"

Tommy lifted it up and looked inside. "Just a bunch of loose papers and some books and stuff. Oh, and a few pencils," he said, holding them up.

"Give me one," Kenny said, grabbing it from him. "Duck! There's Sister Carmelita. That was close," Kenny said. He kept his eyes on her, lit his smoke, and stretched his arm back to pass it to Tommy.

"It's not lit," Tommy said.

"It is so," Kenny said, turning and blowing smoke in his face.

Tommy hauled on the end. "Well it ain't anymore."

Kenny took it from him, lit it again, and handed it back.

"Kenny, Mr. Spencer's gonna come lookin for us and we haven't cleaned the erasers yet," Tommy said. Kenny, once again, peeked out the window. "Okay. Coast is clear. Grab the erasers," he said.

The two of them slid out the back, walked to the side of the school, and began clapping the chalky brushes. The bell sounded for the end of recess. Mr. Spencer was in the doorway waiting for them when they ran up the hallway covered in chalk dust.

"They were pretty chalky," Kenny said. He stood in front of Mr. Spencer and gave them one final clap. "See, good as new," he said, as a cloud of fine, white dust rose in the air. Mr. Spencer stepped back, glared his disapproval, and ordered Kenny and Tommy to their seats.

"Put your readers away and take out your math scribblers," Mr. Spencer instructed. He was writing an equation on the blackboard when Principal Gillis charged through the door and the two ran out and down the hall. Teachers were pouring out of their classrooms and screaming at their students to stay put. That's when they heard the siren. Kenny and his fellow students rushed to the window. "Holy shit!" Harley said. "Isn't that Mr. Spencer's car?"

School was cancelled for the rest of the day.

Kenny was pushing Tommy's bike up Dominion Street with Tommy lagging behind. He stopped outside the entrance to Greenwood Cemetery and turned to his friend. "Let's take the shortcut," he said. Tommy was crying. "For Pete's sake, Tommy! No one knows."

"But what if someone saw us. We'll go to jail."

"No one saw us. And we're not goin to jail. Reform school, maybe. But not jail." Tommy started to sob. "I'm kiddin," Kenny said. "We're not goin anywhere. If ya ask me, it worked out perfect. We got the day off didn't we?"

Tommy ran his sleeve under his wet nose. "Mr. Spencer was glaring at me when he said the police were gonna investigate."

"So what! He glared at me too. He's always glarin. They ain't got no proof. Hell, for all we know we didn't even start it."

"No!" Tommy said. "It just burst into flames on its own. How else did it catch fire?"

"I dunno. But I'll tell ya this. You go actin guilty and the next thing ya know *we will be shipped off to reform school.* Now smarten up and c'mon."

"I don't wanna go to the *Heaps.* I'm goin home."

"Wanna go to the dam instead?"

"No! I wanna go home."

Kenny figured he better stay close to Tommy so he wouldn't go spilling the beans. "I'll come with ya."

Tommy's father was under the hood of his car when they walked up the driveway. "What are you boys doin here? Why aren't you in school?"

Kenny spoke up. "Strangest thing happened. Mr. Spencer's car just burst into flames. Puff! Just like that," he said, throwing his hands in the air. "They gave us the rest of the day off."

Tommy went in the house. Kenny leaned over the engine as Tommy's father tightened the oil cap. "Nice bike ya got Tommy," he said.

Tommy's father closed the hood. "Present for gradin," he said, rubbing his greasy hands in a rag.

"Yeah, so he said. Better hope he passes. I sure would like a bike like that for gradin," Kenny said. "Likely get the same as I got last year. Nottin."

Tommy's father didn't respond.

"*Sooo,*" Kenny said, "*been to the brook lately?*"

Sam walked the short distance from the courthouse on McKeen Street to his office, thinking about what Mary Catherine had said. Why did Stanley lie about renovating the MacPhees? And where has he been every night and practically every weekend for the past two months? Sam didn't have Stanley pegged for the philandering type, and he and Mabel certainly seemed happy. But stranger things have happened. He stopped in front of his office on Commercial Street and looked across to Mendelsons, recalling the day he saw Stanley talking to a woman he didn't recognize. She was tall and thin, and very well dressed in her long, black coat, and white gloves and flapper cap. Sam had left them to their business and went about his own. When he approached the produce table a good twenty minutes later they were still chatting. The striking, unfamiliar woman had reached into her purse, scribbled something on a piece of paper, and slid it into Stanley's jacket pocket. She then leaned in, kissed him on the cheek, and walked down the aisle. Sam recalled the surprised look on Stanley's face when he approached him from behind and asked who she was.

"Clair. An old friend," Stanley had said, not taking his eyes off her. "She's visiting from the mainland. Her aunt died. Left her a house in Boisdale. Needs someone to fix it up."

"Are you taking the job?"

Stanley threw an onion in the air and caught it. "No. Too much on the go."

Sam thought back, thinking it would have been around two months ago. Right around the same time Stanley claimed he was fixing up the MacPhee property.

Sam entered his office and picked up the phone. "Luke. What are you doing later this morning? How about I pick you up at eleven and we take a drive. Boisdale. Yes, Boisdale. I think Stanley might be there. I'll tell you when I see you." He hung up. "Charlie, get in here," he yelled to his young articling clerk. "Drop whatever you're doing. I need you to check out recent deaths in the Boisdale area.

I don't have a name. Looking for an older woman, likely over sixty who died in the past six months or so. I need her address."

Charlie looked perplexed. "Ya mean where she's buried?"

"No, Charlie. Where she used to live," Sam said, reminding himself that it wasn't all that long ago he might have asked the same question.

It didn't take long for Charlie to return. He tapped on Sam's open door. "Pretty sure this is it, cause there's only one person fitting your description," he said, handing the notepad to his boss.

"Thanks, Charlie." His young clerk was about to leave. "Oh, and Charlie, I need you to handle my afternoon appointments."

"By myself?"

"Yes."

"But —"

"I'll leave the files and my notes on your desk," Sam said. He looked at Charlie's note. *Sophia DiJackimo. Sixty-six. Died in February. Lived next to the abandoned sawmill.* He hoped Stanley was wasn't there, or if he was, he was alone.

An hour later he and Luke were driving along the coast, both thinking about what they would say to their friend if they found him with another woman.

"Sam, you don't really think Stanley's been cheating on Mabel do you?" Luke asked.

"I never thought it was possible. But, then again, Stanley's been lying about his whereabouts. I just can't figure out why."

They passed the sawmill, took the next right, and drove to the white farmhouse near the water. There was a black Chevrolet in the driveway and a pallet of new lumber on the veranda, but no blue truck. They knocked on the door. There was no answer. They were peeking through the windows when Clair came around front. She was wearing a pink robe and matching bathing cap, and holding a shovel in a menacing manner.

"Can I help you?" she asked.

Sam jumped and turned from the window to the voice. "I'm sorry," he said. "I'm Sam Friedman and this is Luke…Luke Toth. We're friends of Stanley…Stanley MacIntyre. We didn't think anyone was home and just thought —"

"You'd *peer* through my windows."

"We were…well… we were wondering if anyone was home. If Stanley might be here?"

"And why did you think you'd find him here?"

Sam glanced at Luke. "Well, he's missing and someone told us to try—"

"Who?" she asked.

"Actually, *I* thought he might be here," Sam clarified, awkwardly explaining about the day he saw her and Stanley at Mendelsons. "He mentioned you needed work done to your property."

"Well, you can see he's *not here.*"

"Yes. Sorry for the intrusion," Sam stammered, heading down the steps with Luke in tow.

She rested the shovel against the side of the house. "Can I ask why you're looking for him?"

Sam and Luke turned to face her. "His son died a few days ago and no one has seen him since," Luke said.

Clair put her head down. "I wasn't aware. What happened?"

"He fell off the cliff behind the family home," Sam said and nodded for Luke to join him at the car.

"It's hot gentlemen. Would you like a cold drink?"

Sam looked at Luke, then Clair. "That'd be great."

Clair pulled her robe around her and they followed her inside. "I'm Clair," she said, turning toward them. "Make yourselves comfortable. I'm going to change."

They were sitting on the sofa when she reappeared wearing a white, short-sleeve blouse, black capris, and white tennis shoes. *She's stunning*, Sam thought. Luke was thinking the same. They stayed longer than planned. Clair explained that her father was Stanley's trainer, she and her parents moved to the mainland, and up until the time she ran into Stanley at Mendelsons, she hadn't seen or spoken to him in years. She didn't reveal they were once engaged.

"I never expected to come back and stay, but my parents are both dead, I love the peace and quiet, and I have an older sister in Dominion."

Sam thought it strange, that a gorgeous woman like her never mentioned a husband or children. He looked at his watch and placed his glass on the table. "Luke? We should get going."

Clair saw them to the door. "When you see Stanley, please let him know I'm thinking about him," she said. Sam nodded and waved. Clair watched her unexpected visitors make their way up the long driveway, bounce over the train tracks, and turn left onto the main road.

"Tell him I'm always thinking about him," she whispered as they drove out of sight.

Mary Catherine tidied up the kitchen. She made herself another cup of tea and sat on the back step, wondering if she should just go home. She could see Myrtle climbing up the bank, stabbing the ground with her walking stick. Mary Catherine sipped her tea, relieved that Myrtle kept walking toward her small bungalow. Mabel's strange neighbour stopped at her shed, pulled on the padlock, then rolled a tree stump over to the side so she could peek in the window.

"What are you doing? Not like you've got anything worth stealing," Mary Catherine whispered. Myrtle stepped off the tree stump and turned to face her. "Damn it," Mary Catherine muttered. She had no choice but to wave. Myrtle was approaching. Mary Catherine pretended she didn't notice and stood to go back inside.

"Hey! Have you seen Lucky?" Myrtle yelled.

Mary Catherine had her hand on the screen door. "What?"

"Have ya seen my cat?" Myrtle repeated. "Ugly little thing. No tail. Half an ear."

Mary Catherine gave her an exasperated look. *How could she be so thoughtless at a time like this?* "No," she said curtly.

Myrtle pointed to the water. "Ya ask me, the boy ain't out there."

"And what makes you say that?" Mary Catherine asked, growing more agitated by the minute.

"My gut. Just too many boats out there. The waters have been calm last few days. Body shoulda popped up by now. Ya see, once the body starts to decompose, the gases—"

Mary Catherine put her hand up to stop her from going on. "So you think he just vanished into thin air?"

Myrtle looked out at the ocean. "Just think they shoulda found the body. And I saw a man watchin the house."

"When?"

"A few weeks ago. He was parked on other side of the road. Saw him there a coupla times. He'd just sit there in his truck and stare up at the bluff. So I rapped on his window and asked what he was doin. He tore off like a pit rat looking up at the flat side of a pan shovel."

Mary Catherine was thinking that if Myrtle knocked on her window, she would have done the same. "Lots of folks park across the road on their way to the shore. Maybe he was picking up his kids or something."

Myrtle shrugged. "Wasn't anyone I ever saw before. Anyway, just thought ya should know. Tell Mabel I got some more preserves for her. No charge." She started to walk away.

Mary Catherine called after her. "Myrtle! I'd appreciate it if you don't share this with Mabel. She's having a hard enough time as it is. She needs to come to grips with what's happened. And…well… I'm sure you understand…nothing good can come from giving her false hope."

Myrtle waded back through the field. She turned back and looked at the house on the bluff. "Hope is hope," she said, sticking her tongue out and thumbing her nose in Mary Catherine's direction.

Mary Catherine didn't see her. She was already back inside, rinsing her cup and thinking about how much she missed the kids and her own bed. She'd call the store and see if Luke could come and spend the night.

Alice's father, Corliss, answered. "What do you mean Luke and Sam went for a drive?" Mary Catherine asked. "Did he say where? Is Mabel there? How does she seem? Good. Can someone drive her home? Alright." She placed the receiver down and immediately picked it back up. "Charlie. It's Mary Catherine. Do you know where Sam is? Boisdale? Did he say why? He's checking on a dead woman? No, that's fine, I'll talk to him tonight."

Mary Catherine jumped to her feet when she saw Sam and Luke turn up the driveway. Sam had barely stepped out of the car, when she asked why they were in Boisdale. Sam was going to keep his suspicions to himself, but felt he had no choice now but to share them with his inquisitive wife. Mary Catherine listened to him with a mixture of surprise and relief.

"He'd never cheat on her. He loves her," she said.

"So, where is he?" Luke asked. "If he truly loved her, he'd be with her. And he wouldn't blame her."

Mary Catherine heard the phone and charged up the steps. "Hello? Amour!" she said, pressing her eyes closed. "Thank God!"

Mary Catherine had to interrupt her. "Amour! Thank God you called. I'm sorry. Amour! JC is gone. He fell off the cliff." She could hear the phone drop, Amour holler to Michael, the muffled voices, and then the cries in the background. Michael came to the phone.

"Four days ago. I wanted to call but she wouldn't let me. Angry. Heartbroken. Won't eat. She's at the bakery. Yes, the bakery. No. He's not here. He left shortly after it happened and we haven't seen him since. We don't know. No, no arrangements yet. They haven't found the body. I doubt they ever will. Yes, I will."

Mary Catherine hung up the phone. Sam and Luke were standing next to her. "That was Amour and Michael." She turned to Luke. "Can you stay with Mabel tonight?"

"Of course."

"Try and get her to eat. I left a couple of plates in the refrigerator."

Mary Catherine looked at Sam. "Let's go home."

Wednesday, May 29

CHAPTER 5

Liddy toddled along the kitchen floor and climbed on top of the clothes in the wide-rimmed wicker hamper. Mary Catherine handed Liddy her rag doll, rolled her wringer washer next to the sink, connected the hose, and filled the tub. She pulled the dirty clothes out from under Liddy, tossed them in the water, added a cup of Oxydol, and pulled out the agitator gear. She smiled as Liddy toppled out of the hamper and crawled under the table, playing at her feet. A half-hour later, Mary Catherine closed her six-month old issue of Chatelaine and pushed the agitator gear back in place. The swooshing of the Maytag rumbled to a halt and she began to feed the wet clothes through the wringer. Liddy was unusually quiet. She bent down and looked under the table. She was curled up, fast asleep. Mary Catherine was about to stand up when she spotted the tiny blue dot on the white linoleum floor. "Liddy!" she said, grabbing her by the arms and pulling her out from under the table. Liddy was as limp as her rag doll. "Oh my God!" Mary Catherine screamed as she picked up the empty vial of *Luminal.* Mary Catherine ran to the phone. "Please! I need help! Send an ambulance!"

Mary Catherine was at her daughter's bedside. "Please, Liddy! Please, honey! Wake up." she said, brushing her hair away from her forehead.

Sam was huddled with Dr. Cohen. "So you found three on the floor?"

"Yes."

Dr. Cohen nodded. "And we know Mabel had four."

"Sam, I'm not going to sugarcoat this. She had at least a dozen. It's a powerful sedative. A lot for an adult, let alone a child her size. One thing we know for sure, she's not going to wake anytime soon."

"But she will wake up! Right?" Sam said, tears building in his eyes. Dr. Cohen touched his arm and smiled. He walked out, thinking the child would be dead before morning.

Mabel walked down the long hallway as nurses in their crisp uniforms, starched white caps, and soft-soled shoes side-stepped the whirring buffer gliding across the freshly waxed floor. She could see Liddy's grandparents, aunts and uncles, and older cousins whispering and anxiously pacing outside room 4B.

The whispers stopped when Mabel came into view. Everyone bracing themselves for the hollow-sounding words they knew they were about to offer a mother who had just lost her son; everyone praying they would not be called upon to repeat similar words of sympathy to Sam and Mary Catherine. Mabel greeted them with a hug and a knowing smile. She then looked into the room at the small child lying in a bed meant for an adult. Sam was staring out the window. Mabel laid her hand on Mary Catherine's shoulder, then kissed Liddy's cheek. "Let's take a walk," she said, reaching down and taking her friend's hand.

They walked quietly down the hall, took the stairwell to the main floor, and pushed the heavy wooden doors open. The bright sun and fresh air, providing a welcome relief from the heavy atmosphere inside. Mary Catherine sat down on the concrete steps and watched a dozen or more seagulls land on the front lawn and stomp their feet. Mabel sat down beside her. "They're searching for worms."

"How do you know that?" Mary Catherine asked, reaching for Mabel's hand and placing it on her lap.

"I've watched them. They're not just garbage gobblers, you know."

"I'm terrified," Mary Catherine said bluntly.

"I know."

"If my baby dies, I will too. I'm not strong like you."

Mabel closed her eyes. Mary Catherine had no idea that she was so overcome by her own grief that she wanted to jump to her death.

Mary Catherine started to cry. "I should have been more careful. I should have put the pills away."

"Mary Catherine! Please! It's not your fault. If anyone's to blame, it's me. JC's dead because of me. You had the pills because of me. Liddy is *here* because of me! I feel as if my only purpose in life is to bring misery—"

"Stop it! Stop it!" Mary Catherine said. There was a harshness to her voice. "Mabel," she said more softly. "I don't deny it. It's like there's a black cloud following you around. But you're a kind, loving and generous person. You don't deserve it. Any of it!"

Mabel smiled at her friend. "Liddy is going to come out of this. I know she is. You have to believe. You have to have faith."

Mary Catherine turned to her. "In *the doctors* you mean?"

"Yes."

"And God?" Mary Catherine asked.

Mabel put her head down. "You need to believe in whatever gives you strength."

"You give me strength," Mary Catherine said, resting her head on Mabel's shoulder. "I just don't understand. First, your son. Now, my daughter. Why?"

"I don't know," Mabel said.

"I was thinking about our conversation. You know, when you told me about what you said to James the night before he died. You're right, Mabel. It's easy to give advice and to be so sure of yourself when bad things happen to other people. But when they happen to you, it's altogether different. If Liddy dies, I'll die. I may live to be an old woman, but I'll never draw another happy breath."

"But you still have hope," Mabel said. "And hope is hope. I'm sure that when you're an old, grey-haired woman with no teeth, you'll be singing Jewish lullabies and rocking Liddy's children to sleep."

Mary Catherine stood and looked down at her friend. "I pray you're right. I need to get back inside."

Mabel started to get to her feet. "Look!" she said.

Mary Catherine turned around, shielding her eyes from the sun. There was a gull with its neck stretched up. It had a worm dangling from its beak.

They were walking back to Liddy's room when Mabel heard someone call out to her. It was Captain Dunphy. "You go. I'll be in shortly," she said to Mary Catherine.

"Mabel," Dunphy said, reaching for her hand. "How are you managing?"

"I've had better days."

"I would imagine. Have you heard from Stanley?"

"No."

"I've told the boys to keep an eye out for him."

"Thank you," she said.

"Mabel," Dunphy said, then paused. "I thought you should know… Billy Guthro's dead. Died about an hour ago."

Images of filthy hands reaching for mustard and sardine sandwiches, an empty rum bottle on her bedroom floor, and a mound of yellow vomit flashed in Mabel's mind.

"He held on for a few weeks, but finally succumbed to his injuries. I can't say I'm sorry. The trouble he caused for you and Stanley."

Mabel smiled at Captain Dunphy, thinking he didn't know the half of it. He didn't know about the rape. It was a secret that she and Stanley would take to their graves. There was a time when she would have killed Billy with her own two hands, yet she blessed herself.

"Anyway, I'm sure he's heading straight to hell," Dunphy said.

Mabel touched his arm. "Sounds to me like he was already there."

"Well, I thought you should know."

"Thank you," she said and walked down the hall. She stopped at the fountain next to the nurses' station and put her mouth to the nozzle.

"He's so handsome," one young nurse said to another. "And it's not just the uniform."

"So why isn't he attached? Kinda makes ya wonder," her co-worker said.

An older, heavyset nurse slammed her chart on the counter. "Cause he's waiting for me. Now stop planning your wedding and get to work!" she barked.

They're talking about Dunphy, Mabel thought. She wiped her wet chin and looked down the hall. He was looking back at her and smiling. She felt herself get flush and turned away quickly. Dr. Cohen was across the hall talking to Rabbi Goldberg. A young doctor joined them. They looked grim.

"Rabbi, this is Dr. McLellan. He's got more experience dealing with these matters than I do. We both agree that the child swallowed enough pills to kill an adult. We're surprised she hasn't already died. It's just a matter of time. Likely just hours. You should stick around. The family will need you," Dr. Cohen said.

Mabel's hand started to shake and she felt faint. She needed to sit down. She pushed on the door to what she thought was the waiting room. It was the chapel. She walked down the short aisle to a middle pew, sat down, and watched the flickering votives on the bye-altar cast a warm yellow glow under the image of the Virgin Mary. She wondered if any of the tormented worshippers who had made their offerings had their prayers answered, then lowered herself onto the kneeling pad and folded her hands together. *Dear Lord, this is the last time I will ask you for anything. You've taken my child. Hold and protect him. I beg you not to take another. Let Liddy live to have babies of her own. Show me a sign of your mercy. Show me you are a loving, merciful God. Spare this child. Prove to me that you exist.*

She made the sign of the cross and sat back against the pew. She sensed a presence behind her and then a hand on her shoulder.

She turned. "Father Gregory?"

"It's good to see you praying," he said.

"Force of habit, Father. I do it without expectation. I suspect it will be the last time I ask *Him* for anything," she said, turning back to face the altar.

"Nevertheless, God will be pleased you've called on him. I know that sorrow can—"

She spun around and glared at him. "Really, Father!" she said sarcastically. "What would you know about sorrow!" Father Gregory smiled and put his head down. "And who brought about my sorrow? Who took my son? And who do you think is responsible for that child…that baby down the hall who is about to take her last breath? Who!" she screamed. She shook her fist at him. "I'll tell you who!" She turned and pointed up at the stark wooden cross hanging on the bare white wall. "He is!" She bent over sobbing.

Father Gregory stood up slowly, made his way down the aisle, and knelt at the altar. Mabel looked up at him. He had a white glow around him. She blinked hard and wiped her eyes. It must be the aura from the candles. She wiped them again. Maybe she's just light-headed from not eating. She thought she could hear her name; faint at first, then louder. She turned just as the door flew open. It was Mary Catherine. She was crying and fell to the floor. Mabel ran to her, knelt down, and wrapped her arms around her. "I'm so sorry," Mabel said.

Mary Catherine lifted her head. "She's… she's awake! She's going to be fine!" she said, laughing and crying at the same time.

Mabel looked at the altar. There was no sign of Father Gregory.

Stanley was outside McRae's Hardware. He slid the two-by-fours next to his twenty pound bag of gypsum plaster and closed the tailgate. He was about to hop in the cab when he saw her stepping out of her car. She walked up to him and gave him a hug. "I heard about your son. I'm very sorry."

Stanley felt himself well up. "Thank you, Clair. I thought you would have been back on the mainland by now?"

"I decided to stay. You have folks worried. They're looking for you?"

Stanley was taken aback. "But, how —"

"Sam and Luke came by my place looking for you. Sam remembered seeing us talking at Mendelsons and somehow thought...well, he somehow thought you might be renovating the farmhouse." She placed her hand on his forearm. "How are you coping?"

"How does anyone cope?"

"I see you're working through it," she said, nodding to the supplies in the back of his truck.

Stanley put his head down. "Either that or drink myself to death."

"I can't imagine."

"So, are you still at your aunt's?" he asked.

"Yes. I've hired some locals to do the repairs, but it's been slow. And well...well let's just say their carpentry skills aren't what I had hoped for. I came for some paint. And you? Where are you staying?" Clair asked.

There was an awkward silence. "About thirty miles up the road. Sorry, I should be going. I got a ton of work and I'm running behind."

She closed her eyes and nodded.

"It was good seeing you again" he said. He got in, closed the door, and started up the truck.

Clair walked up to his open window. "If you need a home cooked meal, or just someone to talk to, you know where to find me."

"Thank you, Clair. Good luck with your repairs." He pulled away slowly, thinking she was just as sweet, but even more beautiful than he remembered.

***

Sam turned up Brodie Avenue. "It's hard to explain. Even Dr. Cohen says so. He said they called in Rabbi Goldberg because they didn't expect Liddy to live through the night. He said there was no explanation for it. That it must be the result of some sort of divine intervention."

Mabel put her head down and closed her eyes, recalling the image of Father Gregory kneeling at the altar, surrounded by light. *Was it the work of God or my mental fatigue? But then, how do you explain his disappearance and Liddy's miraculous recovery?* She looked out the passenger window and smiled. *Maybe God did hear my prayers. Maybe JC* is *at peace with the Lord.*

"I'm sorry," Sam said.

She turned to face him. "For what?"

"For being so thoughtless. For sounding so happy knowing everything that you're going through."

"Don't be foolish, Sam. Happiness is all too rare. It's meant to be shared."

Sam reached for her hand. "So is misery," he said. "If you ever need to talk… anything? I hope you know that Mary Catherine and I are always here for you?"

"You know, Sam. I was having my doubts. I mean about…about whether God exists. Liddy's recovery has given me hope that He really does. That He hears our prayers. At least some of them. It helps make my grief… more bearable."

Sam stopped the car and smiled. "Well, *I have no doubt.* Not after tonight."

"Want to come in for some tea?" Mabel asked.

"Thanks, but I need to check on Irwin and get back to the hospital."

"Goodnight, Sam."

Luke and his two younger brothers, Mark and John, were waiting in the living room. John got up from the footstool when Mabel entered and awkwardly approached her. "I made this for you." Mabel smiled and took the folded paper from him. It was a picture of a large red heart with sad eyes. Tears flowed down the page. The penciled inscription below read, *I Love You.*

Mabel laid the paper on her chest and kissed the top of his head. "I love you too." She looked up and smiled, as Alice walked in from the kitchen. "Liddy is going to be fine. It wasn't looking good, but she's been spared." No one said anything. Mabel looked at their glum faces. "For goodness sakes, it's wonderful news. Alice," she said, "let's make some tea."

It was quiet at first, the only sounds were the clinking of cups on saucers and the whispered voices pointing out where to find things. Eventually the conversation picked up. But no one spoke about JC, fearing it would bring too many emotions to the fore.

"You can talk about him, you know," Mabel finally said. "I know this may sound odd, but Liddy's recovery has helped me come to terms with JC's death. As my mother once said, as hard as it is, life goes on. It will never be the same, but it *will* go on."

Alice burst into tears.

Thursday, May 30

CHAPTER 6

Mabel crept downstairs and tiptoed down the hallway to the kitchen.

"Morning," Luke said, sitting up.

"Sorry. Didn't mean to wake you," Mabel said.

"I've been awake for hours. You're up early?"

"Tired of my bed. Spent too much time in it lately. And I want to stop in and check on Liddy before I go to the bakery. Wash up and I'll make breakfast," she said.

Luke was in the kitchen twenty minutes later. He pulled out a chair and watched Mabel prepare their fare.

"Hope you like your eggs over hard," she said, putting the plate in front of him. She pulled out the chair next to him and sat down. "Kind of got used to making them that way. Stanley hates runny eggs." She watched him eagerly dig in. "Thank you," she said.

"For what?"

"For spending the night. For stopping me from—" She took a deep breath, "doing the unthinkable."

Luke put his fork down. "I thought about it too. Kind of crazy when you think of it. I was so scared I was going to get killed in the war, then come home and sometimes wish I had. It's just that

I get this feeling. I don't know. An emptiness. Like I'm numb. Not normal. That's why I have the pills."

An image of Luke as a boy, looking down at his feet popped into Mabel's mind. "I'm sorry, Luke. I knew you felt melancholy from time to time. But I really didn't realize how much you were suffering. I'm here for you. You know that, *right?*"

Luke nodded.

"And your pills…they help?" Mabel asked.

"Mostly. But honestly, Mabel. If you had jumped, I might have been right behind you."

Mabel smiled and put her hand over his. "So, in a way we saved each other," she said.

Luke dropped his head. "I guess so."

"Or God did?" Mabel asked. "You did say God sent you to me that night?"

Luke shrugged. "I don't know. I just felt I had to come. But I didn't think I'd find you at the edge of the cliff."

"But you do believe in God? You *did say* you felt as if *He sent you.*"

"I would have said anything at the time. Honestly, after all the carnage I witnessed overseas…so many young men…younger than me…mowed down… beaten down. Let's just say there's room for doubt."

"I never questioned my faith until last week," Mabel said. "But then, yesterday, I had the most incredible experience." Mabel told Luke about what happened in the chapel. "How do you explain the unexplainable? It must have been some sort of divine intervention. Even Dr. Cohen can't explain Liddy's recovery."

"And this experience you had in the chapel, it helps you accept what happened to JC?"

"No. But it makes it more bearable," Mabel said.

"Like my pills," Luke said.

There was a knock on the front door. It was Fred Clarke. Dirty Willie and Ten-After-Six were standing next to his truck.

"Mabel," he said. "I'm so sorry for your loss. The wife made this for you," he said, passing her a Corningware dish. "Hope you like lamb stew?"

"Yes. Thank you, Fred. And please thank Aggie for me."

"Any word from Stanley?"

"Afraid not."

Fred glanced back at the truck. "Well, me and the boys thought we could get started on the barn. Just wanted to make sure you're good with that."

"Of course, Fred," she said, waving to the guys. Mabel walked back into the kitchen. "Well, Luke," she said. "Time's a ticking and I've got baking to do."

Stanley looked in the mirror and ran his wet hand over his chin and down his neck. He looked like shit and he felt like shit. He needed a razor. He dried his face and threw the hand towel in the sink. He walked into the kitchen, picked up an empty rum bottle, and put it on the floor next to the others. He opened the refrigerator, then closed it, grabbed his keys, and jumped in his truck. He needed to escape his angry solitude. He drove off and pulled into the first place he saw. Marg's Diner offered full breakfasts for forty-five cents. It must be decent, he thought, there were a good number of cars out front. He waited at the door for a chance to take a seat in Marg's popular eatery. He finally took a booth.

An older woman with a hairnet holding her wiry, grey mane in place moved from one table to the next, taking orders without the benefit of pen and paper. She finally got to him. "What'll ya have?"

"I'll have the special. Eggs over hard. I can't eat them runny. And I'll have the ham."

"Have the corned beef hash. It comes with a green chow."

"No thanks. I'll have the special."

"Nah! Have the hash." She leaned in and whispered. "Regular cook's psoriasis is actin up. Murray's on the grill. He knows how to get a good crisp on the hash. He burns everythin else to shit."

Stanley looked at Murray sweating over his grill. "I'll have the hash."

A father walked in with his young daughter and placed her on a stool that had opened up at the counter. His wife joined them holding her son's small hand. They were looking around for a place to sit. The noisy chatter that had momentarily helped Stanley escape his anguish, suddenly went quiet. He couldn't swallow. He stood, threw a five dollar bill on the table, and approached the mother of the small boy. "Here, take my booth," he said, gently laying his hand on the child's head. He walked out, climbed back in his truck, and headed to North Sydney. He passed the sign for Boisdale and spotted the abandoned sawmill. He slowed to a crawl, looked down at the white farmhouse by the shore, then sped up. He got a mile down the road, pushed on the brakes, and turned around.

"Stanley!" Clair said.

"Got any eggs?" he asked.

Mabel walked down the corridor and stopped outside the chapel. She opened the door and looked in, picturing Father Gregory at the altar. The room was small. Too small for him to get past without her noticing. She let the door close and continued to 4B. Sam and Mary Catherine were both there. Liddy was sleeping.

"She okay?" Mabel asked.

"She's fine," Mary Catherine said. She gave Mabel a hug. "Doctor said she'd be pretty groggy for a while but that we can take her home."

Mabel walked over to Liddy and lightly touched her arm.

"No one can explain it," Mary Catherine said. "Doctor MacLellan said it's a miracle."

"Maybe it was," Mabel whispered.

"How are *you* doing?" Mary Catherine asked.

"Better. Happy for you."

Mary Catherine felt a pang of guilt knowing her happiness was matched by Mabel's torment.

"I should be going," Mabel said. "I just wanted to check on Liddy. Luke is waiting for me out front."

"Thank you," Sam said.

Mary Catherine gave her another hug. "I'll drop by this evening."

"No," Mabel said. "Stay with Liddy. Really, I'm doing much better." She was walking out and turned back. "I really am happy for you," she said.

Sam hugged his wife. She was crying.

Mabel and Luke entered the store. Corliss picked up his metal hand crutches and noisily made his way around the counter. "I couldn't sneak up on a dead man," he said.

Alice came from the kitchen, pulled up on his pant leg, hanging loosely below his knee, and re-pinned it under his belt. "That's better," she said.

"I'm goin to the doctor's, not dancin," Corliss said. He looked at Mabel. "Got an appointment with a fancy doctor from Halifax. Ferget what ya call him."

"He's an orthopaedic doctor. A bone specialist. He's gonna measure Da up for a fake leg," Alice said.

Luke looked at Corliss. "I can give you a lift."

"No need. Bert's pickin me up. But maybe you should come too. With Bert's bad hip, your limp, and my missin leg, we'd make quite the sight bangin into one another hobblin down the hall. We could call ourselves The Gimp Gang."

"Da!" Alice said, dropping her arms to her sides.

"What? He knows he ain't no Fred Astaire."

Alice went back to the kitchen. Mabel followed.

"I feel so bad for him," Alice said.

"I think your father's doing —"

"Not Da! Luke."

"Oh?" Mabel said.

"He's so self-conscious about his limp and then Da goes and says that to him."

"Luke didn't take any offense. He's fine," Mabel said.

"No, Mabel, he's not! He's hurting and I don't just mean his leg. He's lonely and troubled. My heart breaks for him."

"Do you ever talk to Mark about it?"

"Mark! Mark's a self-centered ass. He's never around to help Luke with the store. Too busy with his rugby or baseball buddies. And we both know it's Luke that's raising John. Mark thinks of no one but himself."

"I thought you two were an item?"

"Hardly! I go to the movies with him and some of his friends from time to time, but not as his date. He tried to kiss me once and I made it clear I wasn't interested."

"But Mark has suggested as much to me and to—"

"I know. And I told him to stop. He won't listen. Says I'm playing hard to get."

Mabel started dusting her kneading table, wondering if Alice might like to go to the movies with Luke.

Stanley sopped up his runny egg yolk with his store bought bread, and popped it in his mouth.

"You were hungry?" Clair said, resting her head on her hand and smiling.

"It hit the spot. Thank you." He took a sip of coffee.

"I'm glad you stopped in," Clair said.

Stanley patted his stomach. "Me too."

"So, what are your plans for the day?" she asked.

"Need to pick up some supplies." He scratched at his neck. "Starting with a razor."

"Then what?"

"Then, I suppose I turn around and head back the same way I came."

"So you still haven't been home and nobody knows where you are?" Stanley wiped his mouth. Clair sensed she was making him uncomfortable. "I'm sorry. It's really none of my business."

"No. I haven't been home. Just don't feel ready. I'm still…" he paused.

Clair finished his thought. "Hurt? Angry?"

"Yes."

Clair nodded. "Well, I need a few things in town myself. And since you're going to be heading back this way, maybe we can go together?" Stanley didn't respond. Clair stood and walked to the stove. "Or maybe it's not such a good idea after all," she said, reaching for the coffee pot.

Stanley hesitated, then walked toward her holding out his cup. "Why not."

Stanley waited on the veranda while Clair got changed. He was standing over the pallet of lumber when she came out. "Still waiting on my carpenters to do my floors. I fear it will be one big pile of sawdust by the time they get around to it," she said.

Clair insisted they take her car and that she drive. She sensed his discomfort. "Are you okay with this?" she asked.

Stanley smiled and nodded. "Why wouldn't I be?" he lied.

Stanley's initial unease gave way as Clair filled in the years since she and her family moved away. Her father took a job as a longshoreman. She went to Sacred Heart School for Girls. Eventually she got her secretarial diploma, got hired as a clerk with the Bank of Nova Scotia, and worked her way up to assistant to the local manager. She did some traveling, volunteered at the Red Cross, and lived at home with her parents until they died within six months of each other. When she came back home to see to her aunt's property, she fully expected to return, but decided she preferred the peace and quiet of the country to the hustle and bustle of the city.

Stanley couldn't figure out why she never got married. "So what will you do now?"

"The bank has offered me a transfer. Not in the same position mind you. It will be an entry-level job. Probably as a clerk. But I'd rather start at the bottom in a place I'm happy, than stay at the top in a place I'm not. And since I sold the house and have no family of my own to support, I have sufficient means to get by. At least for a while."

"Why *don't you* have a family?" Stanley asked, surprising himself. "I mean, I'm sure you must have had plenty of guys asking you out?"

She turned to him and smiled. "Obviously not the right one."

Clair drove down Archibald Avenue, found a parking spot on the street, and pulled over. "Do you just want to meet back here? Say at twelve-thirty?" she asked. Stanley agreed and watched her walk up the street and enter Vooght's Department Store. When she reappeared an hour later, Stanley was leaning against her car and smoking his pipe. She was struggling under the weight of three grocery bags, one tearing away at the side. He ran toward her. "Here!" he said, handing her his pipe and taking the over-stuffed bags from her. "Did you clean them out?" he asked.

Clair laughed. "No. Just my bank account."

Stanley opened the back seat and put her bags next to his. Clair held up her keys. "Do you want to drive?" she asked. Stanley took them from her and waited for the traffic to clear so he could step around to the driver's side. He didn't notice the paddy wagon drive by.

"Turn around and go back!" Dunphy screamed at McEwan.

"What?"

"I said go back! I just saw Stanley MacIntyre!"

McEwan found a place to turn into and threw the bulky, black wagon in reverse. He was trying to back into traffic. The driver of an oncoming car slammed on his breaks, laid on the horn, yelling "Arsehole!" The drunken passenger McEwan and Dunphy were returning home for the third time that week poked his head up and rested his face against the metal screen keeping him at bay. "What the fuck's gonin on?" he slurred.

"Jesus, Geezer! Back off! You stink!" McEwan said, banging the side of his fist against the screen.

"Yeah, well which one of you dicks shit in my pants?" Geezer said, falling backwards and landing with a thump.

"Forget it!" Dunphy hollered. He opened the door and began running up Archibald Avenue. "Damn it," he said, as the red signal light come on and the black Chevrolet turned the corner and drove out of sight.

Clair drove over the tracks and parked beside the house. Stanley got out, gathered up Clair's bags and followed her into the kitchen. Clair began putting her groceries away.

Stanley looked to the door. "Thanks for breakfast and the ride to town. It was great catching up."

Clair pulled her head from the fridge. "You're not leaving? Look! It's a beautiful day. Stay and have some lunch. We can eat on the shore. You can go for a swim."

Stanley grinned. "I really should hit the road. Besides, no trunks."

Clair sifted through her bags. "Will these fit?" There was an awkward silence. Clair rolled the swim trunks into a ball and put them back in the bag. "I'm sorry. I shouldn't have been so…presumptuous."

Stanley walked over and pulled the trunks back out. He held them up to his waist. "Looks like a perfect fit."

He was sitting on the wharf with his feet dangling above the water. Clair placed a tray of sandwiches, two tumblers, and a frosty pitcher down on the wharf. "You okay?" she asked, sitting beside him.

Stanley leaned back on his outstretched arms and squinted into the bright sun. "The waves washed my son out to sea," he said.

"Yes, Sam told me. I don't know what to say." Clair turned her head and looked back at the farmhouse. "Maybe we should eat inside?"

"No. We live on an island and I have a house on the bluff. Not like I can escape the reminder."

Clair picked up the pitcher. "Lemonade with just a hint of gin," she said, filling their tumblers. "It's beautiful here. Isn't it?" she said, passing him his drink.

"Yes."

She needed to lighten his mood. "Now you know why I couldn't go back to the mainland. I remember the first time I came here. I must have been seven or eight. Da paid the coal train operator a pretty penny to drop us off. He was supposed to pick us up on the way back from Christmas Island, but apparently he got drunk and forgot." She started to laugh. "I can still remember me, Da and my sister watching the train whistle by and Da running down the tracks hollering for him to stop. Anyway, I was happy. We got to spend another day."

"And now you get to spend the rest of your life here," Stanley said. "Sure is nice in the summer. But I dunno," he said, shaking his head, "the winters can be pretty brutal."

"You just have to prepare for it. And I love to skate. I'll have my own rink." She jumped to her feet. "But today I have my own pool." She dropped her robe and dove in.

Stanley waited for her to come up. "How is it?" he hollered.

"Like the ice just melted," she said, floating on her back and kicking up the water. "Seriously! It's not that bad. It's refreshing. C'mon in."

Stanley stood, but hesitated.

"C'mon, it's—"

Clair closed her eyes as the salty water splashed up. Stanley came up choking. He frantically swam back to the wharf and quickly climbed the ladder. Clair came up behind him. He was lying face up on the wharf, shivering and panting. She put her robe over him and rubbed her hands up and down his arms. "Too cold?" she asked.

"No," he said, rocking his head back and forth, and struggling to talk. "Too…too soon."

Mabel couldn't put the incident in the chapel out of her mind. It had to be a sign from God. He was telling her that He was merciful and to believe in Him. Maybe Father Gregory wasn't even in the chapel and it was God who had laid his hand on my shoulder and spoke to me in the handsome, young priest's image. Or maybe it was just my tormented mind and empty stomach playing tricks on me. But then, how do you explain Liddy's miraculous recovery.

She took two apple pies out of the oven and put them on the cooling rack. I'll go see Father Gregory, she thought. She turned as the water bubbled up and over the sides of the pot, sending tiny white beads dancing along the top of the black coal stove. She wrapped her hand in a tea towel and slid the pot to the side. She then placed her egg on a spoon and carefully laid it in the water. Then another. She thought of Stanley. *Make sure they're not runny*, he would say. She wondered where he was and if he was okay. If he would just listen to what happened to her in the chapel, maybe he'd be able to cope better. Maybe even forgive her.

Alice came in and looked at the pies. "Are they ready to go out front?"

"I'd wait for them to cool," Mabel said. Alice surprised her with a hug.

"Thank you," Mabel said. "Not sure what I did to deserve that?"

"You just looked like you could use one," Alice said.

"Nothing better than an unexpected hug," Mabel said.

Mark rapped on the door jamb. "My two favourite girls. Busy bakin up a storm I see."

"Hi, Mark," Mabel said.

Mark kissed her on the cheek and squeezed her arms. "Guess what ladies? Savoy's got a new movie in. *Double Indemnity*. So, Alice? Whatcha think?"

Mabel glanced at Alice. She had her head down, wiping the counter. "You go. I got other plans."

"What plans?"

"None of your concern."

Mark pressed on. "Humphrey Bogart's in it."

Alice was losing her patience. "I don't care. I'm not interested."

Mark walked up beside Mabel, stuck his finger in her bowl of boiled icing, and licked his finger. "She likes to play hard to get," he said.

"No, Mark," Alice said harshly. "You're hard to get through to. I'm not interested. Period! And I'd appreciate it if you wouldn't lead people to believe that we're a...a couple."

He looked at Mabel. "I guess I've been told," he said. He dipped his finger in the bowl a second time and walked out. When he entered the store he kicked a cardboard box across the floor and stormed out.

Luke jumped down from his stool behind the counter and limped into the kitchen. "What's got him so hot under the collar?" he asked.

"I'm sorry," Stanley said, still shivering.

"No need to apologize," Clair said. She placed a blanket over his shoulders. "Here," she said, passing him his glass. "It's scotch."

He took the glass from her. "It's just that as soon as I dove in… I had…I had an image of JC underwater."

Clair knelt in front of him and rested her hands on his thighs. "It's my fault. I should have known better."

"You didn't push me," he said and downed his scotch.

"I did in a way." She got back on her feet. "Why don't you get changed? I'll bring our lunch up here."

Ten minutes later, Clair joined Stanley on the front porch. She was wearing a pretty yellow dress and a fresh application of glossy, red lipstick. She put down her tray and passed him his plate. "Ham and mustard. And of course, a little something to help warm you up," she said, handing him another glass of scotch.

Stanley put his glass down on the small table they shared and bit into his sandwich.

"I think I added to your misery," she said.

"More like I ruined your day. Stopping in unannounced. The episode on the shore. I'm sure you had better things to do than—"

"I'm happy you're here," Clair said, reaching over and placing her hand on his arm.

Stanley reached for his scotch. "Then you must be a dog for punishment."

"Don't be silly. I'm really glad you stopped by. I love it here, but…well sometimes…sometimes it can get a little lonely. It's great to spend some time with an old friend. I often wondered how you were. Even thought about getting in touch with you when I visited my sister," Clair said.

Stanley looked surprised. Clair put her head down. "Always chickened out. I don't know. So much time had passed. Well… I just thought you had probably forgotten all about me."

"Clair, you're not easy to forget."

"So, did you ever wonder about me?"

"Yes," Stanley said, knowing it was true, at least until he met Mabel.

Clair smiled and then started to laugh. "My father would have been impressed with all that you've accomplished. Running your own business. He was a great trainer, but a lousy judge of character."

"He was looking out for you. He meant no harm," Stanley said.

Clair shrugged and sipped her drink. She thought of how lonely she was after the family had suddenly packed up and moved away. She put her glass down thinking about the look on her father's face when he had found her at the train station trying to make her way back home. He had told her it was just a schoolgirl crush and that she'd meet a more suitable young man. As the months passed and she became accustomed to life in the city, Clair begin to think he might be right. Plenty of guys came calling, including a good number of the pin-striped, polished-shoe types who worked alongside her at the bank. She even came close to marrying the brother of one of her co-workers. But, in the end, no one ever measured up to her gentle coal-hauler with his broad smile and dark eyes.

"Remember that time Da caught us holding hands on Big Beach?" she asked. "I thought he was going to have a heart attack."

Stanley put his head down and smiled.

They spent the next few hours sharing memories of younger days and happier times, and polishing off the better part of a quart of scotch. Stanley looked at the shadows on the lawn. "What time is it?" he asked.

Clair got up feeling a little tipsy and peeked through the screen door at the clock on the mantel. "It's not even six. Are you getting hungry?"

"I should go," he said.

"Please? At least stay for supper. New potatoes, beet greens, and a huge speckled trout. Too much for one."

"Damn," Stanley said, jumping up and running to Clair's car. He opened the back door and held up a bottle of milk. He removed the cap, put it his nose, and quickly turned his head away.

Clair started to laugh. "Anything salvageable?" she hollered.

He held up a razor.

Mabel couldn't wait any longer. She needed to speak to Father Gregory. She had Luke drive her to St. Anthony's, insisting she wouldn't be long. She knocked on the door to the Glebe House. There was no answer, so she crossed the street and entered the church. There were several nuns kneeling before the altar and an unusually large number of parishioners, their heads bowed and their rosaries in hand, making their way along the Stations of the Cross. There was no sign of Father Gregory. Mabel knelt and waited. She got to her feet as Sister Bernadette genuflected and walked up the aisle in her black and white habit.

"Excuse me, Sister? Do you know where I might find Father Gregory?"

"St. Joseph's," she said. She laid her hand on Mabel's arm. "He could use your prayers."

Mabel realized she was speaking of the hospital, not the church. "I'm sorry, Sister. Did something happen to him?"

"Yes. He's in grave danger. It's up to the Lord now," she said, and continued up the aisle.

Mabel was stunned. She returned to her pew and prayed for JC and for the young priest, the picture of health and vitality just the day before. What could have happened to him, Mabel thought. She left St. Anthony's confused by the latest turn of events.

An older man was talking to Luke. He nodded to Mabel when she approached the car, then walked up the church steps.

"Father Gregory's sick," Mabel said. "Apparently it's bad."

"Willard just told me he was attacked," Luke said.

"Dear, God!" Mabel said and blessed herself. "Who would want to hurt Father Gregory?"

"Not sure yet. Willard said there's a ton of rumours floating around. Some say it was a robbery gone bad. Others think there's more to it. Claim he was attacked by a jealous husband, or that his homosexual lover flew into a rage."

"That's ridiculous," Mabel hissed.

"Probably. But didn't stop whoever did it from tearing the Glebe House to pieces and beating him to a pulp. Willard's sister-in-law found him. I guess he was lying in a pool of blood when she showed up to do her morning cleaning. He took some powerful blows to the head. His jaw was out of place and he had no teeth."

"Luke," Mabel said. "Drop me off at the hospital."

Mabel walked down the familiar corridor lined with worried faces. "Any word?" she asked a young woman holding her Bible. "Not yet." Mabel leaned against the wall and waited with the others, a good number of them either praying or crying. She needed to know Father Gregory would be okay and that she would have the chance to speak with him about what happened in the chapel. She closed her eyes and began to pray, then she heard the stir. Dr. Cohen and Father Cusack were standing outside room *4B*.

Dr. Cohen was shaking his head from side to side.

Friday, May 31

CHAPTER 7

Kenny looked at the clock. It was after midnight. He couldn't get to sleep. He was worried about his friend. Tommy was terrified he was going to get carted off to reform school or forced into the pit, and Kenny was terrified Tommy was going to blab about smoking in Mr. Spencer's car. He needed to talk to him again first thing in the morning. He was also excited about the new bike Tommy's father promised to buy him. Then there was the problem of explaining his new bike to his parents and, of course, that crazy old woman's curse. Wally One-Nut was lying. There was no such thing as witch piss. He rolled over on his back. Tommy and Harley told him they thought there was something wrong with their privates. They both said they were itchy and Harley said he had a rash.

Kenny sat up and looked across the room at his brother. He was out like a light. He laid back down and put his hands down his pants. It did seem smaller. He looked back at his sleeping brother, turned on the lamp, pushed his bed clothes aside, and pulled his pajama bottoms down.

"What are you doing?" his brother asked.

Kenny quickly pulled his bottoms up. "Nothin."

"Checkin for crabs or somethin?"

"Crabs?" Kenny said, thinking about Myrtle's warning. *One of these days you're gonna wake up dickless.* He pictured the claws of the ugly, bug-eyed critter snapping at his penis. "What are crabs?" Kenny asked nervously.

"A guy's worst nightmare."

"How do ya get em?"

"From messin with the wrong woman. Now turn off the friggin light. I gotta be up at five."

Kenny turned the light off. He tossed and turned thinking about Myrtle smiling down at him as she drenched him in her powerful witch piss, Mr. Spencer pointing an accusing finger at him, and the long-nosed headmaster of the reform school shoving him into a dark hole.

Kenny was no sooner asleep when his father whacked him with a dish towel. "Get yer arse in gear! Yer gonna be late for school."

"What time is it?" Kenny asked.

"Almost eight."

"Jesus!" Kenny screamed, scrambling out of bed.

Kenny's father snapped the towel at him. "Watch yer Goddamn tongue!"

Kenny was out the door in less than fifteen minutes. He stopped in for Tommy, but he had already left. Kenny tore off hoping to catch up with him. The last thing he needed was for Mr. Spencer to get to Tommy first. He could hear the bell sound as he ran under the trestle. Everyone was already gathered in two neat lines outside the main entrances to St. Anthony's.

"Shit," Kenny mumbled, spotting Mr. Spencer off to the side. He had Tommy by the collar. Tommy looked terrified. "Get in line," Mr. Spencer barked at Kenny.

Kenny followed the long line as it inched forward through the double doors, denoting the *Boys'* entrance. He was on the steps and Mr. Spencer was still holding Tommy by the collar. Christ, we're gonna be shipped off to reform school before the day is out, Kenny thought. He took his newly assigned seat in the front. Finally, Tommy walked in and sat on the opposite side of the class. Kenny looked over his shoulder. His friend was as white as a ghost. When Kenny turned to face forward, Mr. Spencer was glaring at him. The door opened. Kenny's heart began to pound when she walked in. Her arms were folded under her huge chest and her hands were buried deep inside her baggy sleeves. Her long, black skirt swooshed across the dull, hardwood floor and her heavy, silver crucifix swung forward and then back against her white scapular. Her wimple hid her face, but Kenny recognized the purposeful strut.

She approached Mr. Spencer and whispered in his ear. She then turned to face the class. "Good Morning," Sister Carmelita said coldly.

"Good morning, Sister," the class replied in unison. Kenny looked at Tommy. Tommy was looking back; his eyes as wide as saucers. The jig was up, Kenny thought. He folded his arms and put his head down on his desk.

"Kenny!" Sister Carmelita snapped.

"Yes, Sister?"

"Sit up! I have something important to share with the class."

"Yes, Sister," he said, again. He waited for Principal Gillis to storm through the door and drag him and Tommy off to the office where their angry parents would be standing beside the black-clad, pointy-nosed headmaster of the County Institute for The Reformation of Wayward Boys. Kenny pictured him rubbing his long, skinny hands together as he gleefully prepared to beat the sin and snot out of the latest delinquents to come his way.

Sister Carmelita adjusted her crucifix. "I've just come from a meeting with Principal Gillis. He asked that I speak to you. As you all know, a terrible crime has been committed. A crime of such magnitude and consequent loss that it strikes at the core of each and every one of us. I have no doubt that this vile crime…this terrible sin against our Lord's commandments and His holy church will be met with swift justice here on earth. But only a merciful and loving God will save the perpetrator or perpetrators from the flames of hell."

Kenny's mouth was so dry he couldn't swallow. He looked at Mr. Spencer. He was staring back. There was a bang. Every head turned in the same direction. Tommy was lying on the floor beside his desk. Mr. Spencer rushed to Tommy, picked him up, and carried him out. Sister Carmelita walked to the window, pushed it up, and put the stick in place to hold it in place, thinking Tommy was overcome by the heat. "Principal Gillis will see he's appropriately seen to," she said. *What did she mean by that?* She then picked up Mr. Spencer's ruler and turned it over in her hands. "As I was saying, our community and church have been shaken. But with God's help our hearts will heal over time and we will move on from this tragic loss."

Kenny lowered his head down. "For Christ sakes. It was a Pontiac," he mumbled.

Sister Carmelita was walking toward him. She stopped. "With that said, Principal Gillis has agreed to suspend classes on Monday morning so that we can say our sad goodbyes to our dear Father Gregory. So wear your Sunday best, and please be on your very best behaviour as we see him on his journey home to the Holy Father."

Kenny put his head back down on his desk and rocked it back and forth; thinking Tommy was probably sitting in the big chair across from Principal Gillis, crying his eyes out, and spilling his guts.

Sister Carmelita laid her hand on his shoulder. "Are you okay?" she asked.

"Yes, Sister. I was just …just thinkin about poor Father Gregory."

⊏⊐

"Sam, I know it was him," Dunphy said into the phone. "Yes, North Sydney. We were taking Geezer home again. Tall and slim. Very well dressed. He was helping her put her bags in the car and then the two of them drove off. A black Chevrolet."

Sam knew who Dunphy was referring to. "Thanks, Gordon," he said and hung up. Maybe Clair *had* lied to him after all. Although she did seem genuinely surprised when he told her about JC. There's only one way to find out, he thought. "Charlie, you're on our own again. I'll be back before noon."

Sam slowed down and looked at the white house near the shore. "Damn it!" he said, spotting Stanley's truck.

Clair and Stanley looked at one another when they heard the pounding. "Who in the world?" Clair said, placing her coffee cup down. She tightened the belt of her robe and went to the door. "Sam?"

"Clair. See *you* found Stanley," he said sarcastically.

Stanley walked down the hall. "Sam?"

"Your *wife's* home worrying about you," Sam said with a tone.

Stanley walked past Clair, took Sam by the arm, and pulled him down the front steps. "Don't go jumping to conclusions," he said. "There's nothing going on between me and Clair."

Sam pulled his arm from Stanley's grip. "I don't believe you! Look, I know you're going through a lot. I can't even imagine. But so is Mabel! She's your wife for Christ sakes!"

Stanley grabbed him by the collar. "I don't need you to remind me about who I'm married to. And don't you dare talk to me about what I'm going through!" he said, shoving him to the ground. "Mind your own Goddamn business!"

Sam stood up and swiped at the dirt on the back of his pants. "How's *the MacPhee property* coming along?"

"Fuck you!" Stanley said, walking back to the house and brushing past Clair.

Sam walked to his car. He was about to get in when he looked up. Clair was standing in the doorway watching him. He drove off, cursing himself. I could have handled that better, he thought.

Clair heard the back door bang shut. Stanley walked to the shore and began pacing back and forth. She watched him, thinking about their night together in front of the fire. It wasn't exactly how she had imagined. How could it be? The mood was somber. Only time would tell if he could once again feel for her, what she had always felt for him. And now was not the time. Sam's visit just added anger to his hurt. Give him time, she thought. Give him time.

Father Cusack entered the Glebe House. "Dear God," he said looking around. He blessed himself, walked to the oak desk, picked up a notepad, and sat down, struggling to read Father Gregory's blood splattered notes. *Scripture reference. James 1: 2-11. Homily notes: Scripture is telling us that we must face great challenge secure in the knowledge that God will bring us joy. That he will make us perfect and complete. It is okay for those who suffer to ask for wisdom, but we must do so with faith in the wisdom of the Almighty. We must trust in the ways of our Lord God. Our Creator. Our Saviour. For His ways are beyond reproach.*"

Father Cusack put the notepad back on the desk and opened the top drawer. He removed a handful of envelopes, a calendar, a few pencils, a letter opener, and an address book. He pushed his chair back, pulled the drawer further out, and peered in. He picked up a flask, unscrewed the cap, and sniffed it. "A venial sin at most," he said smiling. He put the cap back on, opened the second drawer, and spotted Father Gregory's Bible. There was an envelope marked *Upon my Death* inside the front cover. He slid the letter opener into the corner pocket, tore it open, and read its contents. *My wishes are few. I hope to be buried in St. Anthony's Cemetery with only the dates of my birth and death noted on a modest headstone. Any income I have is to be given to the Sisters of Charity to be used to support their worthy deeds. All of my other worldly belongings, with the exception of my maniturgium, are to be entrusted to the Archbishop to be used as the diocese sees fit. My maniturgium is to be given to Mrs. Stanley*

MacIntyre with the wish she be advised of its significance." It was signed and dated the night before he died.

Father Cusack folded the paper over and put it in his inside breast pocket. He then knelt and prayed for the soul of his dear, departed brother.

⊏⊐

Mabel was bent over her kneading board. Luke walked in. "Mabel? Phone's for you."

"Take a message," she said, holding up her sticky hands. "You'll want to take it," he said, dipping his head and arching his eyebrows.

Mabel went to the sink, washed her hands, and dried them in her apron. She entered the store. Luke passed her the receiver and left so she could speak privately.

"Hello?" she said. There was a pause.

"It's me."

Mabel closed her eyes. "It's good to hear your voice. How are you?"

"I thought I'd come home."

"I'd like that. Where are you?"

"Up the coast."

"When?"

"This evening."

"I'm glad."

"Mabel. Don't expect too much of me."

"I know. So, I'll see you tonight then?"

"Yes."

"Stanley," she said. There was another pause. "We can make this work."

"I'll see you tonight," he said and hung up.

Mabel put her hand to her mouth and slowly placed the receiver down. She started to cry. Luke walked back into the store and hugged her. "He's coming home," she said.

⊏⎯⎯⎯⎯⎯⎯⊐

"How's Liddy?" Sam asked, putting his briefcase on the floor.

"She's fine. What's all over your jacket?" Mary Catherine asked, brushing the dirt off his back.

Christ, he thought, I walked around all afternoon like that and no one said a thing. "What's for supper?" he asked, changing the subject.

"Holishkes. Wash up and I'll get the kids."

"I need a drink first," Sam said. He walked to the liquor cabinet and poured a rum. Mary Catherine was surprised. Sam wasn't much of a drinker.

"Bad day?" she asked as he downed it and poured another.

"No better than most and no worse than the rest," he said.

Mary Catherine's concern continued to grow over the course of the night. Sam toyed with his food and was unusually sharp with Irwin during supper. She settled the kids in for the night and came downstairs. Sam was pouring another drink.

"What's wrong, Sam?" she asked. He kept his back to her. "I saw Stanley today."

"What?"

"He's in Boisdale."

"With that woman?"

"Yes."

"Dear God," Mary Catherine said. "What did he say?"

"Not much. I didn't handle it well. I was upset when I found him there. I should've been more considerate given what he's going through. He told me not to jump to conclusions. But it's clear he spent the night. They were having breakfast together. Anyway, it got heated, he pushed me down, and I left. That's pretty much it."

"Is he coming home?"

"He never said one way or the other."

"What am I going to tell Mabel?"

Sam spun around. "Nothing! You say nothing!"

"But I can't keep this from her!"

"*Oooh yes you can*! You have to!" Irwin appeared at the top of the stairs. "Get back to bed!" Sam shouted. He tried to calm himself. "Look! All I'm saying is Mabel's going through enough as it is. She doesn't need to know he's with another woman. Especially now."

"I'd want to know. And I'd expect my best friend to tell me."

"Thankfully you don't have to worry about that. Please, Mary Catherine! Just let it be."

Mabel wanted to make a special supper for Stanley's return. She walked from the bakery to the wharf for some fresh cod tongues, then to Mendelsons for potatoes. She couldn't stop thinking of what he had said. *Don't expect too much of me.* She needed to give him time and not press him on his whereabouts or feelings. Everything is still too raw, she thought. Mabel got supper started, then went upstairs to get cleaned up. As she did every time she passed JC's room, she kissed her fingers and placed them on his door; something she knew she would do for the rest of her life. She entered her room and went to her dresser. She picked up Margaret's Bible and thought of Father Gregory. The aura that surrounded him would have appeared around the same time as Liddy's miraculous recovery. Did he call on God to take him and spare the child? And how strange that he died in the same room where Liddy laid dying just hours before. Was it just a coincidence or, like the incident in the chapel, was there more to it. "I'll never really know," Mabel whispered. The one thing she did know was that she was witness to a miracle that only God could have performed. She knelt beside her bed, folded her hands, and closed her eyes. "God forgive me for doubting you and give me strength. Hold dear my son whom you have called to be at your side. And bless the soul of Father Gregory and all who left their worldly station to live with you in your eternal glory. Dear Lord, help me to be patient with Stanley. Help him find a path that will lead him back to me and back to you."

Mabel heard a car door. She got to her feet, walked downstairs, and looked out front. Stanley's truck was in the yard, but she couldn't see him. She walked out on the step as he rounded the side of the barn. She could feel her heart pound. She smiled and waved.

"See Fred and the boys were here," he said.

"Yes."

He stopped beside his truck, reached in back for his duffle bag, and walked slowly up the steps. Mabel hugged him. He wrapped an arm loosely around her waist. She could smell the liquor on his breath.

"I'm glad you're home," she said. He nodded and headed upstairs.

When he came downstairs a half hour later, Mabel was sitting at the kitchen table. She thought he had been crying. "Are you okay?" she asked.

"Hardly."

"You've lost weight."

Stanley lifted the lid off the hot skillet. "Haven't had much of an appetite."

"Cod tongues," Mabel said.

He sat down across from her. "So, you're back to work?"

Mabel suddenly felt on edge. She expected things to be awkward between them, but his words, his tone, and his actions were more than that. They were unsettling. "I find it helps me get through the days."

"Whatever works, I guess. I find rum helps."

Mabel walked to the cupboard, returning with his rum bottle and a glass. She put them on the table.

Stanley poured his glass half full and pointed to the stove. "How long before it's ready?"

"Won't be long. Twenty minutes or so."

He stood and took his rum out on the back step. Mabel jumped when the screen door banged shut. It was going to be a long, painful process, she thought. She blessed herself and whispered. "God give me strength."

"Hello?" Mary Catherine was walking down the hall with a roaster in her arms. "I made some perogies," she said and placed them on the counter. "So, he finally came home," she whispered. "Everything okay?"

"I'm sure it will be. He's out back. Go say hello."

Mary Catherine didn't feel up to chatting with her friend's cheating husband. "I'm not staying. Just wanted to drop these off and check in on you. Sam's waiting for me in the car."

Stanley walked in from the veranda, polished off his drink, and raised his empty glass to Mary Catherine. "Mary Catherine."

"Stanley," she said.

Mabel could sense the tension between her friend and her husband. Mary Catherine hugged her. "I'll call you tomorrow," she said and walked out.

Mabel tried to ease into their conversation over supper. She told Stanley about Liddy swallowing the pills and that Father Gregory was beaten to death.

"You're a ton of good news," he said.

"I'm afraid that's all the news I have. I'm trying. So you know the fire was deliberately set."

"I heard."

"Well, we know it wasn't Billy Guthro. He was in the hospital and has since died. And Dan McInnes is working somewhere out of province. Maybe some kids hiding out smoking." Stanley shrugged and took another drink. "Stanley? Are you ever going to forgive me?"

"Easier said than done. I just don't understand. After all of the times I warned you not to take your eyes off him while he was outside."

Mabel bowed her head and closed her eyes. "I know. If it wasn't for the fire —"

"Goddammit Mabel! It was a barn. A Goddamn fuckin barn!"

Her head shot up. "But your horses! I was thinking of the first fire and your ponies and —"

"And what? A couple of seconds. Two seconds! That's all it would have taken for you to put JC inside. But no!" he fumed, shaking his finger at the side of his temple. "That would have meant you'd have to use that scatter-brained head of yours." He pulled on the corners of his mouth.

Mabel felt herself well up and took a deep breath. "Stanley, I need to tell you something. I was going to wait and tell you at another time, but it might help you come to terms with things. *Like I have."* He glared at her. "Please! Just let me finish?" she said calmly. "Something happened when I went to the hospital to see Lydia." She started to tell him about overhearing the doctors and the scene in the chapel.

Stanley brought his hand to his forehead and began rubbing it. "Stop! Stop!" he screamed, bringing his fist down on the table. "I can't listen to this…this bullshit Bible babble of yours any longer!"

"Why did you come home?" she asked, more sternly than she expected.

"Good question. Obviously I wasn't thinking straight. I thought I was ready, but apparently not. How the hell can you stay here and walk past his room every day? How! And how can you sit here in your…your chair every morning sipping your tea and look out there?" he said, waving his hand at the water.

"This is our home. This is where I feel close to—"

"Well then, I guess you're a lot stronger than me," he said.

"It's my faith that gives me strength! If only you'd let me finish!"

Stanley jumped to his feet, held his hand up to tell her to stop, and then started down the hallway.

"Please, Stanley! Where are you going? We need to plan a service for James!" Mabel watched from the doorway as he sped down the driveway, churning up a dusty orange cloud in his wake. "Goodbye," she whispered and walked upstairs. JC's door was open. Stanley's duffle bag was on the floor. She opened it, pulled out a shirt, and held it to her face. It was damp. So were the unfamiliar swim trunks, sitting on top.

Mary Catherine climbed in next to Sam. "I can't even look at him. Mabel would be a fool to take him back. I wanted to slap him."

"He just lost his son. He's not thinking straight," Sam said, kicking the blankets off. Mary Catherine pulled them back up. "Thinking well enough to…to climb in bed with that…that slut."

"We don't know that for sure."

"*Seriously, Sam*? What about all those nights and weekends away from home? And the MacPhees? God knows how long it's been going on. I'm sick for her. I have to tell her."

Sam sat up. "I know you're her friend and you love her dearly, but he did come home. Please don't make things worse. Give them a chance to work things out," he said, once again kicking the covers off. He rolled onto his side.

"He came home because you caught him in the act."

"I caught him eating breakfast with another woman. That's all."

"That's just the lawyer in you talking. It's as plain as the nose on your face. Tell me you don't believe he's been having an affair?"

"For the sake of argument, let's just say he was, but that he now realizes it was all a big mistake. You know Mabel loves him. Maybe she wouldn't want to know."

"But I'll feel guilty if I don't tell her. It's like I'm hiding something from her."

"In other words, you're prepared to sacrifice her chance at happiness so you can ease your guilty conscience," Sam said.

"It's not that simple," she said, plumping her pillow. "Sam?"

"Go to sleep," he said in a pleading tone. He was just about to nod off.

"Sam? Do you think JC's body will ever be found?"

"No."

"Myrtle said it should have been–"

"Myrtle!" Sam said, this time reaching down and pulling the blankets up over his head. "Please, Mary Catherine! I'm exhausted."

Saturday, June 1

CHAPTER 8

Stanley was sitting at the table drinking tea when Ten-After-Six walked in from his morning walk. "How far did you get today?" Stanley asked.

Peter tipped his head upward. "Just a coupla miles. Wanted to get back and make you breakfast."

Stanley held up his cup. "I'm good. Thanks for putting me up."

"You can stay as long as you like."

"So has Fred been working you hard?" Stanley asked.

"Into the ground. Says we're behind on the job orders and he didn't want you to be fending off angry callers. And he had a big dust up with Mr. Bugden. Refuses to pay him for the last order. Said the lumber's coming in warped and split."

"I'll talk to Bugden. So how's Willie?" Stanley asked.

"Willie's, Willie. Hard to keep him focused at times. You're a good man for keepin him on."

Stanley closed his eyes, picturing Willie twitching on the canvas. "Willie will have a job for as long as I have a job to give."

Peter tried to straighten up enough to drink his tea without spilling it. "It was an accident. It's not your fault."

Stanley's pulled on his lips. "Yeah. It was."

"Nobody else sees it that way. Not even Willie."

"We both know Willie doesn't know any better. I was the one who hit him. I'm the one responsible for his sorry lot in life," Stanley said, looking into his cup and swirling his tea around. He needed to change the subject. "Do you ever think about just packing up and leaving?"

Peter wiped away the tea running down his chin. "No. I like it here. Why, do you?"

Stanley smiled. "Not until a few days ago. Started thinking about going to the mainland and getting into horse breeding. Always been a dream of mine."

"You mean you'd sell the company?"

"Maybe. Don't worry. Whatever I decide I'll make sure you guys are looked after. At least for the short term. Who knows, maybe Larry Mendelson will buy me out."

"Just hope you don't jump too quickly. Sometimes, after a terrible loss, we don't always think so clearly. But don't worry bout me. I got a little money," Peter said.

Stanley grinned.

"What? You don't believe me? I got close to three thousand in the bank and some penny stock." He reached into his pocket and put a couple of dollars in loose change on the table. "I'm not just good at findin dead bodies, ya know. My walkin pays off."

Stanley looked up at the clock and pushed his chair back from the table. "We should get going," he said and headed for the door. Peter followed, bent at a fifty degree angle. Stanley turned and looked down at the top of his head. "And, Peter? Let's keep our conversation between us for now. I'll tell the others if or when the time comes."

"Don't worry. Never believed in makin folks fret before it's time."

"How's the back?" Stanley asked.

"Still a bit bent," Peter said, pulling the door behind him.

Mary Catherine called Mabel but there was no answer. She then called the bakery. Luke answered and said he hadn't seen her. She decided to take Lydia for a walk to the bluff. If Stanley was home, she'd keep going and head for the dam. She rounded the bend and looked up, relieved there was no truck. She knocked on the door. No answer. She pushed the door open. "You home, Mabel?"

"I'm upstairs."

Mary Catherine and Lydia made their way to Mabel's room. She was in bed. "You okay?" Mary Catherine asked.

"No, I don't feel well."

"Is Stanley gone to work?"

"I don't know."

Mary Catherine reached in her purse and passed Liddy her rag doll. "What do you mean?"

"I mean I don't know where he's at. Things didn't go well. I pushed too hard and he left. I have no idea where he is."

Mary Catherine was pretty sure *she* knew where Mabel's husband was. She wanted to tell her everything, but held back. "Can I get you anything?"

"I'm fine."

"You are not! I'll take Liddy home and come back."

"No. Really, I'm fine. Stomach is just off. I'm just waiting for it to settle. Then I'm going to the bakery. Alice has been working like a dog and needs the help. We have a wedding reception tonight."

"Let me at least make you a cup of tea?" Mabel didn't object.

Mary Catherine took Liddy downstairs and began making the tea. She was fit to be tied. Selfish bastard, she thought. His wife at home mourning their son and him gallivanting about with another woman. She looked up at the ceiling. She could hear Mabel running to the bathroom. She then heard the heaving and the toilet flush. She was about to take Mabel's tea up to her when she appeared in the kitchen.

"Thank you," Mabel said, taking the cup from her. "I feel better now."

Mary Catherine sat down at the table. "Have you been throwing up for a while?"

"No. Just this morning. Must have been the fried cod tongues. Don't worry, it's not what you're thinking. We were always very careful. We wanted to wait until JC was two before having another."

"So when was your last period?"

Mabel closed her eyes and shrugged. "I'm not sure. I've always been spotty. With all the emotional turmoil of late, my cycle's probably just all messed up."

"Mabel, the only guarantee is abstinence. Liddy's proof of that." Mary Catherine looked around the kitchen. She jumped up. "Where is she? Liddy!" she yelled and ran down the hall. "There you are," she said, picking her up off the floor. "I feel as if I can't take my eyes off her," she said.

Mabel put her hand on Liddy's head. "It only takes a couple of seconds," she said softly.

Monday, June 3

CHAPTER 9

Mabel and Luke turned off Brookside Street and onto Dominion. Cars lined both sides of the road as far as the eye could see. Luke pulled over. "I'm afraid this is as close as we're going to get." They entered the church and found a spot in the back. Mourners dressed in black took up every pew, lined the walls, and gathered in the open doorway, many fanning themselves with their hymn books. "I've never seen anything like it," Mabel whispered. The only sound came from above, as St. Anthony's huge choir walked up the side stairs to the small balcony hanging over the entrance to the nave. The cross bearer led the procession, followed by a dozen or more altar boys, several priests, and finally Father Cusack.

Luke nudged Mabel and nodded to Father Gregory's casket. "There's no family here."

"Yes, I see that."

Twenty minutes later, Father Cusack stood at the pulpit. "He was a good man. A man of God. *But he was a man,* and like all men, he sinned. We gather today at this Mass of Christian Burial to pray for our brother's soul. But we also come together today as his family to thank him for his devotion to God and for his holy work in His name. The tragic events that have brutally struck down such a good man in the prime of life has no doubt left some of you questioning your faith. How, after all, could a loving and merciful God take someone as kind and giving as our dear brother? I could recite passages of the Bible in an effort to convince the doubters amongst us of the mysterious ways of our Lord, but I'm afraid that on a day of such great sorrow and consternation, my words may fall upon deaf ears. Instead, let me share with you my last moments with Father Gregory."

Father Cusack paused and looked out over his attentive flock. "The night before he was attacked, Father Gregory paid me an unexpected visit. He came to ask that I hear his confession. When I asked, why now and at such a late hour, he told me he sensed it would be his last. That he was being called to the house of the Lord."

Mabel felt her head lighten and her legs go weak. Luke steadied her. "Are you okay?" he asked.

Father Cusack continued. "A calling, Father Gregory told me, he willingly accepted. And while I believe without a shadow of a doubt that God speaks to all of us on a daily basis, I felt, at the time, that he was mistaken. That his premonition was premature. That he was simply experiencing a feeling of unworthiness, a need to set his worldly and otherworldly affairs in order. That he would be with us for many years to come fulfilling his calling as a man of God. But as we now know, it was *I* who was mistaken. And as we now know, God had in fact told Father Gregory he was calling him home."

Father Cusack waited for the whispers to subside. "I want to take a moment to read from the Book of James. *Count it all joy, my brothers, when you meet trials of various kinds, for you know that the testing of your faith produces steadfastness. And let steadfastness have its full effect, that you may be perfect and complete, lacking in nothing. If any of you lacks wisdom, let them ask God, who gives generously to all without reproach, and it will be given him. But let him ask in faith, with no doubting, for the one who doubts is like a wave of the sea that is driven and tossed by the wind."*

Father Cusack looked up from the pulpit. "For those who may be scratching your heads and wondering why I choose to read that particular passage, it's because it was to be the basis for Father Gregory's homily during yesterday's worship. He wanted you to know that no matter how much turmoil you confront, God is with you. That when you hold steadfast in your faith, God will make you whole and complete. He will reward you. And no one lived this truth more than Father Gregory. From the time he was a young boy, Brother Gregory's faith was tested by a life of tragedy and great sorrow. Tested but not broken."

Mabel's mind flashed back to her angry words in the chapel. "*What would you know about sorrow?*"

Father Cusack stopped and looked down at Father Gregory's coffin draped in a plain white pall. "He was an orphan by the time he was ten. Two years later he lost his two-year old sister, in a drowning accident. Enough to make any boy or man turn his back on God. To deny His existence. To denounce the church and its teachings. But Father Gregory was just not any boy or any man. He had a remarkable capacity to love, to forgive, and to believe. Human qualities he knew were imbued in him by a loving and merciful God. And while his senseless death brings us immense sorrow, do not let it question your faith. Instead, let Father Gregory's life and his last conversation with our Lord reassure you that God is with us. That He has a plan for us. And that while His mysterious ways often challenge and confound us, they are without question, unquestionable."

Mabel pulled a hankie from her pocket, patted her tear-stained face, and lightly blew her nose. Luke put his arm around her, as an endless line of parishioners walked with bowed heads to receive Holy Communion and to offer their final goodbyes.

Father Cusack then read the Prayer of Commendation. "Before we go our separate ways, let us take leave of our brother," he said, sprinkling holy water on the coffin. He put down the aspergillum and picked up a smoky thurible, swaying it at his side and circling the bier. "May our farewell express our affection for him; may it ease our sadness and strengthen our hope. One day we shall joyfully greet him again when the love of Christ, which conquers all things, destroys even death itself."

Mabel and Luke stood outside among the tearful congregation of St. Anthony's and watched the grim-faced undertakers slide Father Gregory's casket into the back of MacGillvary's stark, black hearse. Mabel felt a tap on her shoulder and turned. She stifled a gasp as she took in the thin-lined eyebrows, bright blue eyeshadow, and brilliant red lips of the woman seeking her attention.

"Mrs. MacIntyre," Lizzie MacNeil said. "I just wanted to extend my sincere condolences to ya. Terrible tragedy, losin yer son in such a horrible way. And at such a young age. Must have been awful hard for ya to be here sayin yer goodbyes to our dear Father Gregory. I mean with all yer dealin with."

"Actually, Father Cusack's words brought me some comfort," Mabel said.

"That's good, dear," Lizzie said, quickly turning and waving to the newly widowed Gerald Smithers.

Mabel and Luke headed to the car. "There's John," Mabel said. They waited for John and his schoolmates to weave their way through the stream of mourners making their way along Dominion Street.

"Need a lift?" Luke asked.

"No. I'm good. I gotta a coupla hours to kill before school goes back in. Just gonna hang out with the guys for a bit," John said.

Luke opened his car door. "I need your help after school. Don't be late."

"I won't."

"John! Hurry up!" Kenny Ludlow hollered, reaching in his pocket for his box of matches.

Kenny, Tommy, and John made their way down the tracks. Kenny stopped. "We should build a fort." He pointed at an opening in the heavy brush. "Right there," he said, thinking it would be a good place to hide his new bike.

"Build a fort? With what?" Tommy asked.

Kenny turned to John. "You can get us some tools and stuff, cant ya?"

"I guess so. But where do we get the wood?"

"Bugden's," Kenny said.

Tommy peered into the thicket. "How do we pay for it?"

Kenny shoved him. "We don't need no money. We take it. There's always some scrap lumber out back."

"Maybe we can ask him for some?" Tommy said.

"That tight old fart. Nah, he wouldn't give it to us. Let's start clearing it out a bit."

The boys pulled a few bushes away, but quickly surrendered to their thorny stems. They started back down the tracks. John stopped and watched Kenny and Tommy walk the rails; each putting one foot in front of the other with their arms stretched out for balance. "Guys! I think we should head back. School will be going back in soon," John hollered.

"C'mon," Kenny shouted. "I need smokes. We got plenty of time."

John hesitated, then ran to catch up. They stopped on the tracks between Mechanic and Union streets, then turned down Park Street.

"You guy's got any money?" Kenny asked.

John reached in his pocket and handed him eight cents.

"Thanks," Kenny said, grabbing it and disappearing into Daigle's corner store.

"Ask what time it is?" John said. Kenny came out with four smokes and two bubble gum. "Did ya get the time?" John asked.

"Yeah. It's twenty to one."

"Twenty to one!" John yelled. "We're gonna be late!"

"No we're not," Kenny said, pointing to the No. 42 pulling away from the Machine Shop. "We'll hop the train."

The three of them ran back to the tracks and waited for the slow-moving train to approach. "Hurry up!" Kenny yelled, running up beside it. He grabbed the ladder on the back of the last car and climbed to the top. "C'mon! What are you waitin for!" he yelled. Tommy and John hopped on the back and took their spots on opposite sides of the ladder; their feet hugging the narrow ledge and their hands gripping the rungs and metal side rails. Kenny looked down at Tommy and John. "It won't pick up speed until we get to the graveyard. I'll tell ya when to jump!" he hollered.

Tommy and John looked at each other, then down at the gravel bed below. The creosote rail ties began clicking by, faster and faster.

"Kenny! We need to get off!" John yelled up.

Kenny looked down, gripping his hands tighter around the rusty metal bars. "Shit!" he said. "Jump!"

Neither John nor Tommy moved.

"It's goin too fast!" John hollered, trying to be heard above the noise of the train's shrill whistle and the screeching sound of metal against metal. "Jump!"

Kenny yelled again.

The No. 42 was sailing through Gardiner Mines at almost forty miles an hour when an old woman heard their screams and looked up from her garden. She put her head back down and continued her weeding. "Crazy fools," she said, shaking her head. It was almost two-thirty when the train finally rolled into the New Victoria coal piers.

"Get off!" Kenny screamed.

Tommy's face was ashen and his knuckles white. He opened his stiff fingers and joined John who was sitting on the ground, shaking his numb hands in the air. Kenny jumped down from the third rung. "Assholes," he spit. "Why didn't ya jump when I told ya?"

John stood up. "You said it wouldn't speed up till we got to the graveyard."

Kenny pushed him down.

The engineer came around the back of the train. "How was the ride boys?" he asked, laughing.

Mabel liberally sprinkled flour on her kneading board and placed the sticky blob on top. Whatever doubts she had about her experience in the chapel were doused by Father Cusack. There were just too many coincidences. It had to be God's will. The aura, Father Gregory's disappearance in the chapel, Liddy's recovery, both Liddy and Father Gregory occupying room 4B, and now word that he had predicted his own death just one day after Liddy defied all odds. And then there was Father Gregory's baby sister who drowned. She would have been around the same age as Liddy. Did Father Gregory call on God to take his life and spare that of a child he didn't even know? Did He answer her own doubt-filled prayers?

Luke walked into the bakery. "You doing okay?"

"Yes."

"Did you hear anything more from Stanley?"

"No."

Luke gave her a hug. "Give him time, Mabel. He'll come around," he said and returned to the store.

Mabel started back in on her dough. She thought of her transformation since the night in the chapel. Like Stanley, she had been angry and bitter. Now, although her heart still ached, she was ready to get on with life knowing JC *was* with God. If only Stanley would listen to her and open his heart to believe, they stood a chance. If not, she knew they would only drift further apart. Faith, she thought, is a powerful ally in times of great anguish. And doubt, your worst enemy.

"You're giving that dough a good goin over," Alice said.

"A good kneading makes the bread nice and airy. Did you get everything?"

"Yes. I told Mr. Mendelson you'd be by with the payment."

Luke came in, laid Alice's box of baking supplies on the floor, and sat at the table.

"Time for tea," Mabel said.

"I'll get it," Alice said. The kettle hit the floor. Luke jumped to his feet, knocking his chair over. Alice was holding out her hand. Mabel rushed to her. "Are you alright?"

"I didn't realize it was hot."

"Luke!" Mabel said, examining Alice's hand. "Grab the Mecca ointment. Pantry. Top shelf."

"Luke!" she said again, turning to face him.

Luke was as white as a sheet and staring off in the distance. Mabel walked over and put his chair back in place. "Sit here," she said, easing him onto it. Alice watched with concern. Mabel wrapped her hand in her apron, put the kettle on the counter, and went to get the salve. When she returned, Alice was sitting next to Luke. He was bent over the table, sobbing. Alice was crying too.

Mabel felt unusually tired. The heat, the emotional toll of the past week, along with Father Gregory's funeral and the episode in the store with Luke, must be catching up with me, she thought. She'd take a quick nap and have a late supper. She laid down on the couch. She was worried about Luke. Apart from Stanley and Sam, he had no other male friends and never asked a girl out. He was also letting the store fall into disarray. She was near sleep when she thought she heard a car door. She sat up and looked out the window, disappointed it wasn't Stanley's truck. She sat back, waited for her visitor to knock, and went to the door. "Father Cusack?"

"Hello, Mrs. MacIntyre. I hope I'm not disturbing you?"

"No. Please, come in. Would you care for a cup of tea?"

"That would be lovely. Thank you."

Mabel led him into the kitchen, wondering why he came to see her. She put the kettle on the stove, and placed the sugar bowl and cream boat on the table. "It was a beautiful service. It's hard to believe he's gone."

"There were so many people in the church I wasn't sure you were there. I'm glad you were. It must have been difficult for you. I understand you recently suffered a great tragedy of your own?"

"Yes."

"How are you coping?"

"Better. Your words were comforting. I must admit, I've been struggling with my faith."

"And now?"

Mabel hesitated. "Father," she paused. "I've never said this to another living soul. Not even my husband. But…well, sometimes I feel as if JC is still with me."

"Of course he is. He'll always be with you."

"No. I don't mean… like his spirit is with me. I mean like he's not really gone. That any minute now he might come charging round the corner."

Father Cusack smiled.

"You think I'm crazy? It's okay. I sometimes do, too. I know there's no other explanation for his disappearance and that my heart is just slow in catching up with my brain. It's just a feeling I get from time to time."

Father Cusack rubbed his chin. "It's only natural to feel the way you do, especially under the circumstances. I mean not having found his body. And you're certainly not crazy. You're grieving. You're holding on to hope. And hope can be a very good thing. But sometimes, especially when it's a false hope, it can do great harm. I think it would do you good to have a service of remembrance for your son. It will help you accept that, like our dear Father Gregory, he's been called to the Lord." He smiled and patted her hand. "I suppose you're wondering why I'm here."

Mabel nodded.

"Father Gregory sent me."

Mabel screwed up her face. "Father Gregory?"

Father Cusack pulled a purple satchel from his pocket, reached in, and laid a white linen cloth, edged with gold fringes on the table. "He wanted you to have this."

Mabel was more confused than ever. "Me?" She picked it up. "It's lovely, but what is it?"

"It's his maniturgium. A special cloth priests use to cleanse their hands during ordination. It's usually given to the priest's mother and she's buried with it as a sign that she has given her son to God. But, as you know, Father Gregory's mother died well before he became a priest and he had no family to pass it on to."

"But why me? I knew him as our parish priest, but not nearly as well as so many others."

"I'm not sure. Perhaps, because you lent your son to God?"

Mabel turned it over in her hands. "I don't know what to say?"

"It's a great honour," Father Cusack said.

Mabel folded the edges together and ran her hand over the top. "I'll treasure it." She walked to the stove to prepare the tea. "Father," she said, "I wasn't kind to Father Gregory the last time I saw him. In fact, I was mean."

The two had multiple cups of tea and a half dozen oat cakes over the next hour. Mabel explained her experience in the chapel and all of the odd coincidences. "Do you think it's possible he offered himself to God in place of Liddy?"

"I believe in the infinite power of the Lord. We know he spoke with God. How else does one explain his premonition? So yes, anything is possible."

Alice and Luke sat at the table drinking tea.

"Are you feeling better?" she asked.

Luke tried to smile. "Yes. I'm sorry."

Alice shook her head. "Don't be ridiculous. There's no need to apologize."

"It's just that sharp noises sometimes set me off." Luke dropped his head "Remind me of things."

"You mean the war?"

Luke nodded. "Dr. Cohen said it's battle fatigue. Shellshock. Says it's more common than you'd think."

"It must have been awful," Alice said, taking her cup to the sink. *The Post* was on the counter. She flipped it open.

Luke looked down at his feet, ashamed of himself for appearing so weak, particularly in front of Alice. She had no idea that she was the girl he dreamt about during the war. He remembered the first day he had seen her. James had just hired her to help Mabel in the bakery. He closed his eyes remembering her as she walked around the store with a tray of sandwiches. It was the day he shipped out for basic training. They hardly spoke, but yet he couldn't get her out of his mind. He planned to ask her out when he came back from the war. He never imagined his younger brother would beat him to it.

Alice walked up, spread the newspaper out on the table, and pointed to the bottom corner. Luke looked up at her and then down at the advertisement.

"I'd love to see it. And look! Humphrey Bogart's in it. He's my favourite," Alice said.

Luke gave her a puzzled look. "Are you asking me to go with you?"

"Yes. Why not? It starts at seven. I just need to run home and get cleaned up?"

"What about Mark?" Luke asked.

"What about him?"

"I got the impression you two were an item."

"Then you got the wrong impression. So, are we going to the movies or not?"

Luke smiled for the first time in a long time. "I guess so."

"Great. Pick me up by six-thirty so we can get a good seat. And don't be late," she said and walked out.

Luke felt light. He ran his hand over his stubble. He needed to shave. He walked upstairs, washed up, and put on a clean white singlet. He lathered up and dipped his razor into the basin. He brought the razor to the side of his face. His hand started to tremble. He wasn't sure if it was the battle fatigue or his excitement at the prospects of going out with Alice. He looked in the mirror, thinking about the first time he had shaved. He had borrowed James' razor and came downstairs bleeding from the nicks. *Remember,* he recalled James saying, *the water needs to be really hot.*

Luke turned on the hot water tap and watched his image disappear under the steamy mirror. He bent over the soapy water and looked down at the image of St. Christopher dangling from the chain around his neck. He picked it up, and kissed it. "God, I miss you," he whispered. "If only I had listened to you and stayed out of the fucking war." He swiped the mirror with his hand and continued shaving. He dried his face and was reaching for his best white shirt when he heard the phone. He ran downstairs.

"Hello?" He looked up at the clock. "Christ almighty! Where? No! Oh, for Christ sakes. Yeah. Tell me again. Yeah, I got it. At least an hour." Luke put his finger down on the button, released it, and waited for the dial tone. "Fuck," he said and started dialling. "Hello. Is this Kenny's mother? This is Luke Toth, John's brother."

Tuesday, June 4

CHAPTER 10

Luke entered the bakery. "I'm sorry," he said. Alice kept her head down and cracked her eggs into her mixing bowl. "I called, ya know?"

Alice continued her baking, refusing to look up. "I heard."

"So you know I had to go and get John. Idiot jumped *The 42* and ended up in New Victoria. I thought I'd be back in time. I did call."

"Yeah. Da told me. *At ten past seven.*"

"Then why are you so upset?"

Alice finally looked up. "You should have called me as soon as you hung up from John. Instead, you left me hanging around waiting for you."

"I'm sorry. Like I said, I didn't think it would take that long. Then I had to drop off John's idiot friends. I'll make it up to you. We can go tonight."

"Too late. I went last night."

"So you didn't miss it after all?"

Alice put her head back down. "No. I called… a friend."

Mark walked in and handed Alice a flowered scarf. "Ya left this in Ronnie's car." He leaned over her shoulder and looked into the bowl. "What ya got cooking?"

Alice shoved her scarf into her apron pocket, picked up her bowl, and walked to the stove.

"Hey, Luke! Ya missed a great movie last night. Although I don't understand why everyone's so high on Bogart. Talks like he's got marbles in his mouth," Mark said.

Luke put his head down, thinking that Alice just felt sorry for him after yesterday's episode in the bakery. That's why she asked him to go to the movies. He turned and went back into the store.

John ran downstairs carrying his books. "Thanks again for coming for us. I guess I'll be getting a note from Mr. Spencer."

"Just make sure you get home right after school. No dilly-dallying. And don't go jumpin *The 42,*" Luke said.

⌐———⌐

Kenny, John, and Tommy sat across from Principal Gillis. "I'm not surprised by you two," he said looking at Kenny and Tommy. "But, you?" he said turning to John.

John put his head down. "Sorry, sir."

"You do realize you could have gotten yourselves killed?"

"Train wasn't supposed to speed up until the graveyard. Crazy engineer saw us hop on and sped up. We didn't get a chance to jump off. Then he made us stay and help shovel out the coal cars," Kenny said, kicking the front of Principal Gillis' desk.

"That *crazy engineer* you're talking about is my wife's brother. Have no doubt, I'll be chatting with him too. The question now is how to punish you boys. He looked at Kenny and then Tommy. I spoke to Mr. Spencer about holding you two back a year, but he begged me not to saddle him with you for another year."

"So Kenny, starting tomorrow, you and Tommy will be staying after school for the duration of the school year. The classrooms are to be put in order. The boards are to be cleaned and washed. The erasers clapped. The trash cans emptied. And the desks set out in perfectly neat rows. Oh, and I've talked to Mr. Spencer. He agrees there will be no recess for the *duration* of the school year."

Tommy's mouth fell open.

"And that's not all," Principal Gillis said. "All three of you are to write a five page essay on the dangers of jumping the train. Have it on my desk first thing next Monday."

This time it was Kenny's jaw that dropped. "Five pages!"

"Make that seven. Neatly printed and with no mistakes. And you better practice it, because you'll be reading it in front of every class. Now get your things and get out of here."

The boys stood to leave.

"And guys? Don't screw this up, or I'll have no choice but to hold you back," Principal Gillis said, leaning back in his chair.

John went home. Kenny and Tommy went to Tommy's.

Tommy's father was sitting on the front step having a beer. "You're late, guys?"

"Principal Gillis made us stay after school so he could hand out his punishment for jumpin the train. We gotta write a seven page essay and stay late and clean the classrooms," Tommy said.

"Go tell your mother. Kenny, you wait here a minute." Kenny held back. "Your bike's under a tarp behind the shed," he said.

Kenny started to run to the shed. "Get back here!" Tommy's father shouted. Kenny stopped and turned back. "Now, keep your mouth shut. And not a word to anyone about where you got the bike. Do you understand?"

"Promise," Kenny said and tore off. He pulled the tarp back and there is was. A red CCM Mustang Marauder with shiny silver fenders. No chain guard or handbrakes like Tommy's, but it had a bell. It was the most beautiful thing he'd ever seen. He threw his leg over the crossbar and pushed off. "Tell Tommy I'll see him tomorrow," Kenny yelled. He sat hunched over the handlebars, pumping slowly at first as he maneuvered his treasured wheels along the bumpy, dirt lane. He made a wide turn onto the smooth asphalt surface of the road and began pumping faster and faster. He stood up and closed his eyes, feeling the warm breeze on his face and thinking he was the luckiest kid in town. He was flying down Highland Street, ringing his bell, when Harley Woodward saw him whiz past. How come everybody else is getting a new bike and I'm not, Harley thought.

<hr>

Clair walked up her front steps carrying her freshly picked wild flowers. She stopped on her way inside and looked at the untouched pallet of lumber. She put the flowers in a vase and thought about her night with Stanley. She went to her bedroom, removed the top tray of her jewelry box, and picked up a small garnet brooch encircled with fake diamonds. She sat on the edge of her bed and turned it over in her hands, recalling Stanley's embarrassment at not being able to afford an engagement ring and his promise to make it up to her after his next bout. But there never was another bout, a ring, or a wedding. As she had so many times over the years, she wondered what their lives would have been like, if only Stanley hadn't stepped into the ring with Willie Morrison. Something as innocent as a friendly sparring match changed the course of so many people's lives. Willie's, Stanley's, hers. She shook her head recalling her father saying he'd never allow her to marry a *good-for-nothing* coal hauler. Over my dead body, he had said. Funny, how he thought Stanley was good enough for her when his future as a prize fighter looked so promising, Clair thought. She looked up. "Well, Da? What do you say now?"

She changed into a sleeveless turquoise dress, pinned the brooch to her collar, and walked to the mirror. She brushed her hair, wondering what Stanley's wife was like. Apart from telling her Mabel owned a bakery and that she was considerably younger than him, Stanley said next to nothing about his wife. Was she tall with dark hair, like her? Was she the quiet, reserved sort, or was she fun loving and outgoing? Could they be friends under different circumstances? She reached down, picked her purse off the floor, and headed out the door. She'd visit her sister and stop by Stanley's office. She might even pick up a pie.

———

"Hello. Yes, I'm trying to track down Dan McInnes. I understand he's working the docks. Wondering if you can help me out? No, I don't know which company or what he does. He doesn't have any marine training so he's probably a dock loader or deckhand. No, I don't have a union number. Look, it's a family emergency. His sister died. I'm his uncle. Yes, I can call back. When? And who will I ask for? Great. Thanks, Andrew. No, I understand. Appreciate your help."

Fred waited for Stanley to hang up, then lightly tapped on his open door.

"Come in."

Fred nodded to the outer office. "You have a visitor."

Stanley walked down the hallway and entered the small lobby, cluttered with paint cans and tool boxes. "Mabel?"

She smiled. "How are you?"

He pointed to his office. "Busy. Trying to get caught up."

Fred interrupted. "Sorry boss. I'm gonna head over to Bugdens. Make sure the guys got the order straight."

"Don't be too long. We need to go over those specs," Stanley said, as Fred closed the door behind him. Stanley turned back to Mabel. "Might have a big job at the hospital."

"That's great. Hopefully it will make the days less painful. I've always said it's better to work through your sorrow than…" She stopped.

Stanley finished her sentence. "Wallow in it."

"I'm sorry. I didn't mean to—"

"Anyway, way too early to pop the champagne. Not sure we'll get the job."

"You mean *Champ..pag...nee*," Mabel said, hoping to remind him of their honeymoon. Stanley didn't respond as she had hoped. "Anyway, I won't keep you," Mabel said. "I had to pick up some baking supplies. And I just thought...well...I just thought I'd see how you're feeling?"

"Honestly, I feel like *I* fell off the cliff." Mabel put her head down. Stanley immediately regretted his words. "I guess it's my turn to apologize. You didn't need to hear that."

Mabel wanted to keep the conversation going as difficult and forced as it was. "Where are you staying?"

"Peter's."

Mabel nodded. "Do you have everything you need? I mean, I get the impression you're not coming home any time soon." Stanley didn't answer. "I could pack up some of your things? Some clothes? Shaving gear?"

Stanley closed his eyes. "Mabel, I'm just not ready." He looked at her and spoke softly. "I just can't help feeling the way I do. I'm afraid that if we try and push things before we're both ready, it would just make things harder. You need to give me time to get myself together. To feel less confused. Less —"

Mabel gripped the straps of her purse. "Less angry?"

"Yes."

"Do you ever feel like he's still with us?" she asked.

"No," he said, shaking his head. "I feel dead inside. Like I'm not me anymore. Like I'll never be me again. I never understood why Margaret was so bitter, for so long. I do now."

"But Margaret eventually found happiness. You can too. We both can. We can be us again." He didn't answer. Mabel had hoped to speak to him about a service for JC but knew now was not the time. She looked around. "I'll let you get back to work."

"Thanks for stopping by," he said, walking to the door and opening it for her. She stopped before stepping out, put her hand on his arm, and smiled. He smiled back. It was that same sad smile she had seen so many times in the past.

Mabel walked down the steps and straight ahead. "Thank you, Fred," she hollered without looking back. Fred stepped out from the side of the building and dropped his cigarette on the ground.

"You're welcome, Mabel," he said, twisting his foot over the butt.

It's a start, Mabel thought as she walked up Commercial Street. "Give him time," she whispered. "Give him time."

⌐⟨___⟩⊨

Clair turned off Brookside Street and onto School. She spotted the sign for Cameron's Dry Goods Emporium and Bakery, slowed down, and pulled in front. Corliss was sitting behind the counter. He stood when she came through the door. She smiled and walked to the display in the window.

"Best bread, pies and cakes, ya'll ever eat. Yer taste buds will be dancing on yer tongue," he said, taking in the striking woman he had never seen before.

"I have no doubt," Clair said. She was anxious to see the woman who stole Stanley's heart and broke hers. "Is this the entire selection? I was hoping for a pie," she said, pointing to the window display.

"Pretty sure the pies are all spoken for." Corliss put his hand on the counter for balance and hopped on one leg to the entrance to the bakery. "Got a customer here wants to know if ya got any pies."

"Hello. Can I help?"

This couldn't possibly be Stanley's wife, Clair thought. She's much too young. "Oh, are you the owner?"

"No. But I work here. Sorry we don't have any pies at the moment. If you tell me what kind you'd like, maybe you can come back around two."

"Actually, the chocolate cake looks lovely," Clair said.

"It's my favourite," Corliss said.

"Great. Then, I'll take it. Oh, and I'll have a dozen of the oat cakes."

Alice boxed the cake and bagged the cookies, as Clair settled up with Corliss.

"You from around here?" he asked.

"Boisdale. I used to live in town. Number Six. "

"What's yer father's name?"

"Da!" Alice scolded. "Leave her be!" She put Clair's cake and cookies on the counter and walked away shaking her head.

"Lorenzo Romano."

"Never heard of him."

"We moved away years ago."

Corliss handed Clair her change. "So are ya married?"

Clair smiled. "No. Not married."

"Well, too bad for you. Cause I am." He laughed. "But then, a pretty young thing like you probably ain't too partial to old gimps like me," he said, pointing to his missing leg. "Lost it in the pit. But I'll be cuttin a rug before long. Gettin a new one in a few days."

Clair placed the bag of oat cakes on top of her cake box. She turned back and smiled. "Good luck with your new leg."

Luke was on his way down from his upstairs apartment. He stopped and watched the familiar frame of the well-dressed woman pull the door closed behind her. "Who was that?" he asked Corliss.

"Loveliest thing I've seen on two legs in a long time. Last name's Romania… Rominia… Romito. I dunno. Some sorta Dago name. Said she's from Boisdale."

Luke quickly hobbled downstairs to the window. The tail end of a black Chevrolet was turning onto Caledonia Street.

Clair left her sister's and headed back through town. She smiled when she turned onto Brodie Avenue and saw the blue Ford pickup parked in front of *S&M Design and Construction.* She put the car in park, opened her mirrored compact, brushed the hair back off her forehead, and ran her finger around the corners of her mouth.

Fred greeted her, then stuck his head into Stanley's office. "Yer popular today. Ya got another visitor."

Stanley put down the specs he was studying and entered the outer office. "Clair?"

"Hope I'm not disturbing you?"

He rubbed his eyes. "I could use a break."

"I brought you some oat cakes," she said, handing him the bag. "I was visiting my sister and just thought I'd stop in to see how you're doing?"

"I'm good," he said, putting the oat cakes on Fred's desk.

Fred decided it was time for another smoke. "Back in a bit, boss," he said and walked out.

Clair looked around the cluttered office. "So this is where you make your millions."

Stanley laughed. "Hardly. It pays the bills."

"Any chance you might reconsider freeing up some of your men to replace my hardwood floors. My guys must have decided to take an early summer vacation."

"Actually, we're going straight out."

Clair smiled. "I understand."

Stanley straddled the corner of Fred's desk. "Leave it with me for a day or two. I'll see what I can do."

"Are you sure?"

"I'll talk it over with Fred. See what he thinks."

"Great. So you'll call then?"

"Yes."

Clair looked at the door. "Well, I guess I should get going."

Stanley stood. "It was good to see you again. And thanks for this," he said holding up the bag.

"If your guys find themselves in Boisdale tell them I'll make lots more. Oh, and it wouldn't hurt to mention they can work off a sweat with a dip in the Bras d'Or." Stanley smiled and nodded.

Clair got in her car and put her hand on her brooch. He hadn't seemed to notice, she thought. Stanley was looking out the window and biting into an oat cake when Fred came back in. "Now that was a sight for sore eyes," he said.

Stanley slapped the bag into Fred's chest. "So, I guess you won't mind taking on some extra work. She needs her floors replaced."

Fred reached in the bag, broke off a piece of oat cake, and popped it in his mouth. "Wife said she wants a new mattress," he said, putting his hand under his chin to catch the crumbs.

"See who else might be interested and work up a schedule," Stanley said, returning to his office. He sat down and wondered if the brooch Clair had on was the same one he bought for her so many years ago.

He smoothed down the crumpled paper on his desk, and dialled the number. "Is this Andrew? Yes, we spoke earlier. Yes, Dan McInnes."

Mabel waited outside Mendelsons for Luke to pick her up. She looked up at the sun. It felt like it was ninety degrees and it wasn't even eleven. She was sweating and fanning herself, when he finally pulled up. The two of them loaded up the car and headed for the store.

Mabel started unpacking her supplies. "Alice," she said weakly. Alice turned toward Mabel and watched her slump to the floor.

"Luke!" Alice screamed, squatting behind Mabel and trying to lift her up by the arms. Luke stormed through the door. Alice looked up at him. "She must have fainted!" Luke nudged her aside, lifted Mabel up, carried her upstairs, and placed her on his bed.

Alice came in with a glass of water. "Should we call an ambulance?" she asked.

Luke opened the window. "Give her a minute."

Mabel opened her eyes and looked around. "What happened?" she asked, propping herself up on her elbows.

"You fainted," Alice said, sitting next to her on the bed and urging her to take a drink of water.

"Did you eat breakfast?" Luke asked.

"Yes," Mabel lied, thinking the thought of eating made her nauseous. "It's just the heat."

"Mabel, you work in a bakery that's as hot as an oven. You need to see Dr. Cohen," Luke said. "Do you want me to call him?"

"No. I'm fine."

"You're pretty pale," Alice said.

"I just need a moment to collect myself. Really, I'm fine. Go! I'll be down shortly."

Luke nodded for Alice to come with him.

"I got the bakery covered. So don't worry," Alice said and closed the door.

Mabel laid back down. Morning nausea. Fainting. No period. Maybe Mary Catherine was right. She put her hand on her belly and looked up. "If you've blessed me with another child, please don't take it from me."

Dan McInnes left the Prince Street train station and waited for his drive. He dropped his duffle bag on the ground and was about to light his cigarette when Lenny Slade pulled up. McInnes threw his bag in the back and jumped in.

"Hell. I had to look twice before I realized it was you," Lenny said. McInnes smoothed down his beard and took off his hat, exposing his receding hair line. "Fuck! Ya bulked up," Lenny said.

McInnes curled his arms to show off his bulging biceps. "Yeah. Lifting twenty pound sacks for eight hours a day has its benefits. Everything goin okay?" he asked.

"All's good," Lenny said. He pulled a u-ey, stopped at the intersection, and signalled he was turning right.

"Take a left," McInnes said.

"Why?"

"I wanna go to town."

"But my sister's expectin us."

"Your sister can wait. I haven't been home in years. I want to check things out."

Lenny turned left, drove through Reserve, and into town.

"Turn here," McInnes said, pointing. "Now, slow down." Lenny slowed to a crawl as they passed the police station. "Pricks," McInnes said, glaring at several of his former colleagues gathered on the steps.

"Now where?" Lenny asked.

"Take the next right. I need a beer."

Lenny parked across the street from the Pithead Tavern. He was about to get out.

"Where the fuck do you think yer goin?" McInnes asked.

"I could use a beer," Lenny said.

McInnes opened his door. "Too bad. Wait here."

"But no one knows me here?"

McInnes put his hat on. "That's my point. They don't know ya and they don't need to know ya. Last thing I need is for them to see me with you and start askin questions. Stay put," he ordered and shut the door.

He entered the tavern and looked around at a room full of familiar faces. He went to the bar, ordered three beer, and took a table in the corner. He smiled to himself thinking he had thrown a good number of them in the drunk tank at one time or another, and yet no one seemed to recognize him. He was catching up on the latest gossip making the rounds, including the speculation about the young boy who tumbled off the cliff. *He was left alone to play outside. There was trouble between the husband and wife. They were fighting when the kid ran off.* This was going to be more fun than he thought. He lit a cigarette and took a swig of his beer. A young man he didn't know approached him. "Hey, buddy? Got a smoke?"

"Fuck off!"

"Hey! What's up with you? No need to be so snarly."

McInnes downed his second beer and stubbed out his cigarette. "I said, fuck off."

"No! Fuck you!"

The bar quieted and everyone turned their attention to the table in the corner. McInnes stood, polished off his third beer, and headed for the door.

Skinny wiped his red, sweaty face with his yellowed hankie and nudged Jimmy-One-Eye. "Hey, isn't that Dan McInnes?"

Jimmy's head bobbed as he tried to focus his one bleary eye across the windowless, smoke-filled room. "Yer asking me?"

Stanley hung up the phone. His union contact was adamant that McInnes had been working on the docks up until four days ago when he was fired after another altercation with his foreman. He said he had no idea where McInnes went after he was let go, but that he would have likely been blackballed with little chance of working the docks anytime soon. "Damn it!" Stanley said, slamming his fist on the table.

Fred knocked on his door.

"What is it!" Stanley snapped.

Fred slowly pushed it open. "Sorry. Me and the boys are getting together for a few beers. Thought you might want to come along."

"Thanks, Fred. I'll pass."

"Might do ya some good." Stanley waved him on. "Alright then, I'll see ya in the morning," Fred said and closed the door. He was walking down the steps when Stanley came out. "What the hell," he said.

The two walked the short distance from Stanley's office to the *Pithead*. Ten-After-Six, Dirty Willie and two of Stanley's more recent hires were already sitting at a table cluttered with empty bottles and frothy glasses. Stanley and Fred went to the bar. Stanley waited for his order, keenly aware of the muted whispers and sideways glances of the other patrons. The more intoxicated among them, were more forthcoming, several approaching to slur their sympathies, or to insist on buying his drink. Stanley had his hands wrapped around four beer. He turned sideways to edge past Skinny's table.

"How ya doin, Stanley?" Skinny asked.

"Skinny. Jimmy," Stanley said, nodding.

Skinny ran his sleeve across his mouth and put his beer down. "Didn't happen to run into the bearded guy on yer way in?" he asked.

"Bearded guy? No," Stanley said, shaking his head. "Why?"

Jimmy One-Eye looked up. "Skinny thinks it was Dan McInnes."

Stanley plunked his beer down on their table. He rushed out onto the street just as McInnes was jumping in Lenny's truck. "Anybody recognize you?" Lenny asked.

"Apparently so. That's him," McInnes said, pointing to Stanley frantically running back and forth in front of the *Pithead*.

Lenny waited for an opportunity to pull onto Main Street. "That's who?" he asked.

McInnes grinned. "The dead kid's daddy."

Sylvie Sheppard was angry with herself. She vowed never to play favourites like her mother. She peeked in at her beautiful girls, relieved they were all fast asleep. She walked down the hall and opened a second door. She put her finger to her lips, tiptoed past the playpen, and picked up the baby. "I've been neglecting you," she said, carrying her to the kitchen sink. She gently lowered her into the basin and ran a washcloth over her head. "Oh, dear," she said, quickly reaching for a dry cloth and dabbing at the soapy water that splashed into her eye. "Mommy's sorry."

She was toweling her off when she heard Midas, her brother's golden lab. She looked out the window as he eagerly sniffed and barked at the woodpile. He was going to wake the children and ruin her special time with the baby. She opened the front door. "Shut up!" she screamed, slamming it shut. The sharp, shrill barking continued. Sylvie put her hands over her ears. "Shut up! Shut up!" She grabbed the baby, put her on her lap, roughly urging her arm through her sleeve. The baby's thumb got caught up in her loose-knit sweater. She reached up her sleeve and grabbed her tiny hand. The barking continued. She yanked on her arm. "Fuck!" Sylvie screamed. She tore out of the house and into the barn. Midas kept barking. She stood over him, waiting for him to look up. Midas stretched out his forepaws, put his head down, and whimpered. Sylvie brought the butt of the rifle up to her shoulder and shot him in the head.

Sylvie knelt on the ground next to Lenny's beloved dog. "That's better," she whispered, patting the back of his neck. She abruptly got to her feet, grabbed his front paws, dragged him through the dirt to the back of the barn, and covered him under slabs of corrugated siding and rotting wood.

She walked back to the house, stopping to kick dirt over the wet blood. She then stomped up the steps and flung the door back. The baby was lying face-up on the table, her glassy eyes fixed on the ceiling. Sylvie picked her up. "There, there," she murmured, as she tried to reattach her arm.

"Your sister's okay with me staying for a bit?" McInnes asked.

"Yeah. She's good. Should warn ya though. She got a bit of a temper."

McInnes smiled. "Then we should get along quite nicely."

"Just don't go saying anything about her dolls? Wacky, I know. But no real harm to it. She's always been into her dolls. Became a bit of an obsession after she and Barry lost the baby."

"And she never suspected you with her husband's murder?"

Lenny glared at him. "I told ya! It was an accident!"

McInnes rolled his eyes. "Ya shot him in the gut for Christ sakes."

"I thought I was shootin a deer."

"Why didn't ya just report it?"

"Often wish I did. Wouldn't be shoulderin all this guilt. I dunno. I just panicked. Everybody knew I owed him money. Cheap bastard never let a day go by without tellin everyone within earshot."

"So what does your sister think happened?"

"Like everyone else, figures he just ran off. He was always threatenin to. She still thinks he's gonna come back."

"Lucky for you."

Lenny turned onto the narrow dirt road and drove through the thick trees. He stopped and pointed into the bushes. "Barry's in there. Just over the hill, under the big spruce. Poor bastard. Never did get the chance to leave." Lenny put the truck back in gear and pulled away slowly.

"And the police never checked into his disappearance?"

"Yeah, of course. But everybody heard him say he was going to take off the first chance he got. Eventually everybody just stopped askin bout him. Even his family." Lenny's truck bounced along the winding, tree shaded lane. "See? Told you it's private. Not a neighbour in sight." He shut the engine off and pointed to the barn. "Penelope's in there."

"Penelope?" McInnes said.

"My cow. I also had few chickens but the goddamn coyotes got at em. I shot a couple of em but they just kept coming back. Oh, and I got a gas generator. Kind of sketchy at times, but it mostly does the trick. Like I said, we're in the middle of nowhere." Lenny pointed. "That's the shitter. Barry was always too tight to put in an indoor toilet."

"And nobody comes by?" McInnes asked.

"Barry's family used to drop in from time to time before Sylvie lost the baby, but I haven't seen em in ages. Hasn't been a soul here since Jesus was in diapers." He laughed. "And they were lost."

McInnes grabbed his duffle bag out of the back and followed Lenny up the steps.

Sylvie heard them approach and ran to the door. "Lenny," she said, thrusting her doll into his chest. "Can you fix the baby's arm?"

Lenny gave McInnes an exasperated look. "Sylvie. This is Dan. Dan McInnes," he said, twisting and pushing the rounded knob of the doll's arm into its socket. "There," he said, lifting the arm up and down to show her it was as good as new. He handed it back to her.

"Thank you," she said, hugging it. She positioned its legs so it could sit on the table next to her sewing machine. She carefully gathered up her floral cotton fabric, pinned to a delicate sheet of thin yellow paper, and put it next to her Butterick pattern book on the counter. "I'm being rude," she said with a smile. "Daniel? Would you like some tea? I have some steeping," she said, pointing to the stove.

"Not in this heat," Lenny said. He went to the fridge and took out two bottles of beer. "Hey, Dan? Come see the view from the back."

McInnes followed Lenny outside, sat next to him on the porch steps, and looked out at the uninhabited woods surrounding the lake.

"Nice eh?" Lenny said.

"Yeah, it's perfect. Yer smack-dab in the middle of who the fuck knows and who the fuck cares." He leaned into Lenny. "No wonder your sister's loopy," he whispered.

Lenny shoved him and laughed. "What can I say? She likes her privacy."

"But she's good though? We can trust her?" McInnes asked.

"Yeah. No worries there. She's in her glory."

"And she's got no friends?"

Lenny took a swig of his beer and belched. "Not a one."

"It's a shame, ya know. I mean, she's quite the looker. If she weren't three bricks shy of a load, I'd take a crack at her myself."

Lenny stared at McInnes. "Not sure ya'd live to regret that."

"Does she ever leave the house?"

"Of course. I take her to get groceries and to pick up and drop off her sewing at the Stitch'n Post. But, apart from that, she doesn't leave the yard."

"What about when you were in Dorchester?"

"She was already in the Butterscotch Palace," Lenny said, twirling his finger at the side of his head. "Had to have her locked up. She'd just sit in her chair all day long, rockin and moanin. Wouldn't eat or clean herself. Got up one mornin and she got no top on. She's singing Mockin Bird and holdin one of her dolls to her tit. Anyway, that did it for me. Then I got into that spot of trouble. They kept her in till I got out. But she's a lot better now," Lenny said, draining his beer.

He stood, walked down the steps, and started whistling. "Midas! Here Midas! Midas! C'mon boy! Where are ya? Hey, Sylvie! Did ya see Midas?"

Sylvie walked to the screen door. "No." She put her head down. "Probably out chasing hares. I'm making stew for supper," she said and hurried off.

Lenny walked up the steps and held the door open for McInnes. "Want another beer?" McInnes followed him inside.

Sylvie was walking down the hall, beaming. "See! I told you Uncle Lenny and mommy have a new friend." She squatted beside him. "Ah, don't be scared," she said, taking his hand. "This is Daniel. Say hello, Barry."

⊂▭▭▭▭⊃

Mabel took her pies out of the oven and placed them on the cooling rack. "Alice, *I am* feeling a little tired. I'm going to head out now."

"You should have gone home hours ago. And don't come in tomorrow if you're not up to it."

Mabel took her apron off, laid it on the counter, and picked up her purse. She walked into the store. "Goodnight, Luke."

"Hold on, Mabel. I'll give you a lift."

"No. The walk will do me good. I'm only going as far as town. I'll get the bus from there."

"You sure?"

"Yes, goodnight," Mabel said and closed the door. She was at the brook within fifteen minutes, sitting on the side of the hill and watching the boys. A foul ball bounced in her direction. She picked it up and threw it to the first baseman and continued on to the footbridge. She thought of the morning she first realized she had feelings for Stanley. She was walking along one side of the brook and he was on the other. He called out to her and pointed to the footbridge. They met in the middle. It was the first time they had really talked. The first time she had heard his laugh or seen his smile. So much has happened since then, she thought, feeling herself well up. She put her head down. *Dear God, help him forgive me.*

A sudden commotion made her look up. The boys were running alongside the brook. "Get it! Get it!" they screamed as a white ball bobbed up and down out of reach. One of the boys rolled up his pant legs and waded in. He reached out, but slipped on the rocky

bottom and fell face first into the shallow water. Their ball continued to bounce along, disappearing under the footbridge, destined
for the harbour beyond.

"What do we do now?" one boy asked another.

"We go home."

"It's Hughie's fault. He can't throw for shit. He should get us a
new ball."

Mabel approached them. "It's no one's fault. It was an accident."
She reached into her purse and handed the kid who had braved the
frigid brook a five dollar bill. "Here. Go and get a new one. And buy
some treats for you and your friends."

"Thanks, lady," he said.

"Yeah, thanks lady," the others chimed in.

Mabel walked back over the footbridge and started up the steep
path leading to town. A couple of the boys scurried past her, once
again, hollering their thanks. She felt drained when she reached the
top and briefly sat on the grass. She got back up and was walking up
Commercial Street when they charged out of Woolworth's with their
new ball. Small gestures can bring great joy to the giver, she thought,
watching them run off. She walked past Woolworth's, entered the
next building, climbed the creaky stairway, and opened the door.
"Hello. I was wondering if Dr. Cohen is here and if he might have
time to see me?"

Stanley stopped at the top of Steel's Hill, got out, and knocked
on the door.

"What do *you* want?"

"Mrs. Ferguson," Stanley said calmly. "I'm looking for Dan."

"He's not here. He's working the Great Lakes."

"I heard he was back in town."

"Well, you're as deaf as ever. I'd have heard from him if he were."

"I understand he was just at the *Pithead*."

She looked surprised. "Well, whoever told ya that must be well into their cups. He'd come and see me if he was in town. And I haven't seen hide nor hair of him. Haven't seen him since he left for Dorchester, thanks to you. Anyway, what do you want with him?"

"Just want to have a word with him, that's all?"

"About what?"

Stanley looked back at his truck. "Never mind. Thanks for your trouble," he said, turning to leave.

Gladys Ferguson started to close the door, then quickly pulled it back open. She walked out on her front step. "Hey! That was you who called me pretending to be some guy he met in jail. Wasn't it?"

Stanley was about to get into his truck. She walked off the step. "I know it was! You better not go causing any more trouble. My nephew's a good boy, you pervert! No wonder God took your son! He's punishing you. Just like James Cameron. I bet you any money he's still burning in hell!"

Stanley stopped, closed his eyes, and clenched his fists. He took a few steps toward her. Gladys gripped the sides of her apron and held it up under her chin as if it would protect her.

"Go to hell you fat old cow!" he spat.

"Don't ever set foot on my property again!" she hollered. "Or I'll call the police!" She was watching from the doorway as Stanley started up his truck. He looked back at her, stuck his arm out the window, and held up his middle finger.

Gladys Ferguson gasped and slammed the door shut.

Kenny was grateful for the longer, warmer days of spring. He was going to squeeze out every last second of daylight. He pedalled down Catherine Street and took the path leading to Bicycle Hill, a favourite place for those fortunate enough to own a bike. He looked down from the top of the hill to a quick succession of smaller mounds that promised as much of a thrill as any roller coaster ever could. He stood on his top pedal and pushed down, easily rounding the hills and taking the sharp turn at the top to avoid the thirty-foot drop into the muddy dunes below. Over and over again, he took the exhilarating ride until his legs began to burn from the uphill grind. It was getting dark. He'd take one last loop around and head home. He'd go even faster this time. He set the rubber pedal cover spinning with the toe of his shoe, inched closer to the edge of the hill, gripped his handlebars, and pushed down. He sailed down the first hill, crested the second and then the third. The last hill was in his sights. He'd break his own record. He pumped faster and faster, his bike wobbling from side to side as he hit the final rise. Kenny was airborne. Then, he hit the ground. He was going too fast. He tried to lift his left leg to apply the back brake, but couldn't. He looked down. His pant leg was caught up in the chain. He had no choice. He thrust his body to the right, hitting the ground, and skidding under his bike through the dirt. He stopped just in time; his back wheel spinning midair over the edge of the bank. His right knee and shoulder both ached. He tried to reach his entangled leg, but couldn't. He slowly eased his leg out from under his bike, got to his knee, and pushed himself up, awkwardly straddling the frame. He fell forward. Three times. He finally eased himself back down. His sore shoulder was digging into the ground. He began scraping the heel of his shoe up and down against the corner of the pedal. It finally fell off. He looked around. No one was in sight. He quickly unbuttoned his pants, squirmed out of them, and scampered to his feet. He was sitting on the ground in his underwear, desperately tugging at his ensnarled pant leg when Sally MacNamara and her girlfriends arrived on the scene, laughing and pointing. Kenny gave one last furious yank and fell back. He jumped to his feet and pulled on his tattered pants. He twisted his foot into his shoe and set his bike upright. The back fender was scratched, the front wheel bent, a good chunk of his pant leg was still firmly embedded in the chain, and the girls were still laughing.

Kenny limped along, pushing his bike. He ached from head to toe. He knew he was going to be in big trouble for being so late, but he couldn't wait to get home. He cut through old Mrs. Oickle's backyard and hid his bike behind her shed. He'd look for a better hiding spot in the morning. Please, God, let Ma and Da be in bed or out somewhere, he repeated to himself. His prayers went unanswered.

Kenny's father heard the door. "That you, Kenny?"

"Shit," Kenny mumbled. "Yeah, Da."

"Where the hell have you been? It's a school night, ya know?" his father hollered from the living room. He got up from his chair and walked into the kitchen. "Christ! What in the name of Jesus happened to ya?"

"I was at Tommy's doin school work and I was…I was…attacked by a dog on my way home."

"Whose dog?"

"I dunno. Just some dog."

"Where?"

Kenny hesitated. "Highland Street."

"Where on Highland Street?"

"Just past Harley's."

"Did he bite you?"

Kenny looked down at his torn pant leg. "No. Just tore my good pants to shreds and knocked me down."

"Was it a German Sheppard?"

Kenny thought that sounded reasonable. "Yeah. Pretty sure it was."

Kenny's father drained his beer, grabbed his jacket, and headed for the door.

"Where ya goin, Da?"

"I'm gonna go and make sure that damn dog is put down once and for all!"

"But, Da?" Kenny said, as the door slammed shut.

⊏⎯⎯⎯⊐

Mary Catherine waited for her cash.

The teller to Mary Catherine's right greeted her next customer. "Sadie! How are you?"

"Good dear, good. And you?"

"I'm fine. How's your sister?"

"You know Clair?"

"Yes. We went to school together."

"She's good. She's back home now. Living in Boisdale. We had a nice visit this morning. Brought me a lovely chocolate cake. Gonna be workin for the bank in Sydney come September."

Mary Catherine's teller returned and counted out her cash. Mary Catherine wasn't paying attention. "Is there anything else, Mrs. Friedman? *Mrs. Friedman?*" Mary Catherine looked up. "Oh, yes. I'm sorry. I wonder if you could deposit this in Irwin's account and provide me a new balance," she said, handing her two dollars and Irwin's bankbook.

"Did she ever get married?" Sadie's teller asked. "She was always so beautiful."

"No. Came close once. Was engaged to Stanley MacIntyre. You remember? The boxer that almost killed Dirty Willie? Ya must have heard about the child who fell off the cliff. Well, that was his son."

"I know. So awful."

"Anyway, dear," Sadie said, "I'll just have fifteen dollars to see me through till next week."

Mary Catherine's teller handed her Irwin's updated bankbook.

"Thank you," she said and left. She was getting in her car when she saw Mabel standing in front of The Creamery waiting for the bus. "Mabel!" she hollered. Mabel waved. "C'mon! I'll drive you home."

They drove up the driveway. "So, are you coming in for tea?" Mabel asked.

"Of course."

Mary Catherine sat quietly as Mabel poured the steamy water into the teapot and threw in four tea bags. Clair and Stanley were engaged, she thought. She was Mabel's closest friend yet Mabel never mentioned this to her. Mary Catherine began to wonder if Stanley ever told his wife.

Mabel looked at her friend. "You're quiet. Penny for your thoughts?"

"Oh, don't mind me. Just thinking about this and that. Nothing in particular," Mary Catherine lied.

"How's Liddy?"

"She's good as new. So, I hear Stanley's staying with Ten-After-Six."

Mabel nodded. "Yes. I saw him today."

"And?"

"And he needs time. He's angry. I totally understand. He'll come home when he's ready."

Mary Catherine began to seethe. "He should be here with you now."

Mabel went to get the cups out of the cupboard and to pour their tea. "I need to ask you something," she said with her back to Mary Catherine.

"What?"

"I don't know. It's just that the last time you came by and Stanley was here, I felt…I felt as if you were mad at him."

Mary Catherine wondered how much she should tell her. "Really? I don't know why?"

Mabel handed Mary Catherine her tea and sat next to her. "My overactive imagination, I guess."

Mary Catherine reached for her hand. "You've been through a lot. We both have. Truthfully? How are you coping?"

"I'm fine. My faith is helping me get through things."

Mary Catherine gave her a puzzled look. "I'm surprised. But glad you've had a change of heart. Like you said to me, whatever gives you strength."

Mabel told Mary Catherine about what happened at the hospital, Father Gregory's premonition, and her visit from Father Cusack. She stood up and walked down the hall, returning with Father Gregory's maniturgium. "He left this for me," she said, explaining its significance.

Mary Catherine took it from Mabel. "It's —"

"Hello!"

They both turned and looked down the hallway. "Amour!" Mabel screamed and ran to the door.

Mabel, Amour and Mary Catherine drank tea and cried. Amour cried for Mabel. Mabel cried for Amour. And Mary Catherine cried for the both of them. Everyone's eyes were red and the table was covered in spent tissues. It was going on nine when Mary Catherine reluctantly decided she better get home. She turned at the door. "Ladies, it's supposed to be another beautiful day tomorrow. Let's go to the *Gut*? Just the three of us."

Mabel turned to Amour. "Maybe you need a day to rest up?"

"I'll be fine. Let's do it," Amour said.

"I'll talk to Alice. If she's okay with it, I'll take the afternoon off," Mabel said.

Mary Catherine poked her shoulder. "Listen to you. You're the boss for Pete's sake. Tell her to close for the afternoon."

"I'll pack us a lunch," Amour said.

"Great. So Amour I'll pick you up here, then swing by the bakery for Mabel," Mary Catherine said. "Wear your bathing suits under your clothes." She hugged them and left.

Amour turned to Mabel. "God, I missed you. Honestly, how are you doing?"

"I'm alive and kicking," Mabel said, taking her by the hand and leading her back to the kitchen. She handed her a dish towel.

Amour dried the dishes and put them on the counter. "Do you find it hard to stay here? I mean—"

"I'd find it harder to leave. This is where my memories are. Good and bad. But I'm afraid Stanley feels differently."

"He'll come around. You'll see," Amour said.

Mabel smiled. "So, what do you make of the events in the chapel and Father Gregory's sudden passing?" she asked.

Amour shook head. "I've never heard of anything so strange in all my life. I mean, there are just so many coincidences?"

"Or, maybe they're not coincidences. Maybe they're all part of God's grand plan?"

"Certainly makes you wonder," Amour said. "You're a strong woman, Mabel. Stronger than anyone else I know. You've had so many setbacks in life and yet you always stay so positive."

"Believe me, I have my moments," Mabel said.

"I'm sure you do. Still, when you and Stanley got married and had…had the baby, I thought all of that was behind you. And now this. The greatest heartbreak of all. It's like the sun shines down on you just long enough for you to appreciate its warmth. Then the storm clouds roll in."

"We've all endured our fair share of heartache," Mabel said. "Look what Roddy put you through. And Luke. God, I worry for him."

Amour opened a cupboard door to put the dishes away. "You've changed things around. Where do you keep the teacups?"

Mabel pointed. "Right there." She began wiping down the kitchen table. "You must be tired from the long trip? And If I'm taking tomorrow afternoon off, I need to get an early jump on things at the bakery."

Amour opened the wrong door.

When Mabel turned around Amour was holding the dish towel to her mouth and staring at JC's small, red shovel. Mabel hugged her and led her into the living room. She stopped in front of her wall of photos. "I know it must seem silly, but I like to say good-night to everyone."

Amour put her arm over Mabel's shoulder. "It's not silly. It's beautiful," she said, studying the picture of Ellie flanked by Percy and James in their uniforms. "Your mother and father were certainly a handsome couple," she said.

Mabel smiled. "I always regretted they never got to meet their grandson."

"And now they have," Amour said.

"Yes, I suppose they have."

Amour followed Mabel upstairs and watched her stop outside JC's room, kiss her hand, and lay it on his door.

"Goodnight, Amour," Mabel said, continuing down the hall.

Amour brought her fist to her mouth and pinched her eyes shut. "Goodnight, Mabel."

Sylvie cleared the table of a dozen or more empty beer bottles.

"Grab us a couple more," Lenny barked.

"You drank them all," she said. "Daniel, I put your bag in the spare room. Well goodnight, gentlemen," she said, disappearing down the hall.

McInnes went to his room and came back with a bottle of whiskey. He put it on the table, "She certainly loves the little bastard."

"I'm kinda gettin attached to him myself. First few days were pretty rough. Wouldn't stop cryin."

"I hate kids," McInnes said.

Lenny stood up and went out on the step. "Midas! Midas!" he hollered. He came back inside. "Fuck! Not like him to miss a meal," he said. He went to the kitchen, came back with two glasses, and plopped down on his chair.

McInnes uncapped the whiskey and began pouring. "Like Sylvie said, he's probably tearing into a hare."

"I guess. So, how long ya stayin?" Lenny asked.

"Why? Are ya in a hurry to get rid of me or somethin?"

"Hell, ya can stay as long as ya like. I appreciate the company."

"I need to make one more trip to town. I wanna see my aunt."

"Where ya headin after ya leave here?"

McInnes knew better than to tell Lenny his plans. "Back to the Lakes."

"What about the rest of my money?" Lenny asked.

McInnes took a swig of his whiskey and topped up his glass. "What about it?"

"When am I gonna get it?"

"It's at my aunt's. I'll get it tomorrow. I'll need to borrow your truck."

"Sure. I'll go with ya."

McInnes shook his head. "Not a good idea. How do I explain you to my aunt?"

"I'll wait in the truck."

"No, she's too nosy. She'll start asking questions. Don't worry, I'm not gonna run off or anything. We're in this together."

"Christ, you must really hate the guy? Poor bastard. Thinking his son's dead n' all."

McInnes lit a cigarette, sucked the smoke into his lungs, and blew circles into the air. "That prick and his slutty wife ruined my life. Let's just say it's tit for tat." He slapped Lenny on the back. "Lucky for me, you came along. Just don't fuck things up."

"I won't," Lenny said.

"Yeah, well ya never shoulda torched the barn. Too familiar for my likin."

"Whatcha expect me to do? It wasn't easy, ya know. I almost got caught. Got in the house one mornin and had the kid in my arms. Thought his mother was gettin in the tub. Then I heard her comin down the hall. Musta been runnin the water for the kid. Had to hide in the closet. And there was this crazy old woman always hangin about. She pounded on my window when I was casin out the place. Scared the shit out of me. Christ! You were the one sayin create a diversion." Lenny pushed up his sleeve. "Look at my fuckin arm," he said, pointing to a six inch, crusty gash. "Got that crawlin through the fuckin field. Kid got a few scratches too."

"And you're sure no one saw you?"

"Positive. I snuck in the barn before the sun came up. There wasn't a soul around. Then the kid and his mother come out. I could see her through the cracks in the siding. She had her back to me, yakin away at the kid. Figured it was now or never. So I lit the straw, ran in through the front, and there he was, just sittin on the back step. I just scooped him up, took off round the side of the house, and dragged him through the field. Everybody was focused on the fire and the horses. Hid out behind the neighbour's shed for a bit. Could see the kid's mother runnin round like a chicken with its head cut off. When she ran inside, I grabbed the kid and tore off. Anyway, no one saw us. Christ, *The Post* reported it was a tragic accident. Ain't no one lookin for him. Fuck, everybody figures he's lobster bait."

McInnes took a swig of his whiskey. "All I'm sayin is keep your head down and Sylvie in line."

"Sylvie ain't gonna tell no one. Why would she? She's in her element. She don't wanna lose the kid."

"And she knows not to go paradin him around."

"Yeah, she knows. I don't know why yer so worried. Ya weren't even in the area. Hell, seems to me it's me and Sylvie that got the most to lose."

Stanley held up his glass and clinked it against Lenny's. "We make a good team. Here's to Sylvie's eternal happiness and to Stanley's life-long misery," McInnes said.

Wednesday, June 5

CHAPTER II

The moon was still bright when McInnes drove Lenny's truck up Steele's Hill. He pulled off to the side, got out, and cut through the bushes to his aunt's. A dog started to bark in the distance. He looked up at the house, still in darkness. He darted through the thick brush to the side of the shed, pushed the window open, and hoisted his waist up over the sill. He fell in, toppling over some old paint cans. "Fuck," he whispered. He opened the door a crack and peeked out, then ran to the back of the shed and pushed an old oil drum off to the side. He looked around for something to lift the boards. He picked up a spade, slid the sharp edge between two boards and pushed down. A board popped up, exposing the Crisco can below. He picked it up, slid the oil drum back in place, and looked outside a second time. He ran back the same way he came and jumped in the truck. He removed the lid of the can. "Thank you, Aunt Gladys," he whispered, pulling out dozens of twenties and fifties.

McInnes pulled away, feeling a tinge of guilt. His aunt was always so good to him. So good, in fact, she told him where to find her money should anything happen to her. A good woman for sure, just too stupid to trust the banks. Almost as stupid as Lenny. He wondered if Lenny was up yet and started to laugh. What an idiot. It was a good trip home, he thought. He not only hit pay dirt, he got to make sure things with the kid were well in hand. Hell, he even got a new truck out of it. He looked at Lenny's watch and pushed down on the gas. He'd be on the mainland before noon. A blue Ford pickup approached from the opposite direction. McInnes turned his head to the side until it passed, then looked in the rear-view mirror. The truck's red brake lights came on and it pulled off to the side, not far from his aunt's small, green bungalow.

Lenny crawled out of bed, pulled the piss pot out from under his bed, and relieved himself. He looked at the mirror above his dresser and saw the cover of Sylvie's Butterick Pattern book wedged in the corner. "What the hell," he said, tearing it away and turning it over. *Lenny. Thanks for the truck. If you're looking for your money, it's buried with Barry.*

"Fuck!" Lenny screamed, slamming his fist into the mirror.

Sylvie opened her bedroom door. "Lenny! Be quiet! You'll wake the children!"

"Go back to bed!" Lenny yelled, looking out the window for his truck. He was fit to be tied. He balled up McInnes' note and threw it across the room. "Fuck!" he yelled again, looking at his bloody knuckles. How could I have been such an idiot? I should never have trusted the bastard. Never have shown him where Barry was buried. He went to the kitchen, wrapped a tea towel around his hand, and went back to his room. He sat on the side of the bed, thinking about what he could do. He was out his money, his truck was gone, and now he was saddled with a whiny kid and a crazy sister. He was going to make the bastard pay for what he did. He thought about telling the police McInnes showed up with the kid claiming to be his uncle and just took off. But then McInnes would rat him out for killing Barry. And then there was the problem of what to do about his sister.

Lenny began to pace. He'd need to convince Sylvie she had to give up the kid, and that if she talked they'd both go to jail. And he could easily dig up Barry's bones, put them in the lake, and deny anything McInnes might say. He started to feel he had a way out. Then he remembered there was one gaping hole in his plan. McInnes was working the Lakes when the boy went missing. And then there was that crazy woman who rapped on his window. She'd be able to identify him. He needed to go for a walk, clear his head, and think.

He opened the top drawer of his dresser and pulled out a singlet. It was then he realized McInnes didn't just steal his truck. He stole his watch too. He slammed the drawer shut. Sylvie appeared in the doorway. She was seething. "I told you to be quiet!"

Lenny put his head down.

"Is that my good tea towel?" she asked. She charged at him and tore it away from his hand. "You ruined it!" she screamed and stormed out.

Lenny laid down on his bed. First thing's first, he thought. He needed a car. He'd tell Sylvie he bought it with the money Dan paid him. He decided the Steele City Tavern would be his best chance of picking one up without too much trouble. Then he'd find a way to get rid of the kid. He momentarily considered contacting the parents and asking for a ransom but didn't feel good about his chances of pulling it off. He then thought about dumping him off at a local church. Again, Sylvie was a problem. She'd make him pay for it one way or another. She'd either kick him out or kill him. Poor kid, Lenny thought, he'll be as crazy as Sylvie before long. We both will. He thought of Midas. He sat up and swung his leg over the side of the bed. "Fuck!" he yelled again, lifting up his foot. It was dripping in piss.

Sylvie was back in his room. "Did you do this!" she asked, shaking her torn Butterick pattern book in his face.

Stanley had returned to Steele's Hill and parked just down from Gladys Ferguson's. He had spent half the night driving around looking for McInnes. He went to all of the places he thought he might be. The *Pithead*. *Iggies*. Constable McEwan's. He looked at his watch. It was just past seven. He put his head back, thinking about another time he stalked a man he wanted to kill. He never thought he could hate anybody as much as Johnnie Adshade, the man who beat Mabel and had Billy Guthro burn his ponies. But he did. If McInnes was in town he'd find him. He thought about going to Dunphy, but what would he do? What could he do? For all Stanley knew, Skinny was mistaken and McInnes was still somewhere in Ontario.

Stanley's eyes grew heavy and his head started to bob. He sat up and shook it from side to side, then rested his head against the window. *He was driving Mabel to the shack. He was back in court. James was on the stand, reading a letter and crying. Billy appeared. He had no teeth and was pointing an accusing finger at him and screaming. He was back in his cell with his wrists cuffed, eating pie with his hands, and reading The Great Gatsby. He could hear children laughing.*

Stanley opened his eyes, sat up, and looked out. A bunch of kids were in the middle of the road playing shinny. He looked at the time. It was almost nine. He started up the truck and waited for the kids to move out of the way so he could turn around. He never saw Gladys Ferguson staring at him as she drove past.

Stanley went back to Ten-After-Six's and flopped onto his cot. He was exhausted. He woke two hours later, washed up, and went back to the *Pithead*. If he didn't find McInnes, at least he could drown his sorrows.

"Get your Goddamn sorry arse outa bed?" his father yelled, pulling Kenny's covers down.

Kenny was lying on his side. He hardly slept a wink thinking about his mangled bike, Myrtle's witch piss, Mr. Spencer's Pontiac going up in flames, Sally MacNamara and her friends seeing him in his underwear, and maybe some harmless dead dog. "What time is it?" he asked, pulling the covers back over his sore shoulder.

His father slapped him hard across the ass.

"What!" Kenny said, rolling on his back, and wiping the sleep from his eyes.

"You heard me! Get up! Now!"

Kenny blinked and looked up at his father and his shiner. "Geez Da. What happened to ya?"

"Get up and get downstairs!" Kenny scrambled out of bed and threw on his pants. He hesitated at the top of the stairs. "Kenny!" his father screamed. Kenny crept downstairs and walked sheepishly into the kitchen. His mother was standing next to the stove holding her wooden spoon with an ugly scowl on her face.

"So? You were attacked by a dog?" his father said in a tone Kenny wasn't so sure about.

"Yeah."

"Don't lie to me!"

Kenny was sure now. He put his head down. "No."

"Hear that mother?" Kenny's father said, turning to look at his wife.

"I heard."

"So? How in the hell did ya end up walkin in here lookin like somethin the cat dragged in?"

Kenny swallowed hard. He had to come clean. At least about being on Bicycle Hill. "I was on Bicycle Hill and had an accident. My pants got caught up in the chain and I fell," he said, rubbing his sore shoulder and looking to his mother for sympathy.

"Whose bike?" his mother asked. Kenny knew not to name any of his close friends. He pinched his eyes closed. "Sally MacNamara's."

He waited for the next question. "Well, ya damn well should have told me that to begin with," his father snapped. "First ya jump the Goddamn train! And now this!" He pointed to his black eye. "Look at me! I stormed into Dougie Phalen's threatening to kill his damn dog. He and his two brothers gave me a goin over. Turns out the mongrel was put down weeks ago."

"Well, maybe you should have thought twice before going off half-cocked," Kenny's mother said.

Kenny's father turned to face her. "I thought I was doin good. That damn dog musta taken a good chunk out of a dozen or more neighbourhood kids. Came at me once. I had to give him a good boot in the chops." He turned back to Kenny. "So, this is what's gonna happen. Yer gonna stack every piece of wood out back, clean out the shed, and fill the coal bin. Mother's got a long list of every-thin else that needs doin round here. And yer not to step one foot out of this yard for the next two weeks. You go to school and ya come straight home. You understand me?"

Kenny nodded and was about to leave. "Oh, I forgot. I gotta stay late cause of skippin school. Principal Gillis is makin us stay and clean up the classrooms."

Kenny's father shook his head. "Right after that, then. You get yer ass home lickety-split. And mind yer P's n' Q's. You hear me?"

Kenny went back to his bedroom. He pulled the curtain back to see how much wood he had to stack. "Jesus," he muttered. Old Mrs. Oickle was walking from around the back of her shed, pushing his bike. He rapped on the window. No luck. He tried to open it, but it was stuck. He rapped again, this time harder. Still the deaf old bat didn't look up.

"Kenny! What are you doing up there!" his mother yelled from the bottom of the stairs.

"Nothin, Ma."

"Well hurry up and get ready for school."

Kenny plunked down on the side of his bed and put his head in his hands, thinking about the next wave of trouble he knew was heading his way and wishing he had a smoke.

⊏⊏⊐

Mary Catherine, Mabel and Amour passed two school buses, drove over the one lane bridge, and looked at the crowded beach. "It's busy for a weekday. Must be an end of school field trip. I might have to park in Catalone," Mary Catherine said laughing. She eased her way between cars parked on either side of the road and looked for an opening. They finally found a spot, gathered up their belongings, and settled onto one of the few remaining patches of dry sand.

Amour and Mary Catherine quickly stripped down to their swim suits and struggled with their tight latex bathing caps. Mabel spread the blanket out, sat down, and hugged her knees. "Are you coming in?" Amour shouted.

"Not just yet. You guys go ahead," Mabel hollered, slipping her shoes off and digging her toes into the warm sand.

Amour and Mary Catherine waded in up to their knees, crossing their arms over their chests, and rubbing their hands up and down their arms. Amour turned to Mabel. "It's freezing." Mabel smiled and waved. A group of kids charged in. Amour and Mary Catherine screamed, turned their heads to the side, and threw their hands out in front of their faces as the icy water splashed over them. Mabel started to laugh. She grabbed a fistful of sand, slowly uncurled her fingers, and let it drain from her hand. It was the first time she had laughed since JC died. It *is* possible, she thought.

"Hello, Mabel."

Mabel put her hand over her eyes to block the glare of the sun and looked up. "Mind if I share your blanket?" he asked.

She scooted over. "Sure."

Amour and Mary Catherine inched forward. "So how do *you* find her?" Amour asked.

"She's amazing. I can't imagine how she can put one foot in front of the other. *I know I couldn't.* My heart breaks for her. Of course, I could kill Stanley."

Amour looked at her. "He's devastated, too. He'll come around."

"Don't be so sure."

Amour reached down, wet her hands, and rubbed the salty water over her arms. "Why? What do you mean?"

"I mean he's not the man I thought he was. He's having an affair."

Amour started to laugh. "That's crazy. Stanley wouldn't do such a thing."

"I didn't think so either," Mary Catherine said, before sharing the details of Stanley lying about his whereabouts, Sam finding him at Clair's, and the conversation she overheard at the bank. "Did you know he was engaged to someone else?"

Amour was staring down into the water. "No."

"I'm not even sure Mabel knows. Anyway, I'm convinced he's been cheating on her. So is Sam. I've been wrestling with whether or not I should tell her. What would you do?" Mary Catherine asked.

Amour paused. "I think you and Sam should talk to Stanley. Tell him he either tells her, or you will." She turned to look at Mabel, then elbowed Mary Catherine. "Isn't that Constable Dunphy?"

"You mean Captain Dunphy. Yes, that's him."

"Handsome isn't he?"

"That he is. Well, it's now or never," Mary Catherine said and dove in. Amour followed, quickly jumping back up. She wiped the water from her eyes and watched Captain Dunphy get to his feet, put his hand on Mabel's shoulder, and walk up the beach. Mabel stood and walked to the water's edge.

"Are you coming in?" Amour called. "It's…refreshing," she said and laughed.

Mabel shook her head, thinking the ocean was no longer her friend. "I'll pass," she said, spotting a young woman holding a young boy's hand and leading him into the lapping waves. He started excitedly jumping up and down. It made Mabel as happy, as it did sad. She was returning to her blanket, when she heard the screams, looked down the beach, and saw arms flailing about. She tore into the water, falling face first. She got up, pushed forward, and frantically swam toward them. She reached out, grabbed one boy by the arm and dragged him out of harm's way. She then dove back in to help his friend. She was on her knees, with the water up to her waist, holding the second boy by the wrist. She brushed her wet hair away from her eyes and looked up. The entire beach was standing on the shore, staring at her.

"Lady! What are you doing! They were just playing," a man said, running past her to comfort his son.

She turned to the boy. He was crying. Mabel put her hands over her face and wept.

Mary Catherine and Amour waded in and slowly brought her to her feet. Captain Dunphy met them on the shore and wrapped a towel around Mabel's shoulders. Mary Catherine gathered up their beach trappings and followed Amour, Mabel, and Captain Dunphy back to the car. It was a subdued drive back to town.

⊏▭▭⊐

Harley rounded the side of the house. "Hey, Kenny! Whatcha doin?"

Kenny looked up from the woodpile. "I'm bakin a cake. What's it look like I'm doin? How come you weren't in school today?"

"Had to stay home and look after my baby sister. Ma's back in bed with the ministerial cramps. Wanna go to South Street Beach?"

"Yeah! But I can't. Not allowed outa the yard. Da's workin me like a friggin dog. I gotta stack all this wood."

"Holy shit," Harley said. "All this! Must be three cords?"

"Four," Kenny said.

"Did ya get in trouble for somethin?"

"Yeah."

"What for?"

"None of yer business."

"Ya don't need to be so snarly."

Kenny kept stacking.

"So whose bike were ya on yesterday?" Harley asked.

"What?"

"I saw ya tearin down Highland Street."

"Tommy's."

"It was not!"

"Okay, it was mine."

"Where d'ya get it?"

"Never mind. Why don't ya go ask Tommy to go to the beach?"

"I did. Said he had to stay home and work on an essay for Principal Gillis."

"Shit!" Kenny said, thinking it was something else he had to get done.

"So, where's yer bike now?"

Kenny pointed to it leaning against the side of Mrs. Oickle's house.

"Wow!" Harley said. "Can I take it for a spin?"

"Front wheel's all bent."

"Did ya steal it?" Harley asked.

"No, I didn't steal it!"

Harley started helping Kenny with the wood. "Then where'd ya get it?"

"If I tell ya, ya can't say a word."

"I won't."

"Swear to God?"

Harley blessed himself. "Cross my heart."

"Tommy's father got it for me."

"Why?"

"So I'll keep my mouth shut about what I saw at the brook."

"Ya mean the screwin?"

"Yeah. But don't tell nobody. Or I can get in big trouble."

"Does Tommy know?"

Kenny shrugged. They both turned as Mrs. Oickle and her son walked up to Kenny's bike. Her son squatted beside it. "Looks great, Ma. I just need to fix the front wheel. It might be a little big for Rory, but he'll grow into it," he said and wheeled it away.

Harley's mouth hung open. "Where's he takin yer bike?" Kenny started to cry. "I'll see ya in school tomorrow if Ma's cramps are better," Harley said and ran off. He didn't go to the beach. He went back to Tommy's. Tommy's father opened the door.

"Hey, Harley. Yer back. What can I do for ya?"

"Ya can get me a new bike too."

"Just put the bags down on the table. Want some tea?" Amour asked.

"Sure," Luke said. He put the groceries down, walked to the screen door, and looked out. "Michael like his new job?"

"Yes. He's still learning the ropes. But that's to be expected. It hasn't been that long. So, what about you? Are you seeing anyone?"

"No."

"Handsome young man like you? What's up with that? If I was ten years younger and not happily married, I'd be chasing you around the *Heaps*."

Luke laughed. "Like heck you would."

"You've always been so hard on yourself. You need to get out there and sow your oats. We're only given so much time on earth. No need to waste a minute of it," Amour said. She put her head down, thinking of the ten loveless years she spent with Roddy and the irony of her words.

"I got the jitters. No girl worth her salt wants to be saddled with that."

Amour went to him and hugged him. "You are a beautiful young man with a kind heart who has survived a lot. Any woman would be lucky to have you. I wish you could meet Michael's nieces," she said and kissed his cheek.

"What's this?" Mabel said from the doorway.

"I'm trying to get Luke to run off with me," Amour said. "Are you feeling better?"

Mabel reached for the teacups. "Yes."

Amour began unpacking the groceries. "I'm making supper tonight. Bangers and mash with mushy peas," she said, trying to feign a British accent. "Luke, you should stay? There's plenty."

"He's not going anywhere," Mabel said, pouring three cups of tea and setting out a plate of molasses cookies. They took their tea to the front step. "I made a fool of myself at the beach," Mabel said.

Myrtle appeared out of nowhere, startling Amour. She walked up to Mabel and handed her two jars. "Here's the preserves I told yer friend I'd be bringin ya. I had extras. No charge. Mustard relish and some tomato chutney."

"Thank you, Myrtle," Mabel said. "Are you sure I can't pay you?"

"Like I said, no charge."

Amour took the jars from Mabel and tilted them from side to side. "They'll go great with our bangers," she said.

"Myrtle? Would you like to join us?" Mabel asked.

"Can't," she said. She left and then came back, startling Amour a second time. "Fergot to tell ya Lucky's home, no worse fer wear. Out tomcattin round, I suppose."

"I'm glad," Mabel said.

The phone rang. Luke answered and called Mabel inside. Mabel spoke briefly and hung up. She then placed a call of her own. She looked through the screen door at Amour and Luke sitting on the step. "I thought I'd have a bath before supper."

Amour looked over her shoulder. "Take your time." She turned to Luke. "It wasn't Stanley was it?" she whispered.

"No. Dunphy."

"Captain Dunphy?"

"Yes. He wanted to see how Mabel was feeling?"

Mabel was back in the kitchen within an hour. Amour was pulling a spoon from her mouth. "Mabel," she mumbled, placing her open hand under her chin. "Myrtle's preserves are to die for."

Mabel closed her eyes. "I'm afraid that's a very good possibility," she said. "Oh, and we should set the table for four."

Amour stuck her spoon back into Myrtle's chutney. "Is Stanley coming?"

"No," Mabel said sadly.

"Dunphy?"

Mabel gave Amour a bewildered look. "No! Why would you —"

"Sorry I'm late," Alice called from the doorway. "The bus was running behind. I brought some of Da's Blueberry wine."

Lenny sat at a corner table beside the window. The perfect location to see some unsuspecting schmuck drive up and hopefully walk in alone. His feet ached. He had walked almost six miles before finally hitching a ride into town. He counted his money. He had just over four dollars to his name. He looked through the rainy window at the approaching headlights. The driver got out and ran inside to escape the downpour. *Sit at the bar*, Lenny whispered. He did. Lenny gave him a few minutes to settle in, then pulled out the stool beside him. "Mind if I join you?"

"Fill yer boots," he said, removing his jacket, shaking off the rain and laying it over the back of his stool.

"Pretty nasty out there," Lenny said.

"We could use the rain. I can't remember such a hot, dry spring."

Lenny took a sip of his beer. "Yeah. You from around here?"

"The Pier."

The bait was set, Lenny thought. The two sat, drank and talked about people they thought the other might know, local sports, and the latest rumours about the steel plant's fate. "I gotta take a piss," Lenny's new friend said. Lenny watched him walk around the bar and disappear down the hall. He quickly looked around at the other patrons, then slid his hand into the pocket of the jacket hanging from the stool. He smiled and walked out.

Lenny's friend returned. "Hey, where'd buddy go?" The bartender shrugged. "I'll have one more for the ditch," he said, reaching into his jacket pocket. His wallet was gone. So were his keys. He jumped up and ran to the window. He could see the red tail lights of his McLaughlin turn up George Street. "Call the cops!" he screamed. "He got my wallet and my car!"

Lenny pulled into the yard in his new car, opened the poor schmuck's wallet, and counted his good fortune. "Twenty-two bucks. Better than a kick in the arse," he muttered. He'd lay low for a few days. A green McLaughlin was too noticeable. He'd paint it, or maybe sell it and buy another truck.

He stepped out into the rain and waited for Midas' familiar bark. "Here Midas," he hollered. "Come on boy!" He ducked under the veranda, looked out into the dark, and then went inside. "Hey Sylvie? Still no sign of Midas?"

Sunday, June 9

CHAPTER 12

Stanley woke early. He was beginning to think McInnes wasn't back in town. No one besides Skinny claimed to have seen him. Still, the possibility he was in the area was eating him up inside. He'd make one more trip to Steel's Hill. Again, he parked close enough to keep an eye on Gladys Ferguson's, but far enough away to avoid suspicion. He watched a car come down the hill and pull in front. Gladys came out and settled her stout frame into the passenger seat. The car pulled out. Stanley slumped down, hoping she didn't recognize his truck. When the car was well out of site, Stanley got out and approached the house. He went around back, leaned over the railing of the back step, and looked in the window for any sign McInnes might be there. *A man's coat or shoes.* The curtains blocked most of his view. He tried the door. It was open. He checked to make sure no one was looking and entered. He wouldn't go off the mat. He looked around and saw nothing. A dog started barking. Then he heard the car door slam. He backed out, descended the steps, and peeked around the corner. Gladys Ferguson's neighbours were getting in their car. Stanley waited for them to pull away, then ran back to his truck. He was turning onto Highland Street when he heard the sirens and saw the police fly up Steele's Hill. He wondered if anyone saw him lurking about, then dismissed the idea. He felt totally deflated. He needed a distraction. He'd go to the office and get a jump on the hospital plans while everyone else was enjoying their Sunday dinners or at the beach.

He entered the office and pulled out the specs, but couldn't concentrate. He'd head up the coast and work on the fireplace he had dismantled in his drunken rage.

He passed the sawmill and looked down at the black Chevrolet parked in the yard. He put his blinker on, turned it back off, then put it back on again.

Clair put her book down and smiled as she watched the blue pickup bounce down the hill and churn up a brown cloud of dust. She stood up and walked to the edge of the steps. Stanley got out of his truck and awkwardly smiled. "Looking for more eggs?" she asked.

Luke, Amour, and Mabel stood on the steps of St. Anthony's, squinting from the bright sun as the congregants eagerly made their escape. "Let's go for a drive and grab a bite to eat. My treat," Mabel said.

Luke pulled off the highway and onto the road leading to Marion Bridge. "Let's do takeout and eat outside," he said.

They stopped at a roadside canteen and ate at a picnic table overlooking the Mira River. "There's a great blueberry patch just down the hill," Mabel said, thinking of the day she and Stanley picked three quarts before it started to rain. She smiled remembering it was the day she burnt her pies. She was in the kitchen when Stanley walked up behind her, scooped her up in his arms, and took her upstairs. It took several hours to rid the house of the smoke and the stink from the blackened blueberries and charred crust.

Mabel tugged at the end of her hotdog bun.

"Not hungry?" Amour asked.

"Let's check out the MacPhees? I'd like to see how it's coming along," Mabel said.

Luke looked at Amour. "I think we should get back."

"Why?" Mabel asked. "It's such a nice day."

"I told John I'd help him with his homework," Luke said.

Mabel looked at him. "It's only two minutes down the road. Stanley said it was going to be spectacular. With a lovely veranda and a wall of windows overlooking the water. It won't take long."

Amour pressed her foot into Luke's. "Actually," she said. "I have a bit of a headache. Must be from the sun."

"What's up with you two? Seriously, it won't take a sec. I promise one quick look and then we'll be on our way. We can take our hotdogs with us for that matter," Mabel said and stood up.

Amour looked at Luke and nodded. "It's the first right after the Stitch n' Post," Mabel said. Luke turned down the narrow lane. A downed tree blocked their way.

"That's odd," Mabel said. Neither Luke nor Amour said a word. Mabel opened her door and stepped out. She walked around the fallen tree, down the brush strewn path, and looked at the small bungalow sinking into the ground.

Luke turned to Amour who was sitting in the back seat. "What are we going to tell her?"

"I'm not sure," she said. "She was bound to find out sooner or later. I just wish it was later." She then told Luke about Sam going back to Boisdale and finding Stanley with Clair. They watched Mabel reappear through the trees.

"See. I told you it wouldn't take long," she said and got in. Amour leaned forward and laid her hand on Mabel's shoulder. "I'm sorry."

Luke started to back out. "So you both knew?" Mabel asked.

"Yes," Amour said.

"Who else knows?"

"Mary Catherine and Sam."

Mabel turned her head and looked out the passenger window. "Well, it's not what you're thinking," she said. It was another quiet drive home. Amour followed Mabel inside. "You didn't eat your hotdog. Can I get you something to eat?"

Mabel walked upstairs. "No. I have a bit of a headache. Must be from the sun."

Amour called Mary Catherine to fill her in on what happened and waited for her to arrive. The two huddled together discussing what they should tell Mabel when she came downstairs.

"Everything," Amour said. "She needs to know everything." They were whispering when Mabel walked into the kitchen. "Bet I can guess what you're talking about," she said.

"We're worried about you. That's all," Mary Catherine said.

Mabel sat between them. "So, let's get it all out there."

"I'm sorry, Mabel. I wrestled with whether or not I should tell you. I thought…well… Sam and I both thought we should wait for a —"

"But there's no need to wait any longer. Tell me what you know."

Mary Catherine told her Luke went to the MacPhees looking for Stanley, it was obvious no one was there for years, and that they searched high and low for him with no luck. She said Sam recalled seeing him speaking to a woman some time ago and that he tracked her down in Boisdale. That he and Luke paid her a visit, but Stanley wasn't there, and she seemed genuinely surprised they were asking her if she had seen him. Mary Catherine then told her that Sam went back a second time after Dunphy saw Stanley in North Sydney with a woman driving the same model of car.

"I'm sorry, Mabel. Stanley was there. It was early in the morning. He and Sam had a confrontation."

Mabel remembered discovering the wet bathing suit in his bag. "Boisdale. It's on the water isn't it?"

"Yes," Mary Catherine said.

"And this woman. Does she have a name?"

"Clair. Clair Romano," Mary Catherine said, glancing at Amour.

Mabel smiled and put her head down. "Stanley's old girlfriend."

"So, you knew they had a past?" Amour asked.

"Yes. Stanley told me about her the night you opened the bistro. They were engaged. She was the daughter of his trainer. If her father hadn't come between the two of them, I suppose they would be married by now, with a houseful of kids." Mabel walked to the screen door and looked out over the ocean.

"So, what are you going to do?" Mary Catherine asked.

"Nothing."

Mary Catherine looked at Amour, shrugged, and turned her palms upward. "Nothing?"

Mabel turned back to face them. "That's right. Nothing."

"But —" Mary Catherine said.

"But what?" Mabel said. "Look, I know you must think I'm either blind, stupid, or both. But I don't believe Stanley would cheat on me. And I know damn well he'd never cheat on his son."

"But, Mabel? He was lying to you for months. Why would he say he was fixing up the MacPhees if he wasn't?"

"I don't know. But, I'm sure there's a good explanation. Don't forget, ladies, it wasn't all that long ago everybody was convinced he killed Johnnie. Trust me. Things aren't always as they seem."

Monday, June 10

CHAPTER 13

"Ouch! That's my sore shoulder," Kenny said.

Kenny's brother gave him another shove. "Jesus, yer face is as red as a lobster. Better get crackin. You'll be late for school."

Kenny rolled over on his side and grabbed the clock. "Jesus!" he said and flopped back down. He picked up his scribbler. He had fallen asleep two paragraphs into his essay. There was no way he could get it done now. He closed his eyes. His face felt hot and tight, and his arms and shoulders ached from stacking wood and scrubbing Bon Ami off the windows. He couldn't possibly go to school. That's it, he thought. I'll tell Ma I'm sick from the sun.

Kenny walked downstairs. "Ma. I don't feel so good. Got too much sun stackin the wood. I don't think I can go to school."

Kenny's mother looked at his scarlet face. "You just need some oatmeal."

He rubbed his belly. "But I'm not hungry. I feel a bit queasy."

Twenty minutes later his mother was rinsing the oatmeal from his face and neck, and shooing him out the door. Kenny didn't go to school. He went to the brook. He threw his schoolbag on the ground, rolled his jacket into a ball, and rested his head on it. He was on his back with his knees bent, looking up at the clear blue sky.

He just needed a short nap, then he'd start his essay. He'd convince his brother to forge a note for Principal Gillis. He swiped at his ear and his arm. Then fell fast asleep. On top of an ant hill.

Stanley woke, momentarily confused by his surroundings. "What am I doing," he whispered. He sat up, swung his legs over the side of the couch, and ran his fingers through his hair. He pulled on his pants and walked into the kitchen. He put the kettle on the stove, grabbed his pipe, and sat on the front step. I need to distance myself from Clair, he thought. I need to put a stop to this. He tamped his pipe and brought a match to the dry leaves, thinking about what she had said after her third gin and tonic. *I always missed you. No other man could ever measure up. I treasure my Five and Dime engagement pin as much as I could any diamond.* She had reached for his hand, but he pulled it away. He knew how she must be feeling. He dropped his head, thinking of the time Mabel had frostbite and he was driving her to and from work. He had reached for her hand and she did the same. So much had happened since then.

The kettle started to rattle. Stanley went back inside and poured the hot water over the black coffee grinds, wondering where she was and what she was doing. He needed to talk to her and set things right. He picked up his bucket and filled it with water. He then poured his sand and gypsum mixture onto the cardboard box splayed on the living room floor.

Three rows of beach stone laid and two hours later he slowed down as he passed the white farmhouse by the water. He could see Clair round the side of the house on her way back from the shore. "Take care of yourself, Clair. I hope you find someone to share your life with," he whispered and sped up.

Kenny was back on Bicycle Hill, soaring over the mounds. His legs were burning and the sun was hot on his face. He looked behind him. There wasn't another bicycle in sight. He could see Sally MacNamara waving her arms in the air and urging him on. He was going to win.

Kenny brushed the side of his face, then his forehead. He slapped at his leg. He opened his eyes and looked down. "Jesus!" he said, quickly jumping to his feet and swiping at the swarm of black ants peppering his shirt. That's when he felt his neck and thighs sting. He jumped from one foot to the other, frantically swatting at his legs and rear end. The stinging intensified. He pulled off his pants, running his hands up and down his body, and through his hair. He walked onto the path and looked at his schoolbag. Ants were marching in and out of the corner flaps meant to secure his books and his Bully Beef sandwich. Kenny looked down at his bare legs, covered in tiny red welts. He picked up his pants, turned them inside out, and gave them a good shake. He then pulled them back on, sat well away from the ant hill, put his head in his hands, and cried.

"Kenny? What are you doing home?" his mother asked when he walked through the door. "And why are your pants inside out?"

Kenny walked up to her, wrapped his arms around her waist, and bawled his eyes out.

He was back to the safety of his bed within the hour; his neck, belly, and legs covered in a Bicarbonate of soda paste. His face, once again, plastered in sticky oatmeal. His mother was downstairs writing a note to Principal Gillis, asking that he extend the deadline for Kenny's essay due to illness.

Stanley pulled up to his office and parked next to the police wagon.

Dunphy got up from his chair when he entered. "Stanley."

"Gordon? What brings you by?"

"Got a sec?"

"Sure," Stanley said. Stanley acknowledged Fred and the two went to his office. "Have a seat. What can I do for you?"

"I had a visit from Gladys Ferguson. She claims you've been hanging around her property and that you robbed her."

"What!"

"She claims you robbed her," Dunphy repeated

Stanley smiled and shook his head. "That's preposterous!"

"Were you at her house?"

Stanley paused. "Yes. I was looking for McInnes."

Dunphy gave him a look. "I told you, he's somewhere around the Great Lakes."

"He was. He was fired. Skinny thinks he saw him at the *Pithead*."

"When?"

"Last Friday. Look. It's true. I paid her a visit. But I certainly didn't rob her."

"Ever go near her shed?"

"No! Why? Someone steal her shovel?"

"That's where she kept her money?"

"Now how would I know where she hid her money? Sounds to me like it would be someone who knew her well. Someone she trusted. Maybe her nephew?"

"She said she saw you lurking about. On two separate occasions."

"Listen, Gordon. I just figured if McInnes was in the area he'd go and see her. I certainly didn't rob her."

"So you still think McInnes is responsible for the fire?"

Stanley leaned over his desk. "I did some digging of my own. He was working in Ontario at the time. But I'm sure he had someone start it. Seriously? Two barns? Two fires? We both know he's a vindictive bastard and blames me for his downfall."

"Stanley, you know better than most what happens when you jump to conclusions. If McInnes *is* in town, I want you to stay clear of him," Dunphy said. "I'll ask around myself." He stood to leave.

"So I'm not being charged with robbery?"

"Not yet, at any rate. The old hag left my office in a huff. Said she was heading to the Crown Prosecutor's office to have a word with Mannie. Said she was going to personally see that justice was done and that you're locked up, once and for all. But Stanley, I swear to God, if I hear that you go within a mile of her again *I'll* have you locked up for stupidity, if nothing else."

Stanley stood. "Thanks, Gordon."

Dunphy turned in the doorway. "By the way, how's Mabel?" Stanley pursed his lips and raised his eyebrows. "It must have been awful for her, diving in after those kids," Dunphy said.

"What?" Stanley asked.

Dunphy told him about the episode at the *Gut*. "I just assumed you knew. Anyway, Mary Catherine and Amour saw that she got home okay and —"

"Amour is home?" Stanley said.

"Yes."

"And her husband?"

"Not that I'm aware of," Dunphy said, thinking he knew a lot more of what was happening in Mabel's life than her own husband.

Stanley stood on the front step. He was about to just walk in, but decided to knock. Amour opened the door.

"Hello," she said, giving him a loose hug. "I'm so sorry about JC. How are you coping?"

"I'm surviving. It was good of you to come? Are Michael and Victoria with you?"

"No. I came alone. They send their love."

"I'm sure Mabel was glad to see you."

Amour bit her tongue. "Come in," she said, feeling awkward about inviting him into his own home. She headed down the hall to the kitchen. Stanley followed. "So, is she here?" he asked.

"No. She said she had to stop in town after work. She shouldn't be too much longer?"

Stanley walked to the cupboard and held up a bottle. "Do you mind?"

"Your house. Your rum," she said curtly.

Stanley poured the rum into a mug and leaned against the counter. "When did you arrive?"

"About a week ago."

Stanley could sense her underlying hostility. Her welcome was lukewarm and her answers terse. "How long are you staying?"

"Until Mabel no longer needs me. Hard enough she lost her son. Then, just when she needs her husband the most, he walks out on her. Someone has to be here for her."

Stanley looked into his mug. "Fair enough," he said. "I deserved that."

Amour couldn't help herself. "But you don't deserve Mabel. I always thought you were a decent man. I was happy for you and Mabel. How you could do this to her is beyond me."

"Do what, exactly?"

"I've said enough."

Stanley straightened up. "No, Amour. Sounds to me like you've got a lot more to say. I'm sorry I'm not as strong as Mabel. I was angry and hurt. Truth be told I was furious with *her*. Blamed her for what happened. I needed time away. Frankly, I find it hard being here right now. I don't know how she can stay here," he said. "How she can climb out of bed every morning, come downstairs, and look out there," he said, pointing to the bluff. "I know I can't."

"This is where she feels close to JC. Where he was born. Where her memories are. And she has her faith."

Stanley shook his head. "I used to have faith. Only thing I have now is an empty soul. Happiness is no match for misery." He downed his rum and put his mug in the sink. "I'm glad you're here for her. Anyway, I better get going. It was good seeing you," he said and walked out. He got in his truck and headed off, back up the coast.

Two hours later, he unloaded his groceries and opened a beer. He then picked up his specs and spread them out over the table, grateful for the opportunity to concentrate without a million interruptions. He took a sip of his warm beer, thinking of his conversation with Amour. She was cool to be sure. He walked to the fireplace and picked up four of the smaller beach stones and placed them on the corners of the specs to keep them from springing back into a cylinder. It would be the biggest job he'd ever take on. He thought of JC. He had always hoped that they would work together and that he'd eventually take over the business. He finished his beer, opened another, and began examining the layout of each of the four floors of St. Joseph's Hospital. He then re-read the proposal. *To facilitate a design that includes the addition of three operating theatres within the hospital's existing structure and with the least impact on areas servicing general operations. Proposal should include start and end dates, and all charges for materials and labour. See detailed specifications.*

Stanley poured over the documents, scratching out notes and calculating and recalculating dimensions. He reached for another beer, thinking of Mabel's less than enthusiastic response the first time he brought her to the bluff. *Looks like it'd blow down in a good gale,* she had said. He had bought the old farmhouse hoping that someday they would have a life and family together. He smiled, thinking of the day they painted the newly plastered walls and ate perogies on an overturned box in front of the fire. How happy he was back then, and how utterly empty he felt now. He slammed his fist on the table, knocking his beer over. He grabbed a towel and daubed at the frothy pool blurring the fine blue lines of the fourth floor of St. Joseph's Hospital.

The room darkened. The only light, a brilliant orange beam streaming through the window, exposing the dusty floorboards below. *If only*

Mabel had put JC inside. If only I had finished the fence. He unscrewed a bottle of rum, sat down, and stared at the beam of light inch down the wall until the remnants of day surrendered to the black of night.

Tuesday, June 11

CHAPTER 14

Kenny walked into the bathroom and looked in the mirror. "Holy shit," he said and touched his face. His forehead, cheeks, and nose were peeling, and his lips were sore and cracked. He rubbed his fingers over the dead skin, revealing raw, pink blotches underneath. He pulled his pajama bottoms down. His legs were covered in tiny red welts. He pulled them back up, splashed some water on his face, and walked to the top of the stairs. "Ma! Where's my pants?"

"Wear your shorts," she hollered upstairs.

"I can't wear shorts to school."

"Well ya'll be goin in your underwear. Your last good pair is soakin in the tub for the third time. What in the name of God did you get all over them?"

"I dunno," Kenny said, thinking he better not tell her it was witch piss.

Kenny entered the kitchen and looked at the oatmeal. "I ain't puttin any more of that on my face."

Kenny's mother was at the stove. "Oatmeal's for breakfast, not your face. Eat up," she said, turning toward him. "Jesus!" she gasped. "Ya look like you're molting." She reached in her apron pocket, placed the note she had written for Principal Gillis on the table, and tapped it with her finger. "Here. Put that in your schoolbag."

Kenny was knocking on Tommy's door fifteen minutes later. His father answered, walked out on the step, and closed the door behind him. He grabbed Kenny by his sore arm, and quickly walked him off the step and around the back of the house.

"Ouch! Yer hurting me," Kenny said.

"Listen to me you little bastard! I told you not to tell anybody about the bike."

"I didn't."

"Yeah, well that's not what Harley tells me."

Kenny's eyes widened. "He...he musta just guessed. I swear I didn't tell him!" Kenny said, thinking he was gonna kill the little shit.

"Guessed my arse!" Tommy's father stepped back and looked Kenny up and down. "What the hell happened to you? Ya look like ya stood too close to a pot a grease."

"Sunburn."

"Well yer arse will be burnin if I get word you tell one more person about the bike or anything else. Not only that, but you'll never see Tommy again. Go on! Get the hell outa here," he said. "And keep your GD mouth shut."

Kenny walked away, planning his revenge on Harley. He was approaching the schoolyard when he saw the crowd at the bottom of the hill. They were standing around Tommy and Harley, admiring their new wheels. It should be me, Kenny thought, picturing Mrs. Oickle's son carting his bike away. "Hey, Harley!" he yelled. Everyone turned around at once and started laughing and pointing at his blotchy face and pale, ant bitten legs.

"Jesus, Kenny! Hope it's not contagious," Harley said.

Kenny dropped his schoolbag and charged at him, knocking him off his bike. Harley twisted from side to side with his arms over his head trying to fend off Kenny's blows. Mr. Spencer reached down, picked Kenny up by the back of his collar and seat of his pants, and threw him to the ground. Kenny landed hard on his ass. He then grabbed him by his sore arm, dragging him into the school and down the hall to Principal Gillis' office.

"Kenny, you're the bane of our existence," Principal Gillis said. "Skipping school. Hopping Trains. Fighting. I don't know what's gonna become of you," he said, shaking his head. "Take this note home and give it to your parents. I want to see them in my office first thing in the morning. And where's your essay?"

"I have a note from my mother that explains everything," Kenny said. Mr. Spencer and Principal Gillis exchanged skeptical glances. Kenny flipped the flaps of his schoolbag open and started rifling through it. "It's here somewhere," he said, removing his lunch bag and shuffling his books and scribblers from side to side. He finally turned it upside down and dumped everything out. There was no note from his mother, but there were at least two dozen angry black ants scurrying over the top of Principal Gillis' desk.

Mabel left Dr. Cohen's office. As she suspected, and Dr. Cohen confirmed, the rabbit had died. The thought of another baby both ter-rified and thrilled her. She brushed her wet cheek. JC would have been a big brother. She wondered how Stanley would take the news. Would a new baby help him heal, or add to his sadness? Would it be a constant reminder of his loss, or a welcomed gift that would ease his pain? She wasn't sure. She looked up and saw the *Number Nine* approach. She dropped a dime in the receptacle and, as always, sat at the back of the bus. "Mabel! Ain't this your stop?" the driver called out. Mabel got off and looked up at her home on the bluff and wondered if it could, once again, hold the promise of a happy family. She had to believe it could. She had to have faith.

Amour waved to her from the front step and waited for her to climb the dusty lane. "You look exhausted. Are you feeling okay?"

"I'm fine," Mabel said. They entered the kitchen.

"Stanley was by," Amour said.

"When?"

"About an hour ago."

"How did he seem?"

"I don't know. It's hard to tell. It's like I don't recognize him anymore."

"What do you expect? He's in pain."

"I was cold toward him. I'm sorry, Mabel. I can't help it."

Mabel smiled. "You can't help how you feel, and neither can he."

"Mabel," Amour said, taking the chair beside her. "I don't want you to be hurt any more than you've already been. I know you don't want to believe it, but it's obvious he's been unfaithful."

"You don't know that."

Amour touched Mabel's arm. "We know he hasn't been fixing up the property in Mira, like he said. We know that a woman he was once engaged to is back in town and that he spent the night with her. I know this is hard for you to see or accept, but why else would he lie? I just don't want you to make the same mistake I did and waste your time on a man that doesn't deserve you."

Mabel stood up and smiled at Amour. "Funny thing. I've always felt like I don't deserve him. He's a good man. He's going through a lot right now and he's not himself. Neither of us are. But regardless of how things appear, I believe in my heart that he still loves me. I'm not prepared to throw in the towel."

Mabel walked down the hall, picked up the receiver, and began dialling. "Hi, Peter. It's Mabel. Is Stanley there? Oh, did he leave a number? No, that's fine. Thank you, Peter." Mabel slowly put the receiver down and looked at Amour who was watching from the kitchen. "That was Peter. He said Stanley's not staying with him anymore. He's up the coast."

Amour put her head down, not knowing what to say. Surely, Mabel could now see what was so obvious to her and everyone else. Surely she'd do what had to be done, and move on without him.

"I'm going to take a bath before supper," Mabel said and disappeared upstairs.

Amour walked to the sink and slapped her hand down on the counter. "Selfish bastard," she whispered.

Kenny walked home alone. It was the worst day of the worst week of his life. Tommy and Harley told him they were going to call for a meeting of The Blackheads and get him expelled. Kenny kicked at the ground. "They can't do that to me. I started the club. I'm their leader," he mumbled. Maybe I'll start a whole new club. Least of my worries, he decided, thinking his father was going to kill him. I gotta get to Ma first. He opened back door, dropped his schoolbag on the floor, and kicked off his shoes.

"That you, Kenny?" his father called out from the living room.

"Yeah."

"Grab me a beer."

"Here, Da," Kenny said holding it out to him. His father looked up from his jigsaw puzzle.

"Christ, boy! Yer a mess! D'ya catch scurvy or somethin?"

"If it's goin round, I probably did," Kenny said. "Where's Ma?"

"Next door. She took some tea biscuits over to Mrs. Oickle."

Kenny's head fell. Please, God, don't let her find out about the bike. He walked upstairs and fell on his bed. He heard his mother come in and ran to the top of the stairs.

"That you mother?" his father called out.

"Yes, Father. It's me?"

"Can you catch scurvy?"

Kenny's mother poked her head into the living room. "What?"

"Can ya catch scurvy? Did ya see yer son? He looks like he contracted some terrible disease."

"He doesn't have scurvy, and *no it's not contagious*. He laid down in an ant pile and got a bad sunburn," she hollered from the kitchen.

Kenny's father shook his head from side to side. "I dunno bout that boy. It's like he sniffs out shit to fall into."

"Go easy on him. He's had a rough few days. By the way, the strangest thing. Mrs. Oickle tells me she found a bike behind her shed. Said it was almost brand new. Just had a wobbly wheel."

Kenny's father brought his bottle to his mouth, then put it back down. He pushed his chair back and headed for the stairs.

Kenny jumped back on his bed, grabbed his scribbler, and held it in front of his face.

"Kenny!" his father yelled in a way that Kenny knew spelled trouble. "Get yer arse down here!"

⊏══▭══⊐

Father Cusack spread *The Post* out over his desk.

Captain Dunphy of the Glace Bay Police Department has called upon anyone with any information concerning the recent death of Father Reginald Gregory to contact local officials. "We continue to seek the public's assistance in solving this terrible crime. Anyone who might have been in the area of St. Anthony's Glebe House the night of May 29 and witnessed anything suspicious, no matter how inconsequential it may appear, is encouraged to get in touch with us. Additionally, anyone who may have any knowledge of someone who might have had reason to perpetrate this violent attack is, likewise, asked to come forward with the promise of anonymity," Dunphy said. Captain Dunphy went on to say that the police have no reason to believe that the attack was random. "We believe it was a deliberate attack on the victim. And while we continue to investigate robbery as a possible motive, the viciousness of the attack appears to suggest that the perpetrator or perpetrators were more likely motivated by a personal vendetta of some kind."

Father Cusack looked at the small cardboard box sitting on the floor, marked *FG*. He picked it up, put it on his desk, and pulled back the flaps. He reached in and placed Father Gregory's Bible to the side. He then picked up the envelopes he had taken from the Glebe House. He opened one and pulled out a folded piece of paper with a child's drawing of a cat. *Thank You for Praying for Mindy. This is her now. Love Wanda.* Father Cusack smiled and opened several more. A note with five dollars from Bruce for ministering to his dying mother. A card of thanks from Principal Gillis for helping build the stage for the school Christmas concert. He opened another as he thought of the goodness of his brother in Christ. *Please, if you care about us, stay away.* He opened another. *I beg of you, do not come back. He swore he would kill us.* And then another. *He saw you leave the house. I'm praying for you. He said you were as good as dead.* Father Cusack's hand started to shake. He sifted through the others and began tearing them open. There were five in total, all from an anonymous author, pleading with Father Gregory to keep his distance.

Father Cusack gathered up the letters and rushed out the door. He charged into the police station calling for Captain Dunphy.

Dunphy came out from behind his desk and walked into the hallway. "Father Cusack?"

Father Cusack rushed past him and spread the notes out over his desk. "Here! Read them!"

Dunphy sat down and picked one up. "Thank you for praying—"

"Sorry. Not that one," Father Cusack said, grabbing it from him and passing him the others. "He was being warned!"

Dunphy read the letters. "Well, we now know robbery wasn't the primary motive. Any idea who sent them?"

"None. I didn't realize I had them. I read the piece in *The Post*, then started to go through Father Gregory's box of belongings."

Dunphy turned the envelopes over in his hand. "No postal marks. Not even addressed."

"So somebody handed them to him?"

"Or slid them under his door. Put them in the collection plate. Could have been any number of ways to get them to him. And there was nothing else in the box?"

"No. That's it. Will they help?"

"Can't hurt. But to be honest, it's going to be near impossible to find out who wrote them and who had it in for Father Gregory. And I'm not sure what they mean by *us*. Could mean Father Gregory and the author of the note, or it could mean Father Gregory's actions were endangering others. Hard to tell."

"But why wouldn't he have reported them to the police?" Father Cusack asked.

Dunphy shrugged. "Maybe the rumours *are true* and he was having an affair that he didn't want exposed. Or maybe the author told him something during confession. I'm Presbyterian, but I'm pretty sure you folks frown on repeating anything you hear in the confession box."

Father Cusack nodded. "Knowing Father Gregory, he would have sacrificed himself before breaking a solemn vow."

Dunphy walked Father Cusack to his car. "Keep your eyes and ears open. If you hear of anyone who might have expressed his dis-approval or dislike of Father Gregory, let me know. Might not hurt to raise the attack in church and prey on people's guilt. We know someone out there knows more than we do. You might be the one to help them come forward."

"Are you okay, Father?" Dunphy asked, sensing his sadness.

"Yes. Just thinking. Father Gregory came to me the night before he was killed. Asked that I hear his confession. Said he was being called to the Lord. Now I know that it wasn't a message from the divine, but rather the work of the devil."

Tommy and Harley rode up beside John. "Wanna come back to my place?" Tommy asked. "We got an opening in the club. Thought you might wanna join?"

John was surprised. Except for the day they took their ride on *The 42*, none of the guys ever bothered with him before, other than to call him a *goodie - goodie* or *teacher's pet*. John wondered if they were just being nice so that he could get materials from the store for their new clubhouse. Still, he was glad they asked. "I guess I can go for a bit."

Tommy's father drove in the yard and laid on the horn. "Move yer bikes," he hollered. Tommy and Harley scrambled to their feet, picked their bikes off the ground, and wheeled them out of the way. Tommy's father inched the car forward and got out carrying his pit can. "Tommy! Go get me somethin cold to drink!" he said, and sat on the step next to John. Tommy and Harley went inside.

"You're a new face," Tommy's father said. He shook a cigarette loose from his package of Export 'A's. "Smoke?" he said, holding it in front of John.

"I'm twelve."

Tommy's father lit his cigarette and took a long drag. "Hell, I quit three times by the time I was your age," he said, picking a loose piece of tobacco off the tip of his tongue. "Promised the wife I'd quit. Keeps nagging at me. Says she can hear me wheeze. But it ain't the smoke, it's the Goddamn coal dust. So, what's yer name?"

"John Toth."

"You go to St. Anthony's?"

"Yes. I'm in the same class as Tommy and Harley."

"Are ya gonna grade?"

"Yeah. Pretty sure."

"Good."

"I won't be getting a new bike though."

Tommy's father took his cigarette out of his mouth, put it between his middle finger and thumb, and flicked it on the ground. He glared at John. "I swear to God, it's the last one!" he said and stormed inside. The door banged shut. John looked down at the smoldering butt. He must be trying to quit and it's making him cranky, he thought.

Tommy and Harley came back out and sat beside him. "Here!" Tommy said, handing him a cream soda. The three agreed Kenny could keep the name Blackheads and they'd find a new one. Two hours and twelve scratched out names later, they decided to sleep on it and meet back at Tommy's tomorrow after school. John watched Harley pedal off and stood to leave for home. Tommy's father came back outside and lit another cigarette. John looked up at him. "See you, Mr. Simms," he said, thinking Tommy's old man was never going to kick the habit.

⊏▭⊐

Kenny sat at the kitchen table across from his parents. He still hadn't given them Principal Gillis' note demanding to see his parents in the morning.

"Where did ya get the bike, Kenny?" his father asked.

"I told ya. I found it?"

"Ya just found a new bike lying on the ground?"

"Yes," Kenny said.

"And where was this?"

Kenny had to think fast. "At the brook. It was just lying there in the bushes."

"No, Kenny! I think you're lying," his father said. "No one just leaves a brand new bike round for someone to walk off with."

"Wasn't no one round. I looked. I swear."

"Look, you already lied to us. Ya said you were attacked by a dog. Then ya tell us ya had an accident with what's her face's bicycle. Ya said ya didn't know anything about the bike Mrs. Oickle found, and now yer saying ya just happened upon it at the brook. I dunno bout you, Mother, but I don't believe a word of it."

Kenny looked up at her. She didn't look like she was buying it either.

"Well, mother," he said. "I guess I got no choice. I gotta call the police and report my son's a thief."

Kenny's mouth dropped open. "I swear! I didn't steal it! Ma! I didn't steal it!"

Kenny's mother stood up. "You sit, Father. I'll place the call."

Kenny leaned over the table with his head in his hands and began to cry. Then, he spilled his guts.

Lenny walked up the lane calling for Midas. He started to fear the worst. His dog had wandered off before, but never for more than a day or two. An hour later he returned to the house, stopping to check out a commotion behind the shed. There were two coyotes scratching at the wood. He picked up a rock and threw it in their direction. They looked up, but then resumed scratching. Lenny grabbed a stick and charged at them. They ran off, stopped a distance away, then turned back to face their intruder. "Go on! Get outa here you filthy animals!" he screamed. They sauntered off. Lenny wondered what they were after. Then he saw the tail. He frantically pulled away the rotting boards and rusty sheets of steel. He fell to his knees and sobbed. He then got to his feet, kicked the door open, and stormed into the house. Sylvie cowered in the corner with her arms over her face as he slapped her again and again across the side of the head.

"You crazy, fucking bitch!" he screamed. He finally got tired, walked to the couch, and slumped down. "Why? Why would you shoot my dog? Why!"

Sylvie smoothed down her tangled hair. "He wouldn't stop barking. He was disturbing the children."

"Yer crazy. No wonder Barry left you!"

"Don't say that!" she hissed.

"Well you are! Yer mad! Insane! Deranged!"

Sylvie grabbed her pinking shears and charged at him. Lenny twisted away just in time and rolled onto the floor. Sylvie fell head-first into the couch. Lenny watched her struggle to her feet. "Fuck you!" he said and walked out.

Sylvie looked up and smiled. Barry Jr. was watching from the hallway, holding his blanket.

"Hello, sweetheart," she said. "Did that mean Uncle Lenny wake you?" She took him by the hand and led him into the kitchen. "Are you hungry? Mommy's going to make you something extra special."

Wednesday, June 12

CHAPTER 15

"Mother! I'm not wearing the damn tie. It's Boogers Gillis, for Christ sakes. Snot-nosed little shit. I never liked him and he never liked me. Probably taking it out on Kenny."

Kenny's mother took the tie from her husband. "You're wearing the tie *and it's Principal Gillis*." She put his tie around his neck, knotted it, and drew it tight to his throat. "There," she said, brushing his lapels. "You look as handsome as the day we were married." She kissed his cheek. "It's important we make a good impression. And I expect you to be on your best behaviour."

"Well, makin me wear a damn monkey suit ain't gonna help none. Boogers knows I dig coal for a livin. He's gonna think we're trying to put on airs."

"Do you want your son to lose a whole year of school and end up following you into the pit?"

Father grunted. "Kenny!" he hollered. "Ya got five minutes."

Kenny appeared in the doorway, dressed in his best. Father screwed up his face. "Christ, boy. Doesn't matter what me and Mother say to them. They're gonna take one look at you and think ya got some horrible disease they're gonna catch."

Mother slapped Father's arm. "Boy feels bad enough." She turned to Kenny. "Do you have your essay?"

Kenny checked his schoolbag for the fourth time. "Yes."

"And you have your letter of apology for Harley?"

"Yes."

Mother reached for her purse. "Well, then, I guess we're all set."

Fifteen minutes later they were sitting in Principal Gillis' office. Kenny handed him his essay and said he had a note for Harley. Principal Gillis explained that Kenny had snuck away from school, incited other students to join him, and was found in the schoolyard wailing away at Harley Woodward. "And I've had more than one person report they've seen him smoking in the schoolyard."

Father cuffed Kenny on the side of the head. "So, that's where my smokes been disappearin to."

Mother gave Father a horrified look and began pleading with Principal Gillis. "But it's so close to the end of the year. Kenny will be on his best behaviour. Father and I will see to it. He's sorry for what he did. He's here to apologize and put things right."

Principal Gillis leaned forward and rested his chin on his hands. "So, Kenny? What do you have to say?"

"I'm sorry."

"You see, sometimes saying you're sorry just isn't good enough. You had several warnings."

Kenny kicked at Principal Gillis's desk. Mother pinched his knee to get him to stop. "It's not my fault," Kenny mumbled.

Principal Gillis sat back. "Not *your* fault? Then whose fault is it?"

Mother gave Father a worried look. She started to say something but Principal Gillis held up his hand. "Go on, Kenny. Tell us who's to blame for all the trouble you've managed to get into?"

Kenny put his head down. "Kenny?" Principal Gillis repeated. "I asked you a question."

Father looked at Kenny. "Answer the man!" he said.

"It was the witch!" Kenny yelled defiantly.

Mother, Father, and Principal Gillis stared at him with wide eyes and their mouths hanging open.

"*The witch?*" Mother repeated.

"Yes! The witch! She poured her witch piss all over me and said bad things were gonna happen. And they did." He started to cry.

Kenny's father shook his head and started to laugh. Mother wrapped a protective arm around her son and drew him into her. "Kenny," she said, "What are you talking about?"

"I swear! Ask Wally-One-Nut? She put a curse on him, too! Ma! She said my dick was going to fall off," he said and began to sob.

Mabel reached behind her, untied her apron, and lifted it over her head. She hung it on the back of the door and ran her hands over her belly. Would it be a boy that mirrored JC in looks and temperament, or a girl that was nothing like him. She needed to tell Stanley, but wasn't sure how he'd take the news. She wondered if she really was being a fool for dismissing concerns that he was being unfaithful. Peter did say he was up the coast. Where up the coast? Boisdale?

"Alice," she said, "I'm feeling a little tired. I think I'll call it a day."

"Aren't you going to wait for Luke and Amour to get back from Iona?" Alice asked.

"No. I'll get the bus from town."

"Sure hope they have good news about Ted's wife," Alice said, taking her mixing bowls to the sink. "Not fair that she gets sick so soon after he retired and bought the farm."

"We can only hope and pray," she said.

Mabel gathered up her things, thinking about how quickly happy times can turn to misery and worry. It happened to James and Margaret. They no sooner repaired their marriage when Margaret had her stroke. It happened to Ted and Muriel. And now, it was her and Stanley. Mabel headed for the door, then turned back. "Oops, almost forgot this," she said, holding up a Corningware dish. "Goodnight. See you in the morning."

"Goodnight, Mabel!"

Corliss was sitting behind the counter. Mabel stopped.

"How's the new leg working out?"

Corliss lifted his pant leg to show her the wood and plastic *contraption*, as he called it. "Takes some getting used to, for sure. Gotta test it out on the dance floor. Gonna hop on the Leap'n Lean and go hear Gib and the boys at The Kenwood."

"*The Leap'n Lean?*" Mabel said, tilting her head to the side.

Corliss laughed. "Yeah. The bus to Mira. When Speed gets behind the wheel of that old bucket of bolts and he hits a bump, yer friggin head bounces off the roof. And when he takes a turn, it's like yer gonna keel right over into the bay."

Mabel smiled. "Well, let's hope Speed slows down and you survive the trip. Goodnight, Corliss."

Mabel took her usual route to the brook. She was disappointed when she came down the hill and the boys weren't there. She crossed the footbridge and made her way up Commercial Street. She looked at her watch. She had plenty of time to drop Fred's Corningware dish off at the office and catch the five o'clock bus. She wondered if Stanley was there.

"Goodnight, Fred. I'll see you in the morning," Stanley said, pulling the door closed. He looked up. "Clair?" he said, surprised to see her getting out of her car. "I was just on my way out."

"I won't hold you. I'm staying in town with my sister while the boys work on my floors. Anyway, I thought you might need this," she said, passing him a paper bag.

Stanley looked inside and chuckled. "My razor."

"You left in such a hurry the last time you dropped by. I just thought since I was in town, I'd drop it off."

"Thank you."

Clair smiled. "So, *why did you leave so quickly?*"

Stanley struggled to find the right words. "I'm sorry. I haven't been thinking straight lately. I should have said goodbye. It's just that I was beginning to think–"

"I might be getting the wrong idea?" Clair said.

Stanley smiled and nodded. "Yes. I'm sorry."

She was fighting to hold back tears. "No need to apologize. I know you can't help how you feel."

"That's just it. I don't know what to feel about anything anymore. It's like my whole world has been turned upside down. But, Clair, I love my wife. And I always will. It's just that so much has changed. I don't know how to get on with things."

"I understand. I just got the sense that...well, that perhaps there was a chance for...for us." She put her head down. "I feel so foolish...so ashamed."

Stanley walked up to her and placed his hands on her shoulders. "Don't! You have nothing to be ashamed of. Nothing."

Clair looked up and smiled. "She must be quite the catch?"

Stanley grinned and nodded. "I don't deserve her."

Clair turned her head and looked back to her car. "Well, like I said, I won't hold you."

Stanley opened her door. Clair paused before getting in and unsnapped her purse. "I almost forgot. I should have returned it long ago." She pressed her small garnet brooch into the palm of his hand.

Stanley looked down at it. "You know, under any other circumstances, you'd be beating me off with a stick."

Clair laughed through her tears, placed her hand on the side of his face, and ran her thumb over his stubble. "I'm pretty sure you know more about how you feel than you think. Mabel's lucky to have you. Now, go home and shave, and tell her you love her."

Stanley leaned forward and kissed her forehead, then hugged her. It was a long embrace.

Stanley watched Clair drive off. And Mabel watched Stanley. She watched the entire tender moment unfold from the corner of Commercial Street and Brodie Avenue. *I have been a fool*, she thought. She placed her hand on her belly. "It's just another stab in the heart. You and I will be just fine. We have each other. That's all I need," she whispered to the baby inside her. She wiped away a tear, clutched Fred's dish to her chest, and continued up Commercial Street, vowing to end things swiftly and without rancor.

"Mabel! You on your way home?"

She lifted her head and quickly brushed her cheeks. "I'm just heading to the bus stop," she said, nodding ahead.

"Jump in. I'll give you a lift." Mabel hesitated, then got in. "Another gorgeous day," Captain Dunphy said.

<hr />

Amour and Luke slowed down as they approached the driveway. Dunphy was pulling out. They both exchanged curious glances. "Maybe they found JC's body? Or he has a lead on the fire?" Luke said.

Amour entered the house and met Mabel in the hallway. "Muriel asked that I pick these for you," she said, handing Mabel a bunch of daisies. "She knows they're your favourite."

Mabel put her nose to them. "*I should be bringing flowers to her. How is she?*"

"I'm afraid it's the last time I'll ever see her. She's very thin. Obviously in a lot of pain. But very brave. She knows she doesn't have much time. Obviously worried about you and Stanley. And Ted, of course."

"That's Muriel. Always thinking about others," Mabel said. She put her head down, feeling guilty she hadn't gone to see her. "And how is Ted bearing up?"

"Not well. He walked us to the car and broke down. Broke my heart." Amour unbuttoned her sweater and hung it on the coat tree. "We went by the bakery to pick you up. Alice said you were tired and left early. Are you feeling okay?"

"I'm fine," Mabel lied, thinking she wasn't yet prepared to talk about seeing Stanley and Clair outside his office, or the baby that grew inside her.

"We saw Captain Dunphy leaving. Any word on who started the fire?"

"No. He saw me heading to the bus stop and offered me a lift. He told me that Father Cusack found some notes in Father Gregory's belongings. Apparently someone was threatening to kill him."

"So, that's why he thought the end was near. Honestly, I didn't really buy all that nonsense about getting a message from God."

Mabel put the daisies down on the side table in the hall. "I think I'll lie down for a bit."

"I'm sorry, Mabel. I didn't mean to suggest that…well it's just a little far-fetched to think God told him he was calling him. Don't you think?"

Mabel smiled. "I'm not sure what to think anymore."

Amour watched her mount the stairs, then picked up the daisies. She took them to the kitchen, put them in an empty milk bottle, and added water, cursing herself for being so blunt and worrying about her friend. She didn't look well. Amour missed Michael and Victoria and was hoping to head back to London the following Monday, but was beginning to think her plans might be premature. She remembered how Mabel was there for her after Roddy's suicide. She'd stay as long as she was needed.

The phone rang. "Hello," Amour said.

"I'm afraid she's lying down. Yes. Yes. I'll let her know. Thank you." Amour put the receiver back on the cradle. She walked to the bottom of the stairs and looked up knowing it would likely be some time before she'd see her husband and daughter again.

Tommy, Harley, and John sat on Tommy's front steps, dreaming up and crossing off potential names for their new club. Tommy's father pulled in the yard and got out.

"Tommy! Where's yer ma?"

"I dunno, Da. Probably at the bank. Said something about the account being short and then she just left."

"Christ!" Tommy's father said, thinking he'd have to come up with a good reason to explain his recent withdrawals. He walked up the steps and handed Tommy a dollar. "Here! You and Harley jump on your bikes and go pick up some pop at Murdoch's."

Tommy's father waited for them to tear out of the yard. He grabbed John by the arm, roughly led him around to the back of the car, and opened the trunk. John looked in, unsure of why Tommy's father was showing him a new bike. Tommy's father reached in and set it on its wheels. "There!" He said pushing it into John. "Now take it and get outa here!"

"But?"

"You heard me! Make yerself scarce and don't be tellin any of the other boys."

John gripped the handlebars. "It's for me? But...but why?"

Tommy's father lit a smoke. "Cause you do so good in school," he said sarcastically. "Now go!" he barked.

John walked the bike out of the driveway, turning to see Mr. Simms hauling on his cigarette and angrily staring back at him. Maybe he thinks I'll tell people he's still smoking. Even so, to give me a new bike, he thought. He knew he had to tell Luke where he got it, but why he got it was another story altogether. He jumped up and started pumping. He felt like he was the luckiest kid in the world as he made his way to Bicycle Hill.

Mother angrily slopped the stew into the bowl.

"Mother. I don't know why yer bloomers are still in a bundle. It all worked out, didn't it?"

"I've never been so mortified in all my life. Bad enough Kenny said a witch put a spell on him and his… *dick* was gonna fall off, then you start laughing. And all in front of Principal Gillis. And there was no need to slap Kenny on the side of the head. The two of you are going to put me in an early grave."

"Ah, Mother. It's all good."

"That's fine for you to say! You're not the one who volunteers at the school. I'll never be able to look Principal Gillis in the eye again."

"Just don't look up his nose," Father said laughing.

"And that's another thing. What were you thinking calling him Boogers," she said, turning her back to him and walking to the stove.

Kenny's father got up and wrapped his arms around her waist and nuzzled her neck. "He knows that's his nickname. Everybody calls him that. No harm, no foul."

Mother playfully pushed him aside. "And no nookie for you tonight! Now, go eat your supper before it gets cold."

Father sat down. "Now, Mother. Ya know what happens when a husband can't get his lovin at home. His eyes start roamin. Next thing ya know, yer man's at the brook with some pretty young thing tearin at his clothes."

Mother turned to face him. "Lord, oh, Lord. Now, there's someone else I won't be able to look in the eye. Poor Mrs. Simms. She'd die if she knew her husband was fooling around on her and folks were talking about it."

Thursday, June 13

CHAPTER 16

Mabel was putting her shoes on when Amour appeared on the stairs. "You're heading out early?"

"Yes. I've been neglecting the bakery."

"Did you get the phone message I left on the table?"

"Yes. Thank you."

"Mabel? I'm worried about you."

"Honestly, Amour. There's no cause for worry."

"So why did Dr. Cohen call and say he wanted to see you?"

"It's nothing. Just a checkup."

"But you've been so tired? And you went to bed without supper?"

"Honestly, I'm fine. He's just being overly attentive with…with all that's happened."

Amour sat on the landing. "Oh, and Gussie called. Wanted to know if his nephew should keep the horses a bit longer. I said you'd call him."

"I'll call him this evening," Mabel said.

"I thought I'd come by the bakery later. Give you and Alice a hand."

Mabel smiled at her. "It's not necessary, you know."

"I want to. I miss the bistro and being in the kitchen."

Mabel picked up her purse. "Call when you're ready. I'm sure Luke will come for you."

"Okay. Have a great day," Amour said.

Mabel was walking to the bus stop, trying to rid her mind of images of JC falling off the cliff and Stanley holding Clair in his arms, when she heard the beep. The truck pulled off to the side and the passenger door swung open. Mabel stopped, then quickly crossed the street.

"Hey! Where are you going?" Stanley got out of the truck and watched her scurry off. "Mabel! I stopped by the house so we could talk. Mabel! Wait a minute. Mabel! I'm sorry!" Stanley walked around to the passenger's side and kicked the door closed. "God damn it!"

Mabel didn't go directly to the bakery. She went to the brook, sat on the side of the hill, and cried. She finally stood up and wiped her eyes. "Enough. No more feeling sorry for myself," she whispered. She walked down the hill, across the ball field, and up the steep narrow path that would lead her to the bakery. "Well, little one. I need to feed you. We both need our strength for whatever lies ahead. Life's going to test you. But don't worry. You and mommy are going to be just fine. I promise. I hope you're going to like baseball. And daisies. And blueberry pie. And, of course, mommy's homemade bread. None of that store bought nonsense that tastes like cardboard. And I'll teach you to read. You're going to love *Smokey the Cowhorse* and …

Stanley pinched his eyes. He couldn't concentrate. He called the bakery. Luke answered. Like Mary Catherine and Amour, Luke was short with him. He was unusually terse, simply saying Mabel was busy and couldn't come to the phone. Stanley looked at his watch, then gathered up his specs.

"Fred. I'm heading to St. Joseph's. I'll be back in a couple of hours." Stanley entered the hospital and waited for the Director of Operations to escort him through the building. It took much longer than Stanley expected. He was on his way back to the office when he turned around and headed for the bakery. Not the ideal place to talk to his wife, but he had to see her.

Corliss was behind the counter. "Hi, Corliss. Just dropped by to see Mabel."

"She ain't here. She left early."

"How long ago?" Stanley asked.

"Maybe an hour. Luke drove her and Amour to town."

Stanley went back to the office. He'd wait an hour and then go to the house. Hopefully Amour wouldn't be there and he and Mabel could talk privately. He'd apologize for blaming her for what happened and for storming off when she needed him most. He'd try and convince her to sell the house. He decided he couldn't wait any longer and drove to the bluff. He had no idea Mabel was standing on the scale in Dr. Cohen's office listening to him encourage her to eat more, for her sake as well as the baby's.

Amour and Luke sat at the counter of Woolworth's, waiting for Mabel to rejoin them, and cursing Stanley.

"I could strangle the bastard," Luke said. "I always looked up to the guy. How could he do this to her?"

"I know. I'm worried about her. Not just about her marriage, but her health," Amour said. "Her mother wasn't much older when she died."

"I'm sure it's nothing," Luke said, not sure he believed his own words. "She's been through a lot. Losing JC and now everything that's going on with Stanley."

Amour sipped her cola. "I was surprised she refused to take his calls today. Hopefully, she's finally coming to her senses."

"There she is," Luke said, elbowing Amour.

"What did Dr. Cohen say?" Amour asked.

"He said I'm too thin and need to eat more."

"That's it?" Amour said.

Mabel smiled. "That's it."

The three drove to the bluff. Mabel could see the blue Ford in the driveway.

Amour leaned forward. "Look who's here. Do you want some privacy? Luke and I can make ourselves scarce."

"Just give me a minute. He won't be here long."

Stanley walked out the front door and waved to them. Amour ignored him. Luke gave a curt nod. Mabel got out and made her way up the steps.

"Hi there. I know you're angry with me. I went to the bakery and Corliss said you were in town. I thought I'd wait here for you."

"Are you here for your things?"

"*My things*? No," he said, glancing at Amour and Luke still sitting in the car. "I want to talk. Maybe we can go inside."

Mabel walked past him into the hallway. Stanley followed. "I can see you're mad. I know I screwed up."

Mabel smiled at the irony of his words. "You made your choice. Don't worry about me. I'll be just fine."

"Look, Mabel. I've been messed up lately. Who wouldn't be? I was wrong to blame you for what happened. It was an accident. In fact, if I had finished the fence—"

"How long?" Mabel demanded to know.

"How long, what?"

"How long have you been lying to me? Cheating on me?"

"I haven't! I wouldn't!"

"Where have you been? I mean when you weren't staying at Peter's."

"I told you. I was up the coast."

"Yes. I heard. In Boisdale. So how's Clair?"

Stanley started to laugh. "Oh, so I see Sam's been talking to you. Well, I don't know what he's told you, or Luke, or Amour, but I swear there's nothing going on between me and Clair."

Mabel marched upstairs. Stanley stood at the bottom and listened to drawers bang shut. "Mabel! Please come down! What are you doing up there? I can explain everything. I was drinking too much. Not thinking straight!"

Mabel ran downstairs and thrust his balled up swim trunks into his chest. "Where did these come from?"

Stanley looked at them. "This isn't what it looks like, or what you think. I swear —"

"You didn't answer my question!"

"Clair bought them for me. But, I swear—"

"And you spent the night with her?"

"No. Well, yes. But—"

"I want you to leave. I'll gather up your things and drop them off at the office. Now leave!"

"Do you really believe I would be unfaithful? That I would jeopardize everything—"

"I never would have thought it possible. But then, I also never thought you would have left me to spend the night with another woman while I'm lying upstairs in *our bed* crying my eyes out. I'm not deaf, dumb, *or blind*. I know what I know. I saw the two of you yesterday outside your office for God sakes."

Stanley tried to his calm his voice and his emotions. "Well, you didn't see what you think you saw. I'd never cheat on you."

"I want you to leave. I've been played a fool for far too long. Those days are over," Mabel said, pushing the door open. Stanley smiled. It wasn't the same sad smile she had seen so many times in the past. It was different. It was more of a hurt smile. She felt her chest tighten.

"You're wrong. And you've never been anybody's fool." He looked out at Amour staring back. He put the swim trunks down on the side table and started to head out. He stopped and leaned against the door frame. "Whatever you think you know. Know this. I love you, and I always will," he said softly, and left.

Amour and Luke waited for Stanley to get in his truck and pull out. "Okay, let's go," Amour said to Luke. They entered the house. Mabel was in the kitchen.

"Are you alright?" Amour asked.

Mabel opened the fridge door. "I'm starving."

Luke looked at Amour. "Seriously? How did it go?" she asked Mabel.

"Badly. He denies he's been having an affair," she said matter-of-factly.

"So you now believe that he was?" Amour said, wondering what changed her mind.

"I saw the two of them yesterday. And the eyes don't deceive. How about an omelet for supper? Luke? You'll stay?"

"Maybe I should go," he said, feeling awkward.

"Don't be silly. There's plenty," she said, holding up a carton of eggs.

Amour took it from her. "Why don't you put your feet up? I'll make supper."

Mabel sat down and looked out the screen door at the bluff. "I'm pregnant," she blurted.

Amour spun around. "*You're pregnant!*"

"Yes. Dr. Cohen thinks I'm at least three months along. Funny how things work out, isn't it? I lose one child and lo'n behold I'm blessed with another. In one way the timing couldn't be better. And in another, it couldn't be worse."

Luke sat down next to her. "Did you tell Stanley?"

"No. And I don't want you to. I don't want him to feel any more guilt than he already does. I don't need a man in my life, and *I certainly don't want one* who's in love with another woman. The baby and I will be just fine. We have a nice home. I've got a job doing what I love. I have my friends. And I have my faith. I'm blessed in more ways than most."

Sylvie opened the fridge, looked at the empty shelves, and slammed the door shut. Lenny never came home. She began to worry that he might never come back. She needed to drop off her sewing and pick up some food. She opened the cupboard and emptied the remains of a bag of dried oats into a pot. "Damn," she said, running her finger through the oats and picking out a dozen or more tiny black bugs. She glanced at Barry Jr. lying on the floor, grimaced, and added the steamy water to the pot. "Mommy's making you some porridge for supper. I love porridge. And it's sooo good for you." She knelt beside him and poked him in the belly. "It'll help you to grow up to be big and strong. And after supper, I'm going to read to you. You're going to be so smart. Smarter than even your daddy."

"Daddy," he said.

Sylvie clapped her hands together. "Yes, daddy," she squealed.

"Now! Say mommy. Mommy. Mom…mee"

He put his thumb in his mouth and brought his blanket to his nose.

"Say it! Say mommy! Say it!"

Barry Jr. closed his eyes. Sylvie ripped the blanket away. He started to cry. Sylvie jumped to her feet, roughly hauled him up, and dragged him screaming down the hall. She shoved him in the bedroom, slammed the door, and locked it. He was wailing. She put her hands over her ears, stomped back into the kitchen, and turned the radio up full blast. "Don't disrespect your mother," she repeated over and over again, pacing back and forth across the kitchen. She stopped and looked at the smoke rising from the pot of charred oats and crunchy pantry beetles, grabbed the handle, and threw it off the back step. She then walked back inside and down the hall. She stood outside Barry Jr.'s door. "You were a bad boy! A very bad boy! You made me burn your supper!" She lowered her voice to a whisper. "Mommy had no choice but to punish you. Just wait till Daddy comes home. He's going to be very, very angry."

Lenny left Aubrey's Bar in the Pier and got in his new car. He
opened his wallet. He had two bucks left and no place to go. He
either needed to commit another robbery and risk going back to
Dorchester, or go home to his crazy sister. He dropped his keys,
thinking he had too much to drink. He slammed his hand against
the steering wheel. "Fuck!" He fumbled around for the keys, struggled to get them into the ignition, and started out. He'd find a place
to pull over and sleep it off. Wouldn't hurt to let Sylvie cool her heels
for another night. He drove down the Brickyard Road looking for
the gravel pit. He pulled onto the lane and continued another fifty
feet to the clearing. He then shut the engine off, balled his jacket
into a makeshift pillow, and rested his head against the window. He
wasn't asleep long.

"Hey! Ya can't park here!"

Lenny held his arm up to block the blinding light of the
flashlight.

Buddy started tapping on his window. "This is private property."

Lenny rolled the window down. "Sorry! I was noddin off. Just
needed a place to pull over for a bit."

"Well, ya can't sleep here. Where ya headin?"

"Gabarus."

"Well, ya better get a move on. Owners don't like folks on their
property. Wife saw your headlights and made me get outa bed."

Lenny got out of the car. "Sorry. Wouldn't have a smoke would
ya?"

Buddy reached into his jacket pocket, took out his cigarettes and
lighter, and handed them to him. Lenny lit a cigarette. "Thanks," he
said, blowing the grey smoke into the black air. "I'm running low on
gas. Couldn't lend a guy a few bucks by any chance?"

"Yer drivin a car like this and askin me for money? What kinda
car is it?"

"A McLaughlin."

Buddy nodded his approval. "Well, ya better get goin. Yer wife and kids must be worried bout you."

Lenny laughed. "No wife. No kids."

Buddy shone the light on the toy bunny on the back seat, then walked around to the front of the car and checked out the plates. Lenny started to worry he might be putting two and two together. He held his arm out. "Thanks for the smoke," Lenny said, holding out his cigarette pack. Buddy reached for it. Lenny's fist hit him between the eyes and he went down. Lenny picked up his flashlight and patted him down, hoping to find a wallet. He drove off with a fresh supply of smokes and a sore hand.

Friday, June 14

CHAPTER 17

Luke knocked on the bathroom door. "I'll be out in a minute," John said.

"Where'd the bike come from?" Luke asked.

John knew he had to tell him. He opened the door. "Tommy's father bought it for me."

"What?"

"Tommy's father bought it for me."

"Why?"

John pushed past his brother and headed for his room. "Said because I do good in school."

Luke followed him. "That's crazy. No one buys a kid they hardly know a new bike."

John pulled his shirt over his head. "He did."

Luke sat on John's bed. "Has he touched you?"

"Mr. Simms?"

"Yeah, Tommy's father. Has he touched you?"

"What do you mean?" John asked.

"I *mean* did he touch your...you know...your privates?"

John's mouth fell open. "No!"

"Did he ask you to touch his?"

"No!"

Luke stood. "I'm taking the bike back and having a word with him."

"Luke! Please!"

"Listen, John. Something's not right here. I need to get to the bottom of it."

"Okay. He made me promise not to tell."

"Tell what?"

"Ya gotta promise me ya won't tell another soul."

"Just tell me, or I'm going there right this minute."

"I know he's still smoking?"

"So?"

"So! He's been trying to quit. He bought me the bike so I wouldn't tell anybody."

"That's ridiculous," Luke scoffed.

"But it's true. He told me to take the bike and keep my mouth shut. That's gotta be the reason."

"Sorry," Luke said. "The bike is going back and Mr. Simms and I are going to have a chat."

"Luke!" John cried. "Please!"

Amour ran the facecloth across her forehead and thought about Mabel's predicament. After Stanley's visit she had worried that Mabel would retreat to her bedroom, but she didn't. She had a huge supper and stayed up well past her usual bedtime talking well into the night. There was no bitterness or regret in her voice. She appeared to have made up her mind that her past was past. *What's done is done*, she had said. Amour marveled at her strength, thinking it was born from a lifetime of heartache and one disappointment after the other.

"Amour!" Mabel hollered upstairs. "I'm heading out."

Amour leaned over the banister. "Okay. I'll be home after I meet the old gang from the bistro. I'll see you tonight."

Amour went downstairs and began preparing her breakfast. She wondered if Mabel had any more of Myrtle's tomato chutney. She checked the pantry, with no luck. Amour walked across the field and up Myrtle's steps. All of the curtains were closed. Perhaps she's still in bed, Amour thought. She was about to abandon the idea when she peeked through a gap in the kitchen curtain and saw Myrtle walk to her stove, wrapped in her blue, terry cloth robe. Amour gasped. Myrtle was as bald as an eagle. A cat jumped on the step and started meowing and rubbing up against her. Then another and another. Amour tried to quietly shoo them away and make a run for it. She heard Myrtle unlocking the door and froze.

"Myrtle!" she stammered, "I…I just came by to see if you might have some more of your delicious tomato chutney."

Myrtle quickly closed the door over, leaving it open just a crack. "No! No chutney."

"Okay, then. Have a nice day," Amour said, running down the steps and through the field.

Myrtle ran her hand over her hairless head. "Nosy woman," she muttered, wondering if Amour noticed.

Amour had her breakfast and decided to walk to town. She'd do some shopping before meeting up with the girls from the bistro. She looked in the window of her once beautiful restaurant. It was now a smoky pool hall. She smiled as she remembered the night of the opening. Margaret and James gliding across the floor, Ted and Muriel standing over the display of Isaac Green's tools, and Mabel and Stanley sitting in the corner, deep in conversation and falling in love. She felt a surge of emotions and her eyes tear up. A car backfired, bringing her back to the present. She continued down Commercial Street, stopped, and looked in the window. She hesitated a moment, walked into Martina's beauty salon, and pointed at the short, brown wig resting on top of the faceless, styrofoam head. She pointed to it. "I'll take that one."

Lenny woke up in a fog, looked around, and wondered why his hand hurt. Then he remembered. He stretched his fingers in and out, hoping the guy at the gravel pit didn't call the cops. He reached for his cigarettes and was about to light one, when Sylvie barged through the door. "I need to drop off my sewing and get some food."

"Well, I need to have a piss and eat breakfast."

"There's nothing here."

Lenny threw his covers back and sat on the side of the bed in his underwear. "Any coffee?"

"Yes."

"Then make it," he barked.

Sylvie, Barry Jr., and Lenny pulled up outside the Stitch' n Post an hour later. Sylvie dropped off her sewing and came out carrying a bolt of cloth.

"They pay ya?"

"Yes. Eight dollars."

He knew she was lying and that she was paid at least double that. "Any new orders?"

"Yes."

"Good. I need gas money."

Sylvie reached in her pocket, took out her change purse, and unsnapped it. She handed him two dollars.

"I need ten."

"You need to get a job."

"There's no work to be found."

"Ya won't find it if you don't look."

Lenny waited with Barry Jr., while Sylvie picked up her groceries at Moffat's. He got out, leaned against the car, and lit a smoke.

"Hey! Lenny!" He turned to the familiar voice. Barry's cousin was approaching.

"Fuck," he murmured. He threw his cigarette to the ground and walked toward him, hoping he wouldn't see the kid. "Long time no see. When d'ya get out?"

"A while back."

Barry's cousin looked past him to the McLaughlin. "Nice car," he said, walking over to get a closer look. "Who's the kid?"

Lenny looked toward Moffat's, hoping Sylvie wasn't about to come out. "Just some kid Sylvie's takin care of."

"How's she doin?"

"Good."

"Are ya workin?"

"No."

"Heard they're lookin for some part-time labourers at the plant."

Lenny glanced back toward Moffat's. Sylvie was walking toward him with her arms full. "Thanks. I'll check it out. There she is now," Lenny said, running toward her. He took the bags from her. "I told him you were babysitting the kid," he whispered.

Barry's cousin waved. "Hi, Sylvie," he hollered.

Sylvie waved and headed for the car.

They were pulling out of the parking lot. "That's the last time we take the kid anywhere," Lenny said.

Sylvie unwrapped a Sky Bar, broke off a piece, and passed it to Barry Jr. "We can't leave him home alone," she said.

"Sure we can. We just lock him in his room."

"*I'd never do that!*" she hissed.

Luke knocked and waited for someone to answer. "Mrs. Simms? Is your husband home?"

"He's out back."

Luke walked around the side of the house. Tommy's father was swinging a pick axe into a mangle of stubborn tree roots.

"Got a minute?" Luke called out.

Tommy's father wiped his sweaty forehead and watched the stranger approach. "Don't need any encyclopedias and I already got insurance."

"I'm not selling anything. Just need a minute of your time," Luke said.

Tommy's father rested his hand on the pick handle and ran his arm across his forehead. "Have we met?"

"I'm Luke Toth. John Toth's brother."

Tommy's father shook his head and murmured "Christ!"

"Why did you buy him a bike?"

"Want a beer?"

"No! I want to know why a stranger would buy my brother a bike?"

"Cause he's a good kid?" Tommy's father replied, knowing it wasn't going to satisfy his inquisitor.

"You got a thing for young boys?" Luke asked.

Tommy's father threw his pick to the ground and grabbed Luke by the collar. "What did you say?" he angrily hissed.

Luke tried to pull away. "Why else would you buy him a bike?"

Mrs. Simms watched from the kitchen window as the ugly scene quieted, and her husband and the stranger unfolded two lawn chairs, sat down, and shared a beer. What's going on, she thought, worried that the stranger in her backyard found out about her affair with Principal Gillis and that he was telling her husband. Tommy's father saw her in the window and wondered how much she had seen.

Luke left, satisfied by Mr. Simm's explanation, but furious with John for making a habit of hooking away from school.

Tommy's father walked in the house. "Everything okay, hun?" his wife asked nervously.

"Yeah. Buddy just owes me money from a poker game. Said he needed another week to pay up."

Mrs. Simms let out a sigh of relief. "That's good, because our account is off by nearly fifty dollars. I need to get to the bank and find out what's going on. Make sure he pays up. We need the money."

⊏⟨⎯⎯⟩⊐

"Had a chat with Tommy's father. He told me why he got you the bike." Luke said.

John looked up from his comic book. "Cause he doesn't want me to snitch on him for smoking."

"That's not it!"

John put his pencil down and waited for Luke to go on.

"He said it was so you'd keep quiet about what you saw at the brook."

John had no idea what his brother was talking about. "What did I see at the brook?" he asked.

"You know damn well what you saw. You lied to me!"

"About what?"

"Hooking off school."

"No I didn't! I only missed school that one time. When we jumped the train. And that wasn't on purpose."

"Tommy's father said you and a few of the other guys saw him at the brook when you were supposed to be in school."

John was getting more confused by the minute. "I don't know what he's talking about. I never saw him at the brook. Never! First time I ever laid eyes on him was the other day when I went to Tommy's after school."

Luke believed him. "Okay then. Get back to your school work," he said and headed for the door.

"So can I keep the bike?"

"Yes. It's in the trunk of my car," Luke said and walked out.

John leaned back in his chair. I wonder what the boys saw Mr. Simms doing at the brook, he thought.

⊏□⊐

Mabel knew she needed to pay more attention to the bakery. It wouldn't be long before she'd be a new mother again and Alice was already carrying more than her fair share of the load. Alice was frantically running about when Mabel entered the kitchen.

"Alice. We're going to hire another baker."

"Really?"

"Yes. I once told Mr. Cameron that when supply falls short of demand, you lose money. Time I follow my own advice. I'm going to run a help wanted ad in *The Post.*"

Alice was adding flour to her bowl. "Mary MacDonald is looking for work."

"Mary John Allen McDonald?"

"No. Mary John Angus MacDonald. One's a Mick and one's a Mack."

Mabel started to laugh. "Well, one thing's for sure, if this little one turns out to be a girl, I'm not calling her Mary."

Alice spun around. "Mabel! Are you pregnant?"

Mabel spoke without thinking, but it was too late. The cat was already out of the bag. "Yes."

"Oh my God! That's why you fainted. Are you happy about it? I mean with—"

"Yes."

"And Stanley?"

"He doesn't know."

Alice put her flour bag down. "You haven't told him?"

"No. The only people who know are you, Luke and Amour. And, for now at least, that's how I'd like to keep it."

Alice knew Stanley had been living away from the family home, but little else. "Well, your secret is safe with me. I'm really happy for you. You deserve a little light in your life, especially now. So, do you want me to speak to Mary Mack?"

"Sure. Ask her to drop by and we'll have a chat."

"I know she'd love it here. And she could use the work. Her father got his arm pinned between two tram cars. Lost it from the elbow down. Hasn't worked in four months."

Mabel shook her head. "I'm sure they could stitch a dozen good men together with all the body parts they find in the mine." Mabel watched Alice mix her batter. "Alice," she said, "I don't always tell you how much I appreciate you. You've been holding the bakery together. Coming in early, staying late, and covering off my Saturdays. I'm going to give you a raise."

Alice smiled. "Mabel, I love it here. You pay me better than I'd make anywhere else in town. And you asked Luke to hire Da in the store. We'd be starving to death if it weren't for you. I don't expect a raise."

"Just the same you deserve it. It won't be huge, but it will be gladly given. And when we hire Mary Mack or Mary Mick, I want you to take more time off. You need to get out there and have some fun. Life is too short. You have to make the most of it while you can. Find yourself a nice young man." She hesitated. "I often thought you and Luke would make a great couple," Mabel said, glancing at Alice for her reaction.

"I knew you were up to no good when you asked me to supper. But forget it. I'm done barking up that tree. We were supposed to go to the movies last week and he stood me up. I ended up going with Mark."

Mabel brushed her forehead with the back of her hand. "Mark? I thought you weren't interested in him."

"I'm not. It was stupid of me. I was just ticked off at Luke. Anyway, I've decided I'm not interested in either of the Toth boys. But Captain Dunphy is pretty cute, don't you think?"

＊

Stanley sealed his proposal for the hospital renovations and laid his hand on top. He worried his emotional state might have resulted in serious mistakes that would cost him the job. He was drinking too much and sleeping too little. His mind kept jumping from JC to Mabel, and Dan McInnes to Clair. He was angry, hurt, and lonely. He picked up the phone, then put it back down. She had already refused at least a half dozen of his calls. It was pointless to try again. He thought about going to *The Y* and taking his frustrations out on a punching bag but changed his mind, hoping he'd come across McInnes and take them out on him instead.

"Fred! I'm heading to the hospital and then to the *Pithead* if you want to meet me there?"

"Can't tonight, boss. Wife's makin me go to her brother's birthday party."

"Goodnight then," Stanley said. He dropped off his proposal and was on his way to the *Pithead*. He was almost there when he turned back and headed for the bakery. He pulled up across the street and sat in his truck, debating whether to go in. He lit his pipe and watched a dozen or more people come and go with their bags and boxes of baked goods. He missed her, but he was also angry with her for believing he would be unfaithful. She obviously didn't know him as well as he thought. And he obviously didn't know her. "The hell with this," he whispered and drove off.

Ten minutes later he was sitting alone in the smoky tavern. He sat up when he saw someone with a beard come through the door. It wasn't McInnes. Skinny must have been mistaken. No one else remembered seeing him. But then, who else would know where

Gladys hid her money. He downed his third beer. Then another, and another, and another. He needed to convince Mabel she was wrong about him. Just like he was wrong about her. He got in his truck and drove off. He was drunk as a skunk.

"Hello! Anybody home?" Mary Catherine yelled from the door.

"Come in," Amour said.

"How's Mabel?"

"Good, I think," Amour said, taking a plate of perogies from her.

"Is she home yet?"

"She's on her way. How have you been? We haven't seen you in a while."

The two made their way to the kitchen. "It's been a rough week. Irwin got an ear infection and Sam's been going non-stop at work. So what's the story on Stanley?"

Amour wasn't sure how much to tell her. "Mabel will be home soon. I'll let her fill you in."

"So he hasn't come back?"

"No. I'm pretty sure it's over between them."

Mary Catherine sat down. "I honestly never saw this coming. I always thought they were the tightest couple I ever knew. I certainly didn't believe he would ever fall for another woman."

"None of us did. Least of all, Mabel."

"So what happened?"

Myrtle suddenly appeared on the back step.

"Jesus!" Amour said, putting her hand over her heart. "You scared the daylights out of me."

"I found some tomato chutney."

"Come in."

Myrtle didn't move. "Oh, for goodness sake, Myrtle. We don't bite. Come in!" Amour insisted.

Myrtle slowly opened the door and stood on the mat.

Amour pulled out a chair. "Sit! I was just about to make tea."

Myrtle sat down. Mary Catherine smiled at her. Myrtle didn't smile back. "Chutney is forty cents," Myrtle said.

Amour added water to the teapot. "Have some tea first," she said, intrigued by the strange woman in her plaid shirt and dungarees. It took some prodding, but eventually Amour and Mary Catherine got Myrtle to warm up a little. She told them she was born in Digby, her father was a sea captain, and they lived in Caledonia Heights for eight years. After her father died, she sold the house and bought the bungalow. "I like being close to the water. Just don't like being on it," Myrtle said.

Mabel walked in the front door. "Well hello, Myrtle," she said, surprised to see her mysterious neighbour sitting at her table and having tea with Amour and Mary Catherine. "It's nice to see you."

"Just dropped by with some chutney."

"Great. Well, I'm glad you're here. How are you, Mary Catherine?"

"I'm good. Sorry I haven't been by lately," she said, explaining her circumstances.

Amour left for a moment and came back with a bottle of gin. "Let's have a drink, ladies?" she said.

Myrtle stood to leave, but they all pressed her to stay. An hour later, Myrtle was regaling them with stories of her childhood. How she and her father moved from port to port. That she was pretty much on her own from the age of ten when her father would go to sea for extended periods of time. She didn't get much schooling, but when her father was home, he'd teach her to read as best he could. At one point, she welled up, recalling how good he was to her. Mabel started supper, while Amour, Mary Catherine, and Myrtle polished off the gin. Myrtle stood to leave.

Amour pushed her back down. "Yer not goin anywhere," she slurred. "Yer stayin for supper. Isn't she, Mabel?"

"We'd love for you to stay," Mabel said, smiling at her neighbour.

Mary Catherine suddenly jumped up, ran to the phone and called Sam. She was back in no time. "He said I sounded drunk."

Amour started to laugh. "And he's right."

"Anyway, Myrtle. I'm staying," Mary Catherine said. "And I want to hear more of your stories. Tell us more."

Myrtle got up and walked to the door.

"Myrtle! Please don't go!" Amour pleaded.

"I'm just gonna check on the cats. I'll be right back."

She was no sooner out the door when Amour said, "She's bald. As bald as an eagle. Not a hair on her head!"

"What?" Mary Catherine said.

"That's why she's always wearing the toque," Amour said with a grin.

"How do you know?" Mabel asked.

"I went to her place this morning looking for some chutney and I saw her through the kitchen window. I got her a wig," Amour said proudly.

"What!" Mabel said, dropping her arms at her sides.

Amour nodded. "I got her a wig."

"Well, you just can't say here Myrtle! I know you're bald so I bought you a wig."

Amour gave her a puzzled look. "Why not?"

"Because she'll be embarrassed."

"No she won't! She'll love it! Likely always wanted one but couldn't afford it."

Myrtle returned and knocked on the screen door. "What are ya knockin for! Get in here, you!" Amour said. Myrtle came in holding a bottle of rum.

"Well, look at what Myrtle brought," Amour said, taking it from her. "We're having a party! A hen party!"

Mary Catherine stood on her chair, stuck her rear out, put her hands under her armpits, and started clucking. Everyone was laughing. The girls are lit, Mabel thought. They finished their supper of liver and onions, served with a good smattering of Myrtle's chutney, and took their glasses and the rum to the front step. Mabel was thinking they made a new friend, regretting she hadn't tried harder to get to know her neighbour. Amour left for a moment and came back holding a bag. She walked up to Myrtle, ripped her toque off, and threw it on the step. Myrtle looked horrified, quickly bending over and burying her head in her arms.

"Amour!" Mabel screamed. "What are you doing!"

Amour reached in the bag and stumbled as she tried to plop the wig on Myrtle's head. "I bought you a wig!"

Myrtle snatched it from her and threw it in her face. "It looks like a Goddamn dead muskrat!" Myrtle screeched, picking up her toque, pulling it over her head, and storming off.

Mary Catherine started to roar. Amour started to cry. The party was over.

Saturday, June 15

CHAPTER 1 8

Amour woke up next to Mary Catherine with a bad hangover and a deep sense of shame. "I'm so mortified. I'm never going to drink again."

"What time is it?" Mary Catherine asked.

Amour reached for the alarm clock and held it in front of her. "Shit! It's quarter to ten."

"Oh my God," Mary Catherine said. "Sam's going to kill me. I missed synagogue."

"Dear, Lord! I can't believe what I did. I'm so embarrassed. I need to apologize to Myrtle," Amour said.

Mary Catherine started to chuckle.

"It's not funny!"

Mary Catherine burst out laughing. Amour whacked her with her pillow. "Stop it!"

"A dead muskrat," Mary Catherine said, still laughing.

Amour flopped back down, put the pillow over her head, and screamed into it.

"Mabel's probably already left," Mary Catherine said and sat up. "Just as well, I'm sure she wants to strangle you. You get to go back to London. She's stuck here with Myrtle."

Amour lifted the pillow off her face. "Will you come with me?"

"What?"

"When I go see Myrtle."

"Not on your life!"

"Please! I can't go alone!"

"Forget it!"

"What was I thinking?" Amour said, slamming the pillow against her outstretched legs.

Mary Catherine knew Amour felt awful. "You were trying to do something nice." She tried to stifle a laugh. "You just didn't approach it very well," she said, and once again started to roar.

The two washed up and sat in the kitchen drinking tea. "Up until the wig incident, I think Mabel had a good night," Mary Catherine said. "And *she's not* hung over today. I think she only had one drink."

"And, of course, I had to go and ruin it on her," Amour said, putting her head in her hands.

"Don't be so hard on yourself. I'm sure Mabel's laughing about it."

"Well, I'm not! With everything going on in her life, she deserved a night to forget about everything else." Amour then filled Mary Catherine in on Mabel seeing Stanley with Clair, and his visit to the house. She then told her Mabel was pregnant.

Amour met Mabel at the door. "Are you still talking to me?"

"I am. But I'm not so sure Myrtle is." Mabel handed her a cake box.

"I've been trying to work up the nerve to go over and apologize. I'm so embarrassed."

"I brought the cake home so you could give it to her as a peace offering," Mabel said.

"Will you come with me? Please!" Amour begged.

"Get your shoes on."

The two walked through the field. Mabel held her hand out, her finger tips brushing against the tall grass. She wondered if she'd ever walk through another field again without thinking of the worst day of her life.

Amour plodded behind. "I'll explain that I was trying to do something nice for her. That I didn't mean to embarrass her and simply throw myself at her mercy."

"Amour! She doesn't have a guillotine. At least not that I know of," Mabel said.

"That's not funny."

"Wasn't meant to be. I've never stepped foot in her house before."

"Never?"

"Never."

Amour stopped. "I don't think I can do this. Let's go back."

Mabel took her by the elbow. "There's no turning back."

Mabel walked up Myrtle's back steps and knocked lightly on the door. Amour stood behind her holding the cake. There was no answer. "She's not home," Amour said. "Well, we tried."

Mabel knocked harder. Again no answer.

"See? She's not home. Let's get out of here," Amour said, turning. She screamed, almost dropping the cake box. Myrtle was standing at the bottom of the steps.

"Myrtle! You…you scared the hell out of me," Amour stammered.

"Whatcha want?"

"I came to apologize. I didn't mean to embarrass you. Honestly. I'm really sorry. See, I bought you a cake," Amour said, holding it out to her.

Mabel shot Amour a look. "We're both sorry," Mabel said. "Amour feels awful about what happened."

"I wasn't thinking straight," Amour said. "I was enjoying your company so much. Really! I had too much to drink. I was drunk."

"What kind of cake is it?" Myrtle asked.

Amour looked at Mabel and smiled. "Go ahead, Amour. Tell Myrtle what kind of cake *you bought her*."

"Chocolate?"

Mabel nodded. "With cream filling."

Myrtle walked up the steps and took the cake from Amour. "C'mon in." Amour and Mabel looked at each other with wide eyes. "By the way," Myrtle said, turning to Amour and pushing the door open. "Ya owe me forty cents."

Amour poked Mabel in the side with her elbow. The two stood awestruck and looked around Myrtle's spotless kitchen, painted in pale yellow. The white counters were clear of any clutter and there was a pot on the stove giving off a wonderful minty scent.

"Leave yer shoes on the mat and come in," Myrtle said.

"Your kitchen is lovely," Amour said.

Mabel walked as far as the doorway to the next room and peeked in. The cloaked windows blocked the sunlight, leaving the room unusually dark for this time of day. The only light, complements of two floor lamps on either side of an ornate chaise lounge. Again, the room was beautifully set out, with a baby grand piano, a scroll top desk topped with family photos, and beautiful paintings covering the soft blue walls. A handcrafted table with curved legs and clawed feet, adorned by a large crystal vase of pink and purple lupins, sat over a flowered area rug that accentuated the blue of the walls. There wasn't a cat in sight.

Myrtle put the teapot on the stove. "May I?" Mabel asked, pointing into the living room. Myrtle waved her on. Mabel and Amour walked in, stunned by what they were seeing.

"It's gorgeous," Amour hollered into the kitchen. Myrtle joined them as they looked around the room. "These paintings are incredible. The colours are so vibrant. I've never seen anything like them before. Who's the artist?" Amour asked.

"No artist. Just me fillin my time," Myrtle said.

"*You did these?*" Amour said. "Honestly, Myrtle. They're spectacular! You could make a fortune. Michael and I know people in Boston and London who'd give their right arm for any one of them."

"She's right," Mabel said.

Myrtle grinned. "They're just colourful. That's all."

"It's more than that, Myrtle. Honestly! They're so simple and… and fun. I love them," Amour gushed.

Mabel stood outside Myrtle's bedroom and glanced in. Again, the room didn't disappoint. She smiled when she saw several plaid shirts and dungarees neatly folded on her bed.

"Do you sell your paintings?" Amour asked. "I'd buy a dozen. Two dozen!"

"Never sold one. Never tried. Didn't think they were very good. My jams and jellies get me by."

"Not very good? Myrtle! They're better than good! They're fabulous," Amour said. "Where did you learn to paint?"

"Taught myself. Just before Da died, he showed me these postcards he got from the wife of a fish peddler he knew. Said they lived in this itty-bitty, one-room house and that he had to bend over just to get through the door. Said her hands were all crippled up. Not sure if any of it's true. Da could sow a great yarn. Anyway, he told me I was meant to do more than make preserves. Said I had two good hands and could do just as good as a cripple. So I gave it a try. It helps pass the time. That's him there," she said, pointing to a handsome, bearded man in a captain's hat. "And that's my ma. Don't remember her at all. Died by the time I was four."

Mabel picked up of a photo of a pretty young girl with a head of thick, dark ringlets sitting in a child-sized rocker. "Is this you?"

"Yeah. That's me with hair."

Mabel smiled and put her finger down on one of the piano keys. "And do you play the piano?"

"A little." The kettle started to whistle. "C'mon," Myrtle said, heading back to the kitchen. "Cake's cut and the tea will be ready in a minute."

They sat at the table waiting for the tea to steep. "Myrtle?" Amour said, overwhelmed by her surroundings and forgetting her earlier blunder. "Why don't you open up your drapes and let in the natural light? It would bring out the beautiful colour of your walls and make your rooms... lighter...airier." Mabel wasn't sure her neighbour needed to hear anymore suggestions from Amour. She gently kicked her under the table.

Myrtle shrugged. "When Da would head out to sea, and I'd be home alone, he'd make me promise to keep the doors locked and the windows blocked. Force of habit I guess."

Myrtle, Mabel thought, was as lonely as a child, as she was.

Mabel walked ahead with Amour trailing behind. "Can you believe it, Mabel? Who would have thought she was such an amazing artist and had a grand piano?" Amour said.

"She's a surprise all right. What's more surprising is that you two hit it off so well," Mabel said.

"I know. I love her. She's fascinating. And can you believe she's fifty-six? I would have said forty-eight at most. She's so fit. And she doesn't have a wrinkle. Her skin's so beautiful. Must be the chutney?"

Mabel stopped midway through the field and shone Myrtle's flashlight at Amour's chest. "What? You think she smears it on her face? More likely the salt air and her long walks."

Amour laughed. "Honestly! If it weren't for the fact that she's totally bald and dresses in those God awful dungarees, I think she'd be really quite attractive. I can't wait to tell Michael about her paintings. I'm going to call him first thing in the morning. I'll reverse the charges."

"You'll do no such thing," Mabel said.

"Anyway, I'm going to help her sell her paintings. She said she has boxes of them in her shed. She's going to make a small fortune. Imagine! If I didn't insult her, I'd probably never have discovered her. I feel like I found a diamond in the rough. And I'm going to speak to Sam. See if he'll represent her."

They walked up the back steps and entered the dark kitchen. Mabel switched the light on. There was a note on the kitchen table. *At least take my damn calls. Stanley.*

"Mabel? What are you going to do? You're going to have to tell him about the baby sooner or later," Amour said.

Mabel put the note down, walked to the counter, picked up the sticky rum glass in the sink, and smelled it. "I know. I'm just not ready to share the news." She held the glass up. "And I'm pretty sure he's not ready to hear it. First thing's first, I need to talk to Father Cusack, then see Sam."

"You're going to divorce him?"

Mabel sat down. "I feel I have no choice. The funny thing is, I know he loves me. He just happens to love Clair more. That's why I'm struggling with telling him about the baby. Say what you will, he's a good man. If he knew there was a baby in the picture, I know he'd come home. That's the kind of man he is. I don't want that to be the reason we're together. We'd both end up being miserable." Mabel stood up. "You know, tomorrow is the ninth anniversary of Margaret's death."

Amour looked up from Stanley's note. "What made you think of that?"

"Myrtle. I was thinking about how we judge people without knowing them...without understanding them. I misjudged Margaret and I did it again with Myrtle. Heck! I even misjudged Stanley. When I first met him at the store, I thought he was creepy."

Amour offered her a wry smile. "Well, certainly not creepy. But not entirely truthful either."

"Maybe not. But he was a wonderful father. And he can't help feeling the way he does. After all, Clair *was* his first love. I'm sure that if it wasn't for her father, they'd have been married years ago. Long before I showed up on the scene."

"Just don't make excuses for him, like I did with Roddy," Amour said.

Mabel looked at the clock. "It's getting late and I'm feeling a bit spent," she said, thinking about Stanley's note and feeling another wave of guilt over misjudging Myrtle. "I'm going to head up. I'll see you in the morning." She went to her dresser, pulled the bottom drawer open, and spread Father Gregory's maniturgium out on the bed. She then knelt before it and prayed for JC and Father Gregory, for Muriel and Ted, for the baby inside her, and for Stanley's happiness. "And Lord, please forgive me and grant me strength."

Sunday, June 16

CHAPTER 19

Father Cusack listened to his dwindling, discordant choir sing the final verse of *Almighty God, Beneath Whose Eye*. He stood and walked to the pulpit and gripped its sides. He looked out over the black-suited men, hat-clad women, and their fidgety children; all anxious to get home for their Sunday dinners. "Before you take leave to enjoy the remainder of your day, I have something to say." He paused to allow his restless parishioners time to settle back into their uncomfortable oak pews. "Father Gregory isn't here to enjoy the beautiful sunshine the good Lord has blessed us with today. No, that opportunity was stolen from him on the day he was brutally taken from us. I suspect that one or more of you might know who is responsible. Let me remind you of the words from the Gospel according to Luke. *For nothing is hidden that will not be made manifest, nor is anything secret that will not be known and come to light.* Now, you may hide your secrets from your neighbours, your family, your fellow man, but as Luke tells us, you cannot hide them from an all seeing, all knowing God. If any one of you knows who is responsible for this cowardly act…this violation of one of God's sacred commandments, I urge you to report it to the proper authorities; if not for your own peace of mind, do it as a faithful servant of God. Help the perpetrator see the light, confess his sin, and save his troubled soul. Help *us* identify this misguided and troubled soul so that he can do his penance here on earth before being called to attest before the altar of Our Lord God and Saviour."

Father Cusack prayed the weight of his words didn't fall on deaf ears. He held his hand up and made the sign of the cross. "Go with Christ." The sound of kneeling pads banging in place echoed throughout the church as the hungry, anxious congregants began filing out. Mabel, Luke, and Amour were among the last to make their way down the aisle. Mabel smiled at a pretty young woman in the back. She was sitting with two young children at her side and staring straight ahead. A baby boy, with the same blonde hair as JC, was sitting on her lap.

Stanley chewed his tasteless toast made with store bought bread, relieved he hadn't killed himself on the drive back from the bluff. I'm drinking way too much, he thought. He threw his toast down, took a sip of coffee and tried to piece his foggy night together. He recalled pulling up to the bluff, going into JC's room, and pouring himself a drink. He also remembered rummaging around for something to write on and leaving a note. But he had no idea how long he stayed, or what his note might have said. Thank God she wasn't home, he thought. She wouldn't be too pleased to find me sitting at the kitchen table pissed to the gills. And God knows what I might have said. She made it clear she thinks I'm a liar and a cheat. No need to add drunken sot to the list. I need to watch my drinking and be sober when I speak to her.

Stanley got up, dumped his coffee in the sink, and looked out the window. There was still so much to do, he thought. He'd finish the fireplace and hopefully have time to repair and paint the living room walls. He filled a bucket with water, began preparing his mortar, and thought of Clair. The day they went shopping and she gave him the bathing suit. The morning Luke showed up and found them together. The day he kissed her goodbye outside his office while his wife watched. "If I were in Mabel's shoes, I'd think the same. I'd feel the same. I'd be angry," he whispered, running his hand under his nose.

He picked up a stone, spread the mortar on the underside, and set it in place. He stood back to survey his work. "Damn it," he said, thinking the last row was too uniform. It lacked character and colour. He knelt down. "What difference does it make? I'm probably just wasting my time," he whispered. He thought of the morning he came upon Mabel at the brook and they met on the footbridge. She had asked if he was spying on her. When he told her he was just killing time, he got an earful. *It's a terrible thing. Every minute counts. It's like you're wasting the time God gave you on earth.* He pinched his eyes shut. Tears rolled off the tip of his nose, plopping one after the other onto his makeshift mortar board. He dipped the tip of his trowel into the porridge-like concoction. "It wasn't your fault," he whispered. He pushed the trowel in deeper, then pulled it out, and shoved it back in again. "It wasn't your fault." He began stabbing at the sloppy mixture, slowly at first, then with urgency and anger. "It wasn't your fault," he repeated over and over again.

He was exhausted and sweating when he finally stopped. He looked around. Clumps of drying mortar were splattered on the walls and over the floor. He struggled to his feet, walked to the sink, and waited for the familiar rumble of the pipes. He cupped his hands, gathered up the freezing water, and splashed it over his face, around the back of his neck, and through his hair. He did it again and again, until the grey, gritty water ran clear. He stood up, soaked in water and sweat. "It wasn't your fault," he whispered. "It was mine."

Amour took her tea to the veranda and smiled when she looked across the field. Myrtle's drapes were open. She then sat on the steps and looked out at the water. Like Stanley, she didn't think she could continue to live here if it were her child that went over the cliff. She glanced back at Myrtle's. She was walking through the field. Amour stood and waved. "I just made fresh tea!" she hollered.

Myrtle sat on the steps and waited for Amour to return with her tea. Amour pushed the door open. "Two sugars and a good helping of milk," she said, passing it to her. "And, oh," she said, "here's your forty cents."

Myrtle waved her hand in a dismissive way. "Keep it. I was thinking about what you said about my paintings. Do ya really think I could sell them?"

"Absolutely. I'll help you. I thought we could try some of the stores in town. Sell them on commission."

"I don't know nothing bout that stuff."

"But I do. We could pick out a few and go first thing tomorrow."

"When do you go back to London?" Myrtle asked.

"I'm not sure yet. Why?"

"Just askin."

"Myrtle?" Amour said tentatively. "How did you lose your hair?'

"Just fell out."

"How long ago?"

"Da says it was shortly after Ma died. Don't remember ever havin any."

"So you've worn a hat all your life?" Amour asked.

"In public."

Amour put her head down thinking it must have been hard for Myrtle growing up. She likely never had a date, let alone a boyfriend. She wondered if she ever had a single friend in the world.

Myrtle stared ahead. "I thought I'd try the wig," she said.

"Really!" Amour said excitedly.

"Just curious, that's all. Don't know what I'd look like with hair."

"Well, c'mon," Amour said, pulling Myrtle to her feet. Amour had her sit in a chair in front of the mirror and close her eyes, telling her this one might not be *the one,* but that they'd find a wig that worked. She set it down over Myrtle's head, pulling it this way and that. "Keep your eyes closed," Amour said, brushing it on the sides and in the back. "Okay, you can open them now." Amour smiled. Myrtle didn't. She sat with her eyes fixed on the unfamiliar image staring back. She then touched the side of her head. "So what do you think?" Amour asked. "I think you look fabulous."

"Sure is different."

"Do you like it? I thought you were a natural brunette. But we could try other colours. Maybe even a different style?"

"No!" Myrtle said.

"No to the wig? Or no you don't want a different one?"

Myrtle turned her head from side to side. "This one will do."

"Great!" Amour said. "Now! Let's get you out of that plaid shirt and those God awful dungarees."

⊏▭⊐

Mabel walked in carrying a bunch of daisies.

"That you Mabel?" Amour hollered downstairs.

"Yes."

"I'll be down in a minute." Amour turned to Myrtle. "Wait till she sees you."

"I don't feel right. I haven't worn a dress since I was a kid. And this damn thing," Myrtle said, pulling on the side of her bra. "Never wore one in my whole life. It doesn't feel right. It's digging into my sides."

"We can fix that later. Myrtle, you look terrific. At least ten years younger." Amour grabbed her arm. "C'mon. Let's see Mabel's reaction."

Myrtle held her ground. "I can't. It's just not me. I feel…foolish. I look foolish."

"You do not!" Amour said, sitting down on the bed. "Look! I didn't go through all this trouble for nothing. You're coming downstairs. For goodness sakes, Myrtle. It's just Mabel."

Mabel was arranging the daisies in a vase. She turned to see Amour standing behind her. "Sorry I was gone so long. I stopped by the graveyard to chat with James and Margaret." Amour was grinning from ear to ear. "What's up with you?" Mabel asked.

"Nothing."

"You look like the cat that swallowed the canary. What's with the grin?"

Amour looked at Myrtle standing at the bottom of the stairs and waved her forward.

"What are you doing?" Mabel asked, walking toward her and looking down the hall. She was momentarily surprised by the stranger at the bottom of the landing. "Myrtle?" Mabel finally said. She turned to Amour with her mouth hanging open.

Amour smiled and nodded. "Doesn't she look amazing?"

Mabel turned back to her neighbour. "Myrtle! Oh my God! I can't believe it's you! You are…You're gorgeous!"

Myrtle dropped her head. "I feel ridiculous."

"Well you shouldn't. You should feel wonderful. Because you look absolutely beautiful," Mabel beamed.

Amour grabbed Myrtle's hand and led her toward the kitchen. "Only thing she needs now is a man."

Myrtle pulled her hand away. "That's it!" she said, kicking off her shoes and reaching for her rubber boots.

"I'm kidding!" Amour said, laughing. "Get in here. This calls for a drink."

Monday, June 17

CHAPTER 20

Fred stood in the doorway to Stanley's office and waited for him to get off the phone. "Just wanted to let you know we finished the Boisdale property," he said. He tossed an envelope on the desk. "Client's happy."

Stanley picked up the envelope. "What's this?"

"Your payment."

"God damn it, Fred! I told you not to take her money."

"I didn't. Ten-After-Six did. We were halfway home when he handed it to me."

Stanley held it out to him. "Take it back!"

"What? Now?"

"Yes."

"But's it's almost five. And I—"

"First thing tomorrow then."

"We're supposed to be at Shedden's first thing tomorrow. We're already behind on the job."

Stanley tossed it on his desk. "Never mind. I'll do it. I'm heading in that direction, anyway. Oh, and Fred? I won't be in tomorrow."

"You're the boss," Fred said, thinking the boss wasn't on the job much lately.

Stanley slowed down as he passed the sawmill. Clair's car was nowhere to be seen. "Thank goodness," he said. He then noticed the *For Sale* sign. He pulled up to the house, got out, opened the screen door, and propped the envelope up against the inside door. He was about to get back in his truck when he saw the black Chevrolet bouncing over the tracks. He waved. Clair smiled and got out with an arm full of groceries.

"Well, this is a pleasant surprise," she said, resting her grocery bag on the hood of her car.

"I'm returning your money. Boys weren't supposed to take it."

"Why not?"

"Look, I'm just happy we could help. Let's just say it's for room and board." He pointed to the *For Sale* sign at the top of the hill. "New owners will have brand new floors to scratch up."

"It will be a selling feature," Clair said. She picked her bag back up and started walking toward him. "Are you coming in?"

"Thanks, but I'm heading up the coast. Just wanted to drop off your money."

"It wasn't necessary. I would never have asked for your help if I thought you were going to refuse payment. At least let me make you supper. I picked up some fresh halibut and you can check out my new floors?"

Stanley smiled. "No, I should get going. I want to get back before it gets too dark."

Clair smiled. "I see you shaved."

He rubbed his chin. "Yeah."

"But you're still not back with your wife?"

"Not yet."

"I'm sorry," she said. "I really do hope things work out for you."

Stanley kicked at the ground. "So where are you going? I mean, after you sell the place?"

"Back to Halifax. I've decided, this place really is too isolated. And the winters can be really...well they can be —"

"Brutal?" Stanley offered.

"Lonely," she said and laughed.

"Will you get your job back?" he asked.

"Not likely the same job. But I'll get something."

"When are you leaving?"

Clair tilted her head toward the cloudless sky. "I'm in no rush. Might as well enjoy as much of this weather as I can. And I still have to sell the place." She looked around. "I'll miss it. But…well… it's time to move on."

Stanley looked up to the top of the road. "I should get going."

Clair nodded. "Goodbye, Stanley."

"Goodbye, Clair," he said. He got in his truck, started it up, and smiled. It was a sad smile, Clair thought, as she watched the back of Stanley's blue Ford pickup stop at the top of the hill and turn right. Stanley looked down the hill at the white farmhouse in the clearing. Clair was standing where he left her, clutching her brown paper bag, and watching him slowly drive out of sight.

Myrtle and Amour were playing cards and drinking the remains of Corliss' blueberry wine when Mabel came through the door. Myrtle was wearing her wig and her familiar plaid shirt and dungarees.

"How are the girls today?" Mabel asked.

Amour put her cards down on the table. "Myrtle's trying to teach me Whist. You never know I might join the London ladies for cards after all," Amour said.

Mabel put a bottle of milk in the fridge. "You play Whist, Myrtle?"

"No. Da and some of his friends used to. I got the gist of it."

"You wouldn't believe the day we had," Amour said. "Mary Catherine picked us up and we went to Woolworth's. We sat at the counter. Not a soul recognized Myrtle. Not one. Of course she wasn't wearing *that!*" she said with a dismissive wave of her hand. "She wore her blue dress and black pumps."

"Hate those things," Myrtle said.

"You'll get used to them," Amour said. "Anyway, what's her name? You know? The one that wears the garish lipstick and blue eye shadow? The woman who had her sights set on Michael."

"Lizzie MacNeil?" Mabel said, thinking Armour was a little tight.

"Yeah, her. Anyway she walked in arm and arm with some guy."

"Gerald Smithers," Myrtle said. "He recently buried his wife."

Amour couldn't stop laughing. "Anyway, swear to God, he couldn't take his eyes off Myrtle."

"Not on your life," Myrtle scoffed.

"Nonsense! Ask Mary Catherine. Anyway, Lizzie didn't look too happy. And then Luke walked in and sat with us. You should have seen the look on his face when I told him he was sitting next to Myrtle. He couldn't believe it. Anyway, Woolworth's and Arlies' each took three of her paintings. Only made twelve dollars. But it's a start. She could charge twenty times that much in Boston or London. Even Halifax for that matter."

"Pays better than my jams and jellies," Myrtle said.

"It's not like folks in town have a lot of extra money to spend on fine art," Mabel said, smiling at Myrtle. Myrtle surprised her and smiled back. Her teeth were purple.

"Myrtle ya gotta tell her about the witch piss."

Myrtle shook her head.

"Go on. Tell her! It's a hoot," Amour said, poking Myrtle's shoulder.

Mabel looked at Myrtle, encouraging her to go on. Myrtle told her about how the kids would always taunt her. "I dropped some nickels at my feet. When they went to pick them up, I poured my beet juice over them."

Amour started laughing. "She told them it was witch piss and that their peckers were going to fall off. Can you imagine?"

Mabel smiled and shook her head. The story was as sad as it was funny, she thought. "Good for you, Myrtle. Serves them right."

"That's not the best part," Amour said. "One of the boys who always teased her walked in with his mother." She looked at Myrtle "What did you say his name was?"

"Kenny Ludlow."

"Anyway Kenny Ludlow's mother is holding a pair of pants up to his waist. Then Myrtle walks over to them. Kenny has no idea who she is either. Myrtle waited for an opportunity, then bends down and whispers in his ear. Anyway, he tears off and his mother's standing there with her mouth hanging open wondering what just happened."

Mabel was laughing. "What did you say to him, Myrtle?"

"Just asked him if he still had a pecker."

"It was one of the funniest things I ever witnessed and one of the best days I ever had," Amour said. "Oh, and did you see my paintings in the living room. Myrtle gave me first pick. That reminds me. Mabel, can you tell Luke I need a good sturdy box from the store. Gotta make sure they don't get damaged on the trip home."

"Yes," Mabel said. She opened the oven door and peeked in. "Smells good. Did you book the train to Halifax?"

"Yes. I'll be on *Pier 21* in ten days."

"Well, I'm sure Michael and Victoria will be glad to have you home. But we'll miss you. Won't we Myrtle?" Mabel asked.

Myrtle didn't answer.

"I'll miss you too. More than you know," Amour said. "And, of course, I'm going to miss my new dear friend," Amour said, smiling at Myrtle.

Amour turned to Mabel. "Maybe I'll come back when you have the baby. Maybe all three of–" Amour put her hand over her mouth. "I'm sorry. I didn't mean to."

"That's all right," Mabel said, turning to Myrtle and patting her belly. "Not like I can hide it from folks much longer."

Myrtle looked from Amour to Mabel. "Don't worry. I got no one to tell." She stood up. "I gotta go."

"You're not staying for supper?" Amour asked.

"No."

"But I made quiche?" The door sprang shut. Amour looked at Mabel. "Do you think she's mad at us for not sharing your news sooner?"

"No."

"Then what was that all about?"

"I think she's sad you're leaving."

Tuesday, June 18

CHAPTER 21

Stanley took the pencil from behind his ear, flipped the cover of his small notebook back, and began crossing things off his list. A few more last minute details to take care of. He looked at his watch. He had roughly four hours. He stood beside his truck and surveyed his surroundings. He knew it wasn't perfect, but hoped it would be enough.

Several stops later he pulled up alongside the bakery. "God, I hope this works," he whispered. He checked the time, then tamped his pipe and lit it. He'd wait another ten minutes before going in. He didn't get a chance. She came out. Stanley jumped out of the truck and ran to catch up with her. "Mabel!" he said, running up from behind and grabbing her by the arm.

She pulled it away. "Let go!"

"Sorry. C'mon! I'll drive you home."

"I want to walk," she said.

"Fine. I'll walk with you. We need to talk. I need you to hear me out," he said, trying to keep up with her.

Mabel stopped. "Like the night you stormed out on me because you didn't want to hear any more of my...what did you call it? Oh, yeah! *Bullshit Bible babble.*"

"I'm sorry. I was wrong. I was wrong about a lot of things. But you're wrong too. I didn't cheat on you!"

Mabel stopped. "I know what I saw!"

Stanley looked around. "Look. Let's not do this here. Let me drive you home. If I haven't convinced you by the time we get there, then that will be that."

They walked back to the truck. It was quiet at first. Mabel sat with her mother's brocade tote on her lap. Stanley pointed. "Do you have a book in there?"

"What?" Mabel said. Her eyes were wide and angry.

"A book. Remember the time I drove you back to the shack. You didn't want to talk to me then either, so you pulled a book from that bag and pretended to read it."

"I don't have a book. Wish I did. You're running out of time. So say whatever it is you want to say."

Stanley started in, explaining how he felt after the baby died, and that he took his heartbreak and anger out on the one person he loved the most in the world. He then explained how he ran into Clair at Mendelsons. That she wanted to hire him to do work on a property she inherited, but that he had said no.

"Wait!" Mabel hollered. "You missed the turn."

"I'm taking a different route." Stanley kept talking.

Mabel kept insisting he take her home. "Stop! Let me out!"

"No!" Stanley said. He reached for her hand. She pulled it away. The drive, once again, became quiet.

"Where are you taking me!" Mabel demanded to know as they drove through Reserve.

"You'll see."

Stanley turned onto the road leading to Boisdale.

"I see what you're doing," Mabel said. "I won't talk to her. I won't. What? Things not work out for you two after all, so you think you can just crawl back into my bed. Not a chance! Once a cheat, always a cheat. Take me home!" she screamed.

"I am," Stanley said and sped up.

Mabel looked out the passenger window and wiped her wet cheeks. They came around a corner. Mabel sat up and looked out at the glistening bay beyond and then up at the sunlit knoll. She put her hand to her mouth and looked at Stanley. He was looking back. "You always said you'd like to build a little cabin out here. I wanted to surprise you," he said. They turned up the lane. Mabel said nothing. She couldn't. She got out of the truck, amazed at what she was seeing. There were no bramble bushes or downed trees. No sign of the caved in roof of the farmhouse she grew up in. A lovely white bungalow, with a wall of windows and a wide veranda that stretched from one end to the other, stood in its place.

"I told you I was taking you home," he said.

Mabel looked at her husband, overcome by what she was seeing and feeling. "So this is where you were all those weeks?"

"Yes."

"I had no idea," she said. She put her hand over her eyes and squinted toward the knoll where her mother and baby brother were buried.

"I replaced the markers," Stanley said.

Mabel started down the hill. Stanley sat on the steps and watched her get down on her knees and bend over. He knew she was sobbing. He hoped she now believed him. He waited for almost an hour for her to come back to him. She walked up the steps, sat down, and rested her head on his shoulder. "I'm sorry," she said. He wrapped his arm around her and kissed the top of her head.

"Me, too," he said.

Amour knocked on Myrtle's door and waited. She knocked again. Myrtle finally opened it. "So, *you are home.* I was by a couple of times through the day."

"Was busy."

"Were you painting?"

"No. I was puttin down some jellies."

"Can I come in?" Amour asked.

Myrtle pulled the door open.

"Is everything all right, Myrtle? I was afraid I might have upset you again?"

"All's good."

"You're not wearing your wig?"

"Not wearing my toque either."

"I see that."

"Well ya might as well come in and have some tea," Myrtle said.

Amour pulled a chair out and sat at the table. "You sure everything is okay?" Amour asked tentatively. "If it's because I didn't tell you about the baby, I didn't think it was my place."

"It's Mabel's news to share, not yours. And it's none of my concern," Myrtle said, tightening the lids of her mason jars.

"I just get the sense you're mad at me? And I'm not sure why?"

"Ya didn't do nothin."

"Then what is it?" Amour pressed.

Myrtle put the kettle under the tap and began filling it with water. "I'm just gonna miss ya. That's all."

Amour dropped her head and smiled. "I'm going to miss you too. But we'll stay in touch. I promise." Amour went to the sink and rubbed Myrtle's back. "And when you're rich and famous you can come visit me in London."

Myrtle turned to her. "I don't know what it's like to lose a friend. I never had one before."

Amour's eyes welled up. "Myrtle you're not losing me. We might not always be close in miles, but we'll always be close," she said, hugging her new friend and thinking she was going to miss Myrtle as much as Myrtle was going to miss her.

Stanley held the door open for Mabel. She stood in the doorway and looked at the overturned box in front of the beach stone fireplace, covered in mismatched tea towels. She smiled, remembering the night at the bluff when he surprised her with the perogies. A milk bottle on the heavy mantel held a cluster of daisies and the wide-planked hardwood floors were bare. The only furniture in the living room was a well-used sofa. She peeked into the bathroom and empty bedrooms.

"I figured you'd want to do the decorating," Stanley said, hoping he wasn't wrong.

Mabel smiled and ran her hand along the bare, freshly-painted wall leading to the kitchen. She stopped. "What's this?" she said, putting her hand over a hole.

"A reminder," Stanley said.

Mabel gave him a puzzled look. "To control my emotions. I made that hole the night…the night JC died. The night I left."

Mabel walked to the sink and looked out the window to the knoll. The image of her mother pulling a stool over and telling her to jump up and look out at the water made her tear up. She could almost hear her mother whisper her stories about the magical daisies that would sail away and travel the world.

Stanley walked up to her, put his arm over her shoulder, and pointed. "That's where I thought we'd plant the cherry trees. What do you think?"

Mabel looked down at her expanding belly. "I think our baby is going to love it," she said.

Stanley feel to his knees, wrapped his arms around her waist, and sobbed.

Sylvie Slade sat at the table with her head in her hands.

Lenny came in carrying a bucket of milk. "For Christ sakes, Sylvie! Shut that kid up, or I will."

"I tried. I'm not feeling so good," she said, rubbing her throat.

"I can't stand it!" Lenny screamed. Sylvie got up and walked down the hall. "Where are you goin?"

"I'm going to lie down with Barry for a while."

"What about my supper?"

"Fix your own damn supper," she said and slammed the door.

Lenny ate a sardine sandwich then went to his room. He dropped his pants and crawled in bed. The kid was still crying. He put the pillow over his head. It didn't help. He then reached over to the night table, removed an Export 'A' from its pack, and lit it. "Goddamn kid," he said, thinking what a mess he got himself into. And all for nothing. He should never have trusted McInnes. Fucker was wearing his watch, driving his truck, and laughing at him. He leaned forward and listened. The crying had stopped. "Finally," he said, flopping back down on his back. He dropped his cigarette into a glass of water and turned the lamp off.

"Wake up. Get up Lenny!" Sylvie said, shaking him.

"What?"

"Get up!"

Lenny rolled over and pulled the blanket up over his bare shoulder. "What's that stink?"

"Barry's sick. He threw up on me. He's got a bad fever and there's red spots all over his belly and his neck."

"So. Give him some cod liver oil or somethin."

"I tried. He won't swallow it. He's burning up. He's listless."

"What the hell do you want me to do?"

"We need to take him to the hospital."

"I'm not taking the kid to no fuckin hospital. Now get the fuck out so I can get some sleep," Lenny said, rolling back onto his side.

Sylvie turned the lamp on. Lenny angrily threw the covers back. He was going to kill her. Sylvie was standing over him with the shotgun pointed at his head.

"Oh, yes you are," she said.

Amour came through the door, surprised to see Stanley sitting at the table, drinking tea.

"Stanley?"

"Hi. How are you?"

"I'm fine," she said in a cool tone. "Where's Mabel?"

"Upstairs getting changed."

"I assume she knows you're here."

He nodded. "She does."

Mabel was in her bra and panties, rummaging through her closet. Amour leaned against the open door. "I see he's home."

"Oh, there you are! I was beginning to wonder."

"So, is he home for good?"

"Yes," Mabel said. "We were wrong about him. He hasn't been cheating."

Amour sat on the edge of the bed as Mabel decided what to put on. "Just like that! You're taking him back. I hope you know what you're doing?"

Mabel turned and smiled. "I do." She then told her about their trip to Pleasant Bay. "Amour, we all jumped to conclusions. We all assumed the worst. He wasn't at the MacPhees. He was building a home in Pleasant Bay for me and JC. He wanted to surprise us. Amour it's beautiful."

"Still? What about Sam finding him at Clair's? What about the scene you witnessed outside his office?"

"He explained everything to me. And I believe him. You know, Amour, things aren't always as they seem."

"I hope you're right," Amour said.

"I know I am."

"Did you tell him about the baby?"

"Yes. He's over the moon."

Amour looked at the deep hole in Mabel's leg. "God that must have hurt?"

"Some things hurt more than others. It was so long ago, I hardly give it a thought. It's the whole in my heart that's killing me." Mabel walked to the bed and took Amour's hand in hers. "God I miss him. It's going to be hard for us to go on without him, but we have no choice. I have to have faith we can. I have to believe we can make things work."

Amour dropped her head.

"Amour, I know you still have your doubts. But I know him better than anyone else. And I know he's telling the truth. It's okay if you're not ready to trust him. I just hope you trust me."

"So will you be moving to Pleasant Bay?"

"Stanley would like to. But I don't think I can leave here. And then there's the bakery and the long commute. Anyway, we haven't gotten that far yet."

The two of them went back downstairs. Amour walked up to Stanley and hugged him. "Congratulations."

"Thank you. It means more than you know."

Amour smiled. She still wasn't entirely convinced he was being truthful with Mabel. But for now, at least, and for Mabel's sake, she'd give him the benefit of the doubt.

Lenny was behind the wheel. Sylvie was holding Barry Jr. in back. "Put the window down. The two of you reek," he said. Sylvie moved the shotgun out of the way and did as told. "I can't believe I'm doing this. What the hell are you going to tell them?"

Sylvie ran her hand over the back of Barry's head. "I'm not going in. You are. The doctors might recognize me from…from my time away."

"Sylvie, the doctors at the institution were different doctors. These guys are medical doctors, not shrinks."

"But the regular doctors would come in from time to time. They'd remember me. I know they would. I'll wait in the car. You just go in and ask them to look him over and give him something to make him feel better."

Lenny looked in the rear-view mirror. "They're gonna ask questions. Who I am? Where I live? And ya know they're gonna want money."

"Lenny, you've been lying your whole life. Make something up. Just go in and get them to give him some medicine. It's not that hard. "

"What if he's really sick and they want to keep him?"

"Just get the medicine. They can't force you to do anything," Sylvie said.

They pulled into the parking lot of City Hospital. Lenny opened the back door. Sylvie kissed Barry Jr.'s forehead. Lenny picked the limp bundle off her lap. "I don't have a good feeling about this," he said and kicked the door shut.

He walked down the corridor to the nurses' station, grateful for the late hour and the light traffic. "Kid's got a fever and needs some medicine."

"Follow me," the nurse said, leading him into the room across the hall. She pulled the curtain back. "Put him on the bed." She took one look at the raised rash on his neck and cheeks, then lifted up his shirt. She then opened his mouth and looked at his tongue and throat. "Wait here. I need to get Dr. Metcalf."

"He just needs some medicine, that's all," Lenny called out.

"I won't be long," she said.

Lenny paced back and forth on one side of the curtain, while Ted Collins sat quietly on the other, holding his sleeping wife's hand.

"Is this your son?" Dr. Metcalf asked, approaching his small patient.

"No. I'm his…I'm his uncle."

Dr. Metcalf felt the boy's glands and examined his rash. "I'm Dr. Metcalf." Lenny nodded. "And you are?"

"Dan McInnes."

Ted sat up. It couldn't be the same Dan McInnes, he thought.

"Well, Mr. McInnes, you have a very sick little boy here. What's his name?"

"Barry. We tried to give him some medicine but he wouldn't take it. Maybe you can get some into him."

"Where are the boy's parents?"

"Away. They're in…in Cheticamp."

"And you've been caring for the boy?"

"Yeah."

"For how long?"

"A coupla days?"

"He should have been taken in much sooner."

"Look, I'm kinda in a hurry. Can ya just give him somethin so we can get goin?" Dr. Metcalf walked over to Lenny and felt his neck. Lenny backed away. "What are ya doin?" he asked, slapping his arms away.

"The boy has all of the symptoms of Scarlet Fever. And it's highly contagious."

"I feel fine," Lenny said.

"Just the same, we're going to have to quarantine the boy. And we'd like to examine you more closely. Perhaps start you on some penicillin as a precaution."

"I told ya I'm fine! Forget it!" Lenny said, reaching for Barry.

"Hold on there! You can't take that child," Dr. Metcalf said.

Ted stood and pulled the curtain back an inch. Lenny shoved Dr. Metcalf into the wall and picked Barry up. Dr. Metcalf blocked the doorway. "You can't take this child out of the hospital. He could die! And he's a risk to the public!"

"Get out of my way!" Lenny said.

Ted opened the curtain. "Everything okay?"

"Mr. McInnes doesn't seem to understand the severity of the situation. Nurse, go and get the orderlies."

Lenny tried to get by Dr. Metcalf. "Get outa my way!"

"Do as the doctor said and put the boy on the bed," Ted said, approaching Lenny from behind.

Lenny spun around. "Fuck you!" When Lenny turned back to the door he was facing Dr. Metcalf, his nurse, and two burly orderlies. He spun back around and thrust Barry into Ted's arms, tore back the curtain to Muriel's bed, darted past the orderlies, and flew down the hall.

Dr. Metcalf took the boy from Ted and handed him to the nurse. "Set up the quarantine room and let's get some penicillin into him right away." He turned to Ted. "Thank you, Mr. Collins."

"Poor kid. I'm sure his parents would be worried sick if they knew what was happening. Is he going to be okay?" Ted asked.

Dr. Metcalf put his hand on his shoulder. "Time will tell. Now, let's check on your wife."

Stanley laid his shirt on the back of the chair, slipped out of his pants, and for the first time in almost a month, crawled in next to his wife. "I missed this," he said, curling up next to her and putting his arm across her waist.

"I wasn't sure how you'd take the news," Mabel said.

Stanley closed his eyes. "I wish it were different. I always pictured JC pulling his little brother or sister around the yard in his wagon."

"Stanley, I want you to come back to church. I think it will help. It helped me."

Stanley rolled over onto his back. He didn't want to argue on his first night home. "Maybe over time. Just not now. I'm not ready."

"I need to tell you about the night in the chapel. Maybe then you'll understand why I feel the way I do. I swear, if it wasn't for the miracle in the chapel, I'd barely be able to get out of bed. I needed a sign that God is with us. And that JC is with Him. And He sent it."

Stanley laid his head on her chest. "Go on," he said, understanding it was a small concession after what he put her through. Mabel told him about Lydia swallowing the pills, the doctors saying she wouldn't live through the night, and the aura around Father Gregory as he knelt at the altar. "Then Mary Catherine ran in saying Lydia was going to be fine. Stanley, the chapel is so small. We were blocking the aisle. I never saw him leave. He just disappeared."

"Mabel?" Stanley said.

"What?"

Stanley was about to tell her there was a side door behind the bye-altar into an adjoining room. "Nothing. Keep going," he said, realizing that her faith, no matter how misguided, was helping her accept what he couldn't.

Mabel ran her fingers through his thick, dark hair. "The next thing I hear is Father Gregory is lying in a hospital bed near death. And he's in the same room that Lydia was in. 4B. And, by the way, Lydia was about the same age as his baby sister was when she died. There are just too many coincidences. It's got to be part of God's grand plan. So, what do you think?"

"I think I'm glad to be home with my wife and this little one," he said. He kissed her belly.

"But don't you think it's comforting to know that *there is a God…a divine being*?"

"Yes," he lied, thinking he felt comfort in her, not God.

"So, will you come back to church?"

He paused. "Yes."

Mabel pressed her eyes shut. "Does it matter if it's a boy or a girl?" she asked.

"Honestly, I think it will be easier if it's a girl. There won't be so many… comparisons."

Mabel bit her lip. "And if it's not?"

"If it's a boy, I'll still be counting my blessings." He sat up, leaned in, and kissed her.

Mabel smiled and rested her hand on the side of his face. "Stanley?"

"Yes."

"You need a shave."

Sylvie was lying down in the back seat when Lenny jumped in the car, started the engine, and peeled away. She sat up. "Where's my baby?"

"Shut up!" Lenny said.

"Lenny, Stop! Where's my baby!" Lenny sailed through the intersection. "Lenny! I want my baby!"

"I said shut the fuck up!"

Sylvie started slapping him across the side of the head and gouging his eyes. The car hit the shoulder and veered onto the other side of the road. Lenny straightened it out. He held his arm up to fend off her blows and slammed on the brakes. He threw the car in park, turned around, grabbed her by the hair and roughly pulled her forward. "I should never have listened to you! You crazy bitch!" he said. Sylvie put her hand to her mouth, spewing vomit over herself and the front seat. "Fuck!" Lenny screamed, shoving her back down. He twisted around and slammed his fist on the dash. "Sylvie, they wouldn't let me take him home," he said more calmly. "He's real sick and contagious. Christ, you probably got the same thing. I'm Goddamn lucky I got outa there. Hell, I probably got it now!"

"What's wrong with him?" Sylvie asked, in a low, raspy voice.

"Doctor thinks it's Scarlet Fever."

Sylvie thought of the red rash that was spreading over her chest. "Can it kill you?"

"Why do you think the kid's in quarantine?"

"Lenny! I need my boy. We have to get him back. We just do."

Lenny slid back behind the wheel and started the car. "Yeah, well first we gotta get ya cleaned up. And for fuck sakes, roll down the Goddamn window before I puke."

Lenny was relieved to pull in the yard. The thirty-five minute drive seemed like an eternity. Sylvie cried, moaned, and threw up a second time. The open windows didn't help dampen the stench. Lenny threw the door open, jumped out, and sucked in the fresh air. He waited for Sylvie to get out. She didn't move. Lenny opened the back door. "Are you coming or not?" Sylvie stepped out slowly and followed Lenny. She collapsed on the front steps. "Christ," Lenny said. He picked her up, carried her inside, and put her on the bed. He then took off her blouse and looked at the strawberry-coloured rash covering her chest and neck. He tossed her blouse in the corner, pulled off her skirt, and ran his vomit-stained hands down his pants. Sylvie heaved. He pulled her piss pot out from under her bed. "Try and hit the bowl," he said.

"I got the fever too. Lenny, we need to go back to the hospital. I don't want to die."

"You're not gonna die," Lenny said unconvincingly. "Let's see how you're doing in the morning," he said, knowing there wasn't a chance in hell he'd be going back a second time the same night. "Get some sleep," he said and closed the door. Lenny went to the bathroom, stripped down to his underwear, checked for a rash, and felt his forehead. He thought he felt warm. He then went to the living room, sat on the couch, and lit a smoke. Jesus, he thought, if Sylvie dies I'll have no choice. I'll have to get a job.

Wednesday, June 19

CHAPTER 22

Mabel entered the bakery. "I thought Corliss was working today?" she said to Luke.

"He had an accident."

"Dear Lord," Mabel said. "What happened?"

"Didn't Alice tell you?"

"No."

"Nothing serious. He broke his leg."

"Nothing serious!" Mabel said.

"Not his real one."

"Thank goodness for that. Still he was just getting used to—"

Luke interrupted. "So, I see Stanley dropped you off. You're on speaking terms?"

Mabel smiled. "All is good. He's home."

Luke gave her a disapproving look. Mabel explained the misunderstanding over the MacPhee property and assured him she was satisfied that nothing had happened between Stanley and Clair. "It's not what everyone thought. Including me."

"If you say so," Luke said.

Mabel recognized the skepticism. "I do. Luke, he's been through a lot. He needs—"

"So have you. He should have been there for you."

Mabel smiled. "He knows that. And he's sorry. Is Alice here?"

"Yes. She's been here since six-thirty."

Mabel reached for her apron. "Alice," she said, looping it over her head. "Luke told me about your father. What happened?"

"Speed ran into him."

"And he wasn't hurt?"

"No. Just bumped him. Da was outside the Kenwood. Dumbass was standing in front of the bus when he decided to adjust his leg straps. Anyway, Speed didn't see him and pulled out. Knocked him down and drove over his fake leg. Da got a few bruises, but he's okay. Just pissed he can't dance. Said he's gonna rename the Leap'n Lean the Bruised'n Broken. Johnny Are-So is fixing it for him."

"The dentist?" Mabel asked.

"No. You're thinking of Johnny Am-Not. Johnny Are-So works at the Machine Shop."

Mabel shook her head. "Where in the world do they come up with those names?"

Alice looked up from the oven. "Da said the two were best friends growing up, but always having words. One would say *am not* and the other would say *are so*. It just stuck." Alice started to laugh. "Johnny Are-So came by the house when I was little. I didn't know any better. I called him Johnny Arsehole. Da got such a big charge out of it, he still calls him that. Oh, by the way, I spoke to Mary Mack. She'd like to come by if that's good with you?"

"The sooner the better," Mabel said, thinking her energy level wasn't what it used to be and that she and Alice could both use the extra pair of hands sooner than later.

Ted felt his wife's hand on the side of his face and lifted his head off his outstretched arm. He sat up and smiled. "You're awake. How's the pain?"

"Tolerable. Why don't you head home and crawl into your own bed for a few hours."

"I'm fine," he said and arched his back.

"Honestly, Ted. Go home. Get some sleep. See to the pigs. You can come back this evening. I'm not going anywhere."

He ran his hand over his stubble. "I think I will. I could do with a shave and change of clothes." He leaned in and kissed her. He stood. "You sure you'll be all right?"

"The doctors and nurses will see that I am."

Ted stopped at the nurses' station to tell them he was leaving for a few hours and to ask that they keep a close eye on his wife. He started down the hall. "Mr. Collins," Dr. Metcalf called out. Ted turned and waited for him. "How's Mrs. Collins today?"

"She seems to have rebounded. She's much brighter. Insisted I go home for a few hours."

Dr. Metcalf turned his mouth down and nodded. "The morphine helps to control the pain. But I'm afraid your wife won't be leaving the hospital."

Ted knew the prognosis wasn't good and that it was just a matter of time, but Dr. Metcalf's words still caught him off guard. His throat tightened. He thought they had months, not weeks or days. "No?" he said softly. "But I thought we still had more time to—"

"I'm afraid not."

"But she's doing better. She even sat up and –"

Dr. Metcalf shook his head. "It's not uncommon for terminal patients close to death to have a last minute rally. Almost as if God is giving them time to say their final goodbyes."

Ted's eyes welled up. "Are you sure?"

Dr. Metcalf touched Ted's arm. "Yes. I'm sorry. We'll keep her as comfortable as we can," he said and walked away.

Ted looked back at Muriel's room. He put his head down wondering what to do. He decided he would do as she asked. He'd go home. He'd clean up, but he wouldn't sleep. Instead he'd do what he had been dreading. He'd call her friends and break the gut-wrenching news; his beautiful wife of thirty-eight years would soon be leaving him.

Stanley waited outside the bakery. Mabel opened the door and handed him a bag of oat cakes. "I should have gone to see her sooner," she said and got in. "Poor, Ted. He knows we're coming?"

"Yes."

"Breaks my heart. They were so happy living in the country. It's not fair."

"Life's not fair," Stanley said and squeezed her hand. Mabel smiled. It was a brief happy moment on another day cloaked in sadness. They drove the thirty miles to the hospital, both thinking of their own loss and the pain they would carry with them for the rest of their lives. Stanley turned onto the road leading to the parking lot when Mabel told him to pull over.

"What?" he asked.

Mabel pointed. "Muriel loves mayflowers."

Ted hugged them when they entered the room. Muriel smiled and opened her arms to Mabel. Mabel started to tear up, knowing it was the last time they'd likely be together.

Stanley stood off to the side unsure of what to say. "Are they looking after you okay?" he asked.

"It's not the Waldorf-Astoria, but I can't complain about the care." She took the flowers from Mabel and brought them to her nose. "They're my favourite. Thank you. Ted, get Mabel a chair and put these in some water," she said, pointing to an empty vase on the windowsill.

Ted carried out her wishes then nodded for Stanley to join him in the hall. "Let's let the ladies get caught up," he said.

"Mabel, dear. I don't know what to say. I'm so sorry about the baby. I hope you forgive us for not getting into town. Under any other circumstances we would have—"

"Muriel, please! There's no need to explain," Mabel said, taking Muriel's thin, veiny hand in hers.

"Still, to lose a child. It's one thing to lose a parent or a spouse, but a child. Did you get my card?"

"Yes. It was lovely. So were the daisies."

Mabel sat beside Muriel's bed, praying her emotions would not get the better of her. The two reminisced about their times together with James and Margaret, and Amour and Michael. Playing cards. Going to the Savoy. Dances at the Silver Rail and dinners at the bistro. A half hour later Mabel could see Muriel's eyelids were getting heavy. "Are you tired, Muriel?"

Muriel nodded. "The medication makes be a bit drowsy."

Mabel laid her hand on her friend's arm. "I'll let you get your rest. I'll see you soon."

Muriel smiled. "No, dear girl. I'm afraid you won't. I'll be shedding these mortal coils soon enough."

"Are you scared?" Mabel asked.

"I've always believed in God and the afterlife. But, yes. As the hour draws closer you can't help but wonder what lies ahead."

Mabel told her about her own doubts and her experience in the chapel. "God is there for you, Muriel. I know He is."

Muriel's lower lip started to tremble. "I just wish it wasn't now. It's not fair to Ted. We were supposed to grow old together."

Mabel wiped away a tear. "You've been a wonderful friend. I'll miss you so much. Stanley and I will keep an eye on Ted. I promise."

"I'm so glad you stopped by," Muriel said, grimacing in pain. "I've been so worried about you. But you're a young, healthy woman with your whole life ahead of you. Don't let the loss of one child keep you from the joy of another. Having a child was the one blessing Ted and I never experienced," she said.

Mabel had considered telling her earlier but thought it wasn't the right time. She now realized there was no better time. She patted her belly. "There's already a little one on the way."

Muriel smiled and clapped her hands together. "I'm so happy for you. Your news will make my journey smoother."

Mabel bent down, kissed Muriel's forehead, and squeezed her hand. "I love you, my friend." Mabel picked up her purse and walked to the door. When she turned back for one last look, Muriel's eyes were closed. She was still smiling.

Mabel reached in her pocket, blew her nose, and took a deep breath. Stanley and Ted were in deep conversation at the end of the hall. She approached them and hugged Ted. "I'm so sorry."

"Excuse me," an approaching nurse said, indicating they were blocking her way.

"Sorry," Stanley said, ushering Ted and Mabel to the side. The young nurse pulled the elastic band of her face mask back, brought it down over her white cap, and positioned it to over her mouth. She nodded her thanks to Stanley, then pushed the door open. It had a large sign on it. *Quarantine. Staff Only.*

Lenny sat on the back step, took a drag of his cigarette, and thought of the day he had shot Barry. The blood oozed from his stomach, but Barry wasn't dead. Lenny could still hear him. *Lenny! Why? Why, Lenny? Is it the money?* Barry had pleaded for him to get help. Lenny left, but he didn't get help. Instead, he walked deep into the woods, sat on a fallen birch tree, and waited for Barry to bleed out. He couldn't take the chance Barry would say it was deliberate.

Lenny pinched his eyes shut, trying to rid his mind of Barry's grey face and white lips. "It wasn't about the fucking money. It was a fucking accident," he mumbled. He took another drag of his cigarette, flicked his butt on the ground, and looked over his shoulder at the small cabin he shared with his sister. He went inside and put his ear to Sylvie's door. There was no moaning, crying, or heaving. He knew she was getting worse. He let Barry die, but this was his sister. He hesitated, then slowly opened the door. He walked up to the bed and bent over her. Her eyes were closed, and she was as white as a sheet and shivering. Sylvie reached for his arm. Lenny jumped back. "Help me," she said. Her voice was barely audible but Lenny heard her plea. He reached down, covered her up with a blanket, and carried her to the car. He knew the doctors would connect her and the boy, and that it was only a matter of time before the police came looking for him. He'd drop her off, go back to the cabin, pack up what he could, and go to the mainland. Maybe look for a dock job on the Great Lakes and track down McInnes. Or maybe head south to Maine. He drove to the hospital, half hoping she'd die before the time they arrived. He glanced back at Sylvie trembling on the back seat, then stopped at the intersection leading to the hospital. He laid on the horn. "Go ahead for Christ sakes. Hurry up, arsehole!" he shouted to the driver waiting for an opportunity to turn left. The blue Ford pickup finally pulled out with a grateful wave from the driver and his passenger.

⌐⟨⟩⌐

Mary Catherine, Sam and Amour were sitting at the table when Mabel and Stanley came through the door. It was the first time Sam had seen Stanley since their confrontation at Clair's. The initial awkwardness of their reunion soon gave way to more relaxed chatter when Sam extended his hand. "Amour told us about what happened. As a lawyer, I should have known better than to jump to conclusions. I'm sorry."

Stanley smiled and shook his hand. "I might have done the same," he said.

Mary Catherine still wasn't convinced of Stanley's innocence, but did her best to hide her feelings.

Stanley and Mabel shared the sad news about their visit with Muriel. "It won't be long," Mabel said. She started to cry, but quickly pulled herself together.

"She cried the whole way home," Stanley said.

Mary Catherine held the fridge door open. "It's sad enough. Then add in the raging hormones and you've got—" She stopped, realizing she had just exposed the secret Amour had shared with her.

Mabel looked at Amour then at Mary Catherine. "I was waiting for an opportunity to tell you, but I see Amour beat me to it."

Amour screwed up her face. "I'm sorry."

"Am I missing something here?" Sam asked.

Mary Catherine passed him a beer. "Mabel's pregnant."

Stanley put his arm around Mabel's shoulder and pulled her into him. She couldn't hold it together any longer. Tears streamed down her face. The awkward silence returned. Sam was about to take a swig of his beer, then stopped. "But that's a good thing, isn't it?"

"It's a very good thing," Stanley said, kissing the side of Mabel's head.

Mabel nodded and blew her nose. "Mary Catherine's right. It's just my hormones," she said, knowing it was more than that. Knowing that it was hard to celebrate a new life when another was about to die. Knowing that while a new baby would bring her and Stanley great joy, they would never escape the pain of losing their first child.

Lenny sat in the parking lot waiting for an opportunity to bring Sylvie into the hospital. He looked back at her. Her hair was stuck to her forehead and she was drooling. "Lenny! I'm dying," she begged.

Lenny listened to the familiar plea and, once again, thought of Barry's red blood dripping onto the green forest floor. "Sylvie, Please!" he said, putting his hands over his ears.

He waited another half hour. The parking lot was quiet and there was no one coming or going. He jumped out and scooped Sylvie up from the back seat. Her blanket fell away, exposing her red chest. He opened the heavy glass door and laid her limp body on the floor. "Someone will find you soon. Keep yer mouth shut about the boy, or we'll both go to jail. I'll come back in a day or two. I promise." He touched the top of her head, then looked down at her gold wedding band. "Sorry," he said, twisting it off her finger. He ran back to the car, started it up, and slowly pulled up to the entrance for one last look. He could see a nurse standing over Sylvie. He didn't see Ted Collins getting up from a bench under a maple tree and walking toward the building, wondering if the man driving off in the green McLaughlin was the same man he just saw carry a woman inside.

Ted picked up his pace and pushed the door open. The nurse was bent over Sylvie and waving for the orderlies to hurry up. Ted looked at the red rash. "Scarlet fever?" he asked.

"Yes. I believe so. Are you a doctor?"

"A cop. Retired. Will she be alright?"

"Only time will tell," she said as the orderlies hoisted Sylvie onto the gurney. Sylvie's arm fell loose at her side. Ted looked at her hand and the pale thin band of skin exposing a missing ring. "You should stand back. She's likely contagious," the nurse said.

"So the guy that dropped her off could be as well?" Ted asked.

"Possibly. And he could put a lot of folks in danger."

"He's driving a green McLaughlin. I'll call the Sydney detachment and let them know." Ted went to the pay phone and called the police. He gave them a general description of the person in question, saying he posed a significant risk to public health. He also told them it wouldn't hurt to keep a look out at the local pawn shops for anyone selling a woman's ring. "Likely a wedding band."

Lenny needed gas money. He knew Sylvie had a stash of cash somewhere. She made more than she let on and spent less than she claimed. And Barry was pretty handy at the poker table. Lenny tore the cabin apart, pulling out every drawer, turning over every mattress, and unravelling every bolt of cloth. "Fuck, Sylvie. Where's yer fuckin money!" He walked down the hall, stopping to look at the broken mirror above his dresser, a stark reminder of the mess he got himself into when he agreed to Dan McInnes' ridiculous scheme. He entered the spare room. A dozen or more dolls of various sizes and shapes were sitting on the bed with their legs spread apart and their backs against the wall; their glassy eyes stared back, unsettling him. He pulled each one apart limb by limb, leaving the room strewn with arms, legs and headless torsos. He then grabbed them by the hair, violently shaking them up and down and from side to side. He threw the last one against the mirrored dresser, sending shards of glass flying off in every direction. "Fuck!" He looked around the ransacked room, then stepped over the mess and into the hall. He checked the time, hoping Sylvie hadn't already sent the police his way. He put his hand in his pocket and fingered her ring. "Gotta be worth something," he said.

A half-hour later he had the car stacked with his clothes, canned goods, a roll of bologna, and some silverware. He ran back in the cabin, gathered up his bed clothes, throwing them on top of the shotgun Sylvie had used to kill his dog. "Would have been easier to let ya die and bury ya next to yer damn husband," he muttered and tore off.

Lenny stopped at the corner of Prince and George streets and waited for the traffic to start moving. He glanced across at Steel City Auto. A man who looked vaguely familiar was staring back, waving his hands, and running in Lenny's direction. He was yelling something. "Fuck!" Lenny said as the guy got closer. He quickly threw the car in reverse and backed up. The guy was now pounding on the passenger's window.

"That's my fucking car you prick!"

Lenny shoved the gear in drive, tore around the cars in front, and sped off. He looked in the rear-view mirror. "Dumb schmuck," he said, and turned down the Esplanade.

Ted was back at Muriel's side. He watched her chest rise and fall. Her breathing was becoming more and more laboured. He heard the curtain swoosh open and looked up. "You doing okay?" Dr. Metcalf asked.

Ted nodded. "Will she wake up?"

"Hard to tell. But I don't think so."

Ted's eyes watered. "I never really said goodbye. There was so much more I wanted to say."

Dr. Metcalf wrapped his long fingers around Muriel's small wrist and looked at his watch. "She's still here. You have time."

"You think she'll hear me?"

"Yes, I do. But even if she doesn't, she knows how you feel. You've barely left her side."

"Is she in pain?"

"No. Don't worry. When the time arrives, she'll leave in peace."

Ted's lower lip began to quiver. "Will it be tonight?"

Dr. Metcalf smiled. "Only God picks the time. But I'm sure it will be soon."

Ted brought his hankie to his eyes and blew his nose. "Muriel was asking about the boy. The boy with Scarlet Fever. Is he going to be okay?"

"He's doing much better. Fever has come down."

"Ever locate his parents?" Ted asked.

"No."

"Strange don't you think? The woman who came in today and the boy down the hall? I saw the guy who brought her in. Can't say for sure, but he had a similar build to the boy's uncle. So, does she have Scarlet Fever too?"

"You mean *did she have* Scarlet Fever. Yes. She died about an hour ago. She was septic and her kidneys gave out."

Ted's head dropped.

"Anyway, we now have a few mysteries to solve. Who the boy is. Who she was. And if there was any relationship between her, the boy, and the guy who claims he's his uncle. If he doesn't come back in the next forty-eight hours, we'll post the boy's picture in *The Post*. We need to find his parents. Goodness knows, they might have been exposed and are spreading the fever to others. Last thing we need is an epidemic on our hands." Dr. Metcalf put his hand on Ted's shoulder. "I'll be back to check on your wife before I call it a day."

"Hey, Captain. That green McLaughlin you're looking for. It's hot. Owner just called in and said he saw the guy who stole it across from Steel City Auto. Said he was heading toward the Esplanade."

"Go round up the guys and let them know. Oh, and tell them to check out Porky's on Kings Road. If he's looking for a pawn shop and heading toward the Esplanade, he's likely heading there."

Lenny slapped the ring on the table. "Real gold. Must be worth at least fifty?"

"Is it stolen?"

"No!"

Porky picked it up and squinted. "It's engraved."

"Belonged to my mother. She left it to me."

"I'll give you fifteen."

"Fifteen! It's worth three times that much."

"Not when it's engraved. Cuts down on the resale value," Porky said.

"Don't give me that bullshit. Just buff it out."

"Like I said, I'll give you fifteen and not a penny more."

"Yer crazy!" Lenny said, grabbing it from him. He started for the door, weighing his chances of getting a better deal elsewhere. He needed enough money to get off the Island. He'd figure the rest out later. He turned back at the door and watched Porky shove his sandwich into his fat, pink cheeks. "Seventeen?" Lenny asked. Porky licked his chubby fingers, reached in his pocket, and counted out Lenny's money. Lenny snatched it up and left. He put the car in reverse, placed his right arm over the seat, and turned his head to back out. The police pulled in and blocked his way. "Fuck," he whispered, slamming on the brakes and shoving the gearshift in park. He leaned over the front seat, picked up his shotgun, laid it down at his side, and threw a blanket over it.

A young, red-headed officer got out and rapped on Lenny's window. Lenny rolled it down. "Jesus, Lenny! Not again. C'mon. Step out so we can have a chat."

Lenny didn't move.

"C'mon, Lenny. We both know the car's hot. And we need to talk to you about a woman that was dropped off at —" The blast hit the young officer in the stomach, sending him hurtling backward to the ground. A second officer in the passenger seat scrambled to unsnap his holster. Lenny walked around to the side of the police car with his shotgun aimed at his head. "Put yer fuckin hands up!" he screamed. The officer complied. Lenny opened the passenger door. "Get out!" he said, pulling the gun from the officer's hip and shoving it under his waistband. He kept his shotgun on his target and walked around to the driver's side of the police car. He was just about to get in, when there was a second blast. Lenny's head snapped back and he slumped to the ground.

Porky put his gun down and picked up Lenny's rifle. "Ambulance is on the way," he said to the shaken officer who ran to the aide of his downed partner. Porky glanced behind him, bent down, put his hand in Lenny's pocket, and smiled at his good fortune. He got a ring worth at least fifty dollars and his money back.

Thursday, June 20

CHAPTER 23

Mabel genuflected, got down on the kneeling pad, blessed herself, and rested her chin on her folded hands. Once again, she prayed for those she loved who were at His side, and for Muriel who was soon to be. She then gave thanks for her blessings. "Thank you, dear Lord, for bringing Stanley home to me and for the child that I carry." She heard the woman next to her whisper to her son.

"Go on," she said, shooing him. "The light's off. It's your turn."

Mabel blessed herself and sat back on the pew, waiting to speak to Father Cusack after he'd heard from all of his penitents.

The boy's mother smiled at Mabel and whispered. "He's a little nervous."

"It can be a little intimidating. Even for adults. It's so dark in there," Mabel said, thinking sins committed in the dark would be better shared in the light of day.

"Ain't that the truth," the mother said, turning her head to the confessional.

"Bless me Father for I have sinned. I confess to almighty God and to you Father," the boy hollered into the sliding partition separating him and Father Cusack. Mabel, along with a dozen or more parishioners, shifted uncomfortably and glanced at one another. Several were snickering. The boy's mother put her head in her hands. "Dear, Lord," she said.

"I did bad stuff. I cursed. And oh, I lied to my mother," the young sinner shared with the small gathering.

Father Cusack urged him to speak more softly, not to curse or lie to his mother, and doled out his penance. He shook his head, thinking every child who entered the confessional recited the same sins; most of them likely invented to satisfy their God fearing parents than the Lord to whom they were to atone.

The boy left the box, briefly knelt at the altar, and walked up to his red-faced mother. "You don't have to yell in there, ya know," she whispered, roughly taking him by the arm and quickly dragging him up the aisle. "And when, exactly, did you lie to me?"

Mabel was halfway through her rosary when the final confessor left the box. Father Cusack stepped out. "Mrs. MacIntyre? I'm sorry, I thought that was my last confession," he said, turning to re-enter the box.

"I'm not here for confession, Father. I'm afraid that might take up too much of your time. I'll do it another day. I was hoping to speak to you about a memorial service for my son."

Lenny opened his eyes, looked down at his taped hand, and then up at the bottle dripping clear fluid through the thin tube. He closed his eyes again, knowing he was going back to jail. He tried to sit up, but the shooting pain in his right shoulder and across his back made his eyes water. He leaned back on his pillow. Fuck, he thought. I'd rather be dead than go back to that hole.

"You're awake?" Lenny looked up to see the captain of the Sydney detachment standing in the doorway. "Too bad. I was hoping the doctors would fuck up your surgery."

"Me, too," Lenny said.

The captain pulled up a chair and sat next to him. "Would have been easier all round. Cause, Lenny, you're fucked no matter what way you look at it. If Red dies, and there's a good chance he will, you're gonna hang. But even if he doesn't, you're still fucked. You'll be spending the rest of your life locked up."

Lenny stared at the ceiling.

"So here's the thing, Lenny. Had a half-naked Jane Doe dropped off this morning. And the weirdest thing, she had the same condition as a young boy down the hall. The same boy you brought in a few days ago claiming to be his uncle. Who's the kid Lenny?"

"I don't know what yer talkin about?"

"Sure you do. One of the orderlies identified you as the guy who brought the boy in. Apparently you claimed you were his uncle. And we got a witness who said the person who dumped the woman in the entryway was driving a green McLaughlin. C'mon, Lenny? What are the chances of that?" Lenny's heart was pounding. "So, this Jane Doe? Who is she? And who's the boy?" the captain pressed.

"She's my sister. But I don't know who the kid is. I swear."

"Why did you just dump her at the door? And why did you say you were the kid's uncle?"

"Had no money to pay for their care. Look, I was outa town. Lookin for work. Came home and the kid was just there. Sylvie said she was babysittin. Never mentioned who the kid belonged to. Then they both got sick. I took the kid in didn't I? Go ask Sylvie who he belongs to."

The captain sucked on his upper lip and shook his head. "Well, Lenny. That's gonna be tough. Never did figure out a way to talk to the dead."

Lenny tilted his head to the side. "Sylvie's dead?"

"Yeah, Lenny. Ya shoulda brought her in sooner. Gonna be hard when they slip that noose around your neck. She was your sister for Christ sakes. Ya know you're going straight to hell."

A nurse walked in carrying a tray of gauze bandages. "Sorry, Captain. Time to change his dressings."

The captain turned in his chair. "I'm not done."

"He's not going anywhere," she said. "And I've been on my feet for more than twelve hours. I'm hungry. I'm tired. And I got four kids at home under the age of eight that I'd like to tuck in. It won't take long."

The captain stood to leave. He looked down at Lenny. "Don't make it any harder on yourself than you already have." He turned to the nurse. "I'll wait outside."

Ted looked at his wife. She was sleeping peacefully. He arched his stiff back and walked into the corridor.

"Ted?"

Ted turned to the familiar voice and the officer sitting on a chair in the hallway. "Clarence?" he said, looking at his former counterpart from the Sydney detachment.

The two huddled outside Muriel's room. Clarence put his hand on Ted's shoulder. "I'm so sorry, Ted. I had no idea. Let's grab a coffee," he said, guiding him down the hall. He opened the door to the stairwell. "So how long has she been in a coma?" he asked.

The two old friends drank stale, tepid coffee and spoke of better days long since passed. Both promising to stay in touch; both knowing it would never happen. "I should get back," Ted said and stood. "So what brings you here?" he asked.

Clarence downed the rest of his coffee and put his cup down. "Lenny Slade."

Ted shrugged.

They started to head back to the stairwell. "He shot one of my officers outside Porky's. Red's in recovery, but still not out of the woods. Anyway, Lenny brought a kid in a couple of days ago. Had Scarlet Fever. Then he brought his sister in this—"

"Clarence! I was the one who called the station to report it. You say the guy's name is Lenny? Lenny Slade?"

"Yeah. Been gettin in trouble his whole life. Just got out of Dorchester. Always—"

"Clarence. When the kid first came in, they put him in the bed next to Muriel. This Lenny guy said he was the kid's uncle and that his name was Dan McInnes."

"Yeah. Said he couldn't pay the hospital bills, so lied about who he was. It's all bullshit. There's a lot more to this than Lenny's telling us."

Ted stopped in his tracks. *The barn fire. JC. The kid with Scarlet Fever. Dorchester. Dan McInnes.* It was more than coincidence, he thought. "Clarence, I might know who the boy is. At least I hope I do."

The two ran up the stairwell and down the hall to Lenny's room. There was no sign of the nurse, or Lenny.

Lenny was in the bowels of the hospital. He held on to the wall and peeked around the corner. His odds of escaping weren't good, but he'd rather die in a hail of bullets than go back to his eight by ten cell in Dorchester. It's now or never, he thought. He dashed past the laundry room and pushed down on the handle of the door he hoped would lead to freedom. The bright sun momentarily blinded him and his right shoulder felt like it was on fire. He paused and looked across the parking lot. He slowly made his way out, crouching among a handful of cars. He then ran as fast as his weak legs and bare feet could carry him into the deep woods beyond. He knew he didn't have much time and that it wouldn't be long before the cops realized he was missing and began scouring the area. He frantically looked around trying to decide which way to go. He headed east, hoping to make it to the brook that would lead him to the edge of town. He'd find a barn or shed where he could hide out and rest for the night, then make his way to the Pier and hop a coal train. He plodded along. His arm and shoulder ached. He stepped on a sharp twig and fell forward. He landed on his bad shoulder and screamed in pain. When he stood up, blood was dripping down his right arm. He knew the sutures had torn apart. He didn't know that at least a half dozen officers and a German Shepard were already fanning out and combing the area.

A young officer dangled Lenny's sock in front of Stasi. The dog sniffed, turned west, and started dragging him into the woods. "I told you he was ready," he hollered to his partner as they ran behind the eager dog set on finding its prey. "Jesus Christ! Get back here," the young officer yelled as Stasi broke free of its lead and bounded ahead. The officers ran to catch up, pushing aside the high brush, and thick alder branches. "Ready my arse!" the older officer said. Stasi was violently shaking his head from side to side. He had a small hare clenched between his teeth.

Lenny stumbled into the brook, walked a few feet, and then collapsed against the trunk of a dying birch tree. Blood was streaming down his arm, he felt light-headed, and his recently applied dressing was hanging loosely on one side. He tried to look back at his shoulder, then shivered. He lifted his soaking pant legs and numb feet out of the freezing water, looked up at the fading sun, and wondered if it would be the last sunset he'd ever see. He started to cry and walked a few more feet to a clearing. He could hear the cops off in the distance. "Help," he said weakly. "Help. Please! Help me."

"Okay, boys," the lead officer said to the others. "It's getting dark and cold. One night in the woods will do it for him. Let's regroup and cover off the perimeter. He'll walk out sooner or later."

Lenny fell to his knees. He thought of Dan McInnes sitting next to him toasting their masterful plan, Sylvie standing over him pointing the gun at his head, and of Midas' rotting carcass behind the shed. He looked down at the red drops rolling off his fingertips onto the green forest floor. He could see Barry holding his stomach, looking up at him and pleading for help. "It was an accident," Lenny whispered. He closed his eyes, swayed back and forth, and prayed. Then he heard the snapping branches. They heard me, he thought. He opened his eyes. He was staring into the angry eyes of a snarling coyote; its hot breath visible in the now cool air.

"Wait!" Stasi's trainer yelled, holding up his hand. "Did you guys hear that?" His fellow officers stopped their chatter and turned to see him looking over his shoulder.

"Hear what?"

"I thought I heard a scream." They stood quietly for a moment.

"I didn't hear anything. You?" the lead officer asked. They all shook their heads. "C'mon let's get the hell out of here."

Mabel passed Stanley another plate. He ran the dish towel over it and placed it on the counter.

"How's the new girl working out?" he asked.

"A little clumsy. Keeps dropping pans and spilling things. I'm hoping it's just new job jitters. Anyway, she needs the job and I need the help."

"Any word on the hospital job?" Mabel asked, swishing her washcloth around the sink.

"Not yet. I doubt we'll get it. Up against some bigger companies from Halifax with more experience doing that kind of work."

"Nothing ventured, nothing gained," Mabel said. She hesitated a moment and then plowed forward. "I went to see Father Cusack this morning."

"Oh?"

"I wanted to talk to him about a service for JC."

Stanley put his head down.

"I'm hoping that we can have it before Amour leaves. Just us and a few friends. So, what do you think?" Mabel asked.

Stanley didn't think much about anything involving God or the church, but knew Mabel did. Her faith was her rock. He kissed her forehead. "I suppose we can't put it off much longer."

Amour came in the back door. "Eight more sales!"

"That's fabulous," Mabel said.

"And get this. Myrtle's now wearing lipstick."

Stanley shook his head.

"Wait till you see her, Stanley. You won't recognize her."

"So I hear."

"She's completely transformed. Inside and out," Amour proudly proclaimed. "She even wants to have a party before I go. Told me to invite whoever I want. Can you imagine?"

Stanley laughed. "No."

Mabel hugged Amour. "I think it's wonderful how you've helped her."

"Anyway, I thought Mary Catherine and Sam. And Luke and John."

"And Alice," Mabel said.

"Of course, Alice."

"Stanley? Know of any eligible gentlemen you might want to invite? Myrtle's a catch," Amour said.

The phone rang.

"I got it," Stanley said, disappearing down the hall. He returned less than a minute later. "That was Ted."

"Did Muriel pass?" Mabel asked.

"No. I don't think so. He just sounded odd. Just asked if I could come straight to the hospital."

Mabel put her dishrag down and began drying her hands. "I'll come with you."

"He asked that I come alone."

Mabel gave him a puzzled look.

Stanley pulled his keys from his pocket. "He probably just needs someone to talk to. You know, another guy. Don't wait up. It's likely going to be a long, sad night."

⊏⊐⎯⎯⊏⊐

Stanley took a deep breath and walked down the hall. He pushed Muriel's door open. Ted let go of Muriel's hand. "How is she?" Stanley asked, placing his hand on Ted's shoulder. Ted led him into the hallway. They chatted briefly. Stanley looked down the corridor, then tore past the nurses' station. Ted ran to catch up.

The night duty nurse came out from behind her station. Stanley stood outside the door. "Stop! You can't go in there!" she hollered.

Stanley looked at the surly nurse running toward him, then pushed the door open.

"Stop!"

Ted blocked her way. "I think it's his son."

Stanley could see the back of the small, fair-haired boy curled up in the fetal position. He slowly walked around the bed to see his face. He bent down and gently ran his hand over his head. He picked his small hand up, cupped it between his own, kissed it, and began to weep.

The nurse and Ted watched from the doorway.

"Is he going to be okay?" Stanley asked, tears streaming down his face.

"We think he lost some hearing in his left ear, but otherwise Dr. Metcalf thinks he'll make a full recovery."

Stanley was laughing and crying at the same time. "That's okay. His dad's a little deaf too."

Ted smiled and put his head down. If only I could experience such a miracle, he thought.

Stanley placed JC's hand back on the bed. He walked up to Ted and wrapped his arms around him. "Thank you. Thank you. Thank you," he sobbed.

The once surly nurse smiled. "Well, I'm glad we finally solved that mystery."

"Can I take him home?" Stanley asked.

The response was swift and firm. "No."

"But you don't understand. His mother thinks he's —"

"No! The child stays here. At least till Dr. Metcalf says otherwise."

Ted turned to her. "Call him."

"I'm not calling him at his hour."

"Either you do, or I will," Ted said.

Ted closed the door, leaving Stanley to absorb the incredible joy of the moment. He took the phone from the nurse, apologized to Dr. Metcalf, and explained the happy turn of events. He then walked back to Muriel's room. He smiled, pulled his chair close to her bed, and placed her hand in his. He kissed it. "Hun. I…I have…some…some wonderful news," he whispered. Like his good friend in the room down the hall, he was sobbing.

Stanley stood over the bed and looked down at his sleeping wife. He squatted beside her and gently touched the thin white scar above her right eye, thinking about how strong she was and how much he loved her. Mabel opened her eyes and sat up. She could tell he had been crying. "Is she gone?" she asked.

"No," he said and pulled her bedcovers down. "I need you to come with me," he said.

Mabel looked out into the dark night. "What time is it?"

"It's time to let go of all the pain," he said. He put his hand out to her. "What's going on?" Mabel asked.

"Come with me," he said, clasping her hand." They stopped outside JC's door. Stanley pushed it open. "What are you doing?" she asked.

Stanley nodded toward the small bed. Mabel's legs wobbled. He put his arm around her to steady her. "He's home," he said.

Mabel looked up at Stanley. "I'm dreaming?"

"No. Our boy is home," he said.

Mabel slowly approached the bed and touched JC's head, then his arm and back. Her hand was trembling and tears were streaming down her face. "He's not hurt? He's okay?"

"He's fine."

She picked him up, rocked him in her arms, and kissed his face. "But how? Where has he been? How did you find him?" she asked.

Stanley placed his hand on JC's head. "Ted did."

"Ted?" she asked. JC blinked up at her. "Hello, sweetheart," she murmured, smiling down at him. "I missed you so much." JC turned his head, rested it on her shoulder, and went back to sleep.

Mabel sat in the rocking chair with JC in her arms and Stanley kneeling beside them. "It's a miracle," she repeated over and over again as Stanley told her everything he knew.

Amour woke to the muffled voices. She looked at the clock. It was almost two in the morning. She got out of bed, wrapped her robe around her, and walked into the hallway to JC's room.

"He's home," Mabel said, beaming. "Our baby is home."

Friday, June 21

CHAPTER 24

Mary Catherine rolled the Maytag to the sink and filled it up. She then picked up the wicker hamper and dumped the soiled clothes out on the table. She began sorting the darks from the lights, then set the basket on the floor. She looked down, wondering what she was seeing. She picked the basket up, turned it over and banged on the bottom. Nothing happened. She flipped it upright and began scratching at it with her fingernail, but again it didn't move. She got a knife, slide it between the wall and thick woven base along the bottom and pried it apart. A tiny blue ball rolled forward. She picked it up. Another rolled in its place. She pried more of the braid. Tiny blue dots rolled out, one after another, settling between the thin willow weaves.

"Sam!" she hollered. "Can you come here?"

Sam entered the kitchen. "What is it?'

Mary Catherine pointed at the hamper.

They both stared down into it. "It wasn't a miracle after all," Mary Catherine whispered.

Sam was mentally counting them in his head. There were eight in total. "Oh, my God," he said, running his hand through his hair.

"They were lodged in the braiding," Mary Catherine said. "I need to call Mabel." She had her hand on the phone.

Sam laid his hand on top of hers. "Don't. She doesn't need to know. She believes Liddy's recovery was a miracle. It's helped her cope. Let's not take that away from her," Sam said.

They both jumped, startled at the sound of an incoming call. It was Mabel.

Mary Catherine and Sam shared the receiver, both stunned and overjoyed at the wonderful news. Mary Catherine began rattling off all of the expected questions. Mabel told her everything she knew, assuring Mary Catherine JC would be fine.

"Mabel," Mary Catherine said. "The strangest thing just happened."

"What?" Mabel asked.

Sam shook his head and mouthed *no*.

"Oh, it's nothing. I'll tell you when I see you. I'm so happy for you and Stanley. I can't wait to see JC. We love you."

She hung up and turned to Sam. "Isn't it incredible?" she said. "But why didn't you want me to tell her about the pills? JC's home. What difference does it make now?"

"Let's not tell anyone about the pills. Everyone thinks it was a miracle. Even the doctors. Let's leave it that way. It gives people hope that anything is possible."

Mary Catherine remembered her conversation with Myrtle. Hope is hope, she had said. She put her head down, overcome by a sudden wave of guilt for dismissing Myrtle's suggestion that JC might have been snatched up by a stranger. Perhaps JC would have been found sooner if only she had listened to Myrtle and shared her suspicions.

"Sam," she said. "I need to tell you something."

Nothing could wipe the smile off Mabel's face. Despite being awake since one-thirty she didn't feel tired. She felt exhilarated.

"Hun. You're going to have to put him down at some point," Stanley said, putting on a light jacket.

"Where are you going?" Mabel asked.

"I've got some things to take care of. I'll be back before Dr. Cohen gets here."

Amour put down the phone. "I've told just about everyone. Nobody can believe it. Luke said Alice can't stop crying. Of course, they all wanted to come straight here. I told them they'd have to wait for a bit."

Amour smiled at JC. "I still can't believe it."

Mabel placed JC in Amour's arms. "I'll be back in a minute. Don't take your eyes off of him," she said and went upstairs. She pulled the bottom drawer open, picked up Margaret's Bible, and ran her hand over it. She then removed all of her other treasures. It wasn't there. She pulled the drawer all the way out, stretched her arm in, and felt the bare floor below. She checked the rest of the drawers, tossing her clothes aside. That's strange, she thought. I know I put it right beside Margaret's Bible. She put things back in order and returned to the kitchen.

JC was sitting on Amour's lap. Myrtle was sitting across from them, trying to get JC to play pat-a-cake. "I never thought he drowned," she said. "Body would have been found."

"Are you hungry, JC?" Mabel asked, reaching down to take him from Amour. "Let's have some porridge."

She put the oatmeal in front of him and wrapped his small hand around a spoon. He dropped it. Mabel picked it up, scooped up a spoonful, and brought it to his mouth. He turned his head to the side and started to cry. "That's funny," Mabel said. "He loves porridge."

Amour put a piece of bread on his tray. He picked it up and shoved it into his mouth. "He just missed your homemade bread," she said.

The captain of the Sydney detachment barked out his orders, identifying the areas to be manned around the perimeter and instructing several of his officers to go back into the woods. He made a point of telling them to leave Stasi at the station. "My cat could do a better job," he said to laughter. "I just got off the phone with a cousin of Lenny's brother-in-law, so we have a location for the cabin. Jake and I will check it out. You never know, Lenny might have stolen the car that went missing in Ashby last night. Okay boys, bring him in." Everyone dispersed.

The captain and his second-in-command drove down the secluded lane. There was no sign of life or the 1943 red Plymouth that was reported stolen.

"You take the back," the captain said, unsnapping his holster.

The captain could hear mooing in the barn. He'd check it out first. The only thing he found was a cow that looked emaciated. He quietly made his way up the steps to the cabin and looked in the window. The place was torn apart. "You in there, Lenny?" he called out. "Lenny! Ya need medical attention. We're here to help." There was nothing. He tried the door. It was unlocked. He pushed it open and looked around at the empty cupboards and the floor strewn with pantry items, overturned drawers, and sofa cushions. He stepped over the clutter and opened the back door. Jake was standing with his back to him looking out over the water.

"Nice view, eh?"

"Not inside," his captain replied.

The two went from room to room, surveying the destruction. "Someone was looking for something," Jake said. "And what's up with all this?" he said, picking up a doll's head. "Christ! This place gives me the willies." He let out an involuntary shudder and threw it on the bed. "She obviously loved dolls and sewing," he said, stepping over the severed heads and plastic limbs of Sylvie's doll collection, and wading through the mess of scattered clothes, torn up patterns, and unravelled bolts of cloth. His foot slipped on a glossy Butterick envelope and he stumbled forward. He looked back. "Holy shit!"

"What is it?"

Jake turned to his captain and held the envelope open. "Must be close to a thousand dollars here?"

The captain took it from him. "Keep your mouth shut. Don't tell a soul."

"You're not going to report it?"

"No! And neither are you. Red likely won't be back on the job for a few months. His family needs the money more than the government."

Stanley sat across from Dunphy, filling him in on what Ted had told him. "Gordon, Lenny brought JC into the hospital claiming to be his uncle. He said his name was Dan McInnes. Jesus, they were both in Dorchester at the same time."

"And the Sydney police are looking for Lenny now?" Dunphy asked.

"Yes. Look, I know McInnes put Lenny up to it. So does Ted. And I'm damn sure Skinny was right. McInnes *was* back in town. Dollars to doughnuts he robbed Gladys. Who else would have known where she kept her money. Hell, be probably needed it to pay off Lenny. And why would Lenny take JC in the first place? Not like he came looking for a ransom?"

Dunphy shook his head. "You could be right. But it's all circumstantial. Hopefully they'll find Lenny and we can get him to come clean. I'll give Clarence a call to see if they need a few more officers on the ground."

"So that's it for now?" Stanley asked.

"I'm afraid so."

Stanley stood and walked to the door.

"Stanley? We'll get to the bottom of things. I promise," Dunphy said.

Stanley knew Dunphy would do his best. He prayed they'd find Lenny. He had no idea they already did and that Lenny wasn't talking. His partially consumed corpse was found an hour earlier by a young officer who spotted his pale green, bloodstained Johnny shirt sticking out from under the legs of a pack of feasting coyotes.

Stanley and Dirty Willie drove up the lane to the bluff with his horse trailer hitched to the back. Fred and Ten-After-Six followed in Fred's truck. "I'm going to settle the horses in. Take the lumber out back. I won't be long," he instructed Fred.

Twenty minutes later he entered the kitchen. He kissed Mabel and then JC's forehead. He looked at the strange woman sitting next to Amour. "Hello," he said, extending his hand. "I don't believe we've met."

Everyone started laughing. Stanley looked around, then back at the unfamiliar woman. "Myrtle?"

"Told you she was a catch," Amour said.

Stanley hung up the phone. "That was the Sydney Police. They found Lenny. He's dead."

"So we'll never really know," Mabel said.

"It was McInnes, and no one can convince me otherwise."

"You can't let it eat you up inside," she said.

"I can't help it. I won't sleep easy until he's back behind bars. I'll track him down myself if I have to."

Mabel knew not to argue. Like Stanley, she could kill McInnes herself. But today, she just wanted to relish the miracle of her son's return. Stanley put on his well-warn grey cardigan, reached down, and took JC from Mabel.

"By the way. Did you see Father Gregory's maniturgium?" Mabel asked.

"No," he said, sitting in his favourite chair, settling JC down beside him, and putting his arm around him. "Pass me the book," he said.

Mabel handed him *The Story About Ping*. "It's just…well, I know I put it in the bottom drawer of the dresser. I put it right next to Margaret's Bible. And it's not there now. You're sure you didn't move it?"

"Positive. Why would I?"

"I don't know. It's just the strangest thing."

"It'll turn up," he said.

Mabel put the kettle on, sat down at the table, and thought of the day Father Cusack brought it to her. *He likely wanted you to have it because you lent your son to God*. How strange, she thought. On the same day JC returns home, it goes missing. She shook her head, thinking she had to have misplaced it. It didn't just disappear.

Amour came through the back door. "Well that was fast," she said, pointing to the fence.

"Stanley said there was no point in tempting fate. I'm glad it's done. It does nothing to enhance the view, but it gives us peace of mind. What's all over your arm?" Mabel asked.

Amour bent her elbow forward and looked down at the long red streak. "Myrtle's trying to teach me to paint." She grabbed a cloth, ran it under the water, and began scrubbing her arm. "She says I'm hopeless. I think she's right. By the way, everything's all set for the party. It's pot luck. I'm making quiche. Mary Catherine's making—"

"Perogies," Mabel said.

Amour laughed. "Well, they *are good*. I'll talk to Alice tomorrow. See what she has in mind. The guys are responsible for the libations. Oh, and Myrtle said to take JC. If he gets tired he can curl up on her bed. You okay, Mabel? You seem distracted."

"Just puzzled." Mabel rested her chin on her hand. "You didn't happen to see Father Gregory's maniturgium?"

"Not since you first showed it to me."

"It's the strangest thing. I know where I put it, but it's not there now."

"Did you say a prayer to St. Anthony?"

"At least a dozen times." Mabel, once again, mentally walked through the night before. She had laid it out on the bed, knelt down, and prayed over it. She clearly remembered folding it and placing it next to Margaret's Bible. "I'm sure it will turn up," she said, unsure it ever would.

"Mr. Collins. Mr. Collins." Ted opened his eyes and looked down at the hand on his shoulder and then up at the young nurse standing over him.

"I'm sorry. She's gone."

Ted sat up and looked at his wife. She looked like she was sleeping.

"I'll give you some time alone," the nurse said.

Ted watched the door close behind her. He picked up Muriel's hand and kissed it. "At least you're no longer in pain. You have no idea how much I'm gonna miss you. For as long as I can remember it's just been you and me. *Us.* Now it's just me. What's left of me. I don't know how to do it. I don't know how Io breathe." He began to laugh through his tears. "Who's gonna nag me about my diet? Tell me to get a haircut. Fill the coal bucket?" He leaned forward, brushed her greying hair back off her forehead, and kissed it. "You made me a happy man. I wouldn't have changed a thing. Not one day. You were my world…my everything. Thank you for letting me love you. Thank you for loving me. Rest in peace, my sweet girl. Rest in peace."

Ted pulled out his hankie, wiped his eyes, and blew his nose. The young nurse returned an hour later. "I'm sorry," she said. "Is there anything I can get for you? Tea? A glass of water? Someone I can call?"

Ted shook his head. "No. The only thing I need. The only thing I ever needed was my wife. Now…now…she's gone," he said, and burst into tears. The nurse pulled a chair up beside him, rubbed his back, and offered all of the words meant to console the grieving. *She's in a better place. She was a woman of strong faith who accepted her fate. She obviously loved you so much.* Ted took a deep breath and tried to compose himself. He looked up when the orderlies came through the door pushing a gurney. The nurse helped him to his feet and led him out of the room. "We met when we were fourteen. I loved her from the moment I laid eyes on her. I never thought she'd take a chance on the skinny kid with the big ears. But she did. She was my only girlfriend. I was the luckiest man in the world," he said, as he watched Muriel's thin, ravaged body, draped in a white sheet, roll down the hall and out of sight.

Monday, June 24

CHAPTER 25

To God be Thy Glory
Great things he has done
So loved He the world
That he gave us His son
Who yielded His life
Our redemption to win
And opened the life-gate
That all may go in.

Ted walked behind Muriel's casket, followed by a handful of distant relatives, Captain Dunphy, and a dozen or more uniformed officers, as Muriel's favourite hymn rang through St. Joseph's Church. Stanley walked into the aisle and waited for Mabel, Luke, Amour, Mary Catherine and Sam to join him in the solemn procession. The remaining mourners shuffled behind, mentally preparing for that awkward moment when they would whisper their condolences to the town's latest widower.

Amour hugged Mabel. "Luke and I are going to head back and get the tea started."

"We'll be there shortly," Mabel said, as one person after another hugged Ted, telling them it was a beautiful service. She felt an arm around her shoulder. "Captain Dunphy?"

"Gordon, please."

"Gordon."

"I'm so happy you have your son back. How's he doing?"

"He's still receiving penicillin injections and he's lost some hearing in his left ear, but he's settling back in. Dr. Cohen things he'll be just fine and that he likely won't remember any of the trauma."

Dunphy nodded toward Ted. "He's going to be lost without her."

Mabel bowed her head. "I'm afraid so. He'll need his friends to help him get through things. We're having some folks back at the house. You're welcome to drop by."

"Thank you. I think I will. I was hoping to have a word with Stanley."

Alice entertained JC while Sam and Amour frantically put out the teacups, Mary Catherine's perogies, and an array of squares and pies from Cameron's Bakery. Mary Catherine greeted everyone as they arrived. "They're here," she announced, opening the door and waiting on the step for Ted, Stanley, Luke, and Mabel to join those already gathered.

Amour passed Ted a cup of tea. Stanley took it from him. "I'm sure you can use something stronger," he said, handing him a glass of rum.

The initial whispers and quiet, brought on by the weight of the morning's solemn service, soon gave way to the noisy chatter and laughter of the living.

Dunphy was one of the last to arrive. Alice watched the handsome, unattached officer take off his cap and brass-buttoned jacket and hand them to Stanley. Alice held out a plate of sandwiches. "Captain Dunphy?"

"Thanks," he said. "Love sandwiches without the crust. Have we met?"

Stanley handed him a rum. "This is Alice. She works at the bakery."

Dunphy lifted his glass up and smiled. "Pleasure to meet you, Alice."

Luke approached them. "Can I help with that?" he asked Alice, offering to take the plate from her.

⊏▭▭▭▭▭▭⊐

Stanley threw his pants over a chair and crawled in bed. "Dunphy told me the Sydney police issued a nation-wide bulletin to bring McInnes in for questioning."

"That's great. You must be pleased?" Mabel said, unclipping the cameo broach Margaret had left her. She ran her fingers over it, thinking of the dear friends she had lost. She placed it in the same small cloth bag that held the treasured star shaped pin Mrs. Greene had given her years before.

"I'll be pleased when he's back in Dorchester," Stanley said, watching his wife strip down to her slip.

"Still, at least we know they're looking for him," Mabel said.

Stanley sighed. "Looking and finding are two different things."

"They'll find him. I know they will. He can't hide out forever," Mabel said.

"I told Dunphy they should focus on the Great Lakes. Likely back there trying to get work on a freighter. Also told him to keep in touch with Gladys Ferguson."

Mabel pulled her slip over her head and ran her hand over her growing belly. "Let's not talk about McInnes or Gladys Ferguson. The day was hard enough without thinking about those two." She looked to the door. "I hope Ted settled in okay."

Stanley plumped his pillow. "He's fine. He wants us to go to Iona for the interment. Said it would just be a handful of Muriel's closest friends."

"Of course we're going. I'll pick some mayflowers. Did he say if he was going to stay on the farm?"

"Yes. Said he had no plans to leave Muriel. Wants to live out his days where they were happiest and be buried next to her."

Mabel smiled. "I'm glad you talked him into staying."

"It didn't take much convincing. I think he was dreading the long drive and going home to an empty house. It was good of Amour to give up her bed."

"She didn't mind. Gives her more time to spend with Myrtle."

"Yeah. *They're* spending a lot of time together. So what's up with that?" Stanley asked.

"What are you saying?"

"Not saying anything."

Mabel rolled her slip into a ball and threw it at him. "Yes you are. Put it out of your head."

"Look, I know Amour's not that way. Just not so sure about Myrtle. The way she used to dress. And you gotta admit they're an odd pair."

"Don't be so quick to judge. They're good friends. That's all. Myrtle never had a friend before. And Amour finds her…fascinating. So do I for that matter. She's had a hard life. I feel so badly for her. I also feel guilty that I didn't try to get to know her better. She's going to be as lost as Ted when Amour leaves." Mabel started to laugh. "Did you see everyone's reaction when they realized it was her? I thought Dunphy was going to faint. He couldn't take his eyes off of her."

"And Alice couldn't take her eyes off of him," Stanley said.

Mabel dropped her arms to her side. "I was hoping that she and Luke would get together. He needs to find a girlfriend."

Stanley nodded his agreement. "He's so self-conscious about his limp. And then his *episodes* as he calls them."

"I know Alice likes him. She told me as much. Maybe you just need to give Luke some encouragement," Mabel said.

"I'll leave the matchmaking to you."

"At least do more things with him. Next time you and the boys go to the *Pithead* ask him along. He needs to get out more."

"Done," Stanley said.

Mabel opened the bottom drawer and looked one last time for Father Gregory's maniturgium."

Stanley shook his head. "It's not there. I checked. Even pulled the dresser out and looked behind it."

"It's the strangest thing," Mabel said, shutting the drawer. She turned. Stanley was grinning at her. She reached for her nightgown. "What?" she asked.

"I can see your baby bump."

Mabel looked down at her bare belly. "Won't be long before I'm as big as a house."

Stanley threw the covers back and patted her side of the bed. "I find it sexy."

Tuesday, June 25

CHAPTER 26

Kenny Ludlow sat up straight in the front seat with his hands folded in front of him. He glanced at Tommy while he waited for Mr. Spencer to pass out the latest test results. He needed a good mark, not just to move on to grade seven, but to show his parents he had mended his ways. Mr. Spencer loomed over him holding Kenny's test in his hand. Kenny looked up. Mr. Spencer was shaking his head from side-to-side. Kenny's heart sunk and his shoulders fell. "Kenny?"

"Sir," Kenny said.

"How do you think you did?"

Kenny had never studied so hard. "I thought I did okay."

"You *thought* you did okay?"

"Guess not," Kenny said, thinking he was destined for the pit.

"Actually, Kenny, you got the third highest mark in the class. Second time this week. See what you can do when you set your mind to it? You might just grade after all." Mr. Spencer handed him his test. Kenny's mouth fell open when he saw ninety-one percent circled in red. He couldn't believe it. He would have settled for a pass. He looked up at the clock. He couldn't wait to show his parents. He looked back at Mr. Spencer standing beside Harley. "Not your best, Harley. But not your worst either."

Finally, the bell rang. Kenny's excitement got the best of him and he scrambled for the door. "Kenny!" Mr. Spencer hollered. "Where do you think you're going? You're on blackboard duty. You and Harley clean the board and clap the erasers. Tommy! Straighten up the desks."

Kenny and Harley stood beside each other, wiping the board. Kenny looked at the yellowed bruise on the side of his friend's face. "I am sorry," he said. Harley shrugged. They went to the windows, held their arms out, turned their heads to the side, and began clapping the erasers. The chalk dust blew back in covering their faces. Kenny pointed at Harley and started to laugh. Harley looked at Kenny and did the same.

"What's so funny?" Tommy asked.

The two white faces turned in his direction. Tommy started to laugh. Mr. Spencer looked up from his desk. Now everyone was laughing.

The three former members of the Number Eleven Blackheads walked out on the front steps of St. Anthony's. Tommy looked at the paper proudly clutched in Kenny's hand. "Aren't gonna go all goodie goodie on us, are ya?"

Kenny unfolded his test and looked down. "Nah! Just a fluke."

"Good." Tommy pointed at the chalk dust in Kenny's hair and on his forehead. "Maybe we should call ourselves The Whiteheads?"

Harley shook his head. "Nah. I'd rather stick with Blackheads. What do you think, Kenny?"

"Blackheads."

"Okay, it's settled," Tommy said. "We're the Blackheads again. But I'm the leader."

Kenny watched his best friends walk to their bikes. Still, it was a good day, he thought. He was about to head down the hill when Harley pedalled up beside him. "Jump on the crossbar. I'll give you a ride."

⊏⊂_____⊐⊐

"He's not too heavy on your lap?" Stanley asked.

Mabel ran her hand over JC's head. "I'm fine. Just glad he's here with me."

Stanley stopped at the intersection and turned onto the Boisdale-Iona turn-off. "After the interment let's take a drive to Pleasant Bay?" he said.

"We won't have time. I have things to do for Myrtle's party. You forgot, didn't you?"

"No. But I'd like to. I'll be a fish out of water with all you girls."

"Luke and Sam are coming," Mabel said.

"I'm sure they're as excited as I am."

"Don't be so negative. And wait till you see her house. It's lovely. We should ask Ted. No point in him sitting home alone. Particularly today."

"I doubt he'll come," Stanley said. He looked at Mabel thinking that if anything ever happened to her, he wouldn't want to be around anyone.

Mabel adjusted JC on her lap. "I'm worried about JC. He's not saying anything?"

"He never said much to begin with?" Stanley said, trying to reassure himself as well as Mabel.

"Still, he's unusually quiet. Look, JC," Mabel said, pointing into a field. "Cow. Can you say cow?"

JC closed his eyes and rested his head on her shoulder. They passed the sawmill. "Some lovely properties out this way," Mabel said. Stanley looked down at the white farmhouse near the water with the black Chevrolet in the yard, then at the sign marked *Sold*. He sped up. "Not so fast!" Mabel said. "What's your hurry? We've got plenty of time."

Mabel squatted in front of the sofa, pulled the tongues of JC's white shoes back, and urged them onto his chubby feet. She pinched the toes, recalling the day she thought this simple pleasure was lost to her forever. She touched the side of his face. "Your mommy's sweet boy."

"Mom..my."

"Mommy. Yes, mommy," she said, beaming.

Stanley walked into the living room. "This okay?" he said, hoping Mabel wasn't going to insist he wear a tie.

She stood up quickly. "He just said mommy!" she said.

"Atta boy," Stanley said, picking him up and throwing him in the air. "See, I told mommy she had nothing to worry about."

"Mom..my," JC repeated.

Stanley laughed and pointed at his wife. "That's her. Isn't she beautiful?" JC buried his head in Stanley's chest.

Mabel welled up, overcome by the pure joy of the moment. Stanley leaned in and kissed her on the cheek. "You do look fabulous."

"And, you," she said, squeezing his arm, "need to put on a tie."

Stanley walked around the room bouncing his son in his arms. "Mommy sure is beautiful." He put his mouth to JC's ear. "But she's also a nag." Amour came downstairs. "Look, JC! There's another beauty," Stanley said.

"Are you all packed?" Mabel asked.

"All done."

"You must be excited to see Michael and Victoria," Stanley said.

"I am. But I still have the crossing. It's going to be a long five days."

There was a knock on the door. Mabel answered it and led Fred inside.

"Fred?" Stanley said. "C'mon in."

"Just wanted to tell you we got a call from the hospital. Sorry, we didn't get the job. I know how much you wanted—"

"Don't be sorry, Fred. I got everything I want right here." He kissed JC and passed him to Amour. "We're heading next door for a party." He looked at Mabel. "But I think we can squeeze in a quick drink."

"A quick one," Mabel said firmly.

Fred looked at Mabel and nodded to JC. "I'm glad he's home safe and sound."

"Thank you. Me too," Mabel said.

Stanley walked back from the kitchen and placed four glasses on the coffee table.

"So, I guess you guys heard about the arrest?" Fred said.

"What arrest?" Stanley asked, unscrewing the cap of the bottle and pouring the rum.

"They caught the guy who murdered the priest."

Mabel blessed herself. Stanley handed Fred his drink. "Who?"

"Guy from Number Two. Wife turned him in. Apparently she told the priest he was abusing her and the kids. I guess the priest was at her house quite a bit."

"Father Gregory. His name is Father Gregory," Mabel said sadly.

"Anyway, the guy's wife told the police he…Father Gregory was just trying to convince her to leave her husband and go to the authorities. Husband thought there was more to his visits and that they were having an affair. I guess she's quite a mess. Blames herself for getting Father Gregory mixed up in everything. A few of us have taken up a collection to help her out, given she's got three young mouths to feed. But I get the sense most folks are blaming her for what happened and aren't too willing to help out."

"Well, I'm just happy they caught the bastard," Stanley said. He took two twenties out of his wallet and handed them to Fred. "I'll also hit up the guys next pay day."

Mabel picked her glass up and held it out. "To Father Gregory," she said. "A kind and caring man who endured far too much sorrow."

Fred put his glass down. "Well, I better get a move on and let you folks get to your party."

Mabel followed him to the door. "Oh, Fred. Just a minute," she said. She went to the kitchen and came back a short while later. "Here," she said, passing him his Corningware dish. "I meant to get it to you sooner. Tell Aggie her stew was delicious."

"I will."

"Oh, and Fred?"

"Yes?"

"There's a little something inside."

Fred lifted the lid. "But Stanley just gave—"

"I know."

Mabel closed the door. She was glad the person responsible for Father Gregory's murder was caught, but saddened by the senselessness of it all. And then there was the mysterious disappearance of his maniturgium; the gift she vowed to treasure. Stanley walked up behind her. "You okay, hun?"

Mabel wiped her hand under her wet eyes and turned around. "Just the hormones," she said and smiled.

"So, are we all set?" Stanley said, looking from Mabel to Amour.

"Not quite," Mabel said. "You need a tie."

Stanley looked around the subdued room, thinking it was going to be a long night. He popped one of Amour's tiny quiches in his mouth, licked his fingers, and sat next to Luke. He waved his hand around. "Pretty nice eh?"

"Yeah. Very nice. Not what I expected."

"So how's business?" Stanley asked.

"Okay. Can always be better."

"And the leg?" Stanley asked, trying to draw out the conversation.

"Like the store. Okay, but it could be better."

"Thought I'd round up some of the guys after work on Friday. Go to the *Pithead*. Want to come?"

Luke shrugged. "I'll think about it," he said, wishing Alice would come through the door.

"So, I was hoping to borrow your car tomorrow to take Amour to the train station. You can have my truck."

Luke handed him his keys.

"Thanks," Stanley said, thinking Luke was unusually sullen. "Alice coming tonight?"

Again, Luke just shrugged. Stanley was relieved when he heard Mary Catherine and Sam arrive. He waited for them to stop gushing about Muriel's beautiful home, before greeting them. Eventually, the atmosphere began to resemble a party. Drinks flowed, trays of finger foods were replenished as quickly as they were depleted, and more guests joined the now boisterous gathering, including Ten-After-Six, Captain Dunphy with a woman Stanley didn't recognize, and several others who had dropped by the bluff following Muriel's funeral. Alice was among the last to show up. She brought a date too. Corliss.

Stanley looked at his pregnant wife holding their son. He passed her a drink and whispered in her ear. "Not such a bad party after all." He pointed across the room. "Even Luke's smiling."

"Look who I found," Amour said.

"Ted!" Stanley said, hugging him. "I'm glad you came. Muriel wouldn't want you to be home alone."

Corliss sifted through a stack of vinyl records, pulled one out, and cranked up the gramophone. He put his hand out to Myrtle. "What's a party without dancin?"

"I don't dance," Myrtle huffed.

"I'll teach ya."

"I'd be all over your feet."

Corliss lifted his pant leg, exposing his fake leg. "Darlin, I won't feel a thing." Despite his persistent efforts, Myrtle flatly refused.

"I love to dance," Amour said. Corliss put his arm around her waist. "A girl after my own heart," he said and led her into the living room.

Ten-After-Six decided to join them. He offered his hand to Mabel, who happily obliges. Stanley smiled as Peter turned his head to the side and tucked it under Mabel's armpit. "One thing's for sure, I won't be stepping on anyone's toes," Peter said to gales of laughter.

Three dances later Mabel joined Alice on the couch. "You're quiet. Everything okay?" Mabel asked.

Alice caught sight of Captain Dunphy laughing with Sam in the kitchen and smiled. "I'm better now," she said. A woman they didn't know approached.

"Mrs. MacIntyre?"

"Yes."

"I'm Charlotte Rogers. I work at St. Joseph's. I saw you there the day you visited the Friedman child."

"Of course. I thought you looked familiar."

"I just wanted to say how happy I am that you have your son back."

"Thank you…Charlotte. This is Alice."

Alice briefly turned her attention from Dunphy. "Hello."

"So you obviously know Myrtle?" Mabel said.

"No. We just met. I came with my new boyfriend. Captain Dunphy."

Luke pulled a chair up next to Alice. "Can I refill your drink?" he asked.

Alice passed him her glass. "Make it a double."

It was after twelve by the time most of the guests left and the cleanup began. Ted sat at the baby grand and pushed down on a key.

"Do you play?" Myrtle asked.

"No. But Muriel did."

"Scooch over," she said. Myrtle handed him the song book. "Anything you want to hear?"

"How about this one?"

"Don't know that one."

"This one?"

Myrtle scrunched up her nose and shook her head. "Hate that one."

Ted stopped at another page. Muriel took the book from him, rested it on the sheet rack, and cleared her throat.

Mabel dropped her dishrag in the sink. Amour pulled her head out of the fridge. And Stanley stopped boxing up the empty bottles. They stared at each other, then joined Ted and Myrtle in the living room.

Oh Lord my God
When I in awesome wonder
Consider all the worlds
Thy hands have made
I see the stars
I hear the rolling thunder
Thy power throughout
The universe displayed

Stanley tiptoed out. Mabel smiled when he returned holding their sleeping son. She kissed JC's forehead, rested her head on her husband's shoulder, and joined Ted, Amour and Myrtle in the chorus.

Then sings my soul
My saviour, God to Thee
How great thou art
How great thou art

⊂⊃

Stanley settled JC in his room, and Ted, who this time refused to take Amour's bed, on the couch. He went to the back door to turn off the light. He was surprised to see Luke sitting on the step with his arm over Alice's shoulder. He smiled, quietly walked upstairs, and crawled in next to Mabel.

"Did you get Ted a pillow?" Mabel asked.

"Yes."

"It was a wonderful party," Mabel said. "Myrtle's certainly a woman of many talents."

"She sure is. I think I see a romance blooming."

"What! Between her and Corliss?"

Stanley drew Mabel into him. "Amour did say she was a catch."

Mabel sat up. "Don't be ridiculous. Corliss is a bit of a flirt but he'd never cheat on —"

Stanley started to laugh. "Don't worry. I'm not talking about Corliss and Myrtle."

"Who then?"

"Luke and Alice."

"Really! Why do you say that?"

"They're out on the back step. He's got his arm around her."

Mabel smiled and laid back down, snuggling into him. "God, I hope you're right. I was hoping they'd get together. We should have them over for supper. Maybe next Saturday? I think she'd be so good for him. Help him come out of his shell. He'd be good for her too. She hardly goes out at all. Of course, Mark won't be too happy. But Alice isn't keen on him and I don't think they're a good fit. Mary

Mack would be a better match for Mark." Mabel poked Stanley in the side. "Did you hear anything I've said?"

"Go to sleep! We have an early morning. I've got to tend to the horses and we have to get Amour to the train station by ten."

Mabel rolled over on her back. All in all, it was a great day, she thought. She was tired but couldn't fall asleep. She kept thinking of Father Gregory and his missing maniturgium.

Wednesday, June 26

CHAPTER 27

"Is that everything?" Stanley asked looking at Amour's luggage.

"That's everything. I just have one more thing I need to do. I'll be right back." Amour walked through the field and rapped on Myrtle's door. She waited for Myrtle to answer and took in the breathtaking view of the ocean for one last time. She felt herself well up. Myrtle opened the door. She was wearing her wig and her blue dress.

"Come in."

"I wish I had time. I just wanted to thank you again for last night. It was a fabulous party. But mostly, thank you for giving me the chance to get to know you. You're a wonderful friend." Myrtle put her head down. "Anyway, this isn't goodbye. We'll see each other again. I promise. And we can write. Talk on the phone. I'll need to check on how your sales are going," Amour said, trying to lift her own spirits as much as those of her new friend.

"I'll miss *you*," Myrtle said.

Amour took Myrtle's hand in hers, pressed something into her palm, and wrapped Myrtle's fingers around it. She then hugged her and ran down the steps. "Goodbye, my friend."

Myrtle watched Amour disappear through the field. She opened her hand and looked down at her palm. "It was the forty cents Amour owed her."

Amour sat next to Stanley in the front. "It was good of Luke to lend you his car. I feel like I'm putting everybody out."

"Of course not. Luke's happy to help," Mabel said from the back seat.

Amour looked over her shoulder. "You know you didn't have to come?"

"You came all the way across the Atlantic to see me and *you're* saying I shouldn't drive thirty miles to see you off? Don't be silly," she said, adjusting JC's hat.

"Sil…ly," JC said.

Mabel grabbed his belly and began tickling him. "Yes, silly. Silly goose." JC squealed.

Stanley looked in the rear-view mirror and smiled.

"Besides, we're going to Pleasant Bay after we see you onboard," Mabel said.

Amour checked her purse for her boarding pass. "I'm sorry I didn't get a chance to see it."

"It's beautiful. You'll see it the next time you visit. And hopefully, Michael and Victoria will come with you. I'm sure Victoria would like to meet her new cousin," Mabel said.

Stanley shook his head. "You know, Mabel, Victoria isn't really a cousin."

"Actually," she said and laughed. "I forgot."

"Well, look at that!" Amour said, pointing ahead. "Must have been a sale on bikes."

Stanley slowed as the Number Eleven Blackheads straddled their shiny new bikes on the side of the road, looking up and down for an opportunity to cross. "That's John," Stanley said and stopped. He stuck his hand out the window and waved. John waved back. So did Kenny Ludlow who was sitting on the crossbar of Harley's bike. "Thank you, sir," Kenny hollered.

"What a polite young man," Amour said.

"It's Grading Day," Mabel said. "They must have all passed."

Four Months Later

CHAPTER 28

Stanley was lifting JC into the cab of the truck when Mabel walked out on the front step.

"Careful," Stanley hollered to her. "It's—" Mabel tumbled down the steps. "Jesus!" Stanley said, running to her. "Oh, my God! Are you okay?" He slowly helped her to her feet.

Mabel arched her back and rolled her right shoulder back. "I didn't realize the steps were slippery."

"I should have warned you sooner. You took quite a fall. Let's go back inside. You don't have to go to the bakery today."

"I'm fine. Really!"

Stanley helped her into the truck. "I don't like this. Maybe we should go to the hospital and get you checked out."

Mabel refused, insisting her shoulder was a bit stiff, but that was all. Stanley kept glancing at his wife. He was growing increasingly concerned. Mabel was rubbing her hand over her huge belly. "You look pale," he said, turning onto Brookside Street. "Is the baby kicking?"

"A little."

He turned up Caledonia Street.

"Stanley?"

"Yes?"

"Turn around. Take me to the hospital."

Stanley held JC's hand and watched the orderlies whisk Mabel into the examination room. He walked down the hall, found a bench, and nervously sat with his son on his lap. He waited twenty minutes before approaching the nurses' station. "Any word on my wife?" he asked. There was a sudden flurry as a nurse came out of the room, charged down the hall, and came back with two others. A doctor quickly followed them inside. "What's going on?" Stanley asked.

The nurse tried to reassure him, despite knowing that either the mother, the baby, or both were in distress. "I'm sure your wife is fine," she said.

"Can you check!"

The nurse pushed the examination room door open and disappeared inside.

Stanley picked JC up and walked up and down the hall, cursing her for being so slow.

She finally reappeared. "Mr. MacIntyre? Have a seat. It's going to be a while yet. Your wife is in labour."

"But she's not due for two more weeks. Is she okay? And the baby?"

Myrtle opened her mailbox and reached in. She pulled out the familiar blue-tinged envelop and ran her fingers over the postmark. She smiled and quickly walked back to the house. Lucky and Gowanya were on the back step. Gowanya began meowing and circling at her feet. "Go on ya pesky old thing," Myrtle said, shooing her out of the way. She slipped off her shoes, peeled off her cardigan, and tore the envelope open. A piece of paper fell out and drifted under the table.

My Dearest Myrtle,

I was so pleased to get your last letter and to learn of your fabulous success. I have more good news to share. I've sold every one of your paintings and have orders for more. My Whist ladies adore them. Michael has also sold several to his colleagues. It's so exciting. I'm certain that if you came to London we can find a Gallery in Wandsmith to host a showing. Regardless, please send me more at your earliest convenience. Of course, I'd also love it if you could find room to send along a few more jars of your delicious chutney. I know you don't like the thought of sailing the Atlantic, but remember your father did it all the time. Please think about it. I would love to see you and hear more about your friend Mr. Smithers. Lizzie MacNeil must be fit to be tied. But, I'm sure it won't be long before she finds another widower to dig her claws into.

Myrtle smiled as she continued to read the rest of Amour's four-page letter. She neatly folded it, returned it to its envelope, and held it against her chest. She then bent down, reached under the table, and picked up the paper that had drifted to the floor; a money order for two hundred and sixty-four dollars.

⊏▭▭⊐

Stanley paced the hallway and checked the clock every few minutes. It was over six hours since they rushed Mabel into the labour and delivery room. He thought about going back to the nurses' station and asking about his wife, but knew he'd get the same answer as he did the last eight times he had asked. *I'm sure she's fine. You need to be patient. The doctor is doing all he can. The baby will come when it's ready."* He'd give it another half hour then he'd go in there and find out for himself. He took a seat across from the chapel. Then he heard the screams. He jumped to his feet. And started running down the hall.

"Mr. MacIntyre!" the head nurse yelled. "It's not your wife. It's Annie Peach. She hates needles."

Stanley was about to return to his bench when he saw a nurse leaving Mabel's room. She was carrying a small bundle in her arms and rushing down the hall. Dr. MacLellan was the next to walk out. He turned to Stanley and began slowly walking toward him. Stanley tried to read the young doctor's expression. He suddenly felt weak.

"Mr. MacIntyre? I'm Dr. MacLellan. I'm afraid there's been a few complications," he said.

Stanley couldn't breathe, but he could hear his heart pounding. "Is Mabel okay?"

"It was a difficult delivery. And, of course, the fall —"

"Is my wife okay?" Stanley snapped, looking past the doctor to the door that hid his wife from view.

"As I was saying, the fall likely created some distress."

Stanley lost his patience. "My wife! What about my wife!" he hollered.

"She's understandably exhausted and quite—"

"But she'll be okay?"

"I'm sure she'll be just fine."

"And the baby?"

Dr. MacLellan smiled. "You have a beautiful, little girl. In fact, she's really quite rebellious. The nurses are just counting her fingers and toes, weighing her, and cleaning her up. You'll get to meet her in no time." His expression changed and he laid his hand on Stanley's shoulder. "But I'm afraid your son didn't make it."

Stanley tried to comprehend what he was hearing. He sat down. "We were having twins?"

"Yes. We did all we could. But I'm afraid that sometimes…well, it's not up to us. It's in God's hands."

Stanley felt his stomach sink. "Does Mabel know?"

"Yes. We didn't even get a chance to tell her. She just…she just somehow seemed to know it was a boy and that he didn't survive."

"Can I see her?"

"Let the nurses finish up. It won't be long. Oh, and Mr. MacIntyre? I told your wife the outcome may have been the same with or without the fall, but she still feels responsible. You need to be strong and help her through this. Don't let her blame herself. Even if it was the fall, she needs to know it was an accident."

Stanley thought of the irony of his words and nodded.

He then went to the chapel, where he cried and prayed.

"Mr. MacIntyre?"

Stanley turned to see the nurse in the doorway of the chapel.

"Ready to see your wife and meet your new daughter?"

Stanley wiped his eyes, got off his knees, and followed her down the hall. The nurse pushed the door open. Stanley smiled at his wife holding his baby girl. He walked up and kissed Mabel and then his tiny daughter's forehead. "She's beautiful. Like her mother."

"Where's JC?" Mabel asked.

"Luke and Alice came by earlier and took him home. How are you feeling?"

"Tired. Sore. Sad. Guilty. You name it. Crying tears of joy one minute and tears of heartache the next," Mabel said. Her lips began to tremble and her eyes well up. "If only I hadn't been so careless. I should have known the steps were slippery. I was just so —"

Stanley put his fingers over her mouth. "No! It wasn't your fault. Please! Please don't blame yourself. I should have helped you down the steps. And the doctor…the doctor said the outcome might not have been any different. Mabel we can't turn the clock back and we can't second guess things. Look, we have a beautiful daughter and JC has a little sister. We have each other. We need to count our blessings and be grateful for our family."

Mabel wiped her hand under her eyes. "When the doctor told me there was a second baby, I knew it was a boy and that he wouldn't survive. I had a vision or a dream of some kind. Father Gregory was sitting in his vestments holding a baby in his arms. Then he reached down and passed me his maniturgium. A gift for a mother who lends her son to God."

"It's probably just from all the trauma," Stanley said.

Mabel shook her head. The baby started to squirm and wail. "I don't think so. It seemed so real. Like Father Gregory was right there at the foot of my bed."

Stanley put his hand on the baby's head. "She's got a good set of lungs on her. Dr. MacLellan said she was rebellious."

"Probably missing her brother?" Mabel said. Her lips started to tremble.

Stanley reached down and took the now screeching baby from Mabel's arms. "Hello my little rebel," he said, offering his little finger for her to suck on.

Mabel sat up. "Mary."

Stanley gave her a puzzled look. "Mary?"

"That's what I'd like to call her. It means rebellious one. What do you think?"

"I like Mary. But it's pretty common. There's Mary Catherine, Mary MacDonald at the bakery, Mary McDonald at the bank, and —"

"But it suits her. And so what if the world has one more Mary Mack? We'll call her by both her given names."

"And what would that be?" Stanley asked, rocking Mary in his arms.

"Margaret," Mabel said. "Mary Margaret."

"James and Margaret would be proud our children carry their names," Stanley said. He smiled down at the feisty bundle kicking in his arms. "Well, Mary Margaret MacIntyre. It's nice to meet you. I'm your dad. And see there," he said, turning her to face Mabel, "that's my other beautiful girl. Your mama. I rescued her from a coal shed. She's smart. She's kind. She's patient and forgiving. She makes melt in yer mouth bread and she makes my heart melt. And I can't wait for you to meet your big brother." He put his mouth to her ear. "Your daddy is the luckiest guy in the world."

Stanley placed JC on Mabel's side of the bed, kissed his cheek, and crawled in beside him. He was exhausted but couldn't sleep. There were too many emotions charging at him. The relief in knowing Mabel was okay. The joy in seeing his baby daughter for the first time. And the sadness in losing his infant son. He closed his eyes, picturing the nurse hand his son to Mabel for a final goodbye. She had kissed his downy head as tears streamed down her face. *Our beautiful boy*, she had whispered, running her thumb along his small hand. *You'll always be in our hearts. Stanley, he needs a name. I'd like to call him Gregory?* He couldn't speak. He just nodded. Then they both cried, until they could cry no more.

Stanley thought about Dr. MacLellan's advice and opened his eyes. *It's not her fault. It was an accident. She's grieving. You need to be there for her. We did all we could but sometimes these things are left to God.* He looked at JC sleeping beside him and thought about how his own selfish, angry actions almost cost him the two people he loved most. He reached over and rubbed his knuckle along the side of JC's cheek. "I'll do better," he whispered. "I promise I'll do better for you, your mom, your sister, and your brother Gregory."

He laid awake, thinking of Mabel's vision. It must have been the medication, he thought. He closed his eyes, but still couldn't stop thinking about what she had said. "This is silly," he murmured. He had checked himself. It wasn't there. He kicked his covers off and turned on the lamp, staring at the dresser. He then got up, walked over to it, got down on his knees, and pulled the bottom drawer open. He sat back on his heels.

"Well, I'll be damned," he whispered, picking up the neatly folded linen cloth trimmed with gold fringes.

Epilogue

Dan McInnes paced up and down. He'd give it another ten minutes. He finally saw a boat approaching in the distance. He watched as the captain threw the engine in reverse and the Hunky Dory gently bumped against the slimy green tires mounted on the side of the wharf. The captain picked up his heavy mooring rope and swung it within inches of McInnes' feet.

"Folks at the Screech House tell me yer down a man," McInnes said.

The captain jumped on the wharf. "Ya lookin for work?"

"Yeah," McInnes said, quickly wrapping the rope around the bollard.

The captain looked his muscular helper up and down. "Any experience hauling traps?"

"My uncle had a lobster boat. Used to help out as a kid. Mostly been workin the docks in Ontario."

"Where ya from?"

McInnis paused. "Ya wouldn't know it. It's smack-dab in the middle of fuck knows where and who the fuck cares. Little place called…Forest Haven."

"Yer right. Never heard of it. So, what's yer name?"

McInnes extended his hand. "Barry. Barry Sheppard."

"Well, Barry Sheppard, ya get twelve dollars a day. When the season's done, ya can have all the lobster ya care to eat and all the screech yer stomach can handle. No point in wastin time. Give the boys a hand unloadin the traps. We head out at five in the mornin. So tell me, how the hell d'ya end up in Quidi Vidi?"

That's all for Now

CPSIA information can be obtained
at www.ICGtesting.com
Printed in the USA
LVOW11*1425061117
555213LV00014B/658/P